Old Sins Cast Long Shadows

A Sam Stewart Mystery

by

Elizabeth Housden

For Susie with love,

and

in fond remembrance of Gil, Dr Gil Scott, Susie's late husband
who was the first person to read this story and loved it...
and he didn't guess the dénouement either!

Old Sins Cast Long Shadows

Past...

France, 1944

1

The blue haze hung over the countryside. In the early autumn's noonday heat, the air was heavy and drowsy. The fields were empty of men but here and there a pigeon strutted, looking for left-over husks that would contain the odd ear or two of corn. The fruit was mostly ripened now and wasps crept about, drunk with fermenting juice and the gentle sound of buzzing was all around. In the air, heavy with the scent of wine, hung wisps of smoke from the beginnings of bonfires, the smell of days to come. The house martins gathered in groups, preening their feathers and chattering with excitement about the coming long flight south. They swooped and called to one another, encouraging the young to leave the nest and practise their flying. They performed an aerial ballet for those with time to stand and stare and now and then one could catch the sharp clip of a beak as it closed over an errant gnat or flaunting butterfly.

In the sleepy roadside café William Berkeley sat sipping his wine. The tables under the awning were mostly unoccupied. Business was not good these days and the faces of the men and women around him had a watchful air. They were a subdued bunch, quietly chatting of nothing in particular. William's shirt was open to the waist and he was brown. He had worked in the fields all summer and now the vines had been stripped of their fruit, the juice extracted down to the last pip and, for a short while each day he and the other occupants of Viezy-sur-L'eau allowed themselves to relax and enjoy the last of the summer sun before autumn arrived in earnest. Monsieur le Patron moved easily between the little tables with their obligatory checked cloths, a word here, a smile there, his spotless apron of the early morning now marked with wine and olive oil. He greeted William with a nod and refilled his glass. He moved on again. It was not wise to be seen talking to a spy, you never knew who knew...

The sun was still high in the sky but it did not burn with the fierce intensity of a June day. The drowsy wasps were a nuisance, falling into glasses and alighting on anything sweet in a desperate attempt to bolster up their supplies of sugar. Like drug addicts, demented for a fix, they hung around, crawling from one morsel to another until they were either squashed or fell, dying, in a stupor on the ground. Soon the days would shorten further, the odd bonfire would grow into many and the scent of woodsmoke would fill the air. It lingered longer than it did in far off England, William thought to himself, but the smells were the same. Only the language was different and the wine cheaper, the beer scarcer but apart from that...

But no. There were greater differences. Here on every corner and at every turn was a Nazi soldier - no let-up in the constant reminders that this was occupied France. Not so at home. It was true that the bombs fell, children were evacuated, and the signposts removed. Every evening the blackout out ruined the night and there was rationing. People picked their way through the rubble, searching for what one hardly dared to think but still their spirit remained strong, their resolutions undeterred no matter what was thrown at them from the skies night after night. They set up canteens and slept in Tube stations. They rescued children and animals and sang and laughed and loved to keep the indomitable spirit alive.

However, here were no invading forces, no rape of the land as there had been on the hapless Continent. In spite of all Hitler's rhetoric it was still only our people who walked the streets and inhabited the houses. There were no iron-grey uniforms, no goose-stepping feet. Not like little Viezy with the ignominy of Nazi salutes or the cold and glittering eyes of the expressionless and sinister SS men, no constant tributes to 'Mein Führer'. The people were still free and our land was still ours, William thought, grimly to himself.

He tipped his chair back and surveyed the scene. He'd been here for five months - five months infiltrated into this small community. His French, always perfect, had been just what they had needed and given the valuable entrée that the Allies and the Resistance had needed so badly - a British officer with a perfect cover.

Six sorties he had made into occupied France and six times he had beaten the Nazis at their own game. A rescue here, a bombing raid there, William had been in the thick of it with the Underground Movement. All over France and Belgium he had adopted new roles, his talent for mimicry holding him in good stead and his love of danger and passion for Britain keeping him fighting on. But now it was 1944. Light was at the end of that terrible tunnel for the Allies and all knew it. The Nazis were being backed into a corner but the enemy, like any animal with nowhere to run, suddenly had become even more deadly than before. As he sat there in the autumn sun, William knew as he had all along, that in spite of the balmy days, the wine, and girls in the hay, this was a desperate mission and he was in greater danger every minute of the day and night than he had been at any other time during the war.

As he sipped his wine he contemplated the present stage in the operation. For the moment he was waiting for a message from one of his team, radio operator Pierre DuPont. Maybe Pierre himself would come, maybe Jean-Yves, it would depend on who was able to get away more easily.

Pierre had escaped from Brussels at the start of the war and had somehow found his way to England. Unfit to fight, he was desperate to help his beleaguered country and joined the British underground movement. He had had five tours of duty to Belgium and this was his third trip into France and was to be his last. Enough was enough and Pierre's bravery had won him decorations at every turn.

William stared down into the gathering lees in the bottom of his glass. And what of the others, his fellow outlaws in a foreign land? Hans van Cleef, Dutch, captured in Amsterdam with the rest of his family dead. But Hans was a feather in their cap for now he was actually serving in the German army after working his way in, persuading his Nazi captors that he was "one of them". Here in Viezy-sur-L'eau, he was their man on the inside. As he thought of Hans, William's fist tightened on his glass. As a double agent, the risks he ran were enormous and the consequences of discovery did not bear thinking about but the information he gave them was invaluable. It had taken Hans two years to convince the powers that be in Westminster that he was a bona fide member of the Resistance. This was to be his one and only active job with them, they could not risk it again, but it was to be worth it. Hans would leave France with William and Pierre at the end of the mission.

And finally, there was Jean-Yves de la Flèche, the Frenchman, the local boy. Jean-Yves whose sharp young brain had cooked up this mad scheme and managed to sell it to the Allies. In his mind's eye William thought about them as the Rat, the Mole, the Toad and the Badger. One day he would amuse himself by sketching pictures of them, each in his right role, he thought. But for the moment he was content to think of them collectively and draw parallels later. He lit a cigarette and inhaled the smoke, watching the blue mingle with the grey and cloud his vision of the main street which stretched away, ending in the old mellow-walled château at the end of the village.

Round the corner came a figure on a rickety bicycle in a blue serge jumper, purposefully pedalling in the heat of the day to his rendezvous with William. It was Jean-Yves. Pierre was obviously otherwise engaged. William indicated that he needed another glass and before he arrived, panting slightly with the effort of pedalling in the hot sun, it was on the table, winking in the light, its ruby liquid inviting him, irresistibly, to drink.

Jean-Yves leaned his ancient bicycle against the old wall behind William. Bits of crumbling mortar tumbled down into the dust in the path, causing the earwigs and lizards to dart away and dive for cover. He lowered himself into the seat opposite and took a long pull at the wine. He put down the glass and William watched him lick the red droplets from his upper lip and then lean back in his chair, his eyes half shut.

"It's still hot, my friend, is it not?" Jean-Yves smiled slowly looking at the good-looking Englishman under his eyelashes. "Late September and the sun still with all this heat. Just wait till the war is over! The tourists will flock to La Belle France, just you wait and see!"

William pulled a face. "If only that could be true, Jean! But I fear there will not be enough money for many, many years before people will be able to travel abroad. At least, I'm sure that is true of myself, at any rate!"

"Ah, but you are an aristocrat and they do not have the money these days, I think!"

"Shut up, Jean!" William was suddenly sharp. Like Monsieur le Patron he was instantly on his guard. You never knew who was listening, even though Jean-Yves's practised mode of speech was pitched at just the right level, only to be heard by his companion.

Jean drained his glass and beckoned for another, the bottle was left for them now and the second glass he drank more slowly, allowing himself the pleasure of savouring

the moment. He tipped back his chair and observed his friend, casually. He smiled
a crooked smile. "We are safe among friends here, Guillaume." He used the French
version of William's name, caution coming somewhat belatedly, William noted with a
frown. "Not a Nazi pig in sight. And talking of pigs, Celestine invites you for supper.
We celebrate the end of the harvest and the pressing of the grapes. God knows where she
has found a young pig to roast, but she has. The bastard Nazis take them all! I cannot
imagine who she has bribed to get it, or how, if it comes to that!" Jean's face was sly and
he winked, expressively, raising his forearm in an obscene gesture.

William grinned at the implication. Celestine was a devoted wife and Jean knew it.
She was as faithful to Jean as Jean was to the Cause. His thoughts strayed briefly and
guiltily to ration-torn England but not for long. He was here, risking his life in one of the
most dangerous missions of the war. Why not roast piglet? It was precious little to earn
from it all, when all was said and done. Besides...

"I accept, Jean, of course. And who else is to be there? Is it something of a party or
am I the only extra one invited?" He spoke easily, but hoping that he was not the only
guest.

Now it was Jean-Yves's turn to grin. "Well, you will have to wait, my friend, but I
believe it will be quite a party. But I shouldn't be surprised if Dominique's bright eyes
were there to greet you." He leant forward. "A moment to turn to business, though." His
voice lowered further. "Pierre has heard from Papa," code name for Headquarters in
London, "and the candles," he meant dynamite, "will be here next week, as arranged."

"And the matches?" This referred to fuses.

"Oui. Aussi."

They were silent for a moment, each thinking their own thoughts. The end of their
mission was in sight now and as William felt the approaching operation grow that one
step nearer, his professional soldier's heart gave a flip of excitement and anticipation.
His gaze was still steady though, as he looked down the street, over Jean's shoulder at
the familiar territory. The château, its turrets yellowing in the sun, was covered here
and there in places with Virginia Creeper that was fast turning red. William's thoughts
turned to England and Hampshire and the red of the self-same creeper that crept up the
walls of home. By now, it would probably be bare of the red and the skeleton of little
clinging tendrils would be all that was left till the next Spring when once again the pale
green of the new leaves would put forth and the cycle would begin again. He wondered
if he would see that change or would he, once again, be back in France. Or... maybe not...

He poured himself a third glass. He loved France and had grown to care passionately
for the people of this insular village, touched as it was by world events. Their sorrow
was his sorrow, their fight his fight, their enemy his enemy, but home pulled at his heart
and now he longed for it more than anything. He felt Jean-Yves's eyes rest on him,
searching his face with that quizzical expression of his.

"Not long now and it'll all be over. The Germans gone and peace here once more.

Let us drink to that moment, mon Guillaume!" He turned the glass this way and that. William gave a short laugh and drained the remainder of his drink in one and stood up.

"Till later, Jean and tell Celestine I shall not be late. Roast baby pig is more than mere man can resist!"

"Not to mention my beautiful cousin, eh, mon ami? À bientôt!"

He smiled and left the café, throwing down a couple of notes on the table and picking up his cigarettes in one movement. Behind him he heard Jean hail a friend at another table, heard the reply and a chair scrape against the pavement. Without turning back he strode off down the street back to the room he rented in the house of another sympathiser, Édouard St Vincent, in a tiny cottage off the main high street. He let himself in and went up the stairs two at a time and unlocked the door to his room.

It was peaceful here and still and cool. Even now, months after a fire had been lit, the sweet smell of seasoned logs, burnt in the grates on cooler days, still lingered. He paused for a moment savouring the scent as he always did. That would always be France for him, that scent of wood-burning fires.

He walked over to the windows and flung open the shutters and the sun flooded in. He perched on the window sill and he lit a cigarette, watching the smoke curl upwards and away over the gutter and disappear towards the roof. Doves were billing and cooing high up among the chimney pots as he sat there, looking over the valley. The chateau was over to the left, set apart from the village, holding court, as it were, over the gently sloping hills that stretched away towards the lake.

Amongst the ramparts he could see the odd Nazi sentry on duty, on patrol with a rifle over his shoulder. Here, in the midst of this sleepy village, where on the surface, life had barely changed for hundreds of years, was evil and devilry and plotting that had spread from London to Washington and back again, finally coming to rest in Viezy-sur-L'eau. But it was impossible to believe it, leaning there over the window ledge. The château would soon be no more, the mellow brickwork reduced to rubble and the munitions factory it contained no longer the main supplier of the German war machine, thanks to the Rat, the Mole, the Toad and the Badger.

William turned away and lay on his bed, smoking still, listening to the gentle sounds of the creaking bed-springs from below where Édouard and his wife had retired for siesta. He stretched his arms above his head and grinned. He did not envy them their pleasure for the evening would soon be here and that would bring the only thing that mattered - Dominique...

He stubbed out his cigarette on the ashtray beside him. He lay, listening to the buzzing bees and the sounds of sleepy afternoon. His eyes grew heavy for the wine had been strong. They closed, opened once and then, finally, he slept.

Celestine's party had been as carefree as could be possible, under the circumstances. The wine and the piglet, the cheerful friends and relatives of Jean-Yves made for an evening he would never forget. The old farmhouse kitchen was lively with the sight and sound of feasting, the clinking of bottle neck against glass rim and the smell of roast pork. Just for once, they could pretend there were no Germans, no Occupation, just a normal and cheery post-harvest gathering, such as had been celebrated here for centuries and William was happy to be part of it.

Later, much later on that autumn night, with owls' hoots and the pattering of tiny nocturnal feet in the fields, William lay, staring out at the stars, his arm round Dominique, whispering of a future that they hoped would be theirs. And the girl with green eyes, those curious, unique, siren's eyes, who lay beside him on the hay piled up high in the open barn, propped up on one elbow, listened to him weave that magic spell and gazed at him with love...

3

The undergrowth was damp and smelled of moss and dead leaves. In the stillness of the starless night the slightest sound could be heard - a falling leaf, a mouse scurrying over the earth, the sharp and unnerving cry of a dog fox miles away over the fields. The dank November mists stretched over the downs of Southern England, rolled in eerie waves over the Channel and into the flat lands of Northern France.

Barbed wire littered the landscape, men with lowered eyes and furtive gaze continued to scurry about their work under the all-seeing stare of the ravagers of their land and the real work, the power and the spirit of a proud and passionate people was driven underground. But not for much longer for the pin-prick of light at the end of the tunnel was bigger now and soon would come salvation.

But first, they were going to wound the Nazis where it hurt most and the night was here, quiet and expectant. William lay face down in this undergrowth, waiting, waiting and straining his ears for another sound, the sound of the explosion that would signal the success of their mission.

The moment had come, after all the months of planning and secrecy. Soon the château would be blown to smithereens and with it the largest arms' cache of the German army. It was to be one of the most glorious victories for the Resistance. And in less than an hour, William was going home.

If he had turned his head he would have noted Hans in similar pose a few yards to his left. His lookout was over the fields to the east, watching for the signal from Pierre who was hidden in the next coppice, a mile or so from the edge of Viezy. Their mission all but accomplished, they were waiting for the tiny plane that would land and take the three of them back to England, leaving Jean-Yves behind to carry on alone. But only for the moment. One day William would return, when the signal was sent for him to come, that much he had promised - promised his allies and himself as well as the lovely Dominique, but for now they lay in the wet woodlands, waiting and watching.

The glorious summer had passed. The swallows gone, the wasps dead, save for the queens, buried now in burrows and hiding in attics and crevices until the spring. The little tables outside the café had been moved inside and wind shrieked and howled through the village streets, tossing the striped awnings and driving folks indoors.

And now William lay there, in the dark and dirt, waiting for his last minutes in France to begin, waiting for the end. And there it was, a faint rumble in the air, like distant thunder it might have seemed to one who knew nothing, almost like the beginnings of a storm, but so far away as to be hardly noticed or registered. Then the little world of Viezy-sur-L'eau was torn apart.

The first explosion shot sparks into the night sky like a beacon, like Guy Fawkes night, like a celebration for the birth of a new king. William realised his heart was thumping and he felt terribly sick. His hand grasped the tuft of dying grass in front of him in an effort to stop himself shouting out loud. He allowed himself to turn his head quietly in the direction of the noise that began to rip open the black night. He had to turn his head further than he thought. Surely he was not mistaken? The château had been due west of their hiding place. For weeks they had planned the wires and cables, swiftly laid them and the detonators rushed into place at the last moment. He could have sworn to anyone that he knew that landscape backwards, in any light, or lack of it, in rain, wind or snow. And yet, and yet...?

"William...!"

He turned like a rabbit in a trap at the sound, next to his ear.

Hans snaked his way forward and was lying beside him in the slight hollow beneath the beech. His mouth an inch from his ear.

"What the devil...?"

"William, it's gone wrong, I..."

"Shit!"

William cursed. He knew it. What the hell was happening? That wasn't the munitions factory, it was too far round to the north! As fast as he could muster his thoughts William tried to put them out of his head, the horror of it all. He looked up. By the spasmodic light from each fresh explosion he could see someone. A figure was pushing through the hedgerow, working his way round, out of the glare from the flames that were now leaping hundreds of feet into the air. It was Jean-Yves, it had to be. No one he knew had the ability to run as fast as that, bent absolutely in half.

He raised himself as high as he dared. Jean-Yves came on, working like a terrier through the sparse undergrowth. He dived for the cover of the trees. For a moment or two he disappeared and then suddenly he was next to them, arriving silently, slipping in next to Hans, his eyes blazing.

"We have been betrayed! Those Nazi bastards must have rerouted the fuses, there can have been no other way. It is the village that is burning, not their bloody factory. The children, the screams..." He put his head in his hands.

Pierre joined the other three. "Jean-Yves, you must go back, do what you can. You must not be caught. Do what you can to save your people," his knuckles were white on Jean's arm, even through the dark, lit only by the distant flames, William could see them shining on the blue serge jacket he had learned to love so well.

A shape reared up over the horizon.

"It's the airlift," Hans' voice was high with fright. He turned. "Quick, for God's sake, we must be on that plane and away." He shook William who was rooted to the spot.

Jean-Yves stood up. His face was dreadful. "Go, get out, do to fear for me. I can talk my way out of anything. Come back as we arranged, if and when you can. I will find out who betrayed us and when I do..." He choked on his words and could not speak.

"I'm staying!" William's voice was raised now above the noise of the engines. The plane was on the grass, bumping over the sodden field and slewing dangerously from left to right as the pilot attempted to force it to stay in a straight line.

"NO!" They were unanimous, the other voices.

Jean-Yves went on, "We cannot jeopardise the rest for this. Don't let the bastards win, William. For surely they will if they catch you and question you - torture you. Go back and let us fight another day," he shook him violently. "I will find out who was the traitor and I will kill him, with my bare hands I will kill him for this night's evil."

"I can't let you fight this alone, Jean-Yves, for Christ's sake!"

Jean-Yves stared at him. "This is my country, William. I will avenge her. France is mine." He pushed at them. "Go, get out! I will not forget what you tried to do for France and one day I will tell you who sabotaged this mission. I will let you know, each of you." He screamed at them, "Go, go!"

Somehow they got on board. William never could remember how, thinking later. The side of the plane was open, faces leaned out into the night and strong arms seized them and dragged them inside. William lay on the floor and felt the vibration as the pilot swung the nose round, facing into the direction from whence he had come.

They were flung violently aside and William grabbed hold of the metal casing that held the parachutes in place. The roar of the engines grew wilder and harsher and just as he thought the engine would burst with the effort, they were airborne. He could hear gun fire through the noise of roaring flames and falling buildings and he knew they had been spotted and they were shooting at them. A single bullet found its way into the cabin and buried itself in his leg. He screamed once and passed out.

And the little plane flew out of one hell into another - and that second hell, which came of terrible knowledge, was worse than the first.

And it stayed with him till his life's end.

Chapter 1

1

The explosion ripped the helicopter apart. The noise that filled my ears and mind will stay with me for ever. Ribbons of fire fell among the twisted metal, scorching the green and pleasant land. It killed the pilot and his crew, destroyed my father and broke my mother's heart. In that split second the lives of my brother and myself were irrevocably changed, for on that dreadful day it was my brother who was the pilot.

William. He had always been there. Bearing our father's name and two years my senior, he was tall, good-looking, kind and funny, clever, shrewd, easy with people from all walks of life. He was, in fact, the perfect heir to my father's estate and trained as such from as early as either of us could remember to take over the running of the 7,000 acres of Hampshire that had been home to our family for four centuries. And how he loved the life! Farming, land management, horse shows and open air theatre, even the almost obligatory Open Days when he was generous to the locals and charmed strangers. He breathed new life into the whole set-up and with it came, for the first time in many years, prosperity.

Gradually, my ageing father handed over to him more and more of the running of the "family business" and now, at the age of 32, William was the boss, deservedly so and doing a great job. Making money out of the old heap was the idea and so he went to town on it. There were three day events for the horse riding fraternity, clay pigeon shoots, Arts and Crafts exhibitions, ploughing competitions, archery and falconry demonstrations, you name it, we had it. The hands-on education centre of life on the land since the Stone Age to present day alone attracted not just schools but millions of people - it was a different world from that which we had known as children. We didn't have a zoo, though, no free range big cats or giraffes. "We don't want to put Longleat out of business," William had said kindly. The thing that used to give my father the greatest kick, for some reason, was watching the television advertising. His face would light up as he watched the local station and our ad would appear. Like a small boy, he would look up with proud delight, "There, Phyllis," he'd say to my mother, "that's us. We're on the box again!"

And what of me? Not for me the life of a modern country gentleman, although it was always a joy to go home and see the new lease of life it had all given to my parents. With William running things so well in Hampshire, I was free to do what I wanted, namely run an antiques business and Fine Art centre in Chelsea. I had a partner, Jenny, who ran the business side of it, very well indeed, and allowed me to prowl the world for this and that. An exhibition here, an auction there, New York, Paris, Madrid, Istanbul. Paintings were my great joy and, as the family business became more prosperous, it gave me much pleasure to help my father and William start to build up a considerable collection of paintings with new additions, both ancient and modern. We'd had a lot more pictures when I was a child, I remembered, but gradually, to help with the up-keep, several had been sold. Matisse, Monet and Renoir, glorious works, acquired who knows how but disposed of as quietly as possible, one at a time, over the years.

My father was always a quiet, gentle man, given to long walks alone, with only a couple of dogs for company. The war had taken a heavy toll on his spirit, it seemed. My mother said she had been told he was never the same man afterwards, for it was a long time after the war he married, but that must have been true of many, perhaps all to a greater or lesser extent. What he had done in the war nobody was sure, exactly. When questioned he would either make a joke about it or change the subject gently but firmly, depending on his mood. He loved his house and his land but the responsibility of caring for it all and making it pay weighed heavily on him. When William showed such enthusiasm and proved such an adept manager it lightened his heart much and he became more relaxed than I had ever known him.

My mother worked tirelessly, first for Father and then as a second string for William. "Just till you find someone better at it, darling," she'd say with a hopeful look in her eye. But although William had many girlfriends he showed no sign of settling down with any of them. No more did I, for that matter, so poor mother had only to sigh and go on wishing for weddings and bridesmaids and grandchildren.

So, life was good to us Berkeleys and Forbridge Park grew prosperous and to be a household name under my brother's guidance.

Four hundred years had passed since the family had been in residence. This was an event too good to be missed. A celebration was planned involving every interest and every venture Forbridge had ever hosted. A massive fair, an Antiques Roadshow broadcast (my baby, this!), a horse show, a vintage car rally, cricket and golf tournaments, the whole lot, in fact, was to take place the last weekend in August. Even I was roped in to help, so I knew this was going to be a big one! Television cameras everywhere, loudspeakers, wires trailing - a circus from beginning to end. Actually, I have to admit, I loved it. It was noisy and brash and the sedate old lady that was Forbridge had to let her hair down and bloody well enjoy herself!

Half way through the morning of the bank holiday was to be an air show. On the ground was a fantastic collection of rare and famous old planes. They were lent by a diverse bunch of people from all over the country, surprised at themselves at lending their precious machines, but powerless to refuse once my brother's persuasive tongue had mesmerised them. In the air, trick flyers, parachutists, sky divers and a mock-up of an air/sea rescue over the lake by William in a borrowed helicopter. All events were precisely timed and ran like clockwork.

Loudspeakers blared, the crowd clapped and cheered and the sun shone down and smiled. Modern English pageantry at its best. The policeman who'd volunteered to be rescued was in the water. William climbed into the helicopter and prepared to hover over the lake.

That's when it happened, a flash of brilliant white from the cockpit. Bits of metal and shards of glass and, God help me, bits of human being, fell to earth. After the shattering noise had ceased I could hear screaming, going on and on and on. Someone came up to me, shaking me, hugging me and begging me to stop. It wasn't until that moment that I realised the screaming had been mine.

2

We sat in a daze in the Regency drawing room. The bedlam that existed outside came only dimly to my consciousness. Police were everywhere and the St John's Ambulance people did their best. The summer sun blazed in through the windows and we shivered. My father was sitting, white-faced, slumped into an armchair by the fireplace. Someone had put a blanket round him. My mother was hunched up one end of a chaise longue hugging a cushion and rocking to and fro, another blanket draped over her shoulders. Loving hands put a cup of tea in front of me. I stared at it. Somehow I didn't know what to do with it. A stranger urged me gently to drink.

The door opened again and Eddy Farley, our doctor, came in, an old friend of the family's for many years. Instructions were issued and my parents were gently taken away to rest in bed. I began to come to a little and I managed to answer people who spoke to me. I was deeply shocked but, being young and strong, my constitution could take more than the poor broken old people who now lay twisting in silent horror upstairs.

After several hours of organisation, removal of the crowds, police activity everywhere, Eddy Farley returned to find me. He had been here most of the day, looking after us and others injured. Exhausted, he sank down onto the chair beside me.

"God, Robert, what a terrible business..." He looked at me closely. "Old chap, the police want a word. I've said under no circumstances can they interview either your father or your mother. Really, I fear for your father's life, Rob, after this, I really do." He shook his head. "How are you? Do you feel up to a short chat? You know Adrian, anyway, don't you?" He indicated Adrian Merchant, the Chief Constable who had quietly entered the room with him. Adrian I had known for several years. He shot clay pigeons with us. He was always teased for he very rarely hit anything. He, rather drily, would remark he could only hit live targets and larger ones than clay pigeons.

I nodded.

Eddy patted my arm, kindly, but I was aware of his attentive scrutiny. "I'll be upstairs if you want me, Robert." He left the room.

Adrian took his place beside me on the window seat - looking out at the sea of carnage.

"Robert, I'm so sorry, so desperately sorry. Can you bear it, do you think, but we must ask a few questions? It may give us just that little time that may be vital to catching whoever did this monstrous thing quickly."

His words went in slowly. I had to take it in one word at a time, put them all together and then think about it. My eyes on his face, I repeated like an automaton. "Whoever did this monstrous thing?" I went on staring at him. "The helicopter blew up. It was an accident, surely?"

Adrian watched me closely. He shook his head, "No, Robert." His voice was quiet. He put his hand on my arm, "It will have to be proved by the forensic teams but already I'm 99.9 per cent certain. We have found what appears to be the remains of a detonator. This was no accident. William was murdered."

Murder! The word whirled through my head like a tornado, twisting and winding, driving me near to madness with disbelief. I felt dreadfully sick and then I thought I was going to pass out. I put my spinning head in my hands. "No, it can't be... Why? It's not possible... William..." My mind was filled with whirling shapes and thoughts that meant nothing and there were no more words. Water dripped off my face from somewhere into my hands. I didn't know what it was. I was numb and still and stared at him. There was nothing in my head at this moment.

Adrian continued to be gentle but went on. "We all know how popular he was but is there anything you can think of, Rob, any person who he might have upset or slighted? I know it's hard to believe that of William, but is there anyone at all? Any odd situation at all in recent weeks?" I shook my head dumbly. Adrian persisted. "What about you or your parents? Have you had any strange encounters or had a row with anyone or had any suspicious mail?"

I leaned back against the window frame. Beyond the lawns that ran round the house people were still milling about. They were being herded off the estate by the police, notes taken of them as they went, I could see. I tried hard to apply myself to Adrian's questions. Something reached me in my stupefied state that made me realise how important this was. The crowd surged and sifted as I stared at them. A little red van crossed my line of vision, slowly, slowly edging through the throng. It stirred something in my mind. I frowned.

"Actually, there was something odd, a few weeks ago. It was that red van, it reminded me. The post. It came in the post."

"Right."

I said nothing, thinking still.

"What did, Rob?" Still gentle, Adrian's patience seemed boundless.

"A letter for Father. From France, I think. He started to open it and then stopped and wouldn't look at it in front of us. We teased him about it - you know, begging letters from a French mistress with a shameful bundle on the doorstep stuff. But he was disturbed, genuinely so and we could see that, so we stopped the teasing. And then a couple of hours later, I walked in on him in the picture gallery. I went up to look at two new sketches we'd bought at Sotheby's a few days earlier and I found him, staring into space, the letter was in his hand. When he realised I was with him, he shoved it very hastily into his pocket. I didn't say anything about it but he was obviously very upset. In fact, he was very preoccupied for days afterwards."

"What else can you tell me about this letter? Did you discuss it with him or did William, do you know?"

"I didn't, no. And as regards William, not as far as I know, Adrian. You'll have to ask Father when he's up to answering you. I've told you all I can think of and it may be nothing, anyway. But you did ask about odd things, and that was bloody odd, all in all. I had to go back to London and so it went out of my mind and I've not thought of it again since. William might have said something, but I don't know. It was a funny episode, though."

Adrian tried again. "Did you have business interests in France or friends or relatives?"

"An acquaintance or two, yes but no to the relatives. However, I can't be sure about the business interests. Father and William did all that, really, you know. I only advise them on the sale and purchase of antiquities in connection with the restocking of the house as an investment. Occasionally I'd help with the big events here, like today's. I have quite a bit to do with the Education Centre as History has always been my subject and that's what we do here. William and I went to France last year for a holiday but Father hadn't been since the war. And that's odd, too, now you come to think of it. All that time, helping to liberate France and then never to return. The struggle was too bitter, I suppose. But you ask him later, Adrian. I expect it's all something about nothing." I leant back and closed my eyes. I opened them again quick. In my mind's eye I could only see William. It was too much to bear.

"Anything else? Odd or out of character?"

Out of character. Another jolt in my half-frozen mind. With an effort I spoke again. "Well, in a way, but this morning, very early just after breakfast, William said..." my voice shook and I had to stop for a second. I took a deep breath to continue, "...William said there was something he wanted to talk to me about." I couldn't go on. I was slowly, slowly beginning to realise that I now would never know what it was.

I remembered his hand on my arm as I left the dining room. His voice was lowered and his eyes serious. "Robbie, I must talk to you tonight. Rather an odd thing has happened. It has cut me up no end, I can tell you and I've been forming things in my mind for several days as to what precisely to tell you."

I was struck by his fast, conspiratorial tone and fell in with it at once. But William was never like this. He was mostly joking about something though he could, of course, be irritable and even furious on occasions but this tone from him was rarely heard. "What's it about, Will? Are you in some sort of bother?"

He sighed. "No. No, I'm not but I'm terribly unhappy and I've had a blow, that's all.

But there is something you must know. Don't forget, we must talk before we turn in tonight. OK?"

"Yes, of course. OK."

"Good. Thanks." His normal light-heartedness returned. "Come on, little brother. Let's give the punters what they want!" He struck me a light tap with the rolled up Times.

I smiled and we went out of the room together. I brooded, disturbed for a while but then someone came up to me and started muttering about camera angles and I went off to the gallery with the film crew. And now, now... I allowed my mind to close into a comforting blank once more.

Adrian was watching me thoughtfully. "OK. That's it for the moment. But if there's anything else you can remember, however seemingly small or unimportant, ring me at once, will you?" I nodded down at the card he gave me with the usual contact details on it.

He got up. "I'll go up but I don't expect I'll be allowed to see your parents." At the door he turned. "Robert, I'm so very, very sorry..."

I gave one quick nod and turned away again to scan the seemingly scarcely diminished crowd, searching, searching... but for what? In that moment, I was a small boy again, standing in that same window, staring out across the park. No crowds were there on that occasion, but I could see the huntsmen in their red coats and could hear the cry of the excited hounds. I was waiting for the hunt to return so I could question William about what it was like and had he been blooded, to capture all the thrill of a first hunt. But there was no hunting now, and no William.

And I knew as I stood there that I had always looked for William at that window, and, if I waited for him to the end of my life, now he would never come home again. I collapsed onto the window seat and cried. I cried as I had not cried since I was a small child.

3

Extracted from Police records (1):

The phone on Sam's desk rang.

"Sam Stewart."

"Sam, come and see me, will you?" It was the Chief Superintendent.

"Of course. Straight away?"

"Please."

"On my way, sir."

Sam shut down the computer that displayed reporting of the Berkeley case, knowing exactly what this meeting was to be about. They were taking over. "Correction," Sam thought, heading for the door, "I am taking over," and wasn't sure if this was a good thing or not...

But one thing was for sure, no one else was going to investigate the death of Robert's brother and Sam knew it to be right, however at variance that opinion might be in the official guidelines in such cases.

If they knew the truth...

Chapter 2

1

The nightmare that had begun went on. I couldn't turn on the television or look at a newspaper but to see William's smiling, handsome face looking back at me. "The son and heir to Sir William Berkeley, war hero, murdered", proclaimed the articles and the headlines were so dreadful I put them out of my mind and to this day I cannot recall the exact words. I don't want to. My father insisted on seeing all the papers for some reason. We attempted to limit it to The Times and The Telegraph. As he had been confined to bed by the doctors he had no option but to do as we said but it didn't spare him.

Three days after the horror, he was reading the paper that had arrived with his breakfast tray. When Mother went up to see him, he had collapsed with a stroke. Once again Eddy Farley was instantly there to help us. Initially admitted to hospital, after tests and investigations he was sent home again. Nurses were sent for and the bedroom became a hospital ward for one. Curiously, it gave Mother something to think about and helped her, in a way. She was useful and had a role again, suddenly. She would get him well, she said and we would overcome this awfulness together.

Outside the bedroom door the tray had been placed for collection and I carried it down to Helena, our resident housekeeper, in the kitchen. I took the paper away into the dining room and poured myself a cup of coffee from the pot on the sideboard. Listlessly, I stared at the front page. Father had not opened it. He had only read the headlines. The article about William was brief that morning, although still front page news, explaining police activity and appealing for more witnesses. The other news was depressing, too, I noticed. Stock Market fall in Japan, riots in France over the election, a Dutch businessman and his wife murdered while sailing their holiday yacht in the Dutch West Indies, nothing to cheer one at all. I put down the paper and walked over to the window. A tap at the door and in came Adrian Merchant again.

"Hello," I said. My voice was expressionless.

"Rob, this is dreadful. This second blow. My dear fellow, I don't know what to say to you. How is Phyllis?"

"Coping. She's wonderful. She always has been."

"The shock, it must have been the shock, of course."

I was aware of his piercing glance. I nodded, miserably and shrugged my shoulders. "Must have been. I haven't spoken to Eddy myself in any detail yet, but I can't imagine it wasn't delayed shock." I turned back to the window again. "Have a cup of coffee, Adrian. Help yourself from the sideboard."

He poured one, thanking me and came to stand beside me at the window. Lines of policemen were still combing the grounds, their eyes glued to the grass. They were heading down towards the lower copse and out towards the pheasant pens, I noticed. The area round the lake had been dealt with yesterday.

I thought of my poor father, taxed to the limit, weak and broken. "I wonder why it didn't happen earlier."

"Sometimes in these cases a second shock can bring on a stroke where the first one didn't. Did anything happen to give him another jolt, do you suppose?"

I couldn't imagine what he was talking about. I was almost irritable as I replied. "Another blow? What the hell do you mean, Adrian? Isn't his son's murder enough to do the damage?" I began to pace about. "Jesus, how much more do you bloody policemen want?"

He tried to calm me. "Sit down, Rob. Really, I have to try everything and explore every avenue to help us solve this case. You must see this. The big bods in London are taking over, by the way. I wondered if he'd had any more mail or anything like that?"

"Not that I know of. No, the post hasn't arrived yet. He had the paper but hadn't opened it. I don't know if he'd even read the front page. It just happened." I glared at him. "Quite enough for an old man, without any more shocks, don't you think? Why, it's lucky he's not dead."

"Yes, yes, of course. I had to find out." I sat at the table and he sat beside me. He picked up a teaspoon and fiddled with it. "Robert, can you tell me about your visit to France last year?"

"Yes. But why? Why do you want to know about that?"

"Simply because of the oddness of your father's reaction to an unaccustomed letter from France. We need to examine unusual or bizarre incidents in any shape or form. It's through that more often than not we solve crimes."

I nodded. I sort of understood. I didn't think it had anything to do with anything but it wasn't up to me to solve this awful event. I was there to try to throw some light, any light, on it all.

My holiday with William. Our last holiday together. I stared in front of me in a reverie, remembering many past holidays. Dartmoor with its ponies, sandy beaches all along the south coast of England, Scotland at Hogmanay. That one was worth remembering! We were only about 6 and 8, I supposed. There was another child there with us, as tall as I was, thin and dark with huge, compelling grey eyes, the child of the household, if I remembered properly, but I wasn't sure if it was a boy or a girl, laughing at the prospect of a midnight feast and showing us where to hide to secretly observe the party. We had been allowed to stay up and watch the guests arrive but stayed on, in secret, after the adults had thought we had long since gone to bed. We hung over the minstrels' gallery and in my mind's eye I could see the swirling tartan, watching the reels and hear the laughter. We begged and implored a hapless waiter to come to our rescue and he brought us plates of illicit food and we sat there in the dim light, hidden from view, licking our fingers. I roused myself.

"What do you want to know about our holiday in France?"

"Where did you stay? Did you meet anyone there? How long were you there? That sort of thing. Just tell me what you remember."

We had rented a farmhouse. It was a wonderful old building, crumbling away here and there but what would have been draughty in winter, was cool and fresh in the heat of the Dordogne in June. We had decided to take it for a month and invite a series of friends down. The place had twelve bedrooms and a glorious rambling garden with three tortoises that constantly fell into the swimming pool. In the end, we fixed up a sort of rescue raft for them and they had a wonderful time, struggling out only to plunge back in with a self-satisfied plop. We lazed by the pool, ate the local food and stocked up on local wine.

William had arranged a complicated scheme that involved him only being without a girlfriend for one day of the entire month. How it worked, I shall never know, but it did. One left and another arrived, almost like clockwork. It wouldn't have worked if I'd tried it, that was for sure. But Inno came down to keep me company for the middle two weeks and I was quite content with that. Innogen Harcourt, Ben Harcourt's daughter, our neighbours in Hampshire - "so suitable", everyone thought. Everyone except Inno and I, that is! It was a joke between us and we teased our respective relatives about it. But joke or no, none the less Inno did come down to France and I gained much pleasure from showing her the caves and mediæval walled town and the local cafés. I enjoyed, too, making love to her each night, warm, gratifyingly responsive, affectionate and fun, snuggled up close to me, talking nonsense into the small hours, good friends who had sex every now and then, an uncommon situation, maybe, but it suited us both. At least, it suited me and she seemed happy enough. I have to admit that I missed her when she left, to return to her law practice in the City.

Our various friends came and went and it was our most successful holiday ever. Eventually we closed up the house once more, returned the key to the local agent and William and I set off north again, heading for Le Havre and home. We gave ourselves four days to travel the distance, so our journey was leisurely. We stopped for the night here and there, taking the back routes as opposed to the motorways and selecting suitable 'logis' for our overnight stops. On our last night in France we promised ourselves something special and chose a hotel that was also a château. It was featured in every superior guide book there was and was bursting with stars and chefs' hats to prove it was excellent.

We arrived about four in the afternoon and William pulled up his Aston Martin outside the yellowing stonework of the Château Viezy. An Irish Wolfhound lay in the doorway and raised one eyebrow at us as we climbed, stiffly, from the car. We had to step over him to get in. His tail thumped on the floor and the sound echoed along the hallway and into the dim recesses behind the Reception.

It was cool away from the scorching heat and the stairs wound their way upwards, disappearing in the soft dark above. I filled out the registration form under the helpful gaze of the young fellow who appeared at the sound of the tail thumping. While credit cards etc were asked for and supplied, I looked about me. Across the hall I could see through one of the lounges and out onto the terrace. Chairs were placed beneath sunshades, invitingly, and a dark-suited waiter glided between them, flicking a crumb away from a table top or straightening a chair cushion. Signed in and shown our rooms, opposite each other on the first floor landing, William and I went downstairs again and out to the terrace where, although only the mid-afternoon, drinks were brought. What the hell, why not, this was our last day in France and we weren't going anywhere until the following morning.

The château was built slightly above the surrounding countryside and it was the only building that we could see, except for the odd barn or two, for miles. It was quiet and still, disturbed only by the buzz of bees and the haunting call of the hoopoe. Apart from a woman wheeling her charge in a pushchair the other side of the lawns, there was no one out there. We seemed to be the only visitors. I went back to the Reception to try and find some cigarettes. Another car had pulled up but I could hear the Reception clerk telling the four tourists (obviously and embarrassingly English) that there were no rooms available. I obtained what I wanted and went back outside. It seemed odd to think that this huge, quiet house was full. Oh well... and that was when I saw her, we both saw her, in fact, at the same moment.

2

A girl was coming up through the uncut grass beyond the edge of the lawn. In her hand swung a basket and as she got closer, we could see it was filled with mushrooms. She came up on to the terrace and smiled down at us.

"Good afternoon, monsieur," looking at William, "monsieur," looking at myself. "Welcome to the Château Viezy. Is there anything I can get for you? Please, sit down," for both William and I had instantly risen to our feet.

We ordered two citron pressé this time, more wine could wait now till dinner, and she brought them back, the tall glasses glistening with moisture from the icy contents. We made conversation. She told us about the château and its history. It was interesting. It had been many things over the centuries but none so important as the arms store for the German army in World War Two. She went to fetch a brochure from the reception area, to explain it further.

William looked at me quizzically. "Go on, Rob. Now's your chance. Follow her."

"What do you mean?"

He laughed and said nothing, sipping his drink. He just sat there grinning at me.

I stood up, uncertain, and walked into the hallway. Outlined against the pale curtain behind her, I could see the girl. She had pulled the register towards her and turned it round in order to read it properly. As she read what was written there, I could see her tense. She put her hand over her mouth, staring at the page in front of her. She spun away, staring at the wall, her hands still pressed to her mouth.

I was disturbed. Was it our names she was reading? Why this extreme reaction? It can't have been the fact that we were English. That would have been obvious from our conversation. Both William's and my French was good, but not good enough to have been taken for Frenchmen by one of their own race. I went back outside and sat down again, frowning.

William was still grinning as he looked at me. "Well? You were quick."

I shook my head. "I don't think she was pleased to..." But as I spoke, she came out again and she was smiling.

"Englishmen. Brothers?"

I was right. It was us she was reading about. We nodded.

"Which is which?" She was bright and animated and it disturbed me even more, somehow.

William told her. I was watching her and I saw her look at William - a long look as she chattered about England and suddenly her gaze was on me and from that moment, she, quite clearly, determined I was to be the one.

She was polite to William and friendly and relaxed but with me, she flirted outrageously. I could not pretend that I was not flattered. Her name was Madeleine, she said and she set out to get me, and with William's amused encouragement, I let her know it wasn't a waste of time. It wasn't a situation I was used to, at least not in that very obvious way, but I adapted pretty quickly. Gradually, the vision of her shocked reaction at the sight of the register faded. It was obvious that it was something else that had disturbed her. She was lively and relaxed and happy.

Eventually, saying she would see us later in the dining room, Madeleine took herself and her mushrooms off to the kitchens and we went up to our respective rooms to change for dinner. The shower was refreshing after the day's travelling and the rough towels smelled of lavender. Our rooms were beamed and the walls a mixture of white plastering and exposed brickwork, the beds turned down neatly for the night. I watched the television for half an hour, French television is quite appalling, I thought, and then crossed the landing and thumped on William's door. He opened it at once and we went down into the dining room via the bar.

There was no one else there. Subdued noise came from the kitchen and soon we were subjected to the most superior service from some three or four waiters who flitted unobtrusively about, bringing us this and that and serving the exquisite food and wine.

The evening light grew dim and the sun slid down behind the horizon. As the brandy arrived, Madeleine appeared from nowhere to pour us coffee. Her corn coloured hair hung down on to her shoulders and her bare brown legs went on for ever under her short, sexy black cocktail dress. We invited her to join us for a drink which she accepted, sitting sideways on her chair, resting her cheek in her hand, her eyes hardly ever leaving my face.

William disappeared, making some excuse, with a balloon of brandy in one hand and a cigar in the other and his expression of pure, exaggerated innocence was an infuriation I would take up with him next morning. Madeleine sat down in the chair he had vacated, as opposed to the one opposite and looked at me some more.

I gave her a cigarette and watched her as she leaned forward over the match. I could see the little gold hairs on the back of her hands that went on up her arms. Bleached by the near-constant sun, they showed up against her brown skin. She leaned over further and I watched her cleavage deepen in front of me, inviting and sexy. Her eyes met mine over the flame. They were almond-shaped and brilliant green. They were like the eyes of a mermaid, a siren, and I knew I would never again see eyes like that.

And later on, though not much later, in that gently lit room of mine, with the thoughtful, silky sheets, all through that long night of passionate encounter, in which she moaned seductively and flatteringly, those green eyes looked up at me through half-closed lids and I knew I was bewitched...

3

I woke the next morning and rolled over. I was alone. I could hear the hoopoes crooning and whooping to each other, the most evocative sound of France for me. I lay there for a while, thinking about her. I wondered why me but was somehow humbly grateful for her choice! She was undoubtedly an experienced young women, of that there was no doubt and the sex had been electrifying. And what now? Anything? Or were we to be ships that pass in the night? I sighed. It seemed to me that that is what it would become. I had no time to carry on a long-distance love affair with any kind of success.

I got up, showered and wandered down to the dining room again and found William, already half way through his breakfast and poring over a copy of La Monde. In answer to my greeting he flicked down a corner of the paper and looked at me over the top of it. I couldn't see his mouth but I knew he was grinning at me.

I ordered coffee and croissants and stared at the back of William's paper. The silly season extended to the French papers, too, I thought. There was not much of note. A speculative discussion about the candidates in the forthcoming Presidential election that would be held in the autumn of the following year and an article about a Dutch war hero who had just been declared bankrupt and who appeared to have done a runner. A preview of the autumn fashion collections caught my eye. I was pleased to note that skirts would be even shorter this winter and jeans skin tight. I thought of Madeleine and her long brown legs and what she managed to do with them - well, all her body, really...

Over the top of the paper I suddenly caught sight of William's mocking smile.

"Fuck off," I said in a comradely way and he grinned wider than ever.

"Fuck off and on, I'd say by the look of you. You appear a trifle tired, my boy."

I slid my hand over my face, my first two fingers making a deliberate V sign on either side of my nose and he laughed. The coffee arrived and the smell was wonderful, putting almost all other thoughts out of my mind other than I knew I was starving. Not surprising with the level of activity I had expended half the night.

As I piled our overnight bags into the car, ready to set off, William paid the bill. I let down the soft top and watched it, folding itself carefully and very precisely behind the seats. I heard a step on the gravel and turned. Madeleine was looking at me, fresh and lovely in the early morning sun. She smiled.

"Au revoir, Robert. Maybe I will come to England."

"Do. Don't wait too long."

"You are a wonderful lover, cheri."

"So are you. But you'll want my address."

She laughed softly. "But I have it! It is in the Register. I looked it up yesterday, when I had seen you on the terrace. I was interested even then, you see."

She was still smiling and I pushed away the question mark that formed in my head. I kissed her and she responded, the kiss sexy and intimate and very French. If this went on we wouldn't be leaving till lunchtime, I thought and her hand slid under my tee shirt, heading downwards, her fingers squirming in under the belt of my jeans. I returned the compliment. William appeared. She brought the kiss to an end and stepped away from me. Her eyes were dark and I could see she was aroused again, as I was beginning to be but there was nothing for it, we had to be off. She stood there, waving, as we disappeared round the bend in the drive. When we pulled out into the open road, I looked back again. The front of the Château was in full view once more and I could see her slowly walking up the steps, hands thrust deep into the pockets of her frock. She looked sunk in thought and did not look in our direction again.

Back in England, all returned to normal and life became increasingly hectic with the forthcoming "circus". I travelled a lot, mostly to America, and France did not appear on my itinerary again. Life was too busy for me to think of a holiday fling or to miss Madeleine and there were other girls and other gently lit bedrooms. But now and then, in the odd, quiet moment, the memory of those unforgettable unique almond-shaped green eyes came back to haunt my dreams and disturb more than a few of my waking moments...

"Is that all?" Adrian had been silent as I told the story and I had almost forgotten I had an audience as I talked, thinking my thoughts out loud.

I smiled, slightly sheepishly. I wasn't accustomed to making confessions of such intimacy to people nearly as old as my parents and not often to my own generation. Descriptions of encounters were confined to, 'Got lucky, did you?' or 'Hot, was she?' and possibly, but rarely, the completely unambiguous, 'Fuck her, did you?' All I said to his query now was, "Yes, I think so. Isn't that enough?"

He nodded. "For the moment." He was thoughtful for a moment or two then grinned swiftly, "Lucky young bugger, aren't you? God, you young people don't know you're born, half the time! Back in the day for my generation..." He shook his head, still amused, a trifle envious.

I continued to look mildly embarrassed. "Well, it was fairly unusual, you know. It wasn't a typical encounter, to be honest... Why I remembered it, really..." I attempted some feeble justification.

He laughed and got up. "Hmm. Yes, sure." He was clearly disbelieving. "Anyway, I'll see you soon. Take care of your mother." He went to the door and turned. "By the way, Rob, on an entirely different matter, what are you going to do with the estate? Are you going to come down here and run it?"

I stared at him, shocked afresh. This was Will's role - his destiny not mine.

"Oh, my... God..." I couldn't think of anything to say.

"If you take my advice..."

"Yes?" Anything was welcome.

"Why not appoint a first class manager? At the very least it would give you a breathing space."

A manager? Slowly I took in the idea. "Yes, yes... maybe you're right. I shall need to think about it and not for too long, either, I imagine." I stared at the enormous pile of letters and packets that had appeared beside me from somewhere. He left me and I went out to the kitchen and made more coffee. A nurse had arrived and Helena disappeared upstairs with cups and biscuits on a tray. I took my coffee back to the dining room and miserably addressed myself to the mail.

Extracted from Police records (2):

"They've found a bomb, Sam."

"Shit."

"Yes. So, it's down to us now."

"Yes."

"Do you know this family? I see from info just in both the victim and his brother went to Milldale School. So did you, didn't you?" Sam nodded. "Did you know them?"

"Yes. William was two years above me but, Robert..." a slight hesitation, "Robert was my year."

"So, any personal reason why you shouldn't take this case?"

"No."

"Seen either recently?"

"William, briefly. I've not seen Robert for several years."

"Good. Over to you then, Sam." He handed across a slim document entitled, simply, "Berkeley" and the date. "Adrian Merchant is the Chief Constable of Hampshire. Know him?"

"No, but he has a good reputation, doesn't he?"

"He does. One of the best. You'll get full co-operation there."

"Right. I'll get on to it. Who's in charge of forensics? Do you know, sir?"

"I only know it's the Hampshire team but they're first class."

"Right. I'll get on to them now and start the usual stuff. Searches are on-going already, I understand."

"Catch up the end of the day, right?"

Sam got up, heading for the corridor, "Yes, of course," and left the office, closing the door quietly. Once outside, Sam leaned briefly against the wall, eyes closed, no one about, thinking, thinking. "Oh... my... God. Should I have taken this on? Should I?"

But the die was cast and briskly now, the new officer-in-charge walked back to the office and started to call the team together. It was going to be a long day and without a doubt the most difficult case in Sam's very distinguished, high profile career.

Chapter 3

1

The day dragged on and nurses came and nurses went. Furniture was shoved here and there to rearrange my father's dressing room into a hospital to satisfy my mother's organising spirit and once more I was sitting and thinking, staring out across the park. A car wound its way up the drive and one I recognised for a change. Out of it, immaculately clad, as always, emerged the sad little figure of Inno, my earlier companion on that unforgettable French holiday. She ran quickly up the front path, past the front door and on round the side. She came straight in, as she had always done. I heard voices in the corridor and in another moment, she opened the door. She crossed the room and put her arms round me, saying nothing for a long moment. She held me away from her and I looked down at the floor. I couldn't trust myself to look into her face.

"Robert. Dearest Robert. I'm so sorry. Our beloved, darling, William. I loved him, too. We all did." I turned away from her. Her kindness was so utterly genuine I couldn't bear it. "And now your father. Poor, poor Sir William."

I went over and sat at the table and began to push papers and documents idly, about. I hadn't seen much of her, what with travelling and everything, since my French escapade and having to think about it all in detail earlier had made me feel slightly guilty. And that was all I needed, guilt on top of total misery. I frowned and muttered something, irritably.

She watched me for a moment and then sat down next to me. She glanced at the heap of letters. When she spoke again her tone was different, efficient and firm.

"Robert, you cannot do all this on your own, really you can't. You've your London business to run as well. Have you thought about it?"

Grateful for the change of subject and eager to share this growing dread, I looked at her properly for the first time. She was regarding me rather as a doctor looks at a patient, with a sort of concerned detachment.

"Adrian mentioned it earlier. He suggested getting a manager in. But I know nothing of the qualities necessary for an estate manager. Besides, William did so much more than that. Apart from the Education Centre, which I set up, if you recall, I don't know the first bloody thing about any of it."

My "doctor" continued to look at me with that same look of clinical objectivity, but this time she put her hand on my arm.

"I think you probably know a lot more than you think you do. You've lived in the midst of it all your life but listen, I have an idea. I've thought about it carefully. I rang up Pa, too and he thinks it's a good idea."

I looked up, surprised. "I thought they were away on some cruise ship?"

"They are. But the mobiles work more often than not and they do have ship to shore radios when needed! Now, listen. You already have Mark who helps with the running of the farms, don't you?" I nodded. He'd been with us for about three years, I thought. He was a farmer, really, but William had promoted him as manager of all the estate farms and he was excellent, that much I did know. What he didn't know about animals and grazing and all aspects of farming wasn't worth knowing, I gathered.

I was doubtful. "Yes. But he can't run the other bit, can he? I don't know if he could even run the farming side entirely unsupervised, Inno." I pushed the papers about even more in my anxiety.

Once again her hand on my arm calmed my restless movements. "Wait a minute, I haven't finished yet. Why not ask Martin to help you, to run the business side and liaise with Mark over the farm? Jane's been William's secretary for ages and I think the three of them could manage, certainly to begin with. Pa agrees with me."

I stood up and walked to the windows again. Martin was Inno's brother and Jane his wife of six months. Jane had worked for William for ages but I had never thought of asking Martin. He had recently been made redundant from some huge public relations firm or other. He'd been financial controller, I recalled and they had paid him very handsomely to leave when the firm had been taken over by some newspaper tycoon. They wanted their own man in the job. Martin was probably pleased. He was famously totally Boy Scout straight in business and the new owner was likely not to be, so Martin left with a legitimate handsome payout without having to stalk off without a brass farthing in offended high principles.

I sat down again. I toyed with the idea in my mind. Mark I didn't know too well but if William and Father had been pleased with him enough to keep him in his job for three years he ought to be OK. And Martin? Why I hadn't thought of him myself, I don't know. I'd been his best man and Jane was just wonderful. I frowned again. Why had I been so stupid as not to think of this? I looked at Inno and said as much.

She smiled. "Dear Rob. What have you been thinking about, then?"

I looked down again. "William... and Dad," I said simply.

"Precisely." She jumped up and put her arms round me again and this time kissed my cheek before she sat down. I looked at her some more and her eyes were very bright. "Now," her brisk voice was switched on again. "I hoped you'd see the possibilities in the plan and so Martin and Jane are coming over for supper. You come, too and then if you can agree, all three of you, tomorrow you can speak to Mark and see how it all goes. If the worst comes to the worst, at least you can have two or three days in London each week straight away and later, if it works out, you can start travelling the sale rooms of the world again."

I looked at her and shook my head. "Not yet, Inno. I realise that's quite a way off yet."

"Certainly not yet. But it's what you want to do really, isn't it?"

I glanced up at a Stubbs that hung at the end of the dining room. What a find that had been! Tucked away in some funny sale room in Amsterdam, of all places. I smiled at it, remembering. A private sale from a very private Dutch businessman, who, I assumed, had fallen on hard times. The price had been fair but I still had got a bargain. But...

"I don't know, Inno. Maybe. But my life is going to change a lot. I really will have to help run Forbridge, probably in a fairly major way that I can't envisage at present. It's my home, it's my parents' home, well, it's sort of a national institution. I think I've realised that much in my aimless mental exercises of the last few days, at any rate. I'll work it out but," and here it was my turn to take her hand, "thank you. Thank you for thinking up this plan. I really believe it is the answer. It feels right somehow. But what of Martin, will he be willing?" I looked at her anxiously.

She smiled. "Of course he's willing. Do you think I would get your hopes up only to have them dashed? Whatever do you think of me, Rob?"

Ah, what did I think of her. I was enormously fond of her, really. Perhaps...

She got up. "I'll see you later. Come over about seven. I'm looking after the house and the animals for the parents while they are away on their jaunt. That'll give me time to get something of a meal ready and give us plenty of time to thrash this out."

"Seven, yes. I'll let Mother know and then I'll tell Helena not to feed me this evening."

"Fine."

I took her shoulders in both my hands and kissed her. She smelled wonderful and I buried my face in her hair. I kissed her again, with increasing passion but she gently released herself from me. There was pain in her eyes again, suddenly, but only for a moment. "Dearest Rob," she said quietly. She picked up her keys that had been thrown down onto the papers. "See you at seven, then," her tone was light and social and she was gone, leaving me with very mixed feelings.

2

I spent most of the day poring over papers and letters. There were several heaps. Those to do with the farm, those to do with the education centre, those to do with the rest of it and letters of sympathy. This last pile was the largest. As I read them, one after another, I wondered for whose benefit they were. I know they were meant to be for us but the pain of reading them was excruciating. I put aside uncharitable thoughts as well as the letters for the moment and went to find some tea in the kitchens.

Helena was there, our housekeeper. She had been around for years, ever since I was a boy. I gave her a hug and then sat on a stool at the end of the table and watched her as she made sandwiches and sliced up fruit cake. Helena was an old school friend of my mother's. Many an evening they had spent, they told me, giggling under the bedclothes in their dormitory, reading some forbidden book. Helena had had the misfortune to marry a bounder (Mother's word for him). After he had gone through her money (and there had not been a great deal of that, either) he'd upped and left her for a summer season/pantomime dancer who had won the Pools a few months earlier. They went to South America or somewhere and had never been seen again. Poor Helena was homeless (the house that had been hers had been mortgaged without her knowing) and, of course, being educated as a lady meant she had been taught to do absolutely nothing at all except housekeep and run homes, arrange flowers and entertain.

My parents promptly offered her a home (she had a suite of rooms in the East Wing) and a job - to help look after the family - and that she had done ever since. We all loved her and she was as much part of the family as any of us, and more so than many, particularly those distant cousins and whatnot one only ever meets at weddings.

While I was munching my third piece of fruit cake, amongst everything else Helena was a superb cook, the phone rang. She answered it and listened and then waved it in my direction.

"It's Jane. There's a call for you from France. He's talking French."

"France? I don't know anyone in..." I stopped. Yes, I did. Still, it was unlikely to be her, besides, Helena had said, 'he'. "Oh well, I'll see who it is." I took the phone from her.

"Hello. Robert Berkeley here."

The caller spoke in French and I answered him accordingly. "Robert. We have not met. But I am sure you know of me. I am an old friend of your father. My name is Jean-Yves de la Flèche."

The name rang a bell. I thought he was something to do with the French government, but I wasn't sure. However, it seemed rude to say I didn't really know him from Adam.

"Yes, sir, of course. Er... What can I do for you?"

"Your father has talked about me? You know who I am then, yes?"

"Er... sure..."

He cut in, which was just as well. "I am merely ringing to express my condolences. I understand the eldest son of my great friend has been killed in a plane accident. That is true, yes?"

"He was my brother, and yes, it is true."

"I spoke to a young woman. She is your wife?"

He can't have spoken to my father that recently or he'd know I wasn't married. "No. She is my father's secretary."

"Ah, so that is it. I asked to speak to Sir William and she tells me he is very ill. What has happened?"

"He's had a..." I couldn't remember the word for stroke in French, it isn't a word you use every day. "...I can't think of the word, but it is the shock, it has... how can I put it... A blood clot on the brain."

"Oh, how terrible, terrible.. Yes, I know what you mean now. L'accident vasculaire cérébral. Le AVC. Will he get better?"

"We hope so, sir. The doctors are hopeful but it is too early to say."

"Then I'll not hold you up any more. I could not let this sad event go by without my contacting you. You will tell your father I rang, when he is better?"

"Yes, of course and thank you very much."

"Perhaps I may ring again, for a progress report? My family are all away at the moment on various missions and I am alone. It makes me think even more about you all in this sad case."

"Oh yes, I understand. Do ring, yes, indeed. Any time."

"God's blessings on your family, Robert. I am so, so sad. I think about you. Goodbye."

I put the phone back on the rest I looked at Helena who was looking at me with a certain amount of pride.

"You do speak French beautifully, Robert. Just like your father."

"Thanks, Helena."

"Who was it?"

"I don't know, really. He said he was an old friend of Father's. I didn't know he had any friends in France. This fellow seemed to think we should know all about him. It was a bit embarrassing, really. Oh well..." I shrugged and got off the stool. "Back to the paperwork. Oh, and Helena, I shall be out for supper. I'm going to Inno's."

"Are you, now? That's nice, dear. Do you good." She had a twinkle in her eye. There was nothing Helena didn't know about us all.

I gave her a look and she giggled quietly and turned back to the sink.

I slowly left the room. It was funny we should have been talking about France and French friends such a short while ago and here was one, turning up out of the blue. Only one I had no idea about. Odd. I returned to the dining room and my task.

3

With Father settled comfortably with a night nurse quietly flitting about the sick room, I persuaded Mother to go to bed. Dear, faithful Helena took her up a light meal and I left for the Harcourts reasonably content with things at Forbridge, at least for the evening, if nothing else.

I whistled for my black Labrador, Nell. A constant companion of mine, she was always welcome at Inno's. She looked up at me expectantly as we left the house. I knew what she wanted. "Dad's car, Nell. Dad's car." She raced away from me. It was a game we had. She had learned which car belonged to which member of the family and she never got it wrong. We swapped cars sometimes, just to test her and she still got it right. Mine, Will's, Father's or Mother's and also Helena's. She had recently added Jane's to her collection. She raced off and stood beside my father's Land Rover. I clicked the remote as I approached, unlocking the door and her tail wagged faster. It was my signal to her she had got it right. I made a fuss of her as I always did and pleased with herself, she jumped in and across the front to sit on the passenger seat, her tail still beating a rhythm on the leather. I climbed in beside her. To my rage and dismay, there was a policeman on duty beside it "as a precaution". I felt sick and my hands shook on the wheel as I drove off down the drive. Evil bastards! Who were they, these monsters who made the intrusion necessary, who wrecked peoples' lives? And why, for God's sake? I stopped abruptly before the drive turned into the main road and pulled out a cigarette, something I only rarely did these days. Nell pushed a cold, wet nose against my hand. I sat there for five minutes, the window open, watching the smoke curl up and out of the car, stroking her smooth coat. I was calmed again and drove off to the Harcourts in a slightly less tormented state than when I set forth.

A few minutes later I was pulling up outside the rambling Victorian manor that belonged to our neighbour. Martin's Audi was parked alongside Inno's mini and I stopped next to it. No policemen here, I thought, grimly. However, I set the alarm with a curious mixture of feelings, half-irritation and half-relief that I had the ability to protect myself from whoever might be out there.

Inno was already at the top of the steps to receive me. I kissed her briefly, a social gesture of guest to hostess, not the sort of kiss I had given her earlier (and surprised myself doing it, too). I handed her a pot plant I had fished from the greenhouses as a last minute gift. She buried her nose in its exotic, scentless blooms and I followed her along the hallway. Nell pattered along in front of me, tail waving, the Harcourts' dogs greeting her warmly. She knew her way well but headed, sensibly, for the kitchens and didn't even turn her head as we turned off the corridor.

"Drinks in the conservatory." Inno opened the door.

Martin and Jane both stood up as I went in. He grasped my hand and she hugged me tight. I was quite composed but then I had been prepared for this meeting. We can preserve our veneer when there is advance warning. It is the chance encounter, the unexpected phone call that knocks you sideways and it is those moments that leave one raw and bleeding.

They took their cue from me. I was solemn but calm and I could see them relax in the knowledge that I was, currently, anyway, "all right about it." The gin and tonic, however, was just what I needed and we talked quietly of the events of the last few days. Almost without my noticing, Inno refilled my glass and I, too, for the first time began to feel the tenseness in my muscles subside.

Over dinner, we began to discuss Forbridge. Martin had thought a lot about it. I did most of the listening, with the odd word here and there. Night began to fall and Inno's tapering candles grew slowly shorter, dipping and flickering in the faint breeze that stirred the curtains. The deep red of the Burgundy winked at me from the depths of my glass and the gentle chink of the cutlery on the plates was soporific. The wine was good, the food was good and my spirits lifted a fraction. The heavy weight of responsibility was going to be shared with people who loved William, who loved my family and who wanted to preserve Forbridge as much as he had done.

Suddenly, I knew I wanted that, too. I had never considered myself in any way to be concerned by the mechanics of running the family business, it just trundled its way on as it more or less always had done, simply my family home and where I had grown up. But then, up till now, it had not been threatened. Now it was no longer safe with its guardian gone and suddenly I knew I had to keep it all going - going in a way that William would have wanted. But it was not just for him and his memory that it mattered. It was for its own sake and for mine. For the first time in my life I was possessive about it. A shiver ran through me and disturbed my reverie. The cloak of Elijah? Ah, well, maybe. And now, with these good people to help me, just maybe my shoulders were broad enough to wear it.

So, we made plans. Martin would come over in the morning and we would start to look at things together. Jane would be invaluable for everything that William had started to achieve had had her hand in it too. There wasn't a single thing she hadn't been involved in. Together she would teach us both. I would speak to Mark. We would offer him a rise in salary and an increase in responsibility and see how we got along. I would gradually familiarise myself with the running of everything and spend at least three days a week working in Hampshire and the weekend as well. The other working days I would spend in London and I would reorganise the running of the antiques business round Forbridge. I was satisfied and reasonably hopeful. Martin was fired with enthusiasm.

The important decisions over, I began to relax and Inno dangerously brought out some unbelievably ancient and superb port. I had decided much earlier in the evening that I would summon a cab to take me home. Slowly, quietly and deliberately, with enormous pleasure, I became pretty drunk. The night held me in a velvet grip. I was not maudlin or angry, merely lulled by the warmth of the balmy night and Ben Harcourt's

30 year old anaesthetic. The dining chairs were high backed carvers and I leaned my weight into the one I occupied, relaxed as I hadn't been since before the horror began. We talked of everything, the world and its problems, love and hate and gossip and politics, anything.

I remember vaguely being helped upstairs. I could smell Inno's Chanel Number something or other and the bedroom was full of velvet as had been the dining room. But the rest of the night was lost to me as I lay insensible in their best guest room, the first night's sleep I had had since William's murder that was not punctuated by nightmares.

4

Waking next morning was a slow climb from comfortable oblivion into the pain-filled world of the hangover. Inno was sitting on the edge of the bed when I opened my eyes and shut them again quick. An arc-light was shining directly into my face and six men with hammers were hitting me smartly and rhythmically on the head. I also vaguely wondered why someone had carefully lined my mouth with sandpaper. Through the noise of the hammers I heard Inno speak.

"Coffee, Robert. God, you smell awful!"

It crossed my mind that was not a polite thing to say to the Almighty. I think I said so for I could hear Inno laugh. I caught something about being "not too bad if you can crack terrible jokes." She shook me.

"Come on, Robert, you drunken old soak. Drink your coffee. Martin and Jane are waiting to start work at Forbridge."

I struggled to a sitting position. I sipped at the coffee and obediently swallowed two paracetamols. Gradually some of the hammering men knocked off for lunch and eventually gave up work altogether. I looked at Inno properly for the first time. She was fresh and bright in navy jodhpurs and cream shirt. Her hair was tied back in a clip thing.

I grinned sheepishly. "Oh dear, I'm sorry, Inno. Did I disgrace myself?"

She smiled a secret sort of smile. "Well, you said a lot of rubbish. Really, Robert, you get very amorous when you're drunk!"

Damn! And I didn't remember a thing. Did I...? Had we... er... had we...? I looked at her. "Inno, did I...? er... Oh God, I'm so sorry, I can't remember anything after about my third glass of port. Um... did... did we... ?"

She answered my unfinished question. "No way, Mr Berkeley! I know what you're thinking and most certainly we did not! You fell asleep as soon as your head touched the pillow, maybe even earlier. You were heavy enough. It took all three of us to get you up here." She hesitated. "I did sleep here, though. I was worried you might be sick and choke. I'm glad to say you didn't." She smiled again swiftly. She looked very charming sitting there, demurely beside me on the edge of the bed.

"I'll have to make it up to you." I pulled her towards me.

She wriggled away from me and stood up.

"Come on. Get up. You can come for a ride... "

"Hmm, yes, riding. That's the idea..."

"No, Robert, not that sort of ride! God, you're still at it! Are you sure you're sober? Breakfast first then down to the stables with you! I'll saddle Contessa for you and you can ride... er... no, hack will be a better word. You can hack back over to Forbridge. It'll do you more good than anything."

I tried again, pulling her down onto the bed again. "There's something better than hacking, I can think of. Come on, Inno. I'll be a good boy for you, I promise. I know what you like, naughty girl and I want to say thank you..."

She laughed again and escaped once more. "No, Robert! I mean it. A gentle canter over the hills is called for, not activity all over our best guest bed! Jane has driven the Land Rover back for you. There is an old pair of Martin's jodhs next to your clothes. Put them on. I'm coming over with you. Now hurry or it'll be lunchtime before you've done a thing."

I made another grab for her but she was gone. I could hear her laughing as she closed the door and her footsteps receded down the corridor. I sighed, and struggled out of bed. Staring down at my naked body it made me think afresh about which one of the three it was who had undressed me so carefully and who it was who had placed my clothes, now neatly folded, on the dressing table stool. I walked into the bathroom and stared in the mirror over the basin. I didn't get any answers from the reflection either, as I brooded over the question.

After more coffee downstairs and croissants, shared with Nell, I sought out Inno in the stable yard. Contessa was Ben's huge chestnut mare, as comfortable as a rocking horse, just the thing for a man with a hangover. We mounted and set off at a leisurely pace, Nell trotting along, working her way through the undergrowth, as happy as only a dog can be on such a jaunt.

We talked of the plans we had made the night before.

"Are you sure you're happy with all this? You don't think I interfered, do you?" Her brow furrowed anxiously.

"Of course you interfered but I'm thankful you did. I don't know what I would have done without you. I hope it all works out. I can't think why it shouldn't, though. It seems to have all the ingredients for success." I picked a spray of late honeysuckle from the hedge and gave it to her. She smelled at it, smiling and leant forward in the saddle, tucking it into her horse's brow band. Her mount, Masterman, flicked back his ears as if to appreciate the sweet smell.

"Inno?"

"Yes?"

"Last night..." I stopped. She smiled that funny secret smile again (Why is it women do that? I'll never understand them.)

"Yes? Last night?"

"Er... who put me to bed?"

"I told you. Martin and Jane and I. You were very heavy, you can't think. We..."

I interrupted her. Her mock-innocent expression was infuriating. I knew she knew what I meant but she was making me force the words out. "Inno! You know what I mean."

Silence. Just that bloody smile again.

"Inno, who undressed me?"

She pushed her horse further on, just in front of me. Now she looked back at me again over her shoulder. "If you can catch me, Robert Berkeley, I'll tell you. If you can't, you live in ignorance. Race you!"

And before I could do anything she shot off up the bridleway. Nell gave a short, sharp bark of delight and was off, too.

"Right, you asked for it!" I urged Contessa forward and I could feel her catch the excitement. She bucked once and was away, cantering up the slope after them. But Inno had quite a lead and Masterman was an ex-polo pony and very fast. She just beat me to the stable yard and flung herself off, laughing, breathless.

"Too late, I won!"

I laughed too and dismounted rather gingerly. My head had not yet quite recovered normality. "I'll pay you back, you teasing wench."

"Wench? Is that how you see me? You'll regret that one, all right!"

The banter went on a bit as we went into the house together and the day's work began in earnest.

Mark agreed readily to his part in the reorganisation. He was a pleasant fellow, deeply shocked still over the horror of everything but almost pathetically grateful to be of genuine service to the family. One thing, however, he flatly refused a rise. "I won't be one to profit from William's death, Robert," he said seriously. "See how I gets on, maybe. But not yet. I couldn't take it. I'd be like blood money. No way."

It was very touching. Martin and I did not look at each other. I muttered something about a wonderful thing to say and stared at the desk. I had to swallow a particularly large lump in my throat before I could address myself to any further business.

I couldn't get used to this display of open affection from everyone and there were many examples of it from every quarter. Several times during the day I went out into the garden to have a cigarette and collect myself into some reasonable composure again. Adrian came back and asked a few additional questions regarding the organisation of the Summer Fair. He was pleased with our plan which we had explained to him. As I showed him out, he turned to me.

"Robert, can you be sure to let me know when exactly it is you are to return to London? I shall want to know where I can get hold of you. Besides, the Metropolitan Anti-Terrorist Squad will have to organise your security for you."

I felt outraged again, as I had when I discovered the policeman fawning beside my Land Rover.

"Is that necessary? You can't think how I hate this side of it, Adrian." I was sharp and he glanced at my hands, the knuckles white on the side of the doorframe.

"People often feel like that. But yes, please, it really is necessary and it will help us enormously. This case is in their hands now, you know, not ours. Think of the Royal family. They have to go through this all the time and MPs and all sorts of people."

"Yes, but not ordinary people like me."

He looked at me sadly, "You are no longer ordinary, Robert. This bastard has made it so, not us - those who are trying to catch him or them."

I felt remorse but frowned. "Very well, if it helps you, but only the minimum, right?" I sighed. "More police! I'm sort of accustomed to you and your lot. Now I've got another bunch to get used to." Self pity washed over me. "Why the Anti-Terrorist Branch?"

"The method of the killing. Bombs are not standard equipment for domestic murder, you see. Knives, poison sometimes, guns, yes but bombs are not available to all. They are specialist weapons. They are in charge of this case, now, not the humble local bobbies." He gave me a sympathetic look. "Don't worry. We're setting it up and you'll see them soon. I have your address in London. Let me know the date you're going back. It won't be till after the funeral, I suppose."

The funeral. Christ! Another nightmare. Another hurdle. Oh fuck... bloody fucking hell...

I nodded curtly and left him, more abruptly than I ought but that was one of the unexpected moments. I felt the pain in the pit of my stomach - a feeling akin to stage fright, or the sinking feeling before you take an exam - the anticipation of the coming dreadful occasion.

We worked hard and achieved much. I went up to my father's room and told him our plans, briefly. He was staring at the wall, his eyes bright over the top of the turned-down sheet (he couldn't stand those 'new fangled eiderdowns', duvets, he meant, as he called them). He made no sign that he had understood but the nurse assured me that he could hear and could take in what I said.

"He will be able to react a bit more in a day or two, I should think and shortly after that I hope he'll be able to speak a little. Try not to worry, Mr Berkeley. He's comfortable, at any rate and much better off here at home than in a hospital."

I sat and held his frail, thin hand for a while. Finally, he slept and slightly reassured, I went downstairs again.

This time, I offered the hospitality. It was getting late. Mother was in bed and no one about. We went into the kitchen and helped ourselves to things out of the larder. We sat round the kitchen table, the four of us, exhausted, munching cold game pie and salad.

I poured out the wine. "This reminds me of coming in from late parties when I was younger and sneaking in, starving, at two in the morning!"

Martin laughed. "Yes, I remember! Particularly one New Year's Eve when..."

I was way ahead of him and recalled the occasion. "Right! OK, Martin, that's enough! Not in front of the ladies, specially as one is your lady wife!" And I gave him a broad wink. We laughed and I got the satisfaction of seeing Inno's questioning expression. A small way to pay her back for her lack of communication of the morning, only small but a victory, nonetheless.

Martin and Jane left but Inno stayed on for another half an hour. She left her horse to collect tomorrow. A couple of the policemen, just about to go off duty, had offered to drive her home on their way back to the station as they would pass the door. They had some uses, after all. She sat, holding my hand rather in the way I had held my father's and I could see the pity on he face.

I looked at her. "You can stay, if... if you'd care to. You know I'd love you to and..."

She smiled gently and released her hand, patting me gently. "Not just at the moment, Rob."

I nodded. I wasn't offended. She was smiling at me gently, fondly. "That's OK. Soon though, I hope. Don't leave it too long."

She said nothing but put out her hand and stroked my hair briefly. We heard a car pull up outside. It was her lift, we surmised. I walked with her to the door.

"Now, Inno, just before you go, last night. Tell. Who was it who...?"

She looked up at me, laughing now. "Well..." She hesitated, choosing the right words. We reached the top of the steps. "Let me say this. You're nice and brown, Rob. I wonder how you can get such a tan in London? The mark where your swimming trunks WERE shows up VERY clearly, even by moonlight!"

"Inno! You...!"

"But I have to say you know very well I've seen you naked! Quite a few times, haven't I, so maybe it wasn't me at all!"

I made a grab for her but she dodged me and was gone. She ran down the steps and climbed into the back of the police car. And although I couldn't see her face, I knew she was smiling that damned smile.

Chapter 4

1

I won't and can't talk about the funeral. I got through it by thinking of something else. It helped to support poor Mother but she managed to be loving and generous and brave as ever. The added cruelty was my father not being there to say goodbye to his son. It seemed the final indignity, somehow. There were crowds and crowds of people thronging the little village church. They spilled out over into the graveyard and there were loudspeakers put outside. It was quite the most terrible ordeal I have ever had to face. Afterwards I took Nell out for a walk. We stood together at the top of the beech hangers looking out over the valley and I swore several times, obscenely and with great sincerity, felt a bit better and came home. I consumed two or three whiskies, went to bed and the day was over.

The following day I had to attend another - that of one of the crew who had died alongside William. I didn't know him but I knew I must go to represent our family. Once again, I thought of nothing. The family were touchingly grateful for my presence. But that was the last of it. The other funeral was only for the immediate family and his closest work colleagues and friends, they had said. I felt guilty for feeling a profound relief at not having to attend another nerve-shredding occasion.

A few days later, with things beginning to take some sort of order, I decided I must have a couple of days in London. Father was brighter and had, indeed, said a few whispered words to Mother's great joy and delight. I left her in hopeful spirits.

Martin was really getting to grips with things. Mark had blossomed even further and with Inno back at her law practice in the City, Nell and I set off for the gallery in Chelsea. I had an appointment with someone from the Met's Anti-Terrorist branch. They would accompany me to the flat later that day after having sent in the sniffer dogs and other, less attractive devices to rootle out possible bombs and explosives. I had given a key to the flat to Adrian, who had in turn passed it on to the London men, ready for my return.

Nell sat beside me, looking out. She knew the A3 almost as well as I did, so often had we travelled the route together. I've never known a dog so adaptable to both town and country life. As long as she was near me, she didn't mind. She glanced at me as we drove along and I could feel her simple happiness of being alone with her master.

It was odd, going into my antique shop. Here was all familiarity, surrounded by the purchases I had made. And yet, the last time I was here, William was still alive. I kept having thoughts like that. This time last week we did this or that. This time last year we were at so and so's. The reminders came thick and fast and without warning.

Several items had been sold, I noticed. I walked between the chairs, noting the pictures that had gone, two small oil paintings from the Dutch school and an abstract. The Queen Anne desk I had bought in Sotheby's last sale had sold, too and some

Venetian glass. I knew my stock very well. It was a very personal business, buying antiques. It was rather like buying Christmas presents, I felt. I could never buy anything I wouldn't like to receive myself.

Jenny came to greet me. We pored over the books and the slight edginess I had felt upon my return ceased, as I fell so quickly into the regular routine.

"There's a policeman coming this afternoon, Robert, about two." She pulled the diary towards and glanced at it. "Chief Inspector Stewart of the Anti-Terrorist squad."

"Yes, I know. They told me. I can't get used to all this watching and cloak and dagger stuff. It's so unlike me and William, too. He was the most open of men. It's... it's even more of an intrusion, somehow." I lit a cigarette, a sure sign I was rattled.

Jenny was soothing and we went out to a wine bar for some over-priced plastic quiche and some equally over-priced vinegar which they were pleased to call wine. I was aware of someone else watching me. Were they ordinary members of the public who thought they recognised me - I was quite often on television on stuff connected with the arts - or was it a member of my so-called bodyguard? It was worse in London, I thought. Too many people.

We came back to the office and Jenny set off for a meeting with the accountants. I opened the new Christie's catalogue to see if there was anything of any interest to me. Immersed, as ever, in my passion, I did not hear the shop bell ring. A shadow fell across the page and I looked up.

"Mr Robert Berkeley." A statement, not a question. I stared. The smile was quick and infectious and had not changed. I remembered schooldays, a multitude of visions rushing in on each other. Tennis tournaments, hockey matches, toasting chestnuts over the common room fire on the end of a pair of dividers. Those same clear, grey eyes looked at me then the way they did now, bright and interested. Immaculately dressed as ever, designer suit, the shirt open at the neck, I couldn't believe it.

"Sam?"

"Sam, as ever was."

I continued to stare and then that ringing laugh and the tossing back of the head. There was no one like Sam...

Seriousness returned. "Robert, I'm so sorry to see you again under such circumstances."

I nodded. I was moved to think that Sam had come to see me. But I was beginning to cope with a reasonable amount of graciousness. I held out a packet of cigarettes.

"I'm sorry, Sam. I'm not myself yet, forgive me. Coffee?" I got up and put on the kettle. Then I remembered. "Damn. I've got a meeting in a few minutes but if you can hang on we can talk after he's gone. He's a policeman from..."

"The Anti-Terrorist squad." Sam interrupted me. Again that ringing laugh. "It's me you're meeting, Robert. I'm Chief Inspector Stewart. Didn't you know I'd joined the force?"

"You?" I struggled briefly with the information, dredging up something from my memory. "God, what an idiot I am! Of course! I just didn't put two and two together and when Jenny said a policeman was coming..." I stopped, thoughts crowding in on me, remembering.

Sam had always been an individual, even at school. One of those "one off" people who generally didn't mind being set apart, somehow, even when one was quite young and conforming to the pack was everything. We revered Sam on the games fields, in class, as Head Pupil, everything and not once resented it. It was no particular surprise to those of us who had seen that individuality grow from such an early age, that the eldest offspring of the Earl of Glenmere should enter the police force, of all things. The press had a field day, of course but that had been several years ago now. And now here was Sam, leaning back in my office Chippendale smoking one of my cigarettes, another friend from the past to help me through the awfulness. First Martin at home and now Sam, here in London. I put my head in my hands.

The sun-tanned hand came forward and squeezed my upper arm. The grip was firm and I could feel the strength oozing from it into me. I looked up. A sort of practical sympathy met my gaze.

"Thank God it's you, Sam. I don't think I could have stood for any more strangers."

"I understand. You and William were always so very close and you were always so sensitive, Rob."

"Not me. You've muddled me up with someone else."

No laugh, this time, but a smile. "No, I haven't. I spoke to Adrian Merchant, Hampshire's Chief Constable, a couple of days ago and he confirmed what I had suspected you might be feeling. I didn't speak to you at William's funeral, though. I thought..."

"You came to the funeral?" I had no idea.

"Of course. Many of us from Milldale did, Rob."

"I saw a lot, all Will's year. I didn't realise..."

"You had enough on your plate..."

I shook my head. "I didn't know. I'm sorry. I didn't know you were there. You should have come over." I felt a sort of panic rising, a sort of hysteria.

Again that strong grip on my wrist. "No, no, Robert. You had enough to cope with, without me as well. I came to see if you were all right and to say goodbye to Will, that is all. I was already in the process of taking over the case and knew I would see you very soon. I interviewed the previous investigating officers and forensic team while I was in Hampshire - discussed matters with them, that sort of thing but I left you for another day - today, as you see. I had the beginnings of information to get to grips with things. It's the way I work at the start of a case."

The whistle on the kettle shrieked suddenly and mercifully and I shot to my feet to make the coffee. My hands gradually stopped shaking and I composed myself afresh. I took my time making it to allow myself to feel more normal and put on some kind of cheerful, relaxed front. I returned to the office and sat down opposite Sam once more. We sipped the scalding drinks and spoke a little small talk. Sam looked about.

"Business doing well, Rob?"

"Yes, I'm pleased to say. We're in a first class location here and it's been successful right from the opening." I indicated a chunky ledger beside me. "All sales, right from the outset. We've the accountants digging about at present, hence this is here."

"Can I see?" Sam seemed casually interested.

"Sure." I pushed it over the desk and Sam opened it, scanning the first page idly. "The first item - one Louis Quinze silver snuff box. That was the first thing you sold?"

I smiled, "Yes. Will bought it - for a friend, he said. He said he wanted to buy the first thing I sold and he did. That was it. I thought he'd actually bought it for himself as he never told me who it was for but it wasn't amongst his things, I think, although I've only given them a cursory glance so far - too soon for too much delving..." I looked away, thinking, remembering, but returned to the ledger again, feeling Sam's eyes on me. "Anyway, I'll never forget that snuff box but I doubt if I'll ever know now who was the recipient with Will... gone..." I stopped.

Sam glanced about. "Have you got a piece of paper and a biro or something so I can make a few notes? I never have them. I'm hopeless."

I laughed. "You never did have! You never took notes for classes and yet you still remembered it all! How, I shall never know. So, a member of Her Majesty's Police and still no notebook! Really, Chief Inspector!"

A grin. "Finished?" I fiddled about in a drawer and found a shorthand notebook and a pen. "Thank you, Robert, so kind! I don't write things down because that is the way I remember them. However, I wish to note down a few dates and times and things and before you say it, that is why I was no good at history! I couldn't remember the dates!"

"If you say so but just about the only thing you weren't any good at!" I grinned back, knowing it all to be nonsense. Sam had been just as good at history as everything else.

"Now..." Sam leaned over the book and sucked the end of the pen. "First of all, we will come to the security angle and then, if you don't mind, we will go back to the flat and have a look at the set-up there and then have a talk about everything. My team have been over it pretty carefully. I want you to see it all and understand what it is and why it is there."

I nodded, frowning.

Sam noticed the frown. "I know you hate the invasion of privacy, Rob, but as we talk maybe you will understand a bit more about why, and how, as a result of it, we'll catch the bastards who killed William. You see, I'm here not just to organise your protection, I'm in charge of the team that is trying to hunt down his killers."

The door opened and Jenny came in. She stopped in her tracks and looked anxiously at my companion.

"Oh dear, Robert, I'm so sorry. I didn't realise that... The meeting was cancelled, by the way, only they'd forgotten to tell me. Hopeless lot! I shall be upstairs if you need me." She hesitated, and looked enquiringly at Sam. "I... I'm so sorry to interrupt. Robert was expecting the police, but..."

I grinned. "This IS the police, Jenny. But also, by all that's wonderful, an old school friend as well. Allow me to introduce to you Chief Inspector Sam Stewart."

Sam smiled. "Don't look so surprised! We don't all wear hob-nailed boots and helmets, you know!"

Jenny blushed. "No... er, no. Of course not. But I thought... I was expecting... expecting..."

"Someone older?" A slight warning note sounded in Sam's voice and I could see by the expression on Jenny's face that she had heard it, too.

"Yes, yes, indeed... someone older... I'm so sorry to have interrupted. I'll leave you and get on. Er... 'Bye." She backed out.

I looked thoughtful, taking in this modern enigma before me. "You were quietly reprimanding her, I think."

Sam fiddled with the pen. "Maybe I was but sometimes people deserve it and... er... your Jenny deserved it."

"She's not my Jenny, she's my business partner. She's someone else's Jenny, if you follow me."

Again the grey eyes regarded me and this time the expression was impossible to read. "Yes, Rob, I follow you. Whose Jenny is she, then?"

"Her husband's and her children's, too, I think it right to add. Why do you ask, particularly?"

Sam's answer mirrored my question, "It's my job to ask, particularly, Rob. Now then, where were we..." And Sam addressed the notebook once more, a ghost of a smile hovering there.

It was a funny sort of smile, though and I'd seen it before somewhere, quite recently. But whose smile it was, and on whose face I had seen it, watching Sam in the afternoon sun, I couldn't for the life of me remember.

2

Extracted from Police records (3):

"Darren?"

"Chief?"

"I'm leaving Chelsea in a few minutes. Robert Berkeley has just gone to get his car. Traffic permitting, we'll be with you in, say... 15?"

"OK, Chief."

"How's it going?"

"Fine. Nearly done. We'll be finished when you get here for sure."

"Good. Wait there. I want you to explain to him about what everything is, the watch outside, the bug on the phone, everything, but not the hidden cameras, right? You've put them in the usual places?"

"Yes. As we discussed."

"Is he likely to see them at all?"

"No... He's not to know he's under suspicion, then?"

"Not at this stage, no. Everything working?"

"Affirmative, boss. Like bloody clockwork."

"So I would expect! You're a genius! Lucky you're on the side of the angels or I'd never catch the buggers!"

The voice on the other end could be heard to grin. "Better not tell you I've switched sides then, gov!"

Sam smiled back. "I'll be taking your statement to that effect later then, Sergeant! See you shortly."

The call ended.

3

Sam explained the security carefully. There would be two policemen, armed (God help us. What a world, was my comment) on duty outside my flat 24 hours a day. There would be someone else on duty inside the block of flats, armed as well. They would keep a watch on my car and it was to be locked into the car park behind the building every time I left it there. Similar arrangements had been made at Forbridge but the local Hampshire Constabulary had that in hand and these I already knew about in any case.

We left for the flat. I called up the stairs to Jenny that I was going and she said she'd see me in the morning. Sam and I stepped out from the cool of the shop into the bright street. It was hot and dusty and I suddenly missed Hampshire very much indeed. I made my way to the car, Nell eagerly looking up at me every now and then.

"Find my car, Nell. My car."

She trotted eagerly ahead of me, looking about her. She found it and stopped and I clicked the remote as she looked back at me, her tail wagging furiously.

"Good girl! Clever dog! Well done, Nell." Her tail wagged faster than ever.

Sam glanced at me. "What's all that about?"

I smiled. "It's a game we have. She finds cars. I tell her which one and she finds it."

"How do you mean?"

"I say, or indeed any member of the family can, find my car or Dad's car or Will's - anyone's and she finds it. If, say, Will was with her, he could say, "Find my car", and she'd find his car, or he could say, "Find Rob's" and she'd get it right. She knows the difference between 'his' or 'hers' and 'my'. We acknowledge her finding it by clicking the remote and she knows she's won the game." I stopped and rumpled her head. "Clever girl, aren't you? "

"Remarkable. We should have her in the Force."

"Yes, she is remarkable and, no, you can't have her!"

Sam smiled, pulling a rueful face. There was a plain clothes hovering nearby who acknowledged Sam with a nod but they did not speak. I climbed in, Sam got into the passenger seat and I squeezed Nell into the tiny space behind them. My brother was not the only member of the family to like sports cars. I had a Porsche. She was used to it and wedged herself more comfortably and settled down, her tongue hanging out and panting with the heat. I kept the window down and her nose rested on my shoulder, sniffing the air happily. She loved it blowing in her face. I was always a fast driver and I grinned inwardly as I remembered who was my passenger and as a result, on this occasion, knew I would modify the speed. Sam glanced round, stroking Nell's head.

"Family dog or yours, Rob?"

"Mine. She comes everywhere with me. She's very special."

Her tail thumped at the attention, smiling at Sam, it seemed.

"You and William were always daft about dogs."

"Hmm. Still am. You were, too."

Sam fondled Nell's soft ears. "Hmm. Still am."

I grinned. "Do you have one?"

"Sadly, no. Not fair on the animal in my job."

"What about a police dog, then?" I pulled out into the traffic. "You could have one living with you, I suppose when it was off duty or whatever?"

"God, no! They're very much a one human animal! And dangerous in the wrong hands as many an escaping criminal has discovered! They pull your arm off first and think about it afterwards. Really part of the team, though and a valuable one when handled well."

For once, the King's Road was fairly free of traffic but I drove between the sets of traffic lights below thirty miles an hour. We talked about the new buildings going up and the ever-changing face of London. I turned up towards the Fulham Road. The grubby delicatessens and slightly down-market restaurants of a few years ago had gone. Now it was mostly interior designer establishments and expensive boutiques that displayed their wares. We crawled over Putney Bridge where they were resurfacing the road, working hard to finish the white-lining by the time the rush hour started. We were quite a while there, staring down at the river and we pointed out landmarks to each other, recalling various trips to London when we had been at school. For children brought up in the country, as we both were, there was always an excitement in London, something to quicken the pulse, and the noise and dirt were an attraction rather than something to be tolerated and grumbled at. I turned right at the end of the bridge and pulled up in the street outside my Putney flat. Sam opened the door and glanced at me briefly.

"Perfect driving, Rob. I'll bet you're not usually such a model citizen." I followed the immaculate suit up the steps and in spite of the ironical tone, or maybe because of it, I felt it wisest to say nothing. Nell trotted ahead and admired our very own constable on duty in the hall. I led the way up the stairs and opened the door to the flat. More policemen, these, the plain clothes variety. Upon seeing us, they stopped doing whatever it was they were doing. Sam spoke.

"Jack. Tony." They nodded. "How's it going?"

"OK, boss. We've just finished."

As Nell had done downstairs, I felt obliged to applaud their wiring and bugging and other horrors. I felt ludicrous and faintly hysterical. I felt as I had done when, as a teenager, we had nearly been discovered by the Matron, smoking in the science lab after supper. We had hidden below the benches, hardly daring to breathe and desperate not to laugh. She'd been sure we were there and yet she didn't catch us. Sam had been one of us, I remembered. That was when we were in the Lower Sixth and the dizzy heights of Head Pupil and all that meant had not yet come to rest in Sam's lap. I hadn't thought of that episode for years. Sam's presence stirred many a memory, most of them involving William in some way. I looked at the sergeant while he spoke, but did not really see or hear him.

"Robert?" Sam was speaking.

"Hm?"

"Rob, is there anything else you'd like to know of these officers?" Sam was watching me closely.

"No, I... er... I don't think so." I hadn't heard a word but didn't like to admit it. I smiled at them reassuringly.

Sam nodded. "OK, you can go. I'm staying here with Mr Berkeley for the rest of the evening, probably. You know how to reach me if you need to."

"Sure, Chief."

Chief! I still felt a desire to laugh. It was pure Hollywood. Or perhaps Elstree. No, Ealing comedy, more like. Oh, God, I must pull myself together.

I flung open the doors to the balcony. The noise of London streets rose up from the pavements, along with a wave of heat. I pulled off my tie and threw it onto the sofa.

"I think I'll change before I melt. Help yourself to a drink in the fridge or aren't you allowed to drink on duty?"

Sam grinned. "You watch too much television. I'd love a drink and I'll get you one. What shall it be?"

I asked for a beer. "Oh, and give Nell a drink, too, please. She'll be thirsty."

As I undressed, I thought about my visitor. Sam would be my age, I supposed, same school year and all that. I didn't know much about the promotion plans within the police force but I guessed it was pretty unusual to be so young to be a Chief Inspector. Not to mention the fact that...

"Are you ready for your beer?" The tap on the door disturbed my thoughts and I came out into the sitting room. I took the can that glistened with water droplets and tugged open the ring pull with a satisfying 'phyzzt'. We sat on opposite ends of the sofa, regarding each other thoughtfully. For a few moments we talked small talk and then...,

"Rob, it's wonderful to see you again but I am here for a purpose, a serious purpose. Now, I thought if we could have a good long look at this, we'll see where we get to and try and make some sense of this awful madness. These people have to be caught."

I swigged my drink and nodded.

"If I go too fast for you or if you feel too distressed, we'll stop for a while. OK?" I nodded again. "Good. Oh, yes and when we get hungry, I'll go and get a take away or send one of the men. How about that?"

I laughed. "You're the boss, Chief." I imitated the phone-tapping underling.

It was Sam's turn to laugh. "I'd forgotten you could mimic people. That got you into trouble at school, if I recall!"

More thoughts came crowding in on me - school plays, me as a pantomime dame, William backstage, pulling the curtains or directing, more like. And Sam there, too, principal boy, I remembered, and Peter Pan and Puck. School productions brought forth such an odd assortment of plays and people. It was impossible to recall them all but the flavour of it was there, lingering in the air.

Sam sat back and suddenly I knew this was it. The cross-examination. I prayed that I would do William justice, that I might be able to give the police that extra something that would lead them to his killers. Something of my longing, my hope, even my despair must have shown in my face for concern registered on Sam's and the strong grasp was once again on my wrist.

"Are you all right?"

I gruffly pulled away. "I'm OK. It's just so... fucking awful." I drank some beer. "I'm all right. Let's get on with it."

"I know. I understand." A brief pause then, "Right. First of all, let me explain a little bit about things. I know you have given statements to Adrian Merchant and other officers in Hampshire. I've seen them, within minutes of you making them, actually. So far, there have been no leads to follow. Although the local force don't like it, my department has been brought in. It has had to have been and I know you understand that." I nodded. "Good. I have read all your statements, of course but now this is my enquiry and we have to start from somewhere. OK?" I nodded again.

Sam regarded me thoughtfully, sizing me up, it seemed and after another brief pause, "Well, Rob, tell me about your life - yours and William's."

I looked up, surprised. "You know about our life."

Sam smiled, but there was something sad in it, somewhere I felt. "No, Rob, I know what I know about you. Or... or knew, rather. I don't know what you feel about yourselves. Or how you feel now. Try. Try and tell me."

I felt the beginnings of a curious mesmerisation, the snake with the mongoose, the rabbit in the headlamps, green eyes in a darkened bedroom...

I sat back and began to talk.

Chapter 5

1

I don't know how long it was I talked about my family. I told Sam about my childhood, our times together, about the first hunt and the Highland Ball, about fishing for sticklebacks in the stream that ran through Forbridge. I talked about hunt balls and my college at Oxford, everything and anything that I could recall spilled out and lay around us like the contents of an old trunk. How William had always been there and how he been everything to me and, later on when we were grown up, all things to all men. I talked of the 400 years celebrations. I told of the flying show and that fucking helicopter and the noise and the smell and the blood and the screaming that went on and on and on, that which was still going on but now just inside my head...

Some time later, when I was calm again, I talked of other things. Of my father and his curious isolation from the world, his childish delight in all things modern, how good my mother was at organising things and how the weight of responsibility rested so very heavily on my shoulders now that William was gone. I told of the plan about Martin and Jane and Mark. I said something about Inno. I stopped suddenly and looked about me. I had come out of the trance.

Three empty beer cans lay on the coffee table, two of them mine - maybe the third one was, too, I wasn't sure and it didn't matter anyway. The light was beginning to fade from the room now. The noises outside had diminished somewhat and a red glow from the setting sun glinted from the sluggish waters of the Thames that ran past my windows. Sam was sitting opposite me now, leaning back in the easy chair and watching me.

"Yes? Tell me about Inno."

Something pulled me up short. "Nothing to tell." I mumbled suddenly.

"What sort of nothing? No love? No affair? No what?"

I was cross. "Nothing to do with you."

Sam was bland. "Everything about you is to do with me. You hardly need be coy with me, Rob."

I stared out of the window for a moment. I suppose that was fair and they probably did need to know everything about me. Oh well... "We... we've been together, on and off for years, really."

"Together? She's your current girlfriend?"

"Kind of... No... not really. We just, sort of... I don't quite know how to put it, get together sometimes, for a while, a week or so, a month possibly, that sort of thing. We've been part of each other's lives since we were kids. I think we sort of comfort each other, really. We're just really good friends, very close."

"Oh, so you don't sleep together?"

"Y-yes... sometimes. But ours is a unique relationship, I think. I sometimes think she's my best friend in the world after Will but... it's really strange, I don't actually love her at all. No, let me rephrase that. I'm not in love with her and never have been but I am hugely fond of her."

"Does she feel like that about you?"

"I'm... not sure. I think she has been in love with me, but recently I've thought she isn't really any more, though I was the first guy she slept with. We don't talk about it. It actually doesn't matter. I don't expect you to understand this relationship because I don't myself, actually. I simply don't question it. It's what we are and it's... well, it's what we do. That's all."

"OK. Any other girls?" A smile. "You were never short of girls at school."

I shrugged. "One or two. Here and there. You know the sort of thing."

"Do I?"

"Well, a few weeks here, a couple of months there, holiday romances..." I stopped. I felt I'd walked into a trap.

"Tell me about the holiday romances, Rob."

I thought. I'd had two or possibly three beers but I was not even remotely drunk. I suddenly knew. Adrian must have briefed Sam, he must have done. Sam knew about Madeleine. I was furious. For some totally unaccountable reason I was furious.

"I think you know. I think Adrian has talked to you." I don't know how I kept my voice even. Perhaps I didn't.

"Yes, of course he's talked to me. What do you expect, you stupid idiot? This is a fucking murder enquiry. An enquiry into the murder of your own brother, Robert."

The shock of the speech, the change of mood from gentle lulling, to the obscenity, to harsh, screaming reality jerked me out of my mood of irritable self-pity. I stared in stupefaction.

Sam leaned forward. "I am going to find these bastard criminals. I had hoped you were going to help me, but if you're going to be squeamish about it or go all prim on me or whatever, I'll just have a harder job of it, that's all. Do you think I personally care or am interested in how many women you've screwed in the last few years, hmm? Or Will either? I need to know everything possible to try to get some leads in order to find these dregs of humanity. And by Christ I'm going to find them and if you help me it'll be easier, that is all. It's up to you."

I nodded dumbly. Nothing else mattered, not even my private thoughts about Inno or Madeleine, though I couldn't understand what it had to with William's death. I said so.

My inquisitor spoke more gently. "Rob, if I were a doctor and you were my patient, if you had appendicitis, do you think it would help me in my diagnosis of the problem if you omitted to tell me you had a pain in your side?"

"Well..."

"Or put it another way, if you didn't tell me you had a pain in your side do you think it would help me discover you had appendicitis? I have to know everything about you all. It's the only way."

Finally I saw the point and gave in. "Very well, what do you want to know?"

"You and Will were together on holiday. So, tell me about Madeleine."

And so I told, as I had to Adrian but this time, oddly, more haltingly, which was curious to one my own generation, but leaving nothing out, and when I stopped talking it was dark and I could hear the clock striking ten.

Sam stood up. "I'm going to get that take-away. There's a Thai one just round the corner, isn't there? Anything you don't like?"

"No. Buy what you want." I started to get up. "I'll get some money."

"Sit still and don't be stupid. My shout."

"No, Sam, I can't have that. Damn it, your working, for God's sake."

Sam smiled and headed for the door. "Expenses, Rob. Never heard of expenses?" And was gone.

I opened some wine and poured a glass and went and stood on the balcony, looking down at the darkening river. I could see Sam stop and talk to someone, a girl, and then walk off again in the direction of the High Street, making for the take-away. Opposite the flat were rows of upturned boats, rowing boats, and even at this time of night enthusiasts were out there, polishing and cleaning, calling to one another as they worked. Two or three people sat on the parapet, swinging their feet and drinking from cans or glasses. The pub was close by and its noisy cheerfulness wafted down the street and upwards to my quiet balcony.

Nell's nose pushed into my hand. I patted her head and her tail thumped against the doorframe. A youth in a baseball cap was sitting on a pile of tarpaulins further down by the water line. Someone with a prior claim to the tarpaulins moved him off, selected one and draped his boat with it, carefully tying down the ropes and fastenings. The youth scrambled up onto the walkway and wandered off in the direction of the pub, glancing up at my block of flats as he did so, taking me in, too, I felt, for he hesitated briefly but then went on, looking ahead this time in the direction he was going, no longer at me. Suddenly I realised it wasn't a boy, but a girl, a tall one. Her anorak fell open and I could see her silhouette outlined against the reflected light of the dying sun. I smiled to myself. I must be getting old. But as I watched her disappear amongst the crowd, I observed she walked more like a man. Silly creature. Why hide your femininity behind shapeless anoraks and a masculine walk. No wonder the male of the species was so confused these days!

I looked back towards the High Street. I could see Sam, carrying parcels, returning. The mission had obviously been a success. I turned inside and somewhat belatedly turned on the oven and put two plates in it to heat. I was amused with the thought that when I went out for take-aways I usually came back to someone who had done this task for me. This time it was the other way round and I was doing the waiting. Like the girl who looked like a boy, I was unused to all this role reversal.

Sam dumped the whole lot down on the kitchen work surface. We served ourselves a mixture on the barely warmed plates and sat down again in the sitting room, the meal balanced on our knees. We ate in silence for a while. I hadn't realised how hungry I was. Eventually I looked up, regarding my companion. Sam was looking at me, grinning, as I licked my fingers to catch the last vestige of chilli sauce.

"Why is it one is always starving when one eats this sort of meal?" I said it almost as a means of self-defence.

"I don't know but you're right. And by the same token we'll be ravenous again in a couple of hours!"

"Who was the girl you spoke to out there?"

A quizzical look. "You were watching me?"

"Not deliberately. I was just looking out at the Thames. I like it. Besides, it makes a change for me to watch you. You lot seem to have me under pretty constant surveillance."

Sam nodded. "True. She is a policewoman, a sergeant, actually, under my command. Part of the team. Very good she is, too."

"Why aren't there more high-ranking women police officers? They seem to be as much needed as men."

"How right you are. Mostly they get married and have babies and that's it. It's a difficult job to combine with husbands and children. Impossible to do successfully, really. But you're right, there ought to be more."

I poured some more wine for us both. "Are you married, Sam?" We'd done nothing but talk about me, I thought. Your turn now!

"Not I, sir!"

"The right one not come along yet?"

Sam hesitated and shot me an odd look. "Something like that."

It was funny, in all these hours together and looking back in time, all the years we had known each other, I had never seen Sam discomforted and off balance but that was undoubtedly true now. What nerve had I touched, I wondered? In love with someone married already, maybe? But I was not allowed to speculate further for Sam put down the plate and spoke again.

"Now, Rob, not much more for tonight but let me just ask you one or two things about your father."

I sighed. "Poor old boy. It's not fair, is it? Struggled all those years to keep the old place going, survived the war and have a tragedy like this, right on his own back doorstep at the end of his life." I frowned, thinking of his sad, troubled face, with its bright eyes, peeping over the top of the sheet. His mind an impenetrable barrier, imprisoned within himself.

Sam's face registered sympathy. "Indeed not. I remember him coming down and taking you out for tea in the village. I came with you several times. Do you remember?"

I did. I could see the cream cakes now and the funny old biddy who ran the café, "tea shoppë", as it was advertised outside. And Father, happy, shelling out fivers to all of us at the end of it, quietly slipping me an extra one, outside the school gates. "Yes, I remember," I said.

"Look here, we've got to get to the reason behind this attack. Who was William's enemy and why? If not that, then do you think someone was trying to get back at your father for something? Had he hurt anyone? I know it's impossible to imagine, he's always been such a dear old boy. But can you think of anyone who might want to hurt him enough to kill his son?"

I stared at Sam in horror. The idea that anyone could even think of such a monstrous, evil scheme was beyond me and Sam, cultivated, fastidious, elegant Sam, dealt with scum like that all the time. The Anti-Terrorist Squad! God Almighty! I didn't know how to answer.

Gently now, "Try, Rob. Just try to think."

I tried. I shook my head. "Look, Sam, if I could think of anyone who either Father or William had slighted or hurt, I'd tell you but I can't think of anyone, anyone, do you understand?" I got up and began to walk about the room. "I've already told you about the letter he received and I can add nothing further. Adrian Merchant asked me something similar and it is as incomprehensible to me now as it was then. They didn't do the dirty on people in business, we employ local labour who think they're wonderful. And before you ask, I know they do. The anguish everyone has felt, and shown, over these last few days is totally genuine. It's bowled me over, I can tell you. I never realised how much people really loved..." I choked into silence and turned away.

Sam jumped up and stood beside me on the balcony. Once again that strong hand was on my wrist.

"I'm sorry, Rob, I don't mean to hurt you, you must understand that."

Something made me look up and there was real pain in those grey eyes, the first time I had seen it. I turned back into the room and found my cigarettes. We both took one and inhaled thankful smoke. I stared gloomily at it.

"Bloody cigs. I'll give up sooner or later."

"Me, too. And I rarely smoke these days. But not tonight, Josephine!"

"No way!" I smiled grimly, watching the smoke curl upwards.

A brief silence.

"There was another thing you mentioned to Adrian, Robert. You said William had said he wanted to talk to you about something, urgently, it seemed, that evening after the fête. You must have thought about this." I nodded miserably. "Upon reflection, can you think of anything that it might have been about?"

I realised how important this was. When I could face it, which wasn't often, I had tried to think about why he had spoken to me that way. Nothing came to me. It could have been about money, he might have been ill (though he didn't look it, on the contrary he was very healthy and fit, too). It might have been about a girl - anything. I had absolutely no clue. I said as much.

Sam stayed quiet for a moment, gently fondling Nell's soft, velvety ear - she'd instantly taken to Sam, something she often did when she instinctively trusted and seemingly liked someone new. "It is very difficult but what I would like you to do, not necessarily at this moment, but as soon as you can, try to think back over the last weeks and months and see if there is any pattern at all of uncertainty anywhere. For example, an odd phone call you might have overheard and not understood, meetings missed or taken up suddenly, any odd remarks, however fragmented or distant from each other, that sort of thing. If you can think of anything, write it down and we will look at them together. You may find it a strange thing to do and difficult, too, to start with. But it often works. OK?"

"I'll try." My voice was strained, I could hear it.

"Oh, I'd also like copies of all your bank statements - yours, Will's, your parents' and the businesses - yours and the Forbridge estates', that is - if you don't mind, while I think of it." Sam was casual, "and that sales ledger, too, please."

"Sure, if you need them." I was surprised.

"Just need to tick boxes, you know the kind of thing." Sam waved a vague hand.

"No problem. I'll organise that first thing."

"Terrific. Thanks." Sam stopped being vague and went back to being sympathetic, but firm. "Right. Not much more now. Let me just ask you once more about your father. It may be we need to go further back than the last few years. What did your father do in the war?"

I shrugged. "Bloody hell, I just don't know. He's never talked about it. He actually won't talk about it. He was decorated so he was clearly very brave, he was wounded, a bullet in his leg, that's all I know. We used to ask Mother but apparently he didn't tell her either. He didn't know her then. He is quite a lot older than she is, you know. But," and here I looked up, "he's going to get better. When he has recovered enough to speak more effectively, you must come down to Forbridge and ask him yourself. I won't ask to know anything if he doesn't want me to. Maybe that would make it easier for him." I shrugged. "I don't know."

Sam was looking thoughtful, staring down into the wine glass. "I will do that. I plan to. Indeed I must and as soon as I am allowed. Obviously it is William who is the victim, so associates of his and the business he had built up come under the real scrutiny but there is a small mystery here and we can never allow any mystery, however tiny or seemingly unimportant, cloud the aspect of so serious an investigation as this is. Besides, it is fairly standard in a murder enquiry to look at the family as a whole and individually. I will set a junior on to it and see what we can come up with. The Army records and the old war office are an obvious bet. There must be some record of what he did. You see, it is the only thing about him we can't seem to get any information about at all, not even negative information. There may be nothing in it but until I eliminate it, I can't be sure. My boss will have entrée to all the relevant files and documents. I'll speak to him first thing. Tomorrow I'm going to the City to see the Estate's bankers."

I nodded. I was washed out and had had enough. Any outrage of further intrusion into personal affairs was, at this moment, suppressed by my exhaustion and deep sense of despair and hopelessness.

Sam stood up. "I'm going to leave you now, Rob. Here is my number on your note pad. Ring me at any time you want something or recall anything, however small. By the way, do you know what happened to the letter that came that he wouldn't show you?"

I shook my head. "No. But I'll look for it and ask Mother to look in his pockets or drawers, even though I dislike it very much." I stopped and frowned, something occurred to me for the first time. "Sam... I don't know if it's of any use but..."

"Yes?"

"Well, it's what you were saying just now about remembering odd things. It's about a phone call I had."

"When?"

"A few days ago. It was from a Frenchman who said he was a close friend of Father's. The only trouble was I'd never heard of him. I could hardly ask Father about it. He wanted to express his condolences and was shocked to hear my father had had a stroke." I paused thinking again about the conversation. "L'accident vasculaire cérébral," I added quietly.

"What?"

"Stroke in french. He had to tell me the expression. I was just reminding myself of it, that was all. How we all learn languages, adding things to a vocabulary bit by bit as we encounter them."

"Yes." Sam was regarding me with a shrewd expression, almost knowing. I had no idea why. "Mais oui, vraiment." I smiled. I'd forgotten Sam's french was good, too. "Et tout les activitées, aussi."

Ah. Activities. Now I knew what that dig was about. My smile became a trifle less amused and more fixed and said nothing. I didn't recall any advancement in my vocabulary in my encounter with Madeleine. Actions, possibly. Well, definitely...

"Did he give his name?"

"Yes..." I thought hard. "I can't remember it very well. I had so much in my mind... something like... Oh, shit... Flèche Someone, or Someone Flèche, I think but I can't exactly recall."

"Well, if you remember, let me know. But why is it you thought it odd, particularly? You must have had dozens of calls."

"Yes, I have." I sighed and ran my hands through my hair. I was nearly dropping with tiredness. "People are very kind but, dear God, it's difficult to cope with. Still, I suppose there's no pleasing people at a time such as this. If people didn't make contact we'd be slighted and if they do they're intruding!" Sam just stood there watching me quietly. I thought again. "Oh sorry, Sam. You asked me something. What was it exactly?"

"Why was this call odd to you?"

"Well... I suppose it was his insistence, in his own words, that he was a 'great friend' of my father's and I hadn't heard of him at all. There was something familiar about the name, though."

"In what way, familiar?"

"Oh... bugger, I don't know. I had a vague feeling he was something to do with the French government, but I don't know why."

"Hmm." Sam stared at me thoughtfully. "Flèche something, you said. It wasn't, I suppose, by any remote and strange chance, Jean-Yves de la Flèche, was it?"

Light dawned! How wonderful! "Yes, that was it. God, that's incredible! You're a genius! Who is he?"

"Someone quite important to the French, I think. Now that is enough for the moment. I think it's time you had some rest. You look pretty washed out."

"Do I?" I didn't doubt it.

"One random question. Did William make a will, do you know?"

"I don't know, honestly. I have, so I think he did. We were both left money by our maternal grandparents and when I was eighteen I had a letter from their lawyers informing me of the fact and our lawyer advised me to make a will which I did. I imagine Will was given the same advice."

"What were you left?"

"Half a million."

"Really? That's a lot of money."

"Yes."

"Between you?"

"No, each."

"So Will was left the same."

"As far as I'm aware."

"And who did he leave his money to?"

"I don't know. We never talked about it - ever."

"And you had the same lawyer?"

"I suppose so. I think so. I know nothing of that."

"Very well. I'll look into that." Sam shot me a searching look. "And what did you do with it, if anything?"

"Nothing at first then started my business and bought this apartment."

"Is there any left?"

I grinned. "A bit. Not much. But the business makes money, I'm glad to say, as I said. I've paid off the small mortgage I had, run my car, have holidays and everything. Live, you know, very well, to be truthful."

"And William? What did he do with it?"

"I don't know. Bought his car, I suppose. Invested some of it, maybe. I have no idea. As I said, we never talked about it. I've simply always assumed he was left the same amount. Our grandparents were always scrupulously fair and it was also implied by my lawyers but that's all."

"Hmm. OK. I'll see what I can find out. I shall need the details of your lawyers, Rob, right?"

"Sure. I'll email you their details tomorrow as well as the bank statements."

"Thank you. Yes, please. So, now I'll start various lines of enquiry and speak to you very soon. We haven't a lot to go on, exactly - a letter that upset your father and what William didn't tell you. God, not much! Still I've solved cases with less on the surface to start with!"

"Have you?"

At the door, Sam turned back. We didn't shake hands, just looked at each other. "Good night, Rob. Try and sleep. I'll be in touch." A moment passed where it seemed we both felt we could say something more but somehow, after all the pain there was in the room that night, anything more was either irrelevant or too trite for words. Sam went out and quietly closed the door and I just stood there, listening to the footsteps as they walked slowly away down the corridor. I had never felt so alone or so... so... vulnerable... in all my life.

Extracted from Police records: (4)

Sam rang and a phone was answered.

"Sam?"

"Yes, sir. Just on my way back from interviewing Robert Berkeley. Long session."

"Good. Anything?"

"Maybe. One or two odd things - out of the ordinary rather than odd, would be a better way of putting it."

"Still your chief suspect?"

"Until proved otherwise, he has to be, doesn't he?"

"Right. See you in the morning, right? Oh eight hundred hours, my office"?

"Certainly, sir."

"Good. Sweet dreams, Sam."

Sam smiled. "How kind, sir, but I doubt it."

A slight chuckle the other end and the line went dead.

Sam stared out of the window of the chauffeur-driven police Range Rover as they traveled through darkened streets, still alive with people and frowned. No sweet dreams now until this case was solved. And maybe never again if it all went the wrong way...

Chapter 6

1

I woke next morning to the telephone yelling in my ear. I scrabbled at it and knocked it off the rest onto the floor. It was Sam.

"Good morning, Robert. I'm just testing the listening device. Say something."

"What the bloody hell time of day do you call this, Chief Inspector?"

I heard the familiar laugh again. "It's seven o'clock. Get out of bed! Some people have been awake, and working, for hours! This bug looks as if it's fine. By the way, don't leave the phone off the hook. Not unless you want me to have a lovely transcript of everything you get up to in your bachelor abode! It comes straight through here to my office!"

"Jesus! Talk about Big Brother! But thanks for warning, Chief, he said boyishly!" I was grinning now.

"We did tell you this yesterday, you know, but I knew you weren't listening. You had a very vacant look on your face, so I thought I'd mention it again. Just as well, or I might have got all sorts of peculiar information. Keep my team fascinated for hours!"

"Just piss off, Chief Inspector and go and catch a thief or two before breakfast!"

Even as I said it, I knew the response. "Before breakfast? Why I've been up since..."

"Yeah, yeah! I know!" I interrupted, grinning, "but thanks for the warning and I'm glad you're happy with your gadget."

"Oh, yes, very happy. On a different serious note, though, I've got a meeting with Interpol this morning and we are going to see if they can come up with anything that takes my fancy. They'll supply us with information on European bombers. But I must come down to Hampshire as soon as possible. Are you going to be in London for a while?"

"Just for today and part of tomorrow. I shall return to Forbridge later on tomorrow afternoon for two days and then London again." I swung my feet over the side of the bed, holding the handset under my chin as I attempted to reach my dressing gown. "Now, can you remember that or have you got a pen and paper today?"

"Touché, Rob, touché! And see, I can do French, too, eh, mon brave! I'll see you before you go back to Forbridge. 'Bye for now."

The phone went dead. I listened for a moment but couldn't hear anything, no clicks or whirs or rewinding tapes. I put the receiver back on its rest and sat there on the edge of the bed for a moment longer. It was odd. This morning, with a new day beginning, I felt that I didn't seem to mind being watched quite as much as I had previously. They were efficient and careful and I could feel the responsibility lifted from my shoulders slightly. I'd have to be pretty careful what I said, however, I thought with a grin. Perhaps I'd better make very personal calls from the office. But maybe they'd bugged that, too - ah well. There was something curiously comforting, though, to know that someone was out there, working away quietly on my behalf, closing in on those evil, murdering... bastards...

I got up quickly and headed for the bathroom.

2

Jenny gave me a funny look when I turned up at the King's Road shop that morning. Nell trotted in before me as usual, picking up the newspaper on the mat as was her wont, on the way through to the back. I couldn't think what the funny look was supposed to signify. We opened the mail together and discussed a couple of recent sales. She put down her coffee cup and looked at me.

"Robert...?"

"Yes?" I prised the newspaper from Nell's jaws for the second time that morning. Like searching for cars she took her role as newspaper boy very seriously. "Good girl, Nell. Leave."

She left.

"Rob, do you think I upset your friend yesterday? I didn't mean to. Could you apologise next time you meet? I was just so bowled over. I mean even today one doesn't expect Chief Inspectors in the Vice Squad, or whatever, to be..." She caught my eye and tailed off. I couldn't help smiling at her discomfiture.

"Don't worry, Jenny. Sam must get used to it, I should think. And it's not the Vice Squad."

"Well, whatever they are. Don't be difficult, Rob!"

"Me? I'm not difficult. I thought you would approve of people getting on the way that Sam has."

"I do! That's what makes me so cross with myself!" Jenny's mouth puckered up in self-disgust and anguish. She gathered up some files. "I'm off to that postponed meeting with the accountants." At the doorway she turned. "Please square it with your Chief Inspector, won't you? Please."

I grinned. "All right. But let it be a lesson to you!"

"Pig! You had to get in that gibe, didn't you! But thanks. See you after lunch."

And she went. I squeezed myself into the tiny kitchen at the back where we washed up and made coffee. Alice, our secretary, was on holiday so we were fending for ourselves at present. I sloshed some hot water round the cups and set them to dry on the draining board. It probably wasn't the most hygienic wash they'd ever had, but still... Then I came back into the office.

"Oh, Nell, not again. Leave, bad dog." The newspaper was quite wet in places now. I took it from her and spread it out over the desk. The front page made desultory reading. The usual arguments over government spending, or lack of it, Hollywood star alimony scandal, the usual rubbish. A small item caught my eye.

"Chief Inspector Stewart of the Anti-Terrorist Branch has been appointed officer-in-charge of the Berkeley case. A helicopter, piloted by Sir William Berkeley blew up, apparently by a terrorist bomb, on Bank Holiday Monday. He and the two members of the Air/Sea rescue team on board were killed and several spectators on the ground badly injured. "The investigations are continuing and all leads are being followed up", was the comment from the Chief Inspector's office today."

I could read things like this with reasonable calm now. Why was it the press couldn't get the simplest fact right? It seemed so easy to print 'Mr' instead of 'Sir'. However, I sighed, as I turned the page, considering my poor father's state of health, it might as well have been. There could so easily be two casualties for Father wasn't out of the wood yet. Another shock would kill him, Eddy had said.

I turned the pages, heading for the sale room notices. An article about the French Presidential election attracted my attention. Day by day they were printing full page biographies of each candidate and today was the turn of the oldest contestant. I sat up sharply as I took in the name - Jean-Yves de la Flèche. So that's where I'd heard it. Sam had been right. I gave my attention to the article in greater detail.

Suddenly, as I scanned the page, some words leapt out towards me. There was a photograph, and underneath were the words I read again, this time more carefully.

"M. de la Flèche's home," (it said) "is still today the beautiful Château Viezy set outside the tragic remains of what used to be the village of Viezy-sur-L'eau." I decided to start at the beginning and read it properly.

"JEAN-YVES AND THE ALSO-RANS

Jean-Yves de la Flèche. It is a wonder that there are any other candidates at all in this current race to be President of France. When the other contestants heard he was in the running they must have felt, surely, political allegiance suddenly irrelevant in this case now, there was barely point in even lining up at the starting gate. Jean-Yves is not well known over here in Britain but then we have war heroes of our own and do not have too much time for other people's (lest they be American, perhaps) and French heroes of the Resistance don't raise too much excitement with the modern British. Not so across the Channel.

Jean-Yves was decorated at the end of the war for his sterling work with the Underground Movement. He helped many British to escape back home, he organised sabotage expeditions, liaised with London and corresponded regularly with de Gaulle himself. He was arrested by the Nazis in 1943 but he managed to get himself released. He had the reputation of being able to talk himself out of any tight corner and, failing that, could run like the wind!

At the time, still very young, married at 16, he lived with his equally young wife, Celestine and their baby son, Gaston, in a large farm on the outskirts of the little village of Viezy-sur-L'eau. The Château, built on a small hill just outside Viezy, was taken over by the Nazis shortly after the German invasion and turned into a munitions factory/ arms store. Jean-Yves, accompanied by other members of the Resistance (some British involvement, it is believed) wired the château with explosives and planned to blow the whole thing to Kingdom Come. The date was fixed, the get-away plane arranged for the Allies and the fuses lit. Unbeknownst to Jean-Yves and his companions, a sabotage agent had rerouted the fuses through the village. It was the village that was blown to pieces and the château survived. Jean-Yves' farm, being far enough outside the village also survived, at least partially intact but at the end of the war, in gratitude for all he had done (even though his last mission was a failure) he and his family were given the château. M. de la Flèche's home is still today the beautiful Château Viezy set outside the tragic remains of what used to be the village of Viezy-sur-L'eau. His bravery in rescuing many, many villagers was legendary and as well as the château he was awarded France's highest award for civilian bravery, the Legion d'Honneur.

The château is now a business, run by the de la Flèche family. His son, Gaston continues to farm in the area and the de la Flèche vines are grown on the spot where once the village stood. Gaston's children, Jean-Yves' grandchildren, Jean-Marc and Madeleine, run the château as a luxury hotel. His wife, Celestine, however, was sadly killed some years ago right at the start of what was to have been an extended visit to her sister in Toulouse - it was rumoured there was to be a divorce but Jean-Yves denied this utterly. She was mown down by a hit and run driver who was never traced.

Jean-Yves is a sort of modern St George in the eyes of the French. It is difficult to imagine how anyone can prevail against his reputation, although he has got himself into hot water on occasions with some suspect business deals. Each time, however, he has survived and his reputation remains relatively unsullied. It is hard to envisage..."

The article continued but I only glanced through the rest. French politics seemed even more incomprehensible than our own and there was no more about Madeleine.

It was curious, reading all that. The vision of the château came back to me as I sat there, the mellow brick, the green lawns, burned brown in places in the summer's heat, Madeleine in her tight, black, short-skirted cocktail dress...

So, my green-eyed siren was the granddaughter of the next President of France, or so it appeared, for it did not seem likely that anyone else had so much as an outside chance of clinching the race. The only thing against him was his age as he was certainly knocking on a bit. He looked sprightly enough in the photo, though, a glass of something in one hand looking out of the battlements of what was presumably his château. I had not asked her surname, of course, it hadn't seemed important. I did not recall meeting her brother but then I wouldn't know if I had, there was no reason to suppose I would recognise him. William and I did not look like each other much. I looked more like our mother and he, Father.

So this then, too was the man I had spoken to the other day. The man who claimed to be a friend of my father's - a war hero of the Resistance and the next President of France. It could hardly have been more surprising to me if I had spoken to Mickey Mouse, I thought. And seeing the château's history spread out there in front of me with Madeleine even more personally involved with it than I thought before, I recalled once again her beautiful face, corn coloured hair and strange, unique green eyes and behind it all William's mock-innocent, all-teasing smile...

3

I cut the article about the de la Flèche family out and folded it and put it in my wallet. I kept it for two reasons - one to show to Sam and two, to show my father, if I had the opportunity.

After lunch, I set off for Bond Street. A new gallery had just opened and I was anxious to see what was on offer there. Three days a week Jenny and I were assisted in the shop by Jilly, a suitably briefed twin-setted and pearls young lady, who actually, in spite of her appearance, could sell oil to a sheik. This was one of Jilly's days and after I had escaped her sorrowful gaze, I caught a taxi up to Oxford Street. I would walk down Bond Street and see what was what.

The new gallery was as I had expected it to be - expensively fitted out by the latest whiz-kid in the interior design world and free glasses of champagne for everyone who was admitted through the security doors. I recognised nearly everyone there and instantly realised I'd been a fool to turn up. I spent a miserable half-an-hour thanking sympathetic well-wishers for their kind thoughts. They meant it, of course, but I felt like a freak at a circus and couldn't wait to escape.

Just as I was about to a large lady in flamboyant garb descended on me.

"Dearest Robert. How terrible. How tragic. Your delightful, wonderful brother. What wickedness there is in this world." She dabbed her eyes and seized me in a grip like an iron wrench as she kissed me. Madge Winters was the worst possible sort of female novelist, obsessed with endless, badly-written scenes of explicit, highly contortionistic impossible sex but, in my view undeservedly, hugely successful, and an avid collector of antiques. I'd known her now for several years and she had met William on a few occasions. I muttered something as I wriggled free of an artificial fur wrap thing she had draped herself in. She swayed slightly on her twelve inch heels. I couldn't decide whether champagne or vertigo was the cause of her unsteadiness. Either could have been equally plausible, I thought. She ploughed on.

"Can it really have been only last month I saw him? No, July, that was it. I bumped into him in the foyer of the Savoy - such a pretty girl with him, they looked so happy, hand in hand there. Poor darling must be heartbroken. What was her name, now? I can't remember - Mary, Marilyn, Marianne? A tall, pretty, foreign girl, blonde - adorable. Now Robert, my sweet boy, when are you going to settle down? Nothing like marriage to take your mind of this horror - all that sex, sweetheart, do you a power of good!"

Madge's remark, her books being lurid to the last full stop, was typical of her. I smiled. "Yes, you're right, Madge. It does do me a power of good!" I escaped as I heard her start to shriek with laughter like an express train rushing through a station. God, I thought, trains in tunnels. Half a minute's conversation with her and she's got me thinking like herself. I needed some solitude and squeezed my way across the room to the back of the gallery where there seemed to be less of a crush.

I didn't see a single picture I wanted. I found myself backing into the office and suddenly, mercifully, I was alone. There was another bottle of champagne on the desk and I helped myself to a drop more. I needed some Dutch courage before I fought my way back to the door. Then I turned and saw my reward for enduring all those well-meaning people. It was leaning up against the wall, framed but not hung and it was a watercolour. It depicted a bright yellow gypsy caravan, pulled by a plodding, beautifully expressive horse and beside it walked a Mole. It was an illustration from the Wind in the Willows. We had three of these watercolours at home. They had been done by some obscure painter no one had heard of but it was part of our set and I wanted it. I wanted it for my father who had always loved the book and often read it to William and me when we were small boys, just before lights went out and my parents went downstairs to entertain dinner guests or go out to a do. We had pictures of Ratty, Toad and Badger but Mole was missing.

I picked it up and fought my way out to the owner of the galley, one Lindsay Ferrite-Carr. Where had he bought it, I asked? From a sale room as part of a job lot in Brussels, was the answer. He showed me the sales receipt. I told him I wanted it and why. I beat him down to £75 from £150. He was mildly drunk with the bubbly and, it transpired, grief. His current boyfriend, Jon-Jon, by name, had upped and left him for an able seaman from Portsmouth. He cried a bit as he gave me my receipt, about Jon-Jon, not the price reduction (at least I supposed so, but it might not have been, come to think of it). I commiserated with him and disappeared, leaving him alone with his champagne bottle and his fifty six guests. He shouldn't be too sad for he had made one sale, anyway. But judging by that lot in there, that would the only thing he would sell that afternoon. And he'd be considerably out of pocket as the proceeds from my purchase wouldn't exactly go a long way towards paying for all the vintage Bollinger.

Chapter 7

1

Buying the little watercolour for my father was a satisfying thing to do. The heat of the early September day in Central London sapped my strength and after tidying up some odds and ends at the shop and making a couple of phone calls, I left and Nell and I set off once again for Putney.

I drove slowly along the King's Road and out through Chelsea. Already the streets were beginning to fill with cars although it was early for the rush hour. A charity football match was due to be played in Fulham, so here was one hold up. Cheerful crowds of noisy supporters pushed out into the road. I stared casually at the passers by as I crawled between various sets of traffic lights. I crept across Putney Bridge and turned off along the side of the river. I parked the car behind my block of flats and set the alarm.

"Walk, Nell?" Her ears pricked as she gazed at me with love.

We crossed the road and jumped down onto the shingled, gently-sloping river bank. I picked up a piece of blackened driftwood and threw it for her. She galloped after it with a joyous bark. I headed off towards the rowing clubs. There always seemed to be someone there, I thought idly, at any time of the day or night. I wondered who they were, these rowing fanatics who seemed to have endless spare time to mess about with boats.

I dug my hands in my pockets and kicked at the shingle as I walked. Nell returned with her stick, nudging at me with the end of it. Her insistence was impossible to ignore and I threw it for her again - up and over an upturned dinghy. She shot after it. I heard a bark and a growl and then suddenly Nell came into view, backing away from something, her hackles up. I called sharply and quickened my pace.

Nell stopped but went on muttering to herself, the hair along her spine standing on end. I rounded the end of the dinghy and looked down. A girl was sitting on the ground, leaning against the boat. She was holding out her hand to Nell who for some reason did not like it. She had been startled, I suppose, as I was. I had not imagined anyone to be there. The piece of wood lay at the girl's feet. It had only just missed her.

"I'm most terribly sorry. I had no idea anyone was there. Did the stick catch you?" I regarded her anxiously and she looked up.

Instantly I was transported back to my bedroom in the château. I gazed into those green eyes, those unforgettable, unique, almond-shaped green eyes that laughed at my growing surprise.

"It's all right, Rober-rt. You did not hurt me."

"Madeleine?" I was incredulous.

"Yes, Rober-rt. It is."

"But, what in God's name...?" I tailed off. I couldn't think straight. Nell was still grumbling behind me. "Shut up, Nell. Whatever is the matter with you?"

Madeleine got to her feet. I helped her up and watched as she brushed sandy particles off her calf-length jeans. Her hair was longer than before and blonder, too, the strong French sun having bleached it more than ever. That seemed a lifetime away. I couldn't believe it.

She continued to laugh at my staggered expression. "I have business in London. I arrived some time ago. I did try to see you before but there was no reply from your apartment."

"No, I haven't been here much recently. I... We've had... some family business that I had to attend to." She said nothing but continued to look at me. "Look," I pulled myself together. "Come to the flat and have something to drink. There's so much I want to say, Madeleine."

"That will be love-lee, yes."

We walked back the short distance to where I had jumped down onto the pebbles. I dragged Nell up, her solid Labrador body heavy and awkward and climbed up after her. Madeleine had sprung up on her own and helped me pull Nell onto the pavement. We crossed the road and I ushered Madeleine up the steps and into the hall. I nodded to the policeman on duty.

"This is a friend from France who has arrived on an unexpected visit." I found it somehow necessary to speak to him, to explain the situation, although I felt curiously as if I were talking to a dummy in Madame Tussaud's or one of the Horse Guards on parade.

"Very good, sir." He glanced at Madeleine and glanced away again. He made no other movement but I got the impression he would know her again. I was beginning to get used to policemen, I thought.

Madeleine passed him quickly without looking at him and climbed in front of me up the stairs to the first floor. Nell stumped along behind, cross at having her walk curtailed. I unlocked the door and held it open.

She brushed past me and her scent, that most evocative of senses, brought back a vision of the terrace at the Château and William's mocking smile. I could see her, wandering up through the longish grass on the edge of the lawn and then standing there, looking down at us both. And now she was here, here in my own living room in Putney! I snapped out of it. She was speaking.

"Do all apartment blocks in England have policemen on duty?"

I crossed over to the balcony windows and opened them. The heat came up from the pavement as before, but there was sharpness there, too, underneath, I thought. Autumn was on its way, hidden under the guise of warmth and sunshine that coaxed us all to believe that summer would last for ever.

"No. It's for my benefit. I'll explain in a little while."

Just for now I wanted to go on pretending everything was wonderful, I did not want to break the glorious spell of her sudden arrival with bad news. "Now then, what would you like? Tea? Coffee? Glass of wine?"

She glanced round the room, smiling. "It is charming, Robert and ver-ry you. Ver-ry masculine, I think." Her voiced was husky and low. I had not remembered that about her, particularly. But a long time had passed since I had seen her. In fact, how little I knew of her, and yet... everything... "Coffee would be ver-ry nice."

"Sore throat?" I enquired as I turned into the kitchen.

She attempted to clear it and shook her head. "No, I have had a cold. It will not go away." She crossed the room to the balcony.

I gave Nell a clean bowl of water. She lapped noisily and slopped it over the side. As the kettle filled, I watched her. She looked up, jowls dripping with little droplets, she wagged her tail briefly and put her head back down again.

Madeleine was watching the scene below. I still couldn't believe she was here. "Why didn't you ring? I could have seen you sooner or met you at the airport. Anything."

She smiled a slow smile. "Your address was in the visitors' book, yes, but not the phone number. The telephone operator tells me you are, what is it? I don't know the word..," she thought a moment, "not in the telephone book."

"Oh yes, of course, ex-directory." I turned back into the kitchen and fiddled about with the coffee grinder and cups and whatnot. I left it to brew and went back out to the lounge again. "You are here on business, you said?"

She leaned over the balcony, staring down at the scene below. I took in the picture of her there. She wore a red shirt with the jeans and flat red pumps. They were new, hardly worn and I could see the price label still under the sole. A Louis Vuitton bag, also new by the look of it, lay on the floor of the balcony where it had slipped, unnoticed off her shoulder. I followed her gaze. The rush hour was beginning to build up. Cars lined up along Putney Bridge, the lights changing from red to green and back to red without a movement of the traffic.

"Yes. We are being included in a special brochure put out by the French tourist board and I am visiting them here in London. We have a lot of visitors from England. Now that August is over, the French have all gone back to their work. It is much quieter in France and now I can leave the château. My grandfather cannot come over at present and m-my brother..." she hesitated, "my brother is missing."

"Missing?" I stood and stared at her. It seemed a curious thing to say. I wondered if she really meant missing or not know the right word in English. Perhaps he was just away somewhere.

She turned back into the room and started to wander about, looking at the pictures and books, a trifle restlessly. "Yes, he left a few weeks ago without warning. He said..," she hesitated again, "he said... he was going for a short holiday. He does that sometimes. He is... well... well strung, I think you call it."

"Highly strung." I couldn't help but grin - 'well' going usually with another word, that rhymed with 'strung', when describing the male of the species. She did not notice my sudden mirth which was just as well. I had no desire to explain the reason for my amusement at this point.

"Ah, yes. But he usually tells us where he is and this time he has not. My family are anxious, naturally, but we do not wish to lose this opportunity for publicity for the Château. Jean-Marc would have come in the usual way, he deals with that side of the running of the hotel. Me, I deal with other things." She looked at me, a half smile sending up the corners of her mouth. She shrugged and spread out her hands. "So, this time, I come here instead of Jean-Marc to see the Tourist Board. It has been ver-ry interesting."

I pulled out a packet of cigarettes and offered her one. She shook her head. "No thank you, Robert."

I lit one. I grinned. "Given up?"

"No, I do not..." She stopped and hesitated a moment. "Oh, yes, yes, indeed. That is right. I have given up."

"Good for you. I wish I could, but, well, things are not conducive to the successful abandonment of nicotine at the present time."

This time she looked really puzzled. "Excuse me?"

I laughed. "Sorry. I mean it's not a good time for me to give up smoking at the moment."

The green eyes were steady. "Oh? Why is that?"

I went back into the kitchen and poured out the coffee and brought back the two mugs on a tray with milk in a jug and some sugar. I put the tray down on the coffee table. I offered her a cup and she took it. Again she said, "Why is that, Robert?"

I would have to tell her. Have to break the spell. "It's my brother. My brother, William. You remember him?"

She nodded, sipping at the hot drink and looking at me over the top of it. "Of course."

"He was killed by a bomb a short while back. That is why the policeman is here. He is protecting me."

She nearly dropped her coffee cup. "He is dead? Oh my God, Robert, how awful, how awful... how terrible." She put her hands over her mouth, hunched up in a ball at the end of the sofa. I put down my cup and moved over to sit next to her. I put my arm round her shoulders. She jumped to her feet and rushed out onto the balcony, as if anxious for fresh air. I followed. She turned her horror-struck face towards me. "I did not know. I am so sorry. I should not have come to visit you in such a moment of tragedy."

I was brisk, though I didn't feel it, particularly. I was glad of the cigarette. "Don't be silly. You weren't to know. It's wonderful to see you, Madeleine, wonderful. Why, it's the best thing that's happened for ages."

She leaned against the parapet and shut her eyes. I watched her for a moment, uncertain. Her eyelashes were thick and dark, the eyeliner drawn carefully away in a sweeping, upward movement. They were seemingly augmented by false eyelashes. I noticed, too, that she had plucked her eyebrows and she had inexplicably drawn them in again with eyebrow pencil. Another odd thing that some women did. It struck me how little I knew of her, or indeed, had remembered. "I'll get your coffee." I brought it back out to her and returned for my own. She sipped at it again and made a deep shuddering sigh.

"I am so sorry, Robert. It was such a dreadful shock. I will be calm now and try to help you, not be an emotional, stupid woman."

I smiled, "You're not stupid, I'm glad to say."

The phone rang. I walked back into the lounge and picked it up. "Hello?"

"Robert?"

"Hi."

"Sam. Just making that promised call. Nothing new at present. I'm still waiting for the forensic report on the bomb. I'm off to look at the old war files tomorrow."

"Good."

Sam's voice took on a different tone, some of the warmth went out of it. "I believe you have a visitor."

"How in God's name did you...? Oh, never mind." I was irritated suddenly. The waxwork dummy in the hall below. It didn't need a genius to work that out. But talk about speedy...

"From France, I think. Who is it?"

The irritation continued. " The girl I told you..."

"At the Château? Madeleine? You were not expecting her?"

"No."

"Nice surprise for you, then. Have a good time. But please remember, and this applies to all your friends and business associates, do not under any circumstances talk about the security arrangements. Do you understand? Things can only be secure if they are secret from everyone. Without any exception."

I frowned, "But that is..."

"I mean it, Robert. None of it, and that includes the tapping of the phone. Do you understand?"

"Yes, yes, I'm not an idiot. I understand."

"Fine. Now then, when are you going back to Hampshire?"

"Tomorrow afternoon. I told you."

"Just checking. Your plans might have changed. I'll be in touch before you go, at the shop, I think. Take care, Rob."

"Yes, of course. No chance of my not, really, is there?" I allowed myself half a grin.

Sam's laugh was a trifle forced, but we parted amicably enough which is what I wanted. We couldn't afford not to have Sam on our side. Besides, I didn't want it any other way. I sighed, cross with myself but something almost bordering on disapproval in Sam's voice had irritated me. I don't suppose we differed in our moral behaviour much. We were, after all, both children of our time so a sniff of what sounded very much like old fashioned morality from such a source annoyed me. I put down the receiver and returned to Madeleine and the balcony.

Her eyes were watchful as she looked at me. "Can you tell me what happened? Can you bear it?"

"Yes, yes, I'm beginning to accept that it's happened, but it's been hell on earth, you know - well, continues to be, if I'm truthful."

She nodded. I leaned over the balustrade beside her, watching the boats on the river.

"It was a terrorist bomb, apparently. God knows why. William never hurt a fly. At least he couldn't have known anything about it. I'll tell you this much, Madeleine, I hope the police get the bastard before I do. There wouldn't be much left of him to stand trial if

I found him, that's for sure." I stamped on my cigarette end and ground my heel into it.

I could feel her eyes on me and I glanced sideways at her. Her expression was impossible to fathom. She simply nodded. "Families matter, do they not?"

"Yes, of course. I suppose more than anything. We have a saying in England, 'Blood is thicker than water'. Do you have an expression like that?"

She turned inside again and bending down, picked up her bag from the floor. "We have something like it, yes - le sang est plus épais que l'eau."

"The same, then. By the way, I was very surprised to receive a phone call from your grandfather the other day."

Madeleine was very still, suddenly. I could see her hands tense on the strap of her shoulder bag. "My grandfather? He rang you?"

"Yes. He said he was ringing to say how sorry he was to hear about William. Did he not tell you?"

Madeleine continue to finger the strap. "No, no... He did not tell me but then I have not been around for a while. First in Holland and now in England. I have not seen him for a few weeks. Besides, I live at Château Viezy. These days he spends most of his time either in his apartment in Paris or campaigning. He wishes to become President. Do you know that?"

"Yes, so I have heard. It must be an exhausting business."

"Yes, yes but I do not have too much to do with it. We run the hotel. As I say, I have not seen him. But I am surprised to hear he rang you..." The green eyes were fixed on me. I thought she might be about to say something else but did not. After a moment more she set off across the room towards the door.

I followed her. "You're not going?"

She shrugged. "I must get back to the hotel and make some phone calls."

"Make them from here."

"No, no, they are to France, expensive ones."

"Don't be ridiculous. Make them from here and then we can go out for dinner."

She hesitated. "Well, I will make just one, then. But I must go back to the hotel to change. I cannot go out to a restaurant in jeans."

"OK, but you look fine to me! Make the call then we'll take a cab over there. Where are you staying, by the way?"

"The Grosvenor House in Park Lane. Do you know it?"

"Of course. But you can stay here now, if you'd rather." I took her by the shoulders. She was nearly as tall as I was, something else I hadn't remembered about her. She looked away from me, at the same time twisting herself firmly from my grasp. My hands fell to my sides. I felt the beginning of something like bewilderment.

"I... I... no, I think not, Robert. Not this time, at any rate."

"Why?"

"I... we will talk later. I... I hope you will understand."

I was dumb-struck. I hadn't imagined that since she had bothered to come here at all that she hadn't wanted to take up the relationship where we had left off. She hadn't been slow in beginning it. Something of this must have shown in my face.

She smiled faintly. "We will talk, over dinner, please be patient, Robert."

I turned away. "I'll change for dinner while you make your call." I indicated the phone and left her, awkwardly fiddling with her bag.

While I changed, I thought things over. I was hurt, basically. And cross. I was also staggered. Why? But then, of course, suddenly I knew why. She had someone else. Why on earth had I thought I might be the only one? We had made no plans to meet, only a casual offer to see each other sometime in England. No letters. No phone calls, nothing. I was a fool. She was a beautiful girl and the magnetism between us had been wonderful and special. But I had promised her nothing, no love, no commitment, just, I squirmed inwardly, a one night stand. I hadn't even contacted her again.

I selected a fresh handkerchief from the drawer and grinned ruefully at myself in the mirror. I felt better about it although still more than a little pissed off that I had been rejected, I analysed! Well, I would have to see what charm would do and a little time. I wondered how much time. I sloshed on some aftershave and left the room.

2

The call to France had finished apparently, for she was standing by the window again trying to talk to Nell who obstinately had her back towards her. I tipped dog food and biscuits into her bowl and shut up the windows. Nell's eyes were reproachful as we left her standing in the middle of the room, her tail drooping. We went out into the evening sunlight and walked along beside the river towards Putney Bridge. We stopped and leaned over the side.

I told her about the university Boat Race and how my flat was always crammed with visitors on the day it was raced, one of the best views in London! She asked me about Oxford and listened attentively as I sketched a picture for her. There was no university like it in France, she told me but I knew that already but didn't say so. A cab for hire came round the corner and I hailed it. We climbed in and sat, one in each corner, strap hanging, eyeing each other. She knew London well, it transpired and needed no potted tourists' guide from me. The traffic was heavy all the way and we crept along the Brompton Road, the late night shopping in full flood. She ignored Harrods and Harvey Nichols, I noticed. A most remarkable achievement for a woman!

We drove into the Park Street entrance of the Grosvenor House. I paid the driver and followed her up the steps to the revolving door. She dodged past a clutch of Americans, bristling with cameras and I followed her inside. She turned.

"Wait for me in the bar, Robert. I promise I will not keep you long." She fished the key from her pocket, turned her back on me and quickly walked off towards the lifts. I had been dismissed and I knew it. There was certainly no invitation there to accompany her to her bedroom.

Meekly, I headed for the wood-panelled anonymity of the ground floor bar. I sank into the pale blue velour comfort of a corner seat and gave the waiter my order. Yet more Americans gossiped loudly in another corner, happily anticipating a night in the West End. I swilled the ice cubes round my gin and tonic. So the charm hadn't started to work yet, I thought ruefully. I should just have to go on trying.

I took her to a favourite Italian restaurant of mine in Notting Hill and we pored over the menu, both of us seemingly ravenous. While we waited for the first course, we talked of the hotel and her plans for it. It was quite big business, it appeared. Her father, a quiet, shy man, farmed the land round about and supplied the hotel with his produce. Her parents were separated. She didn't actually know where her mother was. Madeleine and Jean-Marc had run the château, with their grandfather, since they had left school. Twice, by accident she referred to Jean-Marc as her 'sister' and corrected herself hastily to her 'brother', laughing at her stupid incompetence at English. Now, with their grandfather's desire to enter politics they were in charge. It seemed a perfect arrangement.

I told her of the article I had read in a British newspaper and she told me of the election. She talked about her grandfather, of his fierce pride and passionate desire to be President, for this, the greatest honour his country could award him. The wine lowered her reserve and as I listened it was impossible to tell whether the longing she felt was his or hers, for her family or for France. It occurred to me that the families of our politicians would not speak with such passion if such a situation arose. Nothing would stand in his way, she said, and no one would stop him. I said if the article in the British press was anything to go by, he was in there bar the shouting but she was fired up by the thought of it and the strength of her grasp round the bowl of her glass did not appear to diminish.

It occurred to me that I ought to ask her how my father and her grandfather knew each other. But I still felt uncomfortable about it. Here she was talking about the closeness of families and here was I just about to say that although I had implied he was a household name in my home, in fact, I'd barely heard of him and never in context with my father. I felt I'd better leave it. My mother would fill me in, perhaps. I was anxious not to rock the boat in any way.

We ate the main course nearly in silence, appreciating the fine food and Chianti that accompanied it. I had always loved Italian cooking and was interested in their wines as well. I thought it would make a change for her, nothing French or English, either, about the meal, nice and neutral. I steered the conversation round to ourselves. I had to get to the bottom of it. She helped herself to another drink from the bottle and, I was amused to note, poured one for me as well. Was this the ever-present training of the hotelier or another small blow for women's lib?

I leaned forward. "Madeleine, can you tell me why we cannot go on from where we left off? It seems odd for you to look me up if you had not been interested." I decided it better not to mince words.

She watched me cautiously but said nothing.

I had to help her a bit further, it would seem. I took the bull by the horns. "Is there someone else?"

She lowered her eyes. "Since you ask, in a way, yes, there is, Robert," she looked up at me quickly. "Please, do not be too upset. After all, it was only that one night and..." She shrugged and left the sentence unfinished.

So, I had been right. Well... I took a deep breath.

"You and I, as a couple. Is it no good, then? Look, I know it was only a brief affair, but I did think there was something special. Isn't that, honestly, why you've looked me up? You didn't have to, did you? Do you think there might be a chance it would work, you and I?" She made as if to move away. I pressed her further. "Madeleine?"

She turned away. "Maybe... maybe..." She looked at me suddenly with a false, bright smile. "Don't ask me any more now, Robert. We will just wait and see. It is just that, at the moment with... with... Jean-Marc missing and so much at stake for my grandfather, I think perhaps I did not want to be without a friend in England. Perhaps it was selfish of me, but..." She lowered her eyes, "maybe you will forgive me and then, maybe... later... maybe... when I have had a chance to sort things out in my mind..." Once again she left the sentence hanging in the air.

So, it was up to me, I thought, as we pored over the menu again, choosing puddings. But the door was still ajar, just a chink, or so it seemed and I was going to make damn sure my foot was staying in there, wedging it open.

We caught another cab back to the hotel. The streets were busy. I thought of quiet Hampshire. No one would be about much now, on a Wednesday evening. Such a contrast and only some 50 miles distant! The cab wound its way round the back streets of Mayfair. We chatted idly of this and that and we agreed to be in touch and meet again before she returned to France. This would not be till next week. At the hotel, we both got out and I asked the driver to wait. I escorted her up the steps. At the top she turned.

"Goodnight, Robert. Thank you for a lovely meal. I was in need of your friendship this evening. I am sorry, so very sorry about..."

"Don't be silly. I'm not rushing you."

"No, I meant your brother." She stared at the floor. "It must have been so awful for you. Bombs are the instrument of war. You do not expect them in the quiet of the English countryside. And I hope your father will be recovered from his illness soon." Her hands gripped my upper arms, suddenly and the grip was fiercely strong and she kissed me abruptly, on both cheeks. "Á bientôt, Robert," and she was gone, through the revolving door and across the plush, discreet, beige carpeting of the reception area.

I climbed back into the cab and directed the driver towards Putney. As I stared out into the brightly lit streets I wondered what it was that had disturbed me so about that last encounter.

Was it the sudden and unexpected kisses, so lacking in passion, a mere gesture of parting from one friend to another? Why, in France even men parted thus - hardly a good omen for the future. But no, it wasn't this, it was something else but I couldn't for the life of me think what it was.

It wasn't until later that night, when I woke from one of my now customary nightmares that left me wide awake, sick and trembling, that I thought about it again and realised what it had been. I wandered out into the lounge, seeking the comfort of a cigarette. It was then I knew the cause of that feeling of things not quite right.

I thought back again over her parting words. By her reaction, I believed Madeleine had not heard that William was dead until I told her. How then, did she know that the bomb that killed him exploded in Hampshire? I suppose she might have assumed it, but I did not mention, either, that my father was ill. It had not been reported in the papers. The police had wanted to keep it that way, at least for the present. We had not wished it to be common gossip, either so it was kept quite quiet. Her grandfather knew because I had told him. But she told me she had not spoken to him for a while. I had a strange, uneasy feeling for I felt sure she had been lying and for the life of me I couldn't see why.

Chapter 8

1

As is often the case after a broken night, one sleeps late and the morning is even more difficult to deal with than usual. Furthermore, heavy red wine the night before did not improve matters and my head was groggy and aching. I drank a pint of water and took two paracetamols. As I showered I began to wake up properly and by the time I had taken Nell for a brief walk I was beginning to feel more like a human being.

In spite of yesterday's successes, I was uneasy in my mind. I could not pretend to be anything other than disappointed about Madeleine and her revelations and there were other things. She was different, somehow. It seemed as if the passion that had once been for me and filled her mind and heart had been deflected and was now just for her family's pride and family's honour. Perhaps that was it - jealousy! Was I jealous of not merely an unknown lover but the whole of the tribe de la Flèche and the people of France? I smiled grimly to myself. A lover I might be able to cope with but I couldn't take on France as well, that was for sure.

I walked into the little office at the back of the shop and sat down. The mail was already on the desk, as was the newspaper. My lateness had deprived Nell of her paperboy routine. I opened a few letters and the phone rang beside me. It was Sam.

"Good morning, Robert. I trust you slept well." I heard the irony and ignored it.

"Not particularly, thanks. I rarely do these days. Any news?"

"Not really. There seem to be some problems regarding security and clearance on these war records. I have to sort that out this morning. Rob, how do you think your father is? Do you think if I came down to Forbridge on, say, Saturday, I might be able to talk to him? And your mother, too if that is possible. Also, of course, I'd like to look at the scene and talk to staff etc."

I considered this. "I can't see any reason why you shouldn't come down as soon as you like but I can't possibly know about Father. He might be better or he might be worse, it's all very much day to day."

"OK, then. If I can come down early on Saturday morning anyway, and do as much as I can, then if he is feeling up to it, I can ask a few questions of him as well. Is that all right with you?"

"Of course. Mother will be thrilled to see you. She always adored you, you know."

"And I her. She's a special person, Rob, bless her."

Same old Sam, kind and generous and warm. How was it we had lost touch, I wondered? The odd Christmas card and that had been it.

"Thanks, Sam." I stopped. Emotion caught up with me sometimes and this was one of those moments. I thought of something else, quickly. "By the way, our Monsieur de la Flèche. He's going to be the next President of France, it seems."

"Yes, I know. I was amused to see you didn't recognise his name!"

"But there's something else you don't know. He's Madeleine's grandfather. I read all about it in The Times yesterday. I cut out the article. I'll send it to you if you like."

"Really? Well, well, well. What a small world. But I'd like to see the article, yes." Sam's voice was more ironical than ever. I felt myself squirming for some unknown reason. Sam was speaking again. "Oh, one more thing, the phone at the flat."

"Yes?"

"Madeleine made a call, is that right? At least I assumed it was her, about 5.40 yesterday evening. To France."

"Yes. Is there a problem?"

"Oh no, no. Just checking as usual. It was in French, of course, so it's being translated. I didn't have time to myself."

"Is that necessary?" It was tasteless, somehow, this intrusion into other, innocent, people's lives as well as my own, I felt suddenly. I threw down the biro I was fiddling with in a gesture of annoyance.

"Orders is orders, gov'nor."

"Sorry. It's just difficult to get used to, somehow - innocent people caught up in it all, it's... well, shit awful, really."

"Everyone is guilty until proved to be innocent, Rob, in cases like this. It's the other way around from the law at this stage." Sam's voice was quiet, and that quietness seemed to be more telling to me at that moment than anything. A slight hesitation and then, "You didn't mention anything about security to her, did you?"

"No, you told me not to." I knew I sounded rather more cool than I intended it to be. None of this was Sam's fault. The police had to do what they had to do.

"Good, good, that's fine." Sam's voice cut in hastily, anxious not to upset me further.

I smiled. My annoyance had registered, it seemed. It didn't do any harm, I thought. "Why should I tell her?"

Sam was casual. "Oh, I was just thinking of pillow talk, Rob, that's all. Goodbye for now."

The phone went dead, leaving me with a fine old mixture of feelings.

2

Before leaving for Hampshire I rang the Grosvenor House and spoke to Madeleine. The huskiness in her voice was more pronounced over the phone. I asked if her cold was worse. No, no, she was fine. She had a meeting to go to at lunchtime that would last all day and then tomorrow she had to visit three other hotels that would be featured in the brochure. Suddenly I had a thought. Would she like to come down to Hampshire at the weekend? I explained about the police being there, having to ask questions and suggested she came down on Sunday morning and travel back with me up to London on Monday.

I thought she would refuse at first but she agreed quite readily, very readily, actually, which was encouraging. I would meet her from an early morning train and the rest of the weekend would be ours. I put down the phone in a happier frame of mind.

I drove down to Hampshire with the sunroof open. There wouldn't be so many opportunities to do this now that September was here. Nell loved it and would sit there with her eyes nearly shut, her nose resting lightly on the edge of the back of the seat, enjoying the air. I put the seat belt round her and she had learned to stay within it. As I pulled up, clouds were beginning to gather on the horizon and I knew, from the chill in the air that autumn was here and this long, unforgettable summer was over. I walked slowly up the steps. Like the end of all eras one can be glad and sorry at the same time. I was anxious to put aside the horrors of the last few days but part of me wished to savour the last few months I had with William. They were all I had now and would have to last me a lifetime.

My father was doing well and they were pleased with him. No excitements of any kind were allowed, however, as he was still in a frail state. He greeted me, his eyes steady and bright. But his grip was quite firm and there seemed to be little or no paralysis. The doctor was there, which was good timing, and said he would allow a little gentle questioning on Saturday, provided his good rate of progress continued.

I went down to the estate office. Here was buzz and chatter and quite a hive of activity. Martin was bursting with enthusiasm for his new post. Together with Jane we looked at the figures and discussed some plans for the coming season and on into the winter and Christmas. The next major activity for the estate was a three day event in October and we agreed it should continue as planned. William would have wanted it. In fact, he would have been much gratified to see all that he had started continue so comparatively smoothly. I told them Sam would be coming on Saturday. They nodded solemnly, but said nothing.

I opened mail. One letter, addressed to me, was from our family solicitor. I read it once, then twice and pushed it away from me. I stood up and walked to the window, staring out across the park. The letter told me I had a legacy left to me and would I call to make an appointment to discuss it. I knew it would have been from William. I felt sick. Like Mark, it seemed like blood money. But it was his wish, so I'd have to go along with it, whatever it said. At least it was something I knew he had wanted. Everything else had been guesswork, really. Later, after I was less raw, I rang and made the required appointment, put it in my diary for the next day and tried to forget about it.

On Friday, Martin and I did a tour of inspection of the estate with Mark. We visited the four tenant farmers. They all liked Mark and respected him. He talked their language and understood their problems and concerns. He was one of them. This was a great weight off my mind for although I did not doubt Martin's business capabilities, the farming side was new to him, even I knew something of it having been brought up in the midst of it all my life. If Mark could deal with all this successfully, it made our job much easier.

I admired sheep, just white blobs on the horizon normally, which was difficult as my knowledge of sheep was limited and made a fuss of the collie which was easy because I was very familiar with dogs and he was nice. I looked at milk quotas and the backs of black and white cows lowing in the milking parlours. Potato crops were less easy to enthuse about but as I listened to these earnest but anxious men, I gradually began to feel a fraction of their passion and understand anew their fear for an uncertain future. It was good to be able to, genuinely, reassure them that their jobs and livings were safe, that I would carry on as William had done and help them all they needed or leave them alone if that was what was needed, too, as it always is from time to time. It was a worthwhile day and one that brought me, and I hoped them, too, much satisfaction and comfort.

I left Mark at his own farm cottage. His small son came trotting out to meet him. He swung him into the air, kissed him and perched him on his shoulders. His small feet in their green Wellingtons adorned with frog's eyes on the toes hung down over Mark's chest, the classic pose of father and child. Thus they stood, waving, till we were out of sight.

Martin and I parted for the day and I drove slowly back along the road that ran round the perimeter of the estate. I passed a mature piece of woodland and noticed some trees had been marked prior to felling. Here, too were young saplings, the new to take place of the old, bending in the freshening wind. I made my way into the nearby town and parked in the spaces allotted to clients of the law practice. With as blank a mind as I could summon up, I went inside.

I sat in the waiting room and stared at the faded prints on the walls of the little town as it was about a hundred years ago. It was still entirely recognisable, only the names over the shop fronts appeared to be different, the buildings and their ornate, red brick Victorian and Edwardian facades still clearly there. I was summoned into what I assumed would be a dusty office but found it was slick, bright, light with state of the art computers clearly constantly in use. The lawyer, who I had never met but now looked after the family's affairs was young, slick and bright, too. His name was displayed on the door, Dominic Templeton.

"Mr Berkeley, thank you for coming. I thought it best to write rather than ring.

Telephones can often be far too intrusive at such times."

I nodded and muttered something. I didn't want this interview to be a protracted one.

He took up a file already on his desk, selected a long thin envelope, clearly a will and opened it.

"This is your brother's last will and testament. It is a simple document. Apart from a small bequest to your housekeeper, he leaves everything he owns - money, investments, his car and his horse - to you." I stared at him, trying to feel nothing and not succeeding. Curiously, I found I felt angry. I didn't want his bloody money. I wanted him.

"Oh... right... I... I don't quite know what to say..."

He shot me a sympathetic look. "No, I understand." He continued, matter of fact, impersonal, and I went along with it. It seemed to be the only thing to do at this juncture. "I have been in touch with his accountants and his bank. I'm not entirely sure yet how much this legacy will amount to at present and I'm not sure how long it will be before you receive it, as probate..."

"I don't care when I get it! I don't want it at all!" I was livid.

He regarded me mildly. "Are you saying you refuse it?"

"No... no... I mean... I wouldn't be so insulting to my brother to refuse it, if it's what he wanted, I meant..." I couldn't say any more. I doubted if he knew what I meant anyway. Bloody man... Oh God, no, I must pull myself together. This was one of those killing the messenger moments. I took a steadying breath. "Sorry. I didn't mean..."

Once again there was sympathy in his glance. "Nothing to be sorry for, Mr Berkeley," and he continued in dispassionate mode. "Anyway, the sum will be, in total, without valuations done on the car and the horse and assessments of his shares and investments, as a conservative estimate, something in excess of nine hundred thousand pounds."

"Christ!" I couldn't believe it. "But... but... how did he...?" I was at a loss to know what to say. I was staggered.

"As far as I can gather, he spent very little of the money left to him by his grandparents on reaching his twenty first birthday and has had good financial advice over the years. He used some interest, of course for his personal expenditures but of course, he had no property to buy."

"You've discovered that much then." I was still short, though I didn't really mean it to come out like that.

He regarded me coolly. "Yes, but I had a head start. A few days before he died he contacted me to make an appointment to come and see me about making alterations to his will, he said, so I was ahead of the game, as a matter of..."

"Really? Alter his will? In what way?" I was amazed. I didn't care what he did with it but this was really odd and, in that same moment I remembered that thing he wanted to talk to me about that morning. Was it this? But no, he'd said he'd had a blow. Was it money? But it couldn't have been. He must have known approximately how much he was worth. His shares clearly hadn't collapsed which might have been a blow to him. I was floundering and stared at the lawyer.

"He didn't tell me but he did cancel the appointment. Said things had changed and the status quo would stay as it was."

"He said he wanted to change his will and then changed his mind?"

"It seems so, yes."

"But... but why?"

"As to that, Mr Berkeley, I can't say. He didn't tell me in what way I was to change it or why he decided to leave it as it was - as it has been ever since he made it, in fact."

After a few more bits of information regarding the laws of inheritance which I hardly listened to, I left and climbed slowly back into my car in a very thoughtful frame of mind.

However, I knew one thing. This was something Sam needed to know about. I would ring later.

3

I drove slowly home, thinking. I went the long way round, skirting much of the estate. It gave me a chance to collect my thoughts a little. I wondered if I should discuss it with my mother but decided not to. She had enough to cope with and I felt instinctively this was something William had not talked about to her either. While waiting at a T-junction I caught sight of a poster advertising the fête not yet removed and fluttering in the fitful breeze. I pulled the car over into a lay by and walked back to remove the poster from its prominent position by the main road. It offended and disturbed me. All reminders of this should have gone by now.

I frowned as I pulled at it, tearing the paper, damp and beginning to fade, from the board. I walked back to the car and looked down at the crumpled remains. The detail of the words caught my attention properly for the first time and I stopped, staring at it. It announced the fair and listed some of the attractions including "A helicopter air/sea rescue by Sir William Berkeley."

That was the second time that mistake had been made and this time on our own poster. I threw it onto the front passenger seat. I would ask Jane about it and get her to speak to the printer. He shouldn't be allowed to get away with that glaring error and expect to be paid. I was irritated. Why had nobody noticed until now?

I pulled out into the traffic and continued on my way home. Once again, I frowned to myself. Why had William not changed the posters? It was unlike him for, in spite of his easy-going manner, he was more than something of a perfectionist and not likely to agree to that discrepancy without good reason.

In the evening I sat for a while with my father. I talked of the estate and gave him news of the farms he loved so much. There was gossip about this and that and he seemed to be both relaxed and invigorated by my talk. Once, while I was in mid-sentence, his hand came out from under the sheet and grasped me by the wrist. His quiet, "Thank you, Robbie, my dear, dear boy, for all this. It is such a weight off my mind, you can't think," lifted my spirits like nothing else could have done.

I gave him his present of the watercolour I had bought and watched him undo it. His face lit up in childlike delight as he took it from its hastily wrapped covering. He sat, holding the picture at arm's length, a faint smile on his face and we talked of times past but remembered still - of Mole and Ratty and the riverbank, Toad and Poop Poop and the Terrors of the Wild Wood. He traced the outline of the Mole with a shaky finger, gently, reverently. He looked at me gravely and thanked me several times.

"The Mole - the missing one. Now we have him, too. Yes, now we have him... The Mole..." His expression changed to one of deep seriousness. He frowned at it, nodding slowly. "Now we have him..," he said again. This time he seemed to demonstrate some sort of satisfaction and I was pleased.

I propped it up on the top of a chest of drawers, opposite the bed where he could look at it. During the rest of my stay with him that evening his eyes kept straying back to it. Once or twice I thought he was going to say something more about it, but he never did.

Gradually, as he tired, his speech became more rambling and odd. He seemed to take off in flights of fancy or strange reminiscences of which I had no knowledge or maybe they had happened before I was born. I didn't know. He became more dopey and finally lapsed into silence.

After he had fallen asleep, I stood looking down at him and a fierce protective feeling washed for me. As I closed the door quietly behind me, I remembered Madeleine and her passionate eyes, full of longing as she talked of her grandfather. Father's dream had been William's. Now it was mine, too. Perhaps I was beginning to understand her after all.

Chapter 9

1

Early on Saturday morning I stood in the window of my bedroom and stared out across the park. A miserable gust of wind stirred the trees and the greyness of the day affected my mood. In spite of the un-enticing weather, I whistled for Nell, pulled on boots and a wax jacket from the cloakroom and we set off up the hill behind the house. It was still not 7.30. I always marvelled how much easier it is to get up in the country than it is in London even on a day when I might prefer to pull the covers over my head and stay put for another half an hour.

I turned up my collar against the wind and reached the hilltop. The force 6 met me in the face and I felt drops of moisture on the chilly air. I pushed on until I reached the copse and here there was shelter. The little woodland lay under the brow of the hill and the wind raced above it. A worn pathway stretched away under the trees. Here it was that William and I would ride ponies when we were boys, build tree houses and make camps. Almost at every turn I could see a stalker hiding in the undergrowth or a desperate pirate scowl from behind a tree stump, childhood memories crowding in on me. It was a secret, magical place we knew then, inhabited by wood spirits and hobgoblins. As we grew older, we put aside earlier fancies and it became a place where we would creep away to smoke, before we were allowed, or share the odd joint in our teens. Here, too we would bring our girlfriends and hold hands and engage in other intimacies before we persuaded one to "go all the way". As soon as that status had been achieved, we'd find spare bedrooms in our vast, rambling mansion far away from anyone for that purpose and the copse simply became a place where magic merely lingered in the background. But it still remained special.

Last year's leaves lay around, waiting for the fresh fall that would soon begin and cover the old ones with a new carpet. Here amongst the smooth grey-green trunks of the beeches could be seen the beginnings of autumn colourings, pale yellows amongst the green. Here and there a horse chestnut stood, already well on their way towards winter - the first trees to dress for spring, the first to change for autumn. The conkers were virtually ripe. I bent and picked up one from the leafy floor. I peeled back the spiky casing and out from the protective white pith came the glorious red-brown chestnut. It was large and had a bloom of moisture on its beautifully marked skin. I walked on, the conker still in my hand, turning it over and over.

Fungi had appeared and the earth smelt of leaf mould. I paused here and there in my walk. Here was a small grove of fly agaric, their red tops with the white spots, so cheerful and tempting. But I knew better than to touch one - a deadly poison contained within that charmingly deceptive casing. Fungi were often like that, I mused. Delicate and beautiful but some with enough poison to kill you just by picking them, let alone eating them.

Nell raced after a squirrel and I left the copse by the stile, pausing for a moment as I straddled the top of it, looking down towards the lake. It was a perfect view from up here, even on this dreary day. Here was another favourite spot for us to use as a "thinking place". If we had a problem, or had had an argument with someone, or just wanted to ponder on the world and putting it to rights, all of us had, quite independently from one another, allotted this particular place for private moments. Without conscious thought, my feet had carried me here now, I supposed, for I had not deliberately intended to come this way at all.

Nell was on the trail of some hapless woodland animal and I sat on the stile, waiting for her to catch up with me before I launched myself down the hill and home for breakfast and whatever the day held for me. I called her again and here she came, racing along the path, having cheerfully failed in her mission of ridding the copse of another rabbit. I smoothed the conker once more and put it in my pocket. Mark's young son would care for it, I thought.

There were things in the pockets, bits of paper, a hoof pick and a few pony nuts. I pulled out one of the papers and stared at it with mild curiosity. The jacket was my father's, as it happened. We kept them all in the cloakroom and helped ourselves to which ever was nearest or rose to the top of the row hanging on the old pegs. My mother called it "the glory hole", for some reason or other and it was a wonderful muddle of coats and boots, dog leads, tennis racquets and riding crops. The paper was a piece of an airmail envelope and it was addressed to my father.

"Sir William Ber

Forbridge Pa

Hamp

GU

UK

I turned it over. The sender's name was not clear as it had been torn as well.

van Cleef

en Strasse

sterdam

I stared at it. It gave me a curious feeling, this piece of envelope. It reminded me of the foreign letter that I had recalled and its strange effect on Father. But this one had come from Holland, not France. The name, van Cleef, it struck a chord in me somewhere. I don't know... somewhere I had heard it, I was sure. I puzzled for a while but, as is often the case, the more one thinks the less one can recall and so it was now. I must leave it for the moment. Perhaps in the middle of one of my restless nights I would remember where I had heard that name and its associations. I put the envelope in my pocket and set off down the slope. It had begun to rain and I hunched myself into my jacket against the wet.

In the distance I could see a large black car slowly drive up towards the house from the road. I glanced at my watch. It would have been an early start from London, I thought, for it I were not mistaken, the visitor would be Sam.

2

In honour of our guest, if one could describe a formal visit from the police as such, my mother had risen early and come down to breakfast for the first time since William's death. They were sitting together, quite close and Sam was holding Mother's hand. They both looked up at me as I came in and sat down at the head of the table.

"Darling! Good morning! And isn't this wonderful to see dear Sam again?"

I smiled, inclining my head. "It is, indeed."

"Coffee, darling?"

I started to get up to pour myself some from the pot on the sideboard but she stopped me and got to her feet herself, a determined look on her face. I knew better than to try to stop her and sat back in my chair, catching the amused look in Sam's eye as I did so.

Mother lifted the lid of something beside the coffee pot and peered into it. "Kippers! One or two?"

"Two, please", I said meekly, not really wanting even one but wanting the quiet life even more. If I had said none or even one she would be worrying all day that I was sickening for something. I dutifully ate what was placed in front of me and then started on a piece of toast and marmalade. I knew the rules.

My mother was looking at Sam with great fondness.

"It's so long since I saw you, dear. Do you remember the week you spent with us?"

I looked up sharply. Of course! In that moment it came back to me, Sam had stayed here once, half term or something or some special exeat. We would have been about 14 or 15, I thought. How curious I had forgotten.

Sam was speaking. "Certainly, Lady Berkeley. We had a wonderful time. I have often thought of it since, particularly driving up the drive again today. And this is such a beautiful house."

"I think so. I always thought so as a girl, driving past and gazing up at it on the top of the hill as it is, never thinking I'd live here one day! You had such fun, that holiday, all of you. The bonfire you made and cooking things in the embers! And swimming in the lake at midnight! My dear husband talked about it all for weeks afterwards. In fact, do you know, when I told him you were coming down today, he recalled the occasion. I was so thrilled, you can't think! He improves every day and that was yet one more indication he is returning to full strength in body and mind."

Her bright eyes rested on Sam who leaned over suddenly and hugged her again. "He'll be well again, don't worry. We shall do everything to spare him any awfulness, you know. You trust me, don't you?"

"Trust you? My dear Sam, what a question! You can't think what a relief it was to me to hear you were looking after Robert in London and... and everything and now you've come down here to see us all, too. Such a marvellous piece of news after so much terrible sadness."

"Thank you. I'm pleased you feel like that. And now, if I may, can I ask you one or two things? Robert will stay if you like, won't you Rob?" The grey eyes flicked over to me and although it was a question, I knew it to be an order. I felt the authority and was grateful for it, no decision-making for me for the present.

My mother's anxious look was only brief. She sat up even straighter, if that were possible, in her chair. She had been brought up by parents firmly of the era that never slouched over the table. "Ask what you need to know, Sam, dear." She glanced at me. "It would be nice if you stayed, darling. I think perhaps..." She tailed off and I took her hand in mine and squeezed it. She gave me another bright smile and then turned her attention to Sam once more.

"Good. Now, I know Adrian Merchant has asked you a few things and I have read the transcripts of your conversations. To begin with, you didn't think there was anyone you could think of who might want to harm William. Having thought about it again, can you add any more to your original statement?"

"No. No. It is impossible to imagine that anyone would want to hurt him. Really, Sam, you knew him. Can you think it was likely?"

To my surprise, Sam hesitated. "I agree, I think it is hard to imagine that but I am trained, I suppose, to see all things in all men. Everyone has a secret or two, you know. I also know it is difficult for families to view their loved ones objectively. Let me say, then, if he was still the same William that I knew at school, then I think it would be hard to envisage anyone wanting to kill him."

"Well, he was the same William."

I watched her unclasp and re-clasp her hands. Her voice was steady, though. Brave, so brave. And this so cruel, so particularly cruel for her, I thought bitterly. Children shouldn't die before their parents. It was the wrong order. I was made uneasy by Sam's carefully considered reply, however. I would have expected a free denial, even for social reasons, maybe. I frowned, staring into space. I felt Sam's eyes on me and brought myself back to the current conversation. "I suppose..." Mother faltered, "...I suppose it really was a bomb? Not just an engine fault?" Still she was hoping.

"No. The forensic evidence is very explicit and precise. We believe we even know where it was made, and possibly by whom. Bomb makers almost always leave a kind of signature on their handiwork, you know. Not literally, of course, but rather like an artist's work one knows but not actually bearing the name in the corner."

"No, I didn't know." My mother stared at Sam in a sort of horrified disbelief. "Why, you make it sound almost as if they were proud of their achievement."

"Oh, I think they are."

"Good God..." Mother's quiet voice and face said everything.

"Who made it?" This was the first I had heard of this development.

"We believe the components are mostly French - they're good at making explosives - but we think it was actually made in Holland. It looks like the work of a Dutch mercenary we know about. He has supplied several illegal and terrorist organisations with explosive devices, different situations require different tactics. He makes, I suppose what you'd call designer bombs."

I stood up and walked over to the window. I kept my voice as even as I could. "You mean, someone actually commissioned a designer bomb, as you call it, to kill William?"

Sam was matter-of-fact. "It seems like it."

"Jesus Christ." I could have been praying and maybe I was. I stood there thinking for a moment. I tried to visualise someone plotting William's death, choosing what type of devilish instrument to use, coldly ordering it, as one might a hamper from Fortnums. Did he pick it up casually as one collected a suit altered by one's tailor and stroll down the street with it? Did he slip in quietly, by night, to cover his deeds from prying eyes? Was it sent by messenger or Securicor? I was so revolted by the thought I was nearly sick. I felt eyes on me and I turned back, trying not to think any more for the present. "Get through it," my brain screamed at me. My face was expressionless as I put my hand, briefly on my mother's shoulder and held it there a second. She put her hand over mine. We did not look at each other and I sat down.

"Are we getting nearer the truth, do you suppose, Sam?" I spoke almost casually, I had to keep the intensity of my feelings well under control.

"If you mean, do we know who killed him, then no. But we have the maker of the bomb and that is a great help. But unless it had been made by a complete amateur, then we were likely to know that sooner or later, in any case. I have to say, we still have a very long way to go. Now then, Lady Berkeley, can I ask you a different question. Can you think of anyone who wished to hurt you or your husband, or for that matter, Robert?"

She looked up quickly. "You mean, damage us by murdering our son? Oh, Sam!"

Sam was very gentle but pressed on. "I see you understand my train of thought very well. Yes. I'm afraid that is exactly what I mean."

She did not answer for the moment. It was very still in the room. I could hear the grandfather clock in the hallway outside working itself up to striking the quarter. You could hear it puffing and wheezing to itself as it gathered its strength to chime out its four notes. By the time it got up to 12 o'clock you thought it would expire before the end but it never did. It had always been like that, ever since I could remember.

Mother's voice, when it came, was very small. "I do not think anyone wished to hurt me, particularly. But I think, maybe, it is possible someone may have wanted to hurt my husband - once, anyway. But maybe not any more."

I opened my mouth to burst out the question but caught Sam's eyes warning me to be silent. I shut my mouth again. I cupped my chin in both hands, my elbows on the table. It seemed easier to stop the million questions from spilling out and spoiling Sam's investigation if I physically held my mouth shut.

Sam's question was even and quite natural-sounding, almost conversational. "That is interesting. And who might that be, Lady Berkeley?"

"Sam, dear, I only wish I knew. If only I knew! There was something, you know, in his past. Something about the war. There was much he did not tell me about that, but he was different when he came back, people said. I didn't know him then. We met and married several years after the war had ended, you see. People said he was so... so... carefree, I think was the way they described him before he went away. But he was never like that afterwards, never since I have known him." She sighed. "He never told me things, maybe he wasn't even allowed to, official secrets, I suppose and war makes quite normal people into murderers and spies and all sorts of dreadful things. Things you'd never do if there wasn't a war. But you must ask him. I may be imagining things. It is very easy after such a terrible shock such as we have had. The war was over a long time ago but I have often wondered if it was entirely over for him." She looked up with another brilliant smile. "I do not mind if he confides in you and not myself. He should have told someone in all these years."

"Do you mean he has feared this sort of thing ever since the war ended?"

"Oh no. You quite misunderstand me. I do not think he has feared anything, as you call it. It is only myself who has been bothered. And I do not think for one moment he ever believed anyone would hurt either of the boys. In fact, I don't think he ever thought anyone would harm him either. It was just some knowledge he had or had seen or something. Something so dreadful, he could never speak of it. It has weighed down his spirit and he has never forgotten, that is all. There was a secret there and he has never told me. That is all I am really saying. Anything else is, I suppose, mere speculation on my part and I only mention it since it was you who asked me." She stared in front of her, frowning. "No, I do not believe he ever thought anyone would hurt any of us. Whatever it was, just made him terribly, desperately sad."

"And yet it is you, Lady Berkeley, who do not know what it was he did or saw or whatever, who do believe someone might harm him? Why is that?"

I was aware that my heart rate had quickened. I felt I was waiting for something, but I didn't know what.

My mother's face was tragic as she looked at Sam at that moment. "Because of his nature. He trusted people. He always has done. He is easy to dupe, really, you know, though luckily, here at home, he is safe from that for the local people love him so much.

He was never any good at running the business and we were always dreadfully hard up till William took a hand. No, whatever it was, was a serious matter, I believe, and although it would be ridiculous to say I lived in fear of our lives, there were times, oh, I don't know, when one is awake in the night, that sort of thing, that I would wonder and be disturbed for him. It was nothing but female intuition - you understand, Sam dear."

Sam smiled. "Yes, I understand." A slight pause. "One other thing, do you recall a letter arriving that your husband did not like. A letter from abroad that upset him. Robert mentioned it. This letter would have arrived a few weeks before the fete."

My mother glanced at me suddenly. "You remembered that letter, did you, darling?" She looked at Sam. "Yes, I know the letter. It bore a French postmark and William and Robert teased him about it."

"Did you discuss it with Sir William or do you know who it was from or what it contained?"

"I asked him, yes. But he said very little about it. He said it was from the widow of an old friend. This friend had died and she had written to him to tell him about it."

"Who was the friend?"

She shook her head. "I cannot recall precisely what his name was. Something French, though."

"So he was a Frenchman, this friend?"

"I suppose so." She screwed up her face in an effort to remember. "It was Pierre something, I think." She shook her head. "No, I'm so sorry. I cannot remember it. But as I say, ask him. I think he expects questions of that sort, Sam."

Sam nodded. "I will. Is there anything else about the letter, or anything else that disturbed you either then, or now, Lady Berkeley?"

My mother hesitated ever so slightly, but then shook her head.

Sam had seen the hesitation, too. "Sure? Anything, however small may help."

"No. Nothing." She wasn't looking at either of us, deliberately so, I thought.

"Anything particular you remember about the fête or the days leading up to it?"

Here she looked troubled and looked down at her hands. There was silence for a moment, she seemed to be tussling with herself in some way. Finally she gave up the struggle and looked Sam full in the eye. "Well, there was something else. Again, I suppose it might be something but I only mention it because it had never happened before and it was such a dreadful thing it hardly bears thinking about."

Sam was infinitely patient. "Try and tell me."

My mother took a deep breath. "My husband and William quarrelled most bitterly a few days before the fête."

"Good God!" I couldn't help myself. Never had they quarrelled. They had barely ever had a disagreement even when we were at our worst, as teenagers.

My mother looked at me and there were tears in her eyes. "I know, darling. The unthinkable had happened. But they did have a terrible, awful row."

"You're right, Lady. Berkeley. That is an extraordinary thing. What was the argument about?"

My mother's tears spilled out now, over her cheeks. "Oh, Sam, dear, I don't know. I'm appalled to tell you that I don't know. Neither of them would speak about it. William went off for the rest of the day somewhere, I don't know where and my husband wouldn't say a word about it. It took place in the library. My husband was quite ill, really, afterwards. He looked dreadful, as if he'd had a fearful shock. But he wouldn't speak of it."

"And what about William? He said nothing to you either, you said?"

"No. Nothing. I asked him and he said, "Yes, we had a bit of an argument but we've sorted it all out now. It's finished and that's all there is to it." And then he kissed me and shot off somewhere." She buried her head in her hands for a moment, the weeping getting the better of her.

Sam and I looked at each other over the top of her head. I put my arm around her and gradually she quietened herself and became more composed and herself again. The storm was over.

She had nothing else to add. She was tired, suddenly, diminished in spirit and I could see Sam sensed it.

I took charge. "Is that all for now, Sam?" We met each other's gaze in understanding. Sam was cheerful. "That's all for the moment for you, Lady Berkeley, I think that was very helpful. Why not go and see your patient and perhaps you can let me know later what would be a good time for me to see Sir William?"

She smiled and nodded and left, serene once more and her tiredness gone, her tasks for the day once again clear before her. I fished for a needed cigarette and lit it. "You handled her well, Sam. Thank you very much. Poor dear soul. It's so bloody, all this."

"It is. But she's tougher than you think, I believe, Rob." Sam's expression didn't give much away, I thought. "One thing, though, do you think it was this that William wanted to talk to you about?"

I shook my head. I was stunned to think of this revelation. "I don't know. Possibly. Maybe even probably. Nothing like it had ever happened before, that much I can tell you. But I have something new to add to that."

Sam looked up at me sharply. "Oh yes? What?"

I told about the will and the amount and Sam stared at me. "Really? He's left you something in the region of a million pounds and you don't know where it came from?"

"Not really. As I told you, he was left money by our grandparents (our mother's parents, that is, by the way) when we reached the age of 21. I spent most of mine. I suppose he didn't need to or something. I can't think of any other way he'd have come by it."

"Well, we can check that out. And you don't know why he was altering his will and why he didn't?"

"No. I just wondered if that is what he wanted to talk about with me but it doesn't really make any sense in the context of how he spoke to me - not really."

Sam stared at me. "Hmm. Well thank you for telling me. I'll see what I can come up with on that lot elsewhere."

I nodded, staring at the cooling dregs of coffee in my cup and could feel Sam's eyes on me as we both lapsed into silence. I needed a distraction, I thought and stood up to get the coffee jug to replenish our cups once more.

Chapter 10

1

Breakfast over, Sam and I went over to the offices. There were papers to examine, letters to sort through and mull over and all the while clues to be extracted from almost nothing, or so it seemed to me. Jane and Martin were not coming in till later. Sam had wanted to see them both, particularly Jane who had been part of the organisation of the fête from its outset. The estate offices were housed in a separate block, near the stables. I excused myself to fetch a coat of some sorts as the rain by this time was coming down in sheets.

I put on a different jacket from the one I had worn earlier. Dampness still hung over it and there seemed little point in struggling into an uncomfortably wet garment when there were so many dry ones around. Before leaving the glory hole I felt in the pocket of the one I had worn earlier and pulled out the piece of envelope. I pushed it into the pocket of my jeans. I would show Sam and confide my thoughts.

Huddled up against the driving rain, we headed off towards the office. The wind blew the wet into our faces and soon we began to run, arriving out of breath in the large, high, open gateway which had, in time gone by, been used for housing carriages. There had been many horses here, once. But now, as the horse had given way to the internal combustion engine, we took over the lovely, lofty and spacious area for work of a different purpose. The offices now were modern and fully equipped with relevant gadgetry - computers, printers, answer phones, filing cabinets. It was odd, though. Even after all the alterations and the gentle hum of modern machinery at its efficient best there were times, particularly on winter evenings as the light began to fade, sitting here, quietly, I could swear I heard the snort of a horse and the faint, sweet smell of good meadow hay...

I unlocked the door and we hustled inside. It was warm, the central heating as efficient as the office equipment, unlike that in the main house. I opened a door and went into what was now my office and had been William's. We had made a new one for Martin in the next room. Sam walked about, looking at things.

"This is a very impressive set-up. There's nothing amateur or bucolic about all this!"

"Not like the rest of it, you mean." I was teasing.

"You know I don't mean that! No, really, one doesn't expect minor stately homes to be so well managed or equipped. Usually, it's a part time dragon from the WI who generously comes in to answer the phone twice a week and type the odd letter. I know it's like that on my father's estate in Scotland."

"Yes, but he only lets out his grouse shooting, doesn't he? Oh yes, and the odd salmon fishing weekend. We have all sorts of things down here, education centre, three day events, one day events, motor rallies, falconry displays - a million things going on all the year round. Mark you, it used to be a case of Mrs Whatsit from the Mother's Union and her horse-faced daughter every other day but William changed all that. The estate offices weren't here, either. This conversion is new, too."

Sam glanced about and sat in the swivel chair behind the desk. "And what happened to Mrs Whatsit and her horsey daughter? Did she go off in a huff?"

"Oh no. She helps run the cream teas every other Sunday in the season. She was very pleased to be asked. To be fair, although about as useless as it is possible to imagine in the secretarial line, she is a first class scone maker. William worked some of his charm on her and lo and behold, she upped and moved over to teas without a murmur. Apparently she told several people in the village it had been her idea. If I know my brother he'd have let her think it was. Typical William! Got his own way without ruffling a single feather!"

"And the daughter?"

"Married a man with a racing stud in Berkshire. Surprise, surprise, Will introduced them - here - in the office! Perhaps it was just a convenient quirk of fate but I don't think I could ever be sure it was simply that!"

We laughed together. I sat down in the chair the other side of the desk. I stared out of the window across the rain-soaked parkland. "I don't have a gift like that. No one has charm like William or inspired that sort of love, either."

Again I was aware that Sam's gaze was upon me and I could not read its expression. "You underestimate yourself. You have plenty of charm, I promise you and most of it because you do not realise it. It is quite natural. However, I will agree on one thing, I would not describe you as a manipulator."

I frowned. "You are saying William was a manipulator?"

Sam leaned forward in the chair and picked up a biro and began drawing idly on the open shorthand notebook on the desk top. "I don't doubt William was a manipulator. He always was. However, before you start leaping about in his defence, let me say this. He did it more subtly and pleasantly than anyone I had ever known."

I was temporarily pacified but not entirely mollified and thought about this later on when I was alone. It gave me an uncomfortable feeling. When was charm simply charm or when was it a pleasant means of getting your own way? It was rather like the definition of bravery. Was a man really brave or just too stupid to know how foolhardy he might be? Did Will deliberately set out to charm people? I had never seen him like that, but... And if so, did that also include myself?

"Now, Rob, tell me - what are your immediate thoughts about what your mother said to me?" Sam brought me up sharp.

I thought carefully. "I don't know, really. I suppose one of the things is that we always think of our parents as what they are to us. We never really think of them as having a life before we were born. We know they did, but it doesn't really signify at all. The fact that it might have been very important to others or dangerous or difficult or whatever doesn't seem to matter. To the extent, in fact, that it almost didn't happen at all. At least I see it that way."

Sam nodded. "Yes, I know what you mean. Before we existed on this earth then nothing really could have existed for them either, even though they were here. Arrogant, aren't we?"

I grinned. "Yes, very!" I thought again. "My father had a bad time in the war, that much we all know. It seems to me that if he won't tell you when you speak to him you must just try at the War Office or whatever they call it now." I put my hand in my pocket and handed over the piece of envelope. "Look. I found this in one of his pockets this morning. It's something about the name, "van Cleef". It rings a bell somewhere. And there's another thing."

"Yes?" Sam took the envelope, glancing at it and then leaned back in the chair, watching me closely.

"Father had so few letters from abroad. Most of our business was entirely home grown, the attractions, the advertising, it was all based here, although it was beginning to extend into Europe and, of course, the States. No one mentioned this second letter but then maybe none of us saw him receive this one. If Mother had seen anything she would have mentioned it, I think."

"If there was anything to mention, yes. But suppose there was nothing noteworthy in the arrival of this second letter?"

"I think you're wrong there, Sam. He wasn't in the habit of walking about with letters in his hands. Usually he'd open them in the office or, if it was a Saturday, at home, when the mail comes to the house instead. He wouldn't have kept the envelope, torn like this, if he'd opened the letter in the office. It would have gone in the waste paper bin like everything else. The first letter was like that, but he kept it to open in private. I believe he did that with the other one, too."

"I think you may be right. Who knows, we'll make a detective of you yet." Sam smiled and put the envelope away but not before staring at the sender's name once more, "I, too, know of a van Cleef, and if it's the same one, I am very surprised your father knew him. However, for the moment, let me have a look at the files on the fête."

I opened a cabinet and waved a hand at the rows of neat files. "Help yourself. They're all here."

Sam sighed. It appeared that this was going to be a long job.

The door to the outer office banged and I heard Martin call my name. I went out to greet them. Raindrops dripped off them both and they smiled at me, peeling off their soaking outer clothes.

"You didn't ride over in this?"

Jane dug the end of her riding crop into my ribs. "Yes, we did, you lazy old fair-weather rider, Rob! It's lovely if you dress up for it!"

"Hmm. Not my idea of fun. Here, are you both freezing? I'll put on the coffee." We had a plentiful supply over here, quite self-sufficient from the main house in every way.

"Well, I won't say no to your making us some coffee but only because of your disgraceful laziness. Actually, I'm as warm as toast!"

They hung their riding macs up on pegs and left their boots lying about all over the floor. Sam appeared in the doorway. There was no need for introductions, they all knew each other. Jane, in fact, had also been at Milldale with us and they had remained friends ever since. They hugged each other.

We went back into the office, the welcome warmth of the radiators pleasing after the cold draught had rushed in. I filled the percolator and plugged it in, fiddling with mugs and things. The conversation was the kind of general social chit chat such as is typical of old acquaintances, out of touch for a while. We talked of Martin and Jane's wedding. Sam had been invited but could not come at the last minute, crime-fighting somewhere, it seemed.

We sat about sipping the steaming drinks. Under Jane's direction, I was guided to a tin of biscuits and we nibbled at them, taking larger swigs of coffee as it cooled. Sam got up from the window seat and sat again at the desk.

"Now, I'm sad to say, it is business. Martin, I wish to talk to you first, if I may. Initially, it can be on your own, or with Jane here if you prefer. It is also up to you if Robert stays or not. Later I will interview you all separately as well. Joint discussions can stimulate memory, you see which is very helpful."

Martin looked round at us, his expression bland. "Whatever you like, Sam. It's fine by me. Let them both stay. We none of us have secrets and I can hardly imagine there is anything any of us have not said before or thought about, you know."

Sam nodded and stared down at the notepad for a moment, then began. The first questions were all about his previous employment, how and why he left and his feelings about it when it happened. It had been a shock but his settlement had been generous which made it more palatable. They owned their cottage outright and Jane had a job so for the moment, all was fine. The questioning moved on to the current situation, how they had come up with the idea of Martin taking over much of what William did but ultimately under my leadership. I looked up, startled, at this. I hadn't thought they'd envisaged it thus. We were a team, yes, but I hadn't seen myself as the leader, I'd seen it as a partnership, as much as anything. It gave me an odd feeling - alarm mixed with a curious sort of pride.

"So, Martin, briefly, when you took over here, were there any large debts or difficulties in any areas with anyone?"

He leaned forward, both his hands round the coffee cup. He shook his head. "No. Some good-sized sums were borrowed several years ago to start the education centre. These repayments have largely been made. It has done extremely well, much better than the projections. It is likely we shall borrow more for this in the future but not at present. The business has been very well managed and the profits impressive. William certainly had a flair but it is all above board, the money borrowed from impeccable sources, that sort of thing and the accounts properly audited, as you would imagine. I'll show you the books and Financial Reports when you wish."

"I've seen them. Good, what I had observed but I wanted your take on it, too. Now, what about further back. Anything there?"

"Well, there are accounts for the years before. The main source of income once upon a time, apart from farming and one or two minor things like a nursery garden and free range eggs and conducted tours of the house, were selling off minor, far-flung parts of the estate and pictures." He looked at me sheepishly, as if it were his fault. I shrugged. I knew all about that. Enough said. "Also, William negotiated the sale of quite a few acres to one of the local golf clubs to extend their course. That brought in quite a good chunk and there was no problem with change of use as golf is classed as a country pursuit."

"Sales properly recorded?"

"It appears so, yes."

"Nothing untoward, then. Very well, thank you. I have made enquiries in the City and you are confirming what I have been told already. Basically a good business, doing well, founded on straightforward borrowing."

Martin nodded. "Exactly that."

Sam was silent for while, staring down into the coffee mug. The silence grew and I began to feel slightly panicky, for some reason. I found myself listening to anything, a cockerel in the distance, the faint hum of the oil boiler in the next room, even myself breathing. Sam looked up.

"Now, Jane... I have read your statement and you have said that there is no one you can think of who bore a grudge against William in any way. Is there anyone who let him down or he let down or had a row with?"

"Well, no... I don't think so. William rarely had arguments with people. Not serious ones, at any rate. He might get cross if someone overcharged him or did something really stupid like forget to go through the disinfectant on a quarantine farm or something."

"Did he have any dealings with people abroad?"

Here Jane frowned. "Not often in the past but quite a lot more recently, yes. We were expanding advertising in Europe and the States and had more contacts with companies abroad. The three day event for the horsey lot attracted a lot of foreign visitors - followers from overseas interested in their own team - you know the kind of thing. After the first one, two years ago, we began to get quite a stream of enquiries from the Continent."

"Can you recall any of the names, particularly?"

"Not off the top of my head, no. But I can look in the files and the diaries, of course."

"Yes, the diaries, that's important. Did William go abroad himself much?" Sam twirled about on the chair, looking relaxed and I could see how this worked on Jane, too. At the start of the questioning she looked nervous and tense, but now I could see her finding it easier and talked more freely and expansively. Sam was an expert at handling people, I had to admit. First with my mother, then Martin and now Jane. And me? Had I been "handled well", I suddenly wondered?

"No. In spite of what I have said this is still principally really very much a home-grown organisation, Sam. He had a holiday with Rob last year, didn't he?" she glanced in my direction, "and he went to Paris for a conference on European Tourism in February. I still have an itinerary for that if you'd like me to find it."

"Yes. It might be useful. But I'll have a look at the diaries if I may."

Jane nodded. "I'll get them." She started to leave the room but Sam stopped her.

"Oh, Jane, while I think of it, do you have any films of the event? Are there security discs anywhere?"

Jane nodded. "There was security, of course. As you know there always has to be in everything like this nowadays." Christ, I thought. What a bloody, bloody world we have created for ourselves, and it hadn't protected William from the outrage, no matter how intrusive. "We haven't got them here, of course, but I can give you the name of the security firm. They are probably open on a Saturday or at least have a contact number. I should think you could have them by Monday."

Sam actually laughed at this.

Jane looked puzzled. "What is funny? I am sure you could get them by Monday. If you like I can..."

Sam cut her off. "You misunderstand me. I'm sorry to laugh. No, Jane, if I want them and they have them, and they will, I shall have them here by this afternoon at the latest. Police work may seem slow and tedious but we can make people jump, if we have to. And Monday wouldn't be jump. It would barely be a small hop!" Sam swing round the chair till it faced the desk. "Now, then, while you find me the name and telephone number of the security firm, I will ring up Lady Berkeley and see when I might talk to

Sir William."

Jane nodded. She reached over and rifled through a card index system to find the relevant information. She found what she wanted and wrote things down on a yellow post it note. While this hunt was in progress, Sam turned to Martin again.

"Now, how do I ring the house?"

He gave directions. I sat there, feeling useless, twirling a biro back and forth between my fingers. Sam got through to my mother and nodded thanks at Jane who put the post it note next to the coffee cup.

"Lady Berkeley? Yes, it's me. Sam... Fine, thank you... Yes... indeed... Oh dreadfully wet... Now, when do you think I might speak to Sir William?... Just after lunch?... That's wonderful. Give him my best wishes, won't you... yes... Jane and Martin, yes... I'll tell them... We'll see you later. Goodbye... goodbye." The receiver went down. "You two are invited for lunch, she says." We grinned at each other. There was no question of refusal, even if prior arrangements had been made. She was telling them to come to lunch, not asking them!

Sam spoke to the security firm. The relevant videos would be brought to Forbridge that afternoon. Sam looked up at Jane and smiled the knowing smile of 'I told you so'.

"Now, Jane, can I have your diary and do you have the one that was William's?"

Jane left the room and we heard her cross the floor in the next room. The wind moaned round the building but the driving of the rain against the windows had ceased for the moment. We sat silently, each with our own thoughts. Jane came back with two large desk diaries. She put them both down in front of Sam who scribbled out a receipt.

"Thank you. I'll keep them for today and photocopy anything I might want. Is this your diary now, Martin?"

He shook his head. "No, I didn't use William's. I use my old one from my last employment. Surprisingly, they let me keep it. It didn't seem quite right to use Will's so..." he tailed off, unable to complete his sentence.

Sam turned the pages slowly, looking at the entries. "Jane?"

"Yes?"

"What does "M" mean?"

Jane peered at the book, "Where?"

"Here and there, and another one here. It says "M for dinner." That's on Wednesday, 1 August. What have you got in your book?"

Jane turned the pages. "First of August. Yes, here we are. Just one entry. "William, Tourist Board lunch, Savoy, 12.30." She shrugged. "Nothing about M as far as I can see."

"Does M register at all? Is it someone's initial?"

"I suppose it must be but I can't recall anyone that William would think of that way. It could be Mark or Martin or, well, mother, for instance. But then he'd write Mark or Martin or Mother, not just M. Can you think of anyone, Rob?"

I thought and I couldn't. I knew who I might mean by M, but we weren't talking about me.

"What about these other dates when M appears? 27th July and 30th May? Both have a line running through to the next day. What did that mean?"

Jane looked, flicking the pages over. "27th July. Now that says, Farrier, 10.30am. That's for the Education Centre. There was an exhibition of shoeing through the ages. It was terrific. They shod oxen as well as horses and there are even different types of shoes for different kinds of..." She tailed off, Martin stopping her talking, smiling as he gently put his hand on her arm, amused by her enthusiasms but aware of their irrelevance. "Sorry. Just remembering stuff..."

"Don't apologise, Jane and don't stop. I like it when people ramble on like that. It's natural and also we can learn much from casual conversations where people speak without thinking. We glean a lot that way that might otherwise be hidden." Sam was smiling but it had the suggestion of something wily in it, I thought. I felt a strange chill shiver through me. That seemed so underhand, sinister even, to just deliberately let people chatter on, walking innocently into traps, perhaps? It struck me how little we know of sophisticated police work and I couldn't work out if I was impressed and thankful for this or shocked by the duplicity of it. It had the air of ensnaring people unawares and that wasn't me. It also had never been Sam, as far as I was aware and maybe it was that that shocked me more than anything. Had Sam always been like that in reality or was it part of what all police interviewers had to learn?

Jane was continuing to talk, however. "So, William, lunch, Savoy 12.30. When there's a line like that, it meant he'd be out for the rest of the day and whatever it was would run through to the next day, too. It would stop wherever he would be free next."

"So he stayed the night somewhere?"

"Possibly. He just wouldn't be here, that's all."

"I see. And the other one?"

"30th May... Well, there we are again. William, lunch Savoy, 12.30 and the next day blocked out as well."

"Since you are here, Martin, I suppose it wasn't you William was meeting on those days?" Sam looked up at him.

Martin shook his head. "No, not me. I did meet William for lunch some time in May but it wasn't at the Savoy and although I can't remember the date, I know it wasn't the 30th."

"How do you know it wasn't the 30th?"

Martin and Jane smiled at each other. "That's Jane's birthday. I worked all day in the office and left early. Jane came up to London to meet me about six and we went to the theatre and out to dinner." Their eyes met again. The recollection had brought back a particularly happy event for them both. It was a private moment between them, it was plain to see.

Jane was looking back through the diary again. "Yes, here you are, 14th May, lunch Martin, 1.15 Le Bistro. That's somewhere off the Brompton Road, isn't it?"

I nodded. I knew it. Trendy French, very much not nouvelle cuisine, checked table cloths and the wine came from their own vineyards in France. Not a sniff of a New World wine on the list. "Yes. Beauchamp Place."

Sam rifled through the pages, glancing at an entry here, a note there. "Jane? What's this? Something very underlined and with exclamation marks." Sam peered at it, William's writing could be appalling on occasions. "It seems to say, Diamond man off. The date is in March."

Jane took the book and regarded it. Then she smiled.

"Yes, I remember that! That was funny, rather, in an infuriating sort of way." She looked at Sam and started to laugh.

"Why? What was funny?" Martin came and looked over her shoulder at the book spread out before her.

"Now that was something from abroad, Sam. It was this little German chap, at least, we thought he was German. He rang up to organise a conference for his diamond smuggling clients or something!"

"You can't be serious!"

"No, of course not but that was what William called them behind their backs. He thought they were all crooks. Let me explain. The German man rang up and wanted to bring a large party of tourists here for the day. They were having a conference in London and they wanted to come down to the country for some rural sport on their day off. William met him in London at a do and he asked William if he could fix them up at Forbridge. They wanted a full day out - you know, clay pigeons and hampers from Fortnums, all sorts of extras. Anyway, they had it all arranged for some time in the middle of March. Then the man who was organising it started to get funny about the money - he tried to beat us down on everything. For example, he tried to get us to get the food from local supermarkets and put it all in Harrods bags, that kind of thing. He thought up every dodge there was for cutting corners. To cut a not very long story short, William lost his temper with him. He said he didn't care if everything came from the local supermarket but he was damned if he was going to pass it off as something it wasn't and basically he'd chosen the wrong man for that sort of caper." Jane leaned back against Martin who was still behind her. She was laughing. "Well, you should have heard the names he called William! Said he'd let him down and was a snobbish British aristocrat and if he was prostituting his home on the entertainment market, he should get off his high horse, etc, etc! William said if he was a tart then at least he had a heart of gold but there was always an exception that proved the rule and this was it. He told him to bugger off and pester someone else with his cheapskate ideas! As far as we knew, that is what he did!"

Sam was laughing, too. "Good for Will! But why did he think this fellow was a crook or a smuggler or whatever?"

"Well, it was a few weeks after that, William was reading the paper. He suddenly gave a great shout of laughter and said, "Look! I told you that chap was no good! There's a report here about him being arrested and questioned by the Frankfurt police about some massive drug smuggling operation. He seems to have been let off without charge, to their chagrin but I bet he was guilty!" Will thought that's why he wanted to have his conference over here. He said he was going to pick up all the shattered clay pigeons and glue them back together with heroin in the middles instead. That's what all this was about. It wasn't anything, really. It was just a joke."

"Did you meet the man?"

"No. Will only met him once - and that was in London, as I said. But he assured me he looked like a bandit!"

Sam still smiled. "Well, it sounds pretty harmless, albeit somewhat irritating. I'll look into it, though. How soon did he call it off?"

"Oh, with the barest of margins. I think all the delegates or whatever they called themselves were turning up in less than a week."

Sam nodded. "What was your little German's name?"

Jane frowned. "Oh help. Von something. Hans von something, I think. I can't remember."

Sam hesitated but looked at me. "It wasn't, by any chance, Hans van Cleef, was it?"

"Golly, yes, I think it was!"

"Are you saying William had dealings with Hans van Cleef?"

"Well, no, not really. Not dealings. Just this one episode. Who is he?"

"Well, he's Dutch, not German but you very much surprise me. And there is nothing else you can tell me about this episode or any other connected with him?"

"That was the only episode. I'll dig out the correspondence for you. I'll put it in an envelope and give it to you when we come over at lunchtime. Is that all right?"

Sam shut the book with a snap. "Fine. That would be marvellous. Thank you, Jane, that has all been wonderful help. If you can recall anything else, just get in touch with me. I'll leave you all the relevant numbers. One more thing, did William have a personal diary as well as a business one?"

"He had a little pocket one but it was just a copy of this one, really. But I don't know where that is, Sam. I never had it here. I suppose if it's anywhere it would be in his room, amongst all his other things, unless... unless..."

"Unless?"

"Unless he had it on him when he..." Jane couldn't finish the sentence and she didn't need to.

"Quite." Sam looked at me inquiringly.

I knew what was wanted. "Yes, all right. I'll take you back to the house and show you his room. That's what you want, isn't it?"

"Brilliant, my dear Watson. Do you mind, Rob?"

I shrugged and started to leave the room. "Why should I mind?" I did not look at them as I walked back into the anteroom but I could feel them look at each other. I started to struggle back into my wet jacket.

2

I had only been in William's room a couple of times since he died. As I walked up the stairs, leading the way, I found I was none too calm. But it helped to have Sam there. Besides, I wasn't expected to do anything. Sooner or later we would have to go through his belongings and sort and give things away but just for today, just for this weekend, in fact, that would wait. As usual, I opened the door to what had once been not only our nursery but the playroom to many generations of Berkeley children. The toys were still there in profusion - train sets, building bricks, Lego, Scalextric, clockwork this and wind up that, bears and soldiers, jigsaws, a farm, even a dolls' house that William and I were very keen on but pretended not to be, especially on wet days like this one. In fact, everything you could imagine that could amuse a child now or in the past was there. It was almost a toy museum in its way but the public weren't allowed in this part of the house, even though it would have been a fascination for them. But our childhood was special and so we agreed that this should stay as it was, as it had been for us and would be, one day, we felt, for our children. As I passed by these old treasures, I told Sam snippets of this and that, confided our secrets and our reasons for keeping it private and, as I glanced up, I saw Sam's quiet smile and knew that everything I said had been understood.

The long room ran along a section of the front of the house on the first floor and I led the way. The polished boards, faded in many places, creaked here and there as we walked. The wooden rocking horse still stood in the window and I touched his head as we passed, sending him rocking gently to and fro. He rattled. Things, long since stuffed into his insides and lost, rolled about, at variance with the motion of their host. There was a small hole at the back of his mouth and I used to push marbles into it when I was small, pretending to feed him. I was stopped from doing that when it was discovered, I remembered, when I tried it with loose change.

When we were children, we each had a room off this one, mine one end, William's the other. When we grew up, we chose different ones, or at least, I did. My room was further down the corridor on the corner of the house. It was, in fact the main bedroom, that and the inter-connecting one next to it which I used simply as a dressing room, meant originally for the lord of the manor and his lady but my parents had chosen a different set of rooms for theirs, on the other side of the house. I had liked its plastered ceiling, lofty windows and four poster bed and it was a suitably longish trek from my parents' room. I could entertain anyone I liked in it without disturbance, or more to the point, my not disturbing them. The bathroom connecting the two bedrooms was archaic, really, but I liked that, too, as spacious as its adjoining bedrooms. But William had stayed put. I walked the length of the playroom towards the door in the end wall. There were shelves on either side of it, from floor to ceiling, full of well-thumbed children's books - from Winnie the Pooh to Treasure Island, Peter Rabbit to Swallows and Amazons. The door opened silently and I stepped inside.

Although the room had a door to the corridor of its own, this was never used. It had a strange history. Some hundred years or so before, this room had been used as a study for the eldest son, my great-grandfather, prior to going up to Oxford. In order to help accustom him to the life he would lead up there, they had put in an extra door, in order that when he was studying and did not wish to be disturbed, he might "sport the oak" as he would do when he was up at university. After the fiddling about that this entailed, neither of the doors worked properly, the door frames slightly crooked and the handles clashing with each other when they were both shut or opened at the same moment from both inside and out. Thus they were left closed, more or less all the time and the door through to the nursery was used by everyone who had subsequently occupied it.

As boys, it had been a wonderful place in which to hide, for there was a gap of quite a foot between the two, when closed. We could hide in there for ages and as the doors were so ill-fitting, light and air crept through the gaps and we never felt any claustrophobia. Guests never found us and awful cousins or the offspring of friends of my parents we didn't like went away bemused when we disappeared, apparently into thin air. It was a place to hide things in, too, I remembered. I told Sam about a grass snake we had, poor beast, kept in a box till it died of misery or lack of proper food or both. But we kept it still, intending to mummify it but school beckoned once more and we went away, forgetting about it. The ensuing smell had been so awful they had summoned the drains people and the health people and fifty other people but no one ever found it. Eventually, as is usual in these cases, the smell disappeared. But we found the poor corpse when we returned at the end of the term, completely eaten away by maggots, till only the skin was left, all dry and flat and empty. It was quite thrilling, it was so disgusting but we never told and the mystery of the terrible smell was never discovered by the grown ups.

Sam followed me in and I went and stood by the window, looking round. I paused, uncertain and awkward. It was curious. I realised suddenly, how private was this room of Will's. I had never come in here much, there had never been any need and this had very much been his domain. Once an adult, my room was a place to sleep in here and that was all. Not so for William but then I had a flat in London and he did not. This, funnily enough, was the only space he had to call his very own. When he grew up and he brought back the odd girlfriend to stay the night, she would be given a guest room somewhere and he would stay with her there, never here in this room with its single bed. Whether Mother knew or not of this arrangement, neither of us knew but if she did she never said. In all this huge house, where he had lived all his life apart from school and university, this was the only room that he could truly call home. It had never struck me before now. I waved my hand round vaguely.

"Look at what you need to, Sam. I think, if you don't mind, I'll just sit on the bed and watch. I don't think...well... somehow... I think I'll be rather useless. More of a hindrance that a help. In fact, I think I'll go and wait for you in the nursery. Give me a shout if you want to ask something."

Sam's sympathetic face smiled its grave smile and pulling out a radio, summoned the sergeant who had driven them both here who had been left downstairs somewhere. Sam explained. "If I search somewhere I have to have someone else here, too. You understand?" I nodded, the man arrived and I went and sat outside in the window seat, watching the park beginning to come to life after the rain.

I had sat here before like this, feet up on the cushion, arms round lower legs and chin on knees. Moisture was dripping from the trees and the sun struggling out. It was warming up, too and I opened the casement, the red leaves of the Virginia Creeper falling onto the seat beside me. Often we would watch for a change in the weather from this window, the view was panoramic and one could see for miles, ready, as soon as it stopped raining to shout and rush down outside from having been cooped up all morning. A wet nose was pushed into my hand and I knew it was Nell who had found me again. She had been in the kitchen for hours watching Helena prepare things for lunch, ever hopeful for a small something to fall her way from the table top. I fondled her velvet ears and she gently licked the back of my hand.

Sam appeared beside me. "Rob, we've found his wallet and diary. They were in the top drawer of the chest of drawers. I need to have you with me. You must sign for them. I'm sorry. Do you mind?"

"No, no, it's all right." I patted the dog. "Come on, Nell, let's be useful." She padded about the room, restlessly. Once she put her nose against the crack in the bottom of the bathroom door and whined. I called her to me.

"Come here, Nell. Come here, old thing. He's not here now, poor dog," and she came back to me, and sat at my feet, leaning against me, staring in a puzzled way at the closed door, her tail making small movements behind me. She had adored him and attached herself to him whenever I was abroad or left her at home for some reason but always returned to my side when I came back. I turned my attention to William's belongings.

They were in the middle of the bed and I took the wallet and turned it out. There was about £50 in notes, some credit cards, an unused return ticket from London, ages old, the usual stuff. I fished in the pocket that ran along the back and found an opened packet of condoms, with one missing, a rupee and a ticket, much faded, for the Paris Metro. I grinned. "Silly things we keep, isn't it? I wouldn't mind betting that Metro ticket goes back to the time we first went to Paris. William loved the place and was quite silly and sentimental about it. But God knows what he kept the rupee for or where it came from. I make no comment about the Durex!" The silent sergeant smirked.

Sam, expressionless, took the things, turning them over. "I'll make a list of everything and you can send this over to your solicitor. The cards need to be destroyed and the cash is part of his estate - well, yours now, actually." I made no reaction to this, although I could feel a sudden closer attention being paid to me by the sergeant. Sam seamlessly carried on. "As regards the Durex, one is missing which implies he used it. Any idea who with?"

I shook my head. "No. No one serious, I imagine. Not currently, anyway. I'll deal with the cards and stuff and all that later on. Jane can send it over. I'll put it in the safe."

"That's fine. There's nothing here that I can see." Sam turned the pages of the diary. Something fell out of the back of it onto the floor. I picked it up. It was a photograph of William, a bit woolly round the edges as if it had been in a wallet and carried round for a while. I turned it over. On the back was some writing. In the middle, fading now, in William's hand had been scribbled, "To M, always yours, love W." Underneath in new ink, quite recent, by the look of it, were the words,

"W. I do not need this to remember. I shall not forget or forgive. M."

"Seems that not everyone loved William after all." I spoke mildly enough but it was shocking, somehow, to me. The dead have no secrets. Where had I heard that phrase, I wondered. And yet he did. None of us knew who "M" was and unless she made herself known to us, I supposed we never would. I handed it to Sam. "Seems like he gave this to a girl and then, when he ended it, she gave it back to him. I suppose it must have been quite recent, too, as he seems to have still been meeting her for lunch at the Savoy. Is that what you'd make of it?"

Sam did not say anything for a moment. Finally, slowly, "Yes, that's what I'd make of it, or at least something like that," and a strange, troubled look came into those grey eyes as

116

they regarded me. "Rob, tell me something, how much did William confide in you of late?"

I considered this question. "Well, I think we were close, at least I know we were very, very fond of each other. I suppose, though, since you ask, there was quite a lot about him I didn't know."

"That's candid. Good. Did he," Sam hesitated as if looking for precisely the right words, "did he tell you anything about his... his love affairs?"

"No, not really. But I didn't ask him and he didn't ask me much either. I thought he got pretty close to marrying one or two over the years. The last one I thought that about was Jane, as a matter of fact. But it seemed to fizzle out. As you can see, she remained on the best of terms with William. She took up with Martin and they seem very happy, don't you think?"

Sam smiled. "Yes, I think they're very happy. So..." Still the hesitant search for the right phrase, "you didn't know if there was anyone recent, I mean after Jane?"

"No, and he didn't talk about Jane, either, you know. Of course I knew they were an item while it lasted and I knew when they called it a day but that was all. As I said he didn't tell me about his girlfriends much well, not details, anyway. If one became something rather more than a weekend affair, I'd get to know about it and meet the girl, too, obviously usually but not all of them. And as I said in the office, "M" doesn't mean anything to me."

Sam stood up suddenly. "OK, then." No uncertainty now, the old positive Sam. "That's all right for the moment."

Sam was staring at the photograph again. "Rob, was William still keen on photography?"

"Yes. But he'd recently gone over to video cameras. His equipment should be here in his room somewhere, I should think. Try the bottom of the wardrobe."

Sam opened the wardrobe door, pushing about amongst the coats and trousers and pulled out a box amongst the shoes neatly stacked on the rack. "This looks like something. Yes, Pentax Camcorder. Can I take this back to London? There may be something on it."

"Of course." I pointed into the wardrobe again. "There are some discs there, too, by the look of it. You'd better take them, as well."

"Good. Thanks."

I picked up the box and tucked it under my arm. "I'll take this downstairs for you. Do you need me here any more? I've had enough for the moment, Sam."

Sam nodded and they stood watching me in the doorway, as I made my way back across the quiet playroom, where the ghosts of so many children played. Had William joined them, I wondered and I shivered as I walked out again onto the upstairs landing, much more disturbed than I cared to admit to myself.

I walked down the stairs, slowly, examining my feelings. William had not confided much in me and I had not told William much about my girlfriends because, simply, there wasn't much to tell. Even Madeleine, although special in a particular, intimate and earthy way had not been important, exactly. Important to me at the time, of course but not lasting or something I would talk about, I somewhat ruefully admitted to myself. She was just a haunting memory but, if I admitted it, not the sort of affair I'd attach any weight to, when all was said and done. In fact, if she hadn't turned up again out of the blue, in time, I suppose I would have forgotten her all together. The confidences I had shared with him had always been thus and I had assumed it had been like that for him - if there was nothing special, there was nothing to tell. He knew about Inno, of course and she was special to me, but in an unusual way and not the way most people regard as special.

But this photograph, it mattered to her, whoever she was, that was for sure, the venom in the words was plain to see. "Hell hath no fury like a woman scorned", I thought to myself. Also, when I examined the matter more closely in my mind it must have been something reasonably special to him, too. "Always yours," he had written and besides, one didn't go dishing out photographs of oneself to all and sundry like a pop idol. Photographs were intimate, special gifts. Why, then, had he not told me about this, for surely here was a case which I would have expected him to talk about?

So, what did it amount to, then, all this concentrated thought? This much. I did not know my brother as well as I thought I did and I was sad. Sad because I didn't know it at the time and now it was too late.

3

Extracted from Police records (5):

"Griffiths, dig out what you have on Hans van Cleef."

"Yes, boss, sure. Any particular angle?"

"See what contacts you have listed with him on people in this country."

"I didn't think he had any, boss."

"No, neither did I. I'll see you tomorrow but if you find anything interesting let me know ASAP. OK?"

"OK, Chief."

Sam disconnected the mobile and stared ahead, frowning. This was getting more involved than had been thought possible at the start. And yet...?

Chapter 11

1

When my mother did anything, she always did it "properly", as I suppose one would expect. She wasn't born into quite the same social circles as my father but, as with those who are converted to a religion, she became even more particular and zealous about it. Luncheon, therefore was preceded by sherry in the drawing room. Today was no exception even though the circumstances may have been exceptional. We all trooped in about 12.45, arriving from different parts of the house and estate. She was more cheerful than I had seen her for days. My father, she said, was improving daily, she loved entertaining and she was particularly fond of young people. She revelled in it and the simple occasion took on a little warm glow of pleasure to me, watching her there in her usual place at the foot of the table, animated and interested in everything.

The lunch had its standard components, home made soup, fresh salmon and a choice of puddings, one sophisticated and one "nursery". Today's offerings were a chocolate and rum thing and an apple and blackberry crumble, but to me it was a strange meal and nothing standard about it at all. It fell into the category of "meals before events", such as lunch before Speech Day or before playing the piano at a music festival. Setting off for Scout Camp had that feel, too but then Mother was convinced we would all starve if we had to fend for ourselves. She was probably right, too.

Years later, I discovered our survival weekends were a fake. Unbeknown to us the Scout Master always had tins of baked beans and boxes of eggs in the boot of the car, parked surprisingly near our so-called, spontaneous, make-shift camps, to be substituted at the last moment if either we hadn't caught anything or had ruined it in the cooking. "I couldn't bear for them to be disappointed with themselves, Lady Berkeley," I had heard him say. I knew we were all fairly dim in the cooking line but I think even fourteen year old boys could have told the difference between "rabbit caught by hand" and a plate of Heinz beans. But we always managed to catch something and he never was discovered until that chance remark two or three Christmases ago had found him out.

As I ate, I mused to myself on all this and wondered why so many activities in the British way of life had to preceded by eating. I was very aware of the forthcoming interview with my father and so, too, I felt was Sam, nodding at the conversation, quietly getting on with the meal.

Martin and Jane talked to my mother about the estate. They sat one on each side of her. I sat next to Jane, Sam next to Martin, opposite each other. We listened to the three of them but neither Sam nor I said a great deal. We both "spoke when we were spoken to". I caught Sam's eye at one point and caught the quick smile of fellow feeling. Mother took special note of the plans to tell my father later, although one of us went to discuss matters with him every day and engineer the odd bit of decision-making for him. But his memory was erratic. He didn't seem to be able to distinguish in his mind the present from the past. After the meal we returned once more to the drawing room for coffee.

My mother was standing by the window talking to Martin and Jane about the orangery which had recently been refurbished. Last year we had installed a heating unit and she had started to plant what was to be a large collection of rare ferns. Already the graceful stems of one or two of the large varieties nearly reached the high vaulted glass roof in places. This old, elegant building led out from the drawing room and they went through to explore their mutual passion further, Martin and Jane both being very keen gardeners, coffee cups in hand. Sam and I were left alone.

We said nothing for a while, staring out over the park and then Sam spoke.

"Do you mind if I take those videos, Rob?"

"No, if they help. Of course I don't mind."

"If there's something I want you to look at, I'll call you in London and I'll bring them over. Is that all right?"

I nodded.

"By the way, do you know anything about where the helicopter was kept before the day?"

I frowned, thinking. "I'm not sure. I know it was there," I pointed through the window, "in that still roped off bit next to the lake on the Sunday. But that was the day I came down, if you remember. I don't know where it was before that."

"Well, I don't think that would matter so much. After all, it seems likely that the bomb was attached before it could be moved again."

"Oh, you mean the detonator was tied in with the ignition?"

"No, it was a timed device. If it had been attached to the ignition it would have exploded when he switched on the engine."

We were curiously detached about it. I suppose the police develop that way with dealing with things and I caught the mood from Sam.

"Jane will be able to tell you about where it was beforehand. She's a fount of all knowledge here as you saw this morning. I don't know what we would have done without her, you know."

"I think it would have made a lot of extra work, that's for sure."

I drained my coffee and put the cup and saucer back on the tray. I smiled. "I don't begrudge Martin his wife, since they are obviously so happy but I wonder at my brother's not snapping her up himself when he had the opportunity. He was hardly shy in coming forward!"

Sam laughed but those grey eyes were very watchful, suddenly. "Indeed, I think you are right. Have you any idea idea at all why he did not?"

The question was not frivolous and I was surprised to hear the note of seriousness in Sam's voice. It was almost as if Sam really wanted to know the answer, although I couldn't for the life of me see why this would be the case. However, as it had been put in a serious tone, I felt compelled to resist the temptation to be flippant.

"He told me it was no longer an issue but it had never been serious. They enjoyed each other's company, while looking for someone special. He said she had said she thought she had found him and then, a few months later she announced her engagement to Martin. I told him he should have married her himself and he laughed and that was that. Everyone was quite relaxed about it."

"Was there any awkwardness between him and Jane, working together every day, I mean?"

"No, none but I wouldn't have expected it, considering the way he described it. There seemed to be no difference between them at all, really. William told me it was over, and why and that was that. But he had never been all over her all the time in any case - it wasn't that sort of relationship. They were just pleasantly affectionate with each other and that has never changed." I thought a little more. "To an outsider, it appeared to be almost a brotherly, sisterly thing, I think."

"Oh. Wasn't it a physical relationship, then?"

"Oh yes, of course it was. I knew that much about it."

"So why say...?"

"I didn't mean it was platonic when I said it was a brotherly/sisterly thing. I meant just sort of casually affectionate and rather fond of each other."

"Did he say that to you?"

"Not in so many words. It's just my observation of it, since you asked me to think about it. Aren't you going to ask Jane herself?"

"Yes, I will speak to Jane again. Alone this time. I will do it later without you or Martin breathing down her neck!"

I grinned and Sam asked another question.

"Do you think Martin was jealous of William at all, by the way?"

"No, I don't think so but as I said there was no reason to be. He was terribly shocked by William's death and has been a tower of strength, you know, Sam."

Sam stood up, suddenly brisk, efficient. "Right. Now then, if your mother is in agreement, I will go and talk to your father. Let's see what Sister Berkeley has to say of her patient."

I followed Sam slowly out of the room.

2

At the top of the stairs we met Eddy Farley. During the day, he let himself in usually and needed no ceremony. I introduced him to Sam who explained the purpose of our visit to the sick room. He frowned and beckoned us into a spare bedroom and closed the door.

"Listen, Rob. I haven't said anything to your mother, she's been through enough for the moment. I am more than a little bothered about him. He is restless today and pretty vague. He knows you are here," he gave Sam a quick smile, "and is anxious to see you but I must warn you, he is frail, very ill and anything he may say could be unreliable. I must stress this, Chief Inspector."

Sam looked grave and regarded him, weighing things up. "You mean he'll invent stories, imagine things?"

"No, not exactly but things may get into the wrong order in his mind. He can be very confused. This is partly the drugs we have to use, you understand. It makes it easier for him to cope with the shock. We are dealing with different conditions here, you see, not just one."

I nodded. "I've noticed he can make some odd remarks, often quite unrelated or seemingly so to the matter under discussion. But they are real. He asked me if I'd mended the swing the other day. I remembered the incident he was actually referring to but it happened when William and I were about 10 and 8. He spoke about it as if it were yesterday."

"You understand me precisely. So," he turned to Sam again, "you see what I mean? He can be fine for quite a while and then suddenly make an odd, unrelated remark or, alternatively he can start off in a world of his own and stay there. Take it all with a pinch of salt and you really must not be too long with him. I can't put a time on it. If you're both in there, you can judge when enough is enough." We nodded. He turned to go but stopped. "One more thing, Rob."

"Yes?"

"Keep this from your mother. Obviously she knows he is uncertain in his memory and thinks this is purely due to drugs. I have to say, though, that your father's health is very precarious. I believe he will get better, at least partly, in similar cases that has been the outcome but it will be a slow and frustrating business for you all. In her heart of hearts your mother knows this but for the moment I think it is better for her to handle it

122

her way. But I feel you had to know the real lie of the land. All right?"

I shook his hand. "Thanks. You've been marvellous. I'm glad you told me - well, us."

He glanced at Sam again somewhat curiously this time and left the room. We heard him cross the landing and go down the stairs. We looked at each other.

"So..." I stopped.

Sam was thinking I could see.

"Yes, now Rob, listen. It seems to me I am going to have to try and sort out what it is I think he can really help me with. In other words, I don't want to tax his strength with questions I can find the answer to elsewhere, even though that will undoubtedly take longer, bugger it, and time is not what we have. Trails going cold and all that. Right?"

"OK, yes." I agreed.

Sam walked about a bit, half-thinking out loud, or so it seemed.

"The army must come up with what he did in the war, they must do, although it looks like were going to have to pull rank on them, they are not being easy about it. They like keeping their secrets to themselves. To start with, at any rate, I must glean what I can from records. There will be more, but at least I won't have to take him back through reams of historical stuff that will probably tax him severely, either his memory or, if your mother is right, emotionally too, before I got to the real nitty gritty. I suppose that might be locked away in his memory and nowhere else but we have to pray it's not and there is another source. Besides, it has to be said, that may all be a complete red herring in any case and may have nothing to do with William. It's just one of the mysteries I don't like to see unanswered in an enquiry that I was telling you about. If I can study the background more closely and get a better picture from other sources then maybe, if I thought it important, then I could come back and ask him some more stuff but better prepared. To question him today would have been a shortcut, that's all. However, considering how frail he is I can see that might very well be counter-productive in the long run. So, we'll put that on the back burner for the moment unless I can see a way in there that might either be essential or possible without being too stressful, right?"

"OK. Of course. You're the expert and you know what you want, anyway."

"Know what I want? God, if only..." Sam stared out of the window briefly and then turned back towards me. "Right. I shall start off by asking him questions about people who might have disliked William. Then, I shall ease the questioning round to himself and see if I can't find out something about the row they had. Then I will try to get something on the letters. Phew...!" Sam sighed. "Well, we'll see now we go. Ready?"

"Yes."

I had an odd sensation, almost akin to stage fright as we crossed the landing. My father really was the key witness, perhaps the only one who could really help, I suddenly realised. I took a deep breath and let it out slowly as Sam knocked gently on the door to my father's dressing room.

The day nurse opened it at once. She was a new one and she was expecting us. She simpered at me, girlishly and as she walked past I caught a whiff of cheap scent. I wrinkled my nose and caught Sam's eye, who gave a small half-hidden smile, understanding. We promised not to tire him and she left, anxiously glancing towards the bed where he sat, propped up on some five or six pillows.

Sam went over straight away and knelt down beside the bed on the floor. His eyes grew fond as he looked over the top of Sam's head at me. "Sam's here again, Rob. See?"

I nodded and sat down on the edge of the bed, opposite Sam.

"You had a good bonfire, Sam, down there by the lake!" His eyes were bright. I took his hand in mine and it felt very hot. I glanced at Sam who had gently put his other hand on top of the bedclothes. We exchanged a pointed look.

"We did, Sir William. It was marvellous. One of the best bonfires ever! Now, do you remember particularly why I am here today?" Sam's voice was kind as only Sam's could be. He nodded.

"You want to know if I can help you about William. About the people who killed him." The simple statement from the old man, moved me much. The directness of the very old or the very young can be deeply disconcerting on occasions and so often happens when one least expects it.

"That's exactly it, Sir William. First of all, is there anyone you can think of who didn't like William? Was there anyone who had had a disagreement with him?"

He stared in front of him and his face flushed more. I looked anxiously at Sam, who was watching him intently.

"Yes." He paused for a moment, feeling the sheet between his sparse, greyed fingers. He stared straight ahead of him. "She hated him, she must have... must have... And for the same reason she hated me, too, I imagine. She was bound to have done when he told her. And he, William, didn't like me telling him either, you know - wanting to shoot the messenger, that sort of thing. He ranted and raved, loathed me..." He sighed, "not that that feeling lasted, but it left him so sad, so sad, poor fellow. But he had to know. It would have been a terrible thing if he had gone ahead. Terrible."

Sam was wonderfully patient and gentle. "I'm sure it would have been. Can you tell me what you told William?"

He glanced at me uncertainly. "I don't know that I should. It's Rob, he's... he's only a little chap. He doesn't know about... about things."

Sam took his hand again and drew his gaze away from me again. "Rob is fine about it all and he's quite grown up now, you know. William was going to tell him. Is that not so, Rob?"

"Yes, Dad. William was going to tell me." I was tense, desperate to get to play the game right.

My father's face had a far away expression. "Yes, he would have told you, of course he would. But it was the fact that she was... well, part of HIS past, you see. Families matter, you know, even today and it would have been intolerable. I expect she was pretty, William always liked pretty girls but I never saw her, no. It was enough that I knew her name." He leaned forward slightly, holding tight to Sam's hand. He was making a great effort, I could see. This would cost him dear, I felt. "It was a terrible, awful coincidence that they should meet and love each other. To think of it, his cousin, of all people. But William couldn't marry her, not after what that bastard had done. Besides, it would have been the death of her. He would have killed any member of his family who associated themselves with me. I knew, you see, and he knew I did. Poor William, he was helpless to do anything. The past has affected the future and I was the cause, the impediment, if you like. No wonder he hated me at that moment but we can't undo what we have done or unlearn what we know." He brooded for a moment and then looked at Sam eagerly. "Do you think I'm right, Sam? You can't run people into danger like that, can you?"

"I'm sure you're quite right. You can't take risks with people's lives."

He twisted and shifted and looked distressed. "I hated that quarrel with William, I hated it so. But I had to shock him into understanding but it was very hard for me, to deny my beloved son his happiness... very hard..." He stared at nothing once more, silent now.

Sam tried again, gently. "Who is it who is dangerous, Sir William? It may be important. Who is it you're talking about?" He looked very vague all of a sudden. "Sir William... can you tell me the names?"

He looked at Sam sharply. "No, I can't." His voice was firm and had some of its old military style in it. "Official secrets. I signed the Act, you know."

"Do you think this is to do with your wartime activities, then?"

He shook his head. "No, no, Sam, the war's over now but I'm not allowed to speak of it." He shut up like a clam, suddenly, and I realised Sam had made a mistake mentioning the war. He was trying to remember things that didn't matter, back in a world long since gone. I leaned forward.

"Dad?"

He stared at me. His eyes cleared and he smiled. "Robbie," he went on smiling. He beckoned me to him closer. "Come here, old boy, I must tell you something."

I leaned even closer and he whispered loudly to me. "If you look in my tallboy, you'll find that fiver I promised you."

I squeezed his hand. "Thanks, Dad, that's wonderful of you. Now, can you remember the name of the girl that William..." I glanced at Sam who nodded briefly. I took a risk, "that William wanted to... to marry? He was going to tell me all about it but... but... he didn't have time." I swallowed and could feel the sweat prickle my forehead.

He frowned and thought. He seemed to be trying to remember but it was anyone's guess precisely what. Something seemed to occur to him for he roused himself and looked at me. "Don't tell your mother. It was over before I married her. Why, we weren't even engaged then, hadn't met. But it would make her sad, Robbie." He glanced at Sam and smiled. "Don't make her sad, Rob, she needs to be loved. She's always loved you, you know. William told me." He put out his hand and touched Sam very gently on the arm.

He looked tired suddenly, and very old. He lifted haggard eyes to Sam's. "Can I have some water?" Sam held the cup to his lips and I was surprised to see those capable hands were shaking slightly. He sank back on his pillows for a moment and opened his eyes wide. "Sam," he said in quite a different voice, "make me up some Ribena. I love Ribena." He grinned at me.

Sam mixed the cordial with water and he took it, drinking it himself. He placed it carefully on the tray. "That bloody fool of a nurse. She can't make Ribena. Doesn't make it nearly strong enough. You can barely taste it at all." He looked at me with a wink. "Ghastly girl, you'd loathe her, Rob, priggish, prissy... not your sort at all." He beamed at Sam and patted the brown hand. "Now we know what sort of girl Rob likes, don't we?" He chuckled. The next second he looked politely at us, from one to the other. "Now, what else can I help you with?" He sounded like a shop assistant.

"Do you remember getting some letters from abroad, Sir William? One from France and one from Holland?" Sam sat on the bed. My leg had gone to sleep, curled up underneath me. I was very uncomfortable but did not dare move in case I disturbed his train of thought, such as it was. I was surprised by his reply which came promptly and positively.

"Yes, I do. I knew you were going to ask me about the letters. Phyllis mentioned it. One was from Hans..." He stopped and shook his head. "I couldn't believe it. He said his only crime had been ambition but it was more than that, he was a bad lot, really, or became it, perhaps is a better way of putting it. Joined the wrong side in the end. Interested in the fate of his picture, was he? Hmm. I don't know..." He stayed frowning and preoccupied as before. He roused himself again. "The other was from poor Pierre's widow. He had a stroke, you know. Very sudden. I was very sad."

"Yes, you must have been. Anything further you can remember about either letter?"

He frowned. "He sold out to him. He told me he had to. Hans, all powerful once but no money now. Even the Stubbs wasn't enough for him. What a dangerous man he has always been! Jean wrote too, but that was a long time ago... a long time ago. He'd never write now..." He went quiet once more.

I remembered! The Stubbs! I bought it from a man called van Cleef! That was where I had heard the name and yet, was that the only time I'd heard it? Surely, there was something else connected with that name...

Sam was speaking again. "The letters, do you still have them?"

He stared, vague again. "I put them somewhere... but don't worry, Robbie will find them. Robbie will know..." He tailed off.

Sam tried again on the first tack. "Now, Sir William, are you sure you can't give me the name of anyone who might hurt William, considering everything you've told me?"

His face was puzzled. "William? No, no, not William. He didn't fight in the war, you know. And no one can hurt him any more now, Sam. Can't talk about the war. Official secrets and all that. Can't talk of that, although if I told anyone, it might be you, one day. The police were very kind, very kind. They're nice men. Do you know any policemen, Sam? Nice men. Very kind..." He suddenly looked utterly exhausted. "But not today... I'm tired today. I'll tell you another day, maybe. Those boys wear me out, pushing them in the swing..."

There was silence. We sat there for a while longer but he was asleep, instantly, like a child who has played hard all day. His breathing was strong and rhythmical but his face was pale with two red spots, one on each cheek. Sam signalled to me and we got up and crept out of the room. The nurse came down from her discreet position further up the corridor. No one would ever accuse her of eavesdropping.

"He's fallen asleep, Nurse," I said, "suddenly and in the middle of a sentence."

"That's quite normal, Mr Berkeley." She was bright and cheerful.

"He seems very hot." My brow furrowed anxiously.

"Yes, yes, our temperature goes up and down. We'll be better when we've had a sleep. I'll call you later, if we need you. Don't worry! I'll do the looking after, you're such a busy, busy, Mr Berkeley!"

I nearly smacked her she was so bloody chirpy. It was as if she were humouring a small child into taking its medicine. My father was right, she was a ghastly girl with her fluttering eyes and "Night in Paris" cheap scent. I turned on my heel and marched down the stairs. I heard Sam murmur something to the silly cow and follow me down into the drawing room where I went for refuge from the nurse's round, fat face and round, fat eyes. I took a long breath to sooth my irritation and bathe my shattered wits.

3

Sam followed me in and quietly closed the door. There was silence in the room. I sat for a while, listening to the ticking of the clock on the mantelpiece and staring out at the park.

Sam spoke, quietly. "Can we talk, Rob?"

I roused myself with a sigh. "Yes, Sam, yes. Of course." I brooded for a moment longer. "Where do we start with this lot? A tangled jumble of information, if ever I heard it. And what is real and what is not, I'd like to know? Still, I think you did very well, as far as it went."

Sam smiled a rueful smile. "Apart from my mentioning his wartime activities at the wrong moment. I nearly lost him then completely. Thanks for stepping in! You even have the promise of a fiver in the tallboy as a reward!"

I smiled briefly and stared down at the roses printed on the chintz of the window seat cover. I traced the leaves and flowers with my fingertip. The design of the fabric showed up, clear and well defined, the threads running backwards and forwards, weaving their shape and changing colour precisely where they were needed in order to make the patterns. No disorder there, but this business... The threads that ran through that weren't well defined at all. I didn't know where to begin to think.

Sam sat down in front of me. "Come on, Rob, don't let me down now! We've got some information to shift between us. I can't do it on my own, you know."

With an effort, for I was beginning to feel I was being crushed by the stress and enormity of it all, I tried to think. I stood up and wandered over to the mantelpiece. The fire was not lit. There were fir cones in the grate, neatly balanced one on top of the other. I rested my arm along the length of it, feeling the cold of the marble through my sweater. My mind slowly cleared. Sam was speaking again and I addressed myself to new questioning.

"Firstly, let me say this. You asked me what was real and what was not. All of it was, real, Rob. Every word. It's just the order of events and who precisely he was talking about that are uncertain. But it was all true. Remember what your doctor said. Besides, although muddled, it sounded true, don't you think?"

I thought about this. Yes, I saw what Sam meant suddenly. I nodded. "Yeah. I think you're right."

"Good. Now, I believe we have here the essence of what it was William was going to speak to you about. Do you feel that?" Sam's eyes searched my face.

I nodded again. "Yes. Maybe you're leading me a bit, but yes. I think it was something to do with a girl. But a girl he wanted to marry? I can hardly believe it! You remember what I said about serious relationships? Well, this would fall into that

128

category, for God's sake. He'd never wanted to marry anyone before. Surely he'd tell me that!"

Sam watched me and spoke slowly. "Maybe, but maybe not. It is possible you have just answered your own question. He had never wanted to marry someone before. If it were that special, maybe he couldn't talk about it to anyone, not even you."

I frowned. I could see that theory would work for some people, but William and myself? I wasn't convinced. However, we had to press on for the moment.

"The next thing is, who is she?"

I looked up, mystified. "I don't bloody well know! You know I don't!"

"No, but maybe we can work it out since there's some sort of family involvement here. Someone's cousin... Your father's? Yours? An acquaintance of your father's who has got a cousin that William might have..."

I half shouted at Sam. "You're crazy! It might be anyone!"

"No! It can't be just anyone. It has to be someone your father dislikes, fears even, by the sound of it. I thought you would be bound to know that."

"Well, I don't. Can't you understand, Sam, he never quarrelled with anyone! Do you hear me, not any-bloody-one! Not seriously enough to interfere with William marrying someone, for Christ's sake!"

"What about a branch of his own family?"

"I can't believe you're serious in this but well..." I thought for a moment. "He doesn't get on too well with his cousin in America. He disappeared with a lot of money from somewhere, I think. But that was years and years ago and we still get Christmas cards and send them, too I believe. He looks at them and says things like, "God, that bugger", and shrugs it off. That's all. It's all water under the bridge now whatever it was, I promise you, but Mother knows all about that. Ask her."

"I will. So, is there a branch of the family tree William might have wanted to marry? He said "his cousin". What cousins do you have?"

"Heaps. In total, three or four girls and about fourteen boys. We go in for boys in this family."

"Would any of these girl cousins have interested William?"

I was emphatic, walking up and down in my agitation. "Absolutely not. One's about four years old, I think, two are married and one's a nun! Make something of that, if you will. Besides, friends or relatives apart, Father doesn't... have... arguments... with anyone." I stressed each word carefully. "Got that? He only disliked his cousin, I think disapproved of him, really but I don't think he ever... and in any case he didn't dislike him enough to go to the lengths he obviously did to put William off. He cannot have meant Will's cousin. He must have meant someone else's, not ours. Really. Honestly, Sam, that's a complete red herring. I know it."

"Shit! I thought he meant Will by 'he' - HIS cousin, YOUR cousin, too, obviously, by implication!"

"No. I'm positive. But he doesn't argue with people. That's why his row with William was so extraordinary." I cast my mind back over the strange conversation. I went on, "I'm sure I don't know this girl, whoever she is. I don't believe I can help you here at all." I sighed. "My poor father. There was something he didn't want my mother to know. He's always protected her all these years. He was always saying, 'don't worry your mother with any of this', whatever it was. But I wonder what he was talking about, 'over before they were married and weren't even engaged'? A pre-marital affair, I suppose. He's always looked after her carefully, making sure she was safe and happy. I find that very touching. But he jumps from one thing to another so, it's very confusing. And I don't know what he was talking about when he said William had told him Mother had always loved me. William wouldn't need to tell him that. He knew it. I've never doubted it for one moment and I hope I should never be so unkind as to make her sad..." I broke off, for Sam had leapt up.

"Rob, have you a cigarette? I can't think where I've left mine."

"Sure." I stared, for Sam's composure had quite gone in that instant and I knew that all this rushing about looking for cigarettes was a blind. God knows what that meant but I had enough mysteries to deal with for the moment. But as I lit Sam's cigarette those grey eyes caught mine for a moment and as they did so, for some unaccountable reason Sam looked exceedingly anxious, embarrassed almost, but drew in the smoke and looked away.

For a little while we sat and smoked in silence. It seemed that Sam was thinking very hard what next to say.

"So... as far as you can, you cannot think of anyone who your father has quarrelled with at all, let alone someone he should hate enough, or fear enough, to stop William marrying?"

"Exactly so."

"I see. Damn and bugger it! I didn't press him because I felt sure you'd know." Sam thumped the arm of the chair. "Fuck! That's a wasted opportunity. I will have to try another day and I don't want to wait. We need to get onto something as soon as. So, I must try other sources there, if I can but it doesn't sound as if... Now then, let's try another tack. What about these letters?"

Ah, an excitement! Here was a small piece of information I could help with, I thought. "I know who van Cleef is, Sam. I bought the Stubbs in the dining room from him, or rather through his agent. I knew I'd heard that name before. But if it is the same man, I wonder what he was writing to Father about? Can it have been the picture? Somehow I doubt it. It seemed to be more than that but it seems to me that that is something we can expand on - check, or whatever."

Sam frowned. "Maybe. 'Sold out to him', he said. Could he have meant the picture? Did he mean sold out to you? I don't think so. Even in his muddled state I think he would have said you, if he meant you. But there is something else in my mind. I have also heard of a van Cleef and it was nothing to do with pictures. Did you meet him?"

"No, never. I bought the picture through his agent, an art dealer, that was all. I just remembered his name but I didn't meet him and had no contact with him personally at all. That is common when buying much art work."

"And when was this?"

"A few months back - last year some time."

"Hmm. OK. No more of that for the moment. I need to investigate further and come back to you."

After another brief pause, Sam asked me to think what else my father could have meant about where he had put the letters - something about 'Rob will know?' I hadn't a clue. William might have done, as they worked together, I thought. Safes and bank deposit boxes perhaps. Perhaps even Jane could help but I couldn't think how I would know or why he would suggest I could.

Sam left shortly after this to find Jane and ask her one or two things in private. For my own part, I felt drained and tired. The strain was showing here and there, I could feel it was. I was glad to be on my own again for a while.

4

I whistled for my faithful Nell and we set off, down across the park for a change. I was struck how uncomplicated was the relationship between a dog and its owner. How undemanding were animals - no arguments or secrets just straightforward liking and trust. But there was more than that, too. Loyalty. Nell would have died for me, I thought, quite willingly. It was a humbling thought and I was glad to have her company and no one else for that moment.

The road wound down and over a bridge that arched over part of the lake. It was screened by bushes, now heavy with blackberries and behind them I came across Martin who was leaning over the parapet, tapping with a stick, seemingly idly, at the brickwork. Bits of mortar fell off and splashed into the water below. Police enquiries made us all suspicious, it seemed to me. Sam had put a doubt in my mind. Had Martin cared about Jane's fondness for William? It seemed so silly that I had not even thought of it before. As I had said to Sam, he had no reason to be jealous because there was nothing of which to be jealous. But now, for the first time, I wondered.

He heard my step. He looked up, knowing it was me for Nell had pushed her nose at him in greeting, his expression anxious, kindly.

"Hello, Rob. How was it? I saw Sam who has just collared Jane again for some reason. They packed me off without ceremony, so I thought I'd look at the bridge. I'm a bit worried about it, as a matter of fact. I am worried about the weight of all these modern vehicles that go over it all the time. I believe we should get in a structural engineer to have a look at it." He glanced up in the direction of the house. "The two of them looked set for an involved conversation. That's the trouble, meeting up with old school friends who happen to head a police enquiry! All these huddles they get into! Almost incestuous, it seems to me!"

I had heard more than enough about incest or, at least, close family involvement of the dubious kind for one day and made a lot more noise and bother than was necessary as I climbed down the bank and stood in the water, peering up above me. One or two ominous-looking cracks seemed to be criss-crossing the brickwork. I scrambled out again.

"I think you're right. I don't like the look of it. It's been here for at least three centuries, so I suppose it's entitled to a bit of an MOT. I should think it would be damned expensive, though."

We wandered on together, down towards the lodge cottage. We talked about the tree planting scheme and Martin pointed out various sights for different areas of mixed woodland we planned to plant. Nell rushed furiously about, her coat soaking. She had followed me delightedly into the water. Any excuse to get wet, made her happy - a typical Labrador. Martin looked up in the midst of showing off his new-found knowledge of the Scots Pine.

"Oh, I know what I had to say. I have a message from Inno. She is down this weekend and she wondered if you could come over for supper. We could ask Sam, too - that is, if you'd like to." He faltered slightly, looking at me anxiously, as if he might have offended me in some way.

I smiled at his obvious nervousness. "Well, I haven't any plans for this evening and of course, I can't speak for Sam. Mother will be in bed by 7.30, as she usually is these days, I imagine. She's had an exciting day, what with lunch for five and everything that went with it." I didn't mention the traumatic nature of her questioning and put aside the vision of her earlier, her tears and anguished thoughts about William and my father.

"So you'll come?"

"Yes. Thank you, Martin, I will."

"And shall we ask Sam?"

I shrugged. "Why not? It's not my party. You ask who you like."

Martin looked disturbed again but said no more. I thought he might have said something else, given half a chance, but I did not encourage him to do so and he was silent.

We walked back to where the cars were parked. We could see Sam and Jane had come out of the office and were watching us, waiting for us to come up the hill to meet them. Martin suddenly spoke again. "Oh yes, I almost forgot. Just thought I'd mention there was another guest this evening. Do you know Charles Harrison?"

I thought. Oh yes, cocktail party at the Dorchester, six months ago, old Etonian. "Yes, he's a barrister, I think. Isn't he in her chambers?"

"Yes, that's right. He's... he's come down for the weekend." For the second time Martin looked awkward but this time I could see why.

I smiled. "I see. New boyfriend, is that it? Don't worry, Martin, I shall be a good boy and not chase Inno round the dining table or play footsie with her when I think no one will notice!"

He looked increasingly uncomfortable. "I didn't mean that, Rob. I just thought, well, you might have thought you would have Inno to yourself..." He tailed off.

I couldn't help laughing but I wanted to keep the initiative. I deserved some sort of pleasure, albeit on the malicious side, after all I'd been through that day. "Don't worry, I shall be the soul of discretion. I promise faithfully not to mention the steaming hot romance we had, still going on just a matter of days ago!"

Martin looked really alarmed. "Rob, don't! Inno would do something horrible to me if she thought I'd said anything!"

I laughed again. "Oh ho! So you and Jane thought you'd better have a quiet word in my ear, just in case! What a dutiful brother you are, Martin!" He looked so miserable that I relented. "I'm only teasing. I promise to be good, as I said. Go ahead and ask Sam, too if you like and then I can talk to my old school chum all evening and not flirt with Inno. How about that?"

He looked at me dubiously, a little reassured maybe but I could see he was uneasy. But I left him alone. Poor old Martin. With me in my particular mood he was no match for me. It wasn't fair on him.

We came up to Sam and Jane. Jane looked quickly at Martin. "Have you asked Rob about tonight?"

"Yes, he's coming."

I went over to Jane and put my arms round her, looking down into her face. "And guess what, Janey, my sweet, I have promised to be a good boy and not pinch Inno's bum and make poor old Charles thing jealous. What do you think of that?"

Jane squirmed way from me, a horrified look on her face. "Robert! How could you... Martin, really! What have you said?"   .

I heard Sam's rich laugh behind me. "Jane, can't you tell when he's having you on? Besides he'd better behave, as I'm coming, too. Or I'll have you in irons, Mr Robert Berkeley!"

I shrugged, spreading my hands wide with a look of outraged innocence. We walked with the two of them back to the stables where they saddled the horses and set off back to the neighbouring estate. We watched them go and then turned back to the house.

"It'll be a pleasant party tonight," I remarked lightly.

"Very pleasant. But I can't stay late. It's a longish drive back to London."

I glanced sideways. "Don't you want to stay the night? You're very welcome."

"I have to be somewhere very early tomorrow. I can't keep my driver out all night, anyway, poor bloke. And I'm working here, you see, don't forget. This isn't a social call, Rob. I can stay and eat because I must eat somewhere and I am indulging myself eating with all of you but that is all, I'm afraid." There was regret there behind the brisk words, I thought.

"Oh, yes of course." We walked on. "Some other time, then."

"One day. That would be marvellous."

'One day'. The implication there was when this hell was over. I stared up at the sky briefly, watching the clouds. Life had taken on a surreal aspect, I thought. I had to do something to make it feel more normal or I'd go round the bloody bend. I glanced at Sam's serious face and stopped. "Sam, why are we being so bloody polite to each other?"

Sam's relieved laugh rang out, suddenly and infectiously. "I don't know. Let's stop, for God's sake! And give me a cigarette, while you're at it!"

"You're catching my bad habits, Chief Inspector!" I grinned and lit it and once again the grey eyes looked back at me over it as they had earlier but this time with the same familiar, smiling look of old.

Chapter 12

1

It was a pleasant party and I was a model citizen. At the end of the first course, I carried plates out to the kitchen for Inno. I watched her chatting of this and that as she piled up the trolley with dishes and vegetables and some amazing-looking thing in pastry from the Aga. She was the most wonderful cook and always had been. She most certainly was going to make some lucky fellow a wonderful wife, I thought but didn't say it. Remarks like that these days were not considered de rigeur. She shut the lower oven door with her foot, her hands full of plates. She glanced round, checking.

"I think that's everything. Can you push for me, Rob?"

I caught her by the wrist. "Inno?"

She looked at me, anxious all of a sudden. "Yes?"

I leant over and kissed her cheek. "He's a nice man. He suits you. Much better than I ever could. I hope you're happy. You deserve it. However... " I looked down at her with a degree of mock severity, "you might have told me, you know. You can't think what a state poor old Martin got into!"

To my concern, she burst into tears.

Alarmed I fished in my pocket for a handkerchief and couldn't find one. I handed her a tea towel from the rail running along the front of the Aga instead. She dabbed her eyes. "Damn! My eyeliner will run. Oh, Rob, you are such a dear man, and now you've made me cry." She gave me a watery sort of a smile. "Are you sure you don't mind? I was so anxious not to hurt you, particularly at this moment in your life. But Martin should not have said anything. I was very cross with him. I was going to tell you myself, of course but you... I... wasn't sure if... and you seemed to need me... still. I..." She tailed off, just looking at me, her brow lined and puckered in her obvious anxiety.

"You thought I'd be jealous and hurt? All that wounded pride?" I smiled at her and couldn't resist a teasing moment, besides it lightened what could turn into a heavy conversation and I didn't want that, for her as much as for myself. I gave a theatrical sigh. "I won't pretend I won't be heartbroken, Inno, but... but... There is always the Foreign Legion."

"Robbie? Can't you ever be serious?" She was half-laughing and half-exasperated.

I gave her a huge hug and then let go of her, my hand still round her face, though, smoothing her cheeks, watching her carefully. "Yes, I can be. And I meant it. He's a nice man. I am, I promise, really happy for you." I hesitated, staying where I was. "I told someone once you were my best friend in all the world after Will and you are. I know our relationship has been an unusual one and you need a normal one, I mean a constant, proper, loving man in your life. I suppose you've never stopped, in the back of my mind, being my girlfriend although I knew you weren't, really. It's been odd the way we've sort of dropped in and out of each other's lives in the way we have, never sort of talking about it but just... well... doing it. My fault, of course. I simply assumed... Didn't think, really. I thought you were happy with it all..."

"I was. I... I loved you, you see and that was how I kept you, or thought I did. Don't think about it, Rob. It was different, as you say, but I was content enough to go on with it. Really..."

"Christ, but I feel like a total shit now!"

"Don't. There's no need. I don't think of you like that and never have because I know you're not."

"I know I was the first one for you, Inno and..."

"And I'll never forget that, Rob. You were so kind and patient, and sweet and made it really special. Considering what some of my girlfriends told me of what they went through, it doesn't compare in any way. I loved you so much. I've been in love with you for years but I knew you didn't love me, not like that I mean, not IN love, just very fond of me."

"Oh God, I didn't want you to think I didn't care, Christ, I did - well, do..."

"No, you misunderstand. I knew you cared. For years I hoped you would fall in love with me, too but after last summer, our lovely holiday in France, I knew you'd never love me the way I loved you. If I hadn't changed you then, I knew I never would."

"Oh Inno, I'm so sorry..."

"No, no, don't be. I mean it. No one can force issues like that. Never. You see... af-after I... knew, really knew, I gave myself a real talking to when I got home and made a real effort to move on and it worked. You know we've seen very little of each other in the last year and a few days ago when... when you asked me stay with you, I couldn't say to you then that it was over for always now, in that way, because of the awfulness of William and what hell you were going through but I couldn't stay with you in that way, Robbie, because Charles and I have... well... are... Oh God, I could never sleep with one man and then another at the same time, like that. I couldn't. But... I so didn't want to... to say... to tell you just then..." Her face was tragic and I smiled.

"I understand. I mean it. And I think you've done the best thing for yourself and me, too. It's time I grew up, really. And I think you're wonderful. And I'm more glad than I can say that you've found someone really worthy of you. And he really is 'it', is he?"

"Yes. I really think he is."

"Good! Now then, come on, or they'll think we've eloped or something. Big kiss and that's it..." We kissed, gently at first, then developing into something not in any way chastely and I let her go, still slightly weepy. I squeezed her hand and wheeled the laden trolley down the hallway to the dining room. She held the door open for me and as I pushed it past her, we gave each other an intimate, secret smile. Not secret enough, though for as I looked up from the look, I saw Sam's quizzical look and raised, questioning eyebrows. As I passed Sam the vegetables, I heard, very quietly, "I hope I don't have to get out my handcuffs, Robert."

I smiled, innocently and replied equally as quietly, "Not on this occasion, Chief Inspector!"

"What are you two whispering about?" Jane didn't miss much either, I thought.

"Just planning the perfect robbery," I said. "Who would ever suspect Sam Stewart of the Yard?"

The conversation moved to other things and I fell silent as I ate. I watched Inno, animated, happy, at her end of the table. I felt a slight twinge of regret but I knew she had never been for me, not really although maybe once she could have been but I hadn't done anything about that. Because I hadn't really wanted her. A dear friend indeed, a unique relationship, but it was true, I never had been in love with Inno. He would be good to her, I thought, this quiet, clever and amusing man who looked at her properly, the way he should and I was glad. Once again I looked up and saw Sam watching me and this time, not for the first time today, I found I could not read the expression so well.

After coffee, Sam left, quietly without fuss. I went out to the car too and we walked slowly across the gravel.

"There's a lot for me to do in the next few days." Sam glanced sideways at me. "I'll ring you. When are you returning to London?"

I tried to switch off the party mood and think business. I pushed my hand through my hair which had done its usual trick of falling into my eyes. "I think Monday morning. I have a meeting with a man about some Chinese jade so I'll be leaving here quite early. I think I will be in London till Wednesday afternoon and come down to Hampshire again that evening. That do you?"

Sam nodded. "Fine. I'll be in touch. There are the videos to see some time this week. Maybe..." Sam hesitated, "maybe you'd like to come over to my office or my flat and watch them there. It may be easier for you in an unfamiliar setting."

I was surprised. "Easier for me?"

Sam flashed an intent look at me. "Yes. Sometimes these moments can be quite stressful. If there are films of William, moving and talking, you might find it upsetting, Rob. I think you ought to be aware of that."

I thought about it and decided it had got colder suddenly, for I shivered. Yes, it didn't take too much imagination to understand the stress of this particular ordeal. I decided I wouldn't think about it any more that evening and carefully closed the mental file for the time being. This would have to be addressed in a time of my own choosing. I merely thanked Sam for the invitation and accepted it.

"Very well. Come for supper on Tuesday. I cook a pretty mean Spaghetti Bolognese!"

I smiled. "What an invitation! I couldn't resist! You're on!"

Sam climbed into the back of the chauffeur-driven car. "You know where I live?"

I met Sam's gaze. I felt there was a challenge in it, somehow. I decided to meet it. "Yes, I know where you live, Sam. I send you Christmas cards, remember?"

A faint smile and the challenge had gone. "Yes, Rob. I remember."

I watched the car as it sped away down the drive. Why was Sam such a puzzle? I felt I had not behaved well today on occasion, though, God knows, I had enough excuses, all things considered. I sighed, cross with myself, for I was never happy upsetting people, particularly people as kind and patient and well, loving, really, as Sam. Some thrived on it but not me and for some inexplicable reason I felt as if I had been unfair. I could see the tail lights of the car disappear as it made the turning onto the main road and I swore, quietly, to myself. I should make more of an effort on Tuesday, I thought.

Suddenly, I was really, really tired. I would go in and make my excuses and leave the other four to themselves. I stretched my arms above my head and looked up at the billions of stars, sparkling there. Today had been vile. Tomorrow would be better. It must be. Apart from anything else, it would bring Madeleine with it. I ran back up the steps two at a time and went in to call for a taxi and say my goodbyes.

2

Extracted from Police records (6):

Sam settled into the back seat of the Met's BMW and stared briefly out of the window at the darkening landscape. "Right. My home, please, Jones."

"Right, Chief."

"Sorry to have kept you. Did someone feed you?"

"Yes. The housekeeper at Forbridge Park. Lovely steak and kidney pud. Just like my mum used to make."

"Good. That's something, then. Take the morning off tomorrow in lieu. I'll get myself to the office. OK?"

"That'd be great, boss. My wife's got an antenatal appointment. I'll be able to go with her."

"Good. I'm glad. Doesn't make me feel quite so guilty. I think maybe..." Sam's mobile rang. "Sorry, must take this. Yes, sir?" It was the Chief Superintendent.

"Sam? Where are you?"

"On the way back to London."

"Well, anything new? Any further? What thoughts?"

They slowed at a junction before pulling out onto the A31, heading for London. Sam was thoughtful. "Plenty but nothing concrete."

"Go on."

Sam spoke slowly, watching the gathering night as the car picked up speed on the dual carriageway. "Difficult to say but... well, if I was asked..."

"I am asking."

"Yes... Well, I suppose I'd say I wonder why we've been called in to investigate this."

"What do you mean?"

"Put it this way, if there wasn't a bomb involved then... "

"But there is."

"Yes, but putting that aside, I'd say this isn't a terrorist job at all, I'd say it was a domestic crime."

"Surely it can't be?"

"Well, no, that's why I'm confused. Let me explain. These people, as far as I can gather, have absolutely no connections or imply nothing that can associate any of them with any known terrorist activities. MI5 say the same. It seems on the surface a domestic issue, only one that I cannot fathom at all. They have no apparent animosity to one another, no money worries, although there are one or two money issues that need to be investigated that are a trifle bizarre and..."

"In what way, 'bizarre'?"

"Oh, unusually large amounts in bank accounts, though they're quite up front about them, nothing hidden or attempted to be hidden or fudged in any way."

"No indication of money laundering?"

"Not that I can see at present, no, but... well, I don't know, there's something lurking there. Something to do with associates abroad both past and present, maybe one or two dubious people but nothing to suggest any involvement other than long in the past or minor irritations in the present. As I say, nothing too untoward and absolutely nothing to do with terrorism with the exception of one thing."

"And that is?"

"All three, William, Robert and Sir William have all, seemingly, to a greater or lesser extent had dealings with Hans van Cleef."

"That evil sod? And you say it's domestic?"

"Yes, I do. But apart from Sir William's association, which I can't get to the bottom of at all at present, I can't see anything that connect Robert or William with him in any serious way. He is the only fly in the ointment. The rest of it just has a domestic feel to it, with the exception of a bomb. It's crazy. And I mean crazy. It doesn't make sense at all."

"You don't want to hand it over to homicide, then?"

"No. Certainly not. I don't like mysteries like this and... well..."

"You and your famous intuition then, is it Sam?" The voice held amusement, Sam could hear, irony, more like.

"That's right, sir. But I'll spell it all out in more detail tomorrow morning, yes?"

"Fine. 8.30? My office?"

"8.30, your office."

"Good. See you then."

The line went dead. Sam switched off the mobile and leaned back in the leather comfort and stared into the swiftly darkening night. This was the most difficult case any officer ever had to deal with, the investigation into the murder of a friend. Sergeant Jones glanced in his mirror swiftly at his now silent and brooding passenger and pushed his foot more firmly on the accelerator. Enough was enough for one day and he knew, suddenly, he wasn't the only one in the car who felt like that this evening.

Chapter 13

1

I sat in the car, waiting for the London train. It was early, I thought, for a Sunday - nine o'clock. No one was about and the station unmanned. It was a curious little place. The nearby village from which it took its name was at least a mile away. Here, in the middle of nowhere, there were one or two "railway cottages", an enormous car park for the London commuters and the little station itself. As I sat there, looking at the scene, it seemed to me like a ghost station but not run down and wild as one would expect. Here, in the midst of Hampshire was a sure-fire winner for the "prettiest station in the country" competition. The paintwork was fresh and gleaming, the whole place swept and clean and a pristine yellow line ran along close to the edge of the platform. There were hanging baskets and pots with a wild profusion of coloured plants, all crammed in making a delightful tangle. Further down the platform, set at regular intervals, were flower beds. Here, all summer long had grown petunias, geraniums and dark blue lobelia. Now, with autumn come, springing up and taking over were yellow and russet chrysanthemums and the purple faces of Michaelmas daisies. And yet, although so beautifully tended, there was no living soul and the air of desertion was made stronger and more eerie by the contrast of its obvious cultivation.

I hung my head out of the window and listened. I could hear the faint hum of trembling rails and I knew the train would soon appear round the bend of the single track and the ghost station would come alive again for the duration of the train's visit. Normality would remain with its hustle and bustle until, once again, the people gone and the train on its way to its final stop, it would sink back to be a sanctuary for bees and butterflies and now and then the idle observer, such as myself.

There was no scurrying crowd today, however. Madeleine was the only passenger to alight from the train that morning. She looked up and down the platform. I tooted the horn and she caught sight of me and raised a hand in greeting with a smile. She found her way through the side gate, for the usual exit through what they rather grandly called the Booking Hall was closed when the station master was off duty. She climbed into the passenger seat.

"'Ello, Rober-rt."

Nothing about her, neither facial expression nor body language, invited me to kiss her so I did not. I merely smiled and let in the clutch. "Hello," I said. "Good journey?"

"Yes, there were no problems." She turned her head this way and that. "It is very pretty here. I did not pass through other stations like this."

"No," I pulled out into the road from the station forecourt and started the short journey home, along the winding, narrow country lanes. "The old boy who runs the station is crazy about gardening. He loves his station and does it all himself. It's his life - trains and gardens - his job, hobby, passion, everything."

The autumn morning made the lanes particularly beautiful. It seemed to me that nature had dressed herself in her best that Sunday to welcome a visitor from another land. Cobwebs laden with drops of water hung like diamond necklaces from bushes and grasses and the bloom of moisture covered everything with a blue-grey haze. The air was sharp but the sun already had warmth in it and it promised to be a wonderful day. My spirits rose. The omen was good.

We drove through the gates and up the winding driveway. Madeleine asked me about the house and its history. I stopped the car at a distance so as to be better able to point out the various changes in its architecture, marking the times and seasons and generations as they passed. The middle section, of mellow red brick and half-timbering was Tudor, one wing was Queen Anne and another Regency. The original stable block, now the office, could be seen from this position and was early Victorian. So was the kitchen but being round the back was hidden from view. It was an extraordinary hotch potch of styles and yet, curiously, it worked. Each bit grew out of the next bit, a homage to the age recently passed, but a pride in the presentation of the new. Each generation of Berkeleys was supposed to add something of his own era to the house. My father had not added the conservatory, but refurbished it for my mother and her ferns. It was after all a Grade One Listed building and no additions were permitted now but we were allowed to restore it in the same way as the original had been. Thus it had been Victorian and still looked like it now. I explained all this to Madeleine. I was fairly well practised at reciting the history of my home and had learned it all as if it had been lines or a speech from a play. Once in a while it fell to me to do the odd conducted tour to WI coach parties and the like so we were all well rehearsed on the subject of Forbridge. As I was speaking, it occurred to me that one day I, myself, now should have to add something to it. I stopped my discourse somewhat abruptly and drove on, this latest responsibility having crept up on me when I was not ready to accept it. Something else to be looked at and examined more closely in the future.

Madeleine said nothing much but nodded as I talked. Once in a while she asked a question, such as what all the upstairs windows were and what rooms one had in English country houses. In France, she went on, they were mostly bedrooms as they had such large families. I pointed out the library, the billiard room and the morning room, all on the ground floor and upstairs the nursery and which bedroom belonged to which member of the family. "Cellars?" she asked.

I smiled. Trust a Frenchwoman to ask about wine storage. "Yes, we have cellars. But I'll bet not a patch on the ones at the château! We only drink the wine here. You grow it, harvest it and mature it, too. Far more superior!"

She stared at me and nodded, solemnly. No sign of amusement crossed her face in answer to my smile. She appeared humourless. Something else I hadn't remembered about her. On the contrary, we had laughed a lot, but admittedly not while sitting in a car admiring architecture.

Mother was there to greet us. Madeleine shook her hand and they talked for a while. We went in for a late breakfast.

I sat, watching her eat. She looked curiously out of place there - like a strange, exotic hot house plant amongst a row of cabbages. I wondered why. I felt she was deeply uncomfortable, for some reason. She was not at all relaxed although she talked animatedly enough to my mother and myself.

After she had eaten her fill, I offered to take her upstairs to show her the room Helena had allocated for her stay. She stopped and regarded me in a troubled way.

"Oh, Rober-rt, I do not think... I fear it will not be possible for me to stay here this evening. I must return to France very early tomorrow morning, on the first flight, in fact. Therefore I am staying tonight at one of the hotels at Heathrow. It makes it so much easier." I obviously looked a trifle downcast at this revelation but she said earnestly, holding my upper arm tightly to press home the point, "But the good news is that I will return soon - a week on Monday, and then I will see you again."

"Well, OK, then. But let us make a bargain. If I don't kick up a fuss about you leaving earlier than you promised, let me cook you dinner at the flat that Monday evening and before you start to pull faces, I'm quite good at cooking some things."

She regarded me seriously, nodding. "Ver-ry well. That will be love-lee. It is a date then, oui?"

"It's a date, then. Oui."

"I do not know what time I will be there, though, that is the problem. I could have to wait outside for a long time or maybe turn up later that I need..."

I thought for a moment. "Well, why don't I give you a key, I have a spare one, then you can come in whenever you like."

She nodded. "Yes. All right. That is a good idea, I think."

Happier, I took her for a guided tour downstairs. She paused here and there, looking at various pictures and bits of furniture. She was knowledgable about things, too, I noticed but although the conversation did not flag, I got the strong impression that I was physically and verbally being held at arms' length. I sighed inwardly. I wasn't getting very far. She wasn't staying tonight when I might have got a bit closer to what I wanted but at least she was coming back and, seemingly, quite cheerful about the prospect of spending an evening with me, á deux, at the flat.

I took her along to the kitchen to meet Helena who was, as usual, up to her eyes in preparing a wonderful Sunday luncheon, one of the very best British traditions, I said. Madeleine agreed, most warmly. It was the same in France, she said. In fact today she knew her family would all be together at the château. She looked at me with a smile. "If I had not promised to come and see you, Rober-rt, I would have gone back today to be with them." For the first time my heart gave a lurch of pleasure but when I tried to touch her, she turned away, making an excuse of pointing at something across the courtyard, so I could no longer reach the hand that was nearest to me. I ground my teeth together in silent protest. The progress was bloody slow. Still, it did, at last, seem that I was actually getting somewhere. She had chosen to be with me today instead of back home with the clan de la Flèche and considering how passionate she was about them all I could only assume that to be more than a small compliment.

We went through the kitchens and out towards the kitchen garden. The smell of herbs in the sun was wonderful and she smiled and looked really happy, all of a sudden. "Why, it smells like home," she said. Suddenly, something occurred to me.

"I know what you'd like to do."

She looked at me questioningly but a trifle warily, too, I noticed. "Let's get some baskets and pick mushrooms. I bet you do that in France at this time of year."

She laughed - a high-pitched, sudden, excited laugh, rather like a child. "Yes, yes, I love to do that. That is a wonderful idea, Rober-rt." Her pleasure was so youthful and naïve it made a sharp contrast to the sophisticate I knew her to be. I half expected her to jump up and down and clap her hands. I did not find it attractive, this sudden childishness, although some men might have done. It was off-putting. However, the plan obviously pleased her and I picked up two wicker baskets from the glory hole and set off in the direction of the copse. I whistled for Nell to accompany us.

She came, slowly, from the kitchen and stopped in her tracks on seeing Madeleine. I saw her hackles rise and heard the faint grumble in her throat. I called her again. "Come on, Nell, old girl. It's Madeleine. You know her."

Nell turned her back on us and sat down. Nothing I said or did would make her budge. I laughed. "She's a funny dog. I think she's jealous of you. She doesn't care to share me with anyone!" I tugged at her ears but she still resolutely refused to move. "All right, you daft thing, you stay here with Helena, then. We're going to the woods." Upon hearing Helena's name, she got up and stalked off indoors without a backward glance.

I felt as if I had to continue making apologies for her behaviour, rather as one does when a child has been rude to a visitor. However, in truth, although I pretended she was often like this with people she did not know, I was disturbed a little, for I had never known Nell do this to a person before. She could bark and display some fine teeth if she really thought she (or I, for that matter) was being threatened but this was if she could make neither head nor tail of Madeleine.

It put me in mind of when she was a puppy and had come across a mirror for the first time. As is usual with animals, she jumped at it, expecting to meet the other puppy she saw there, ready to play. After three or four times of banging her nose she tried to get round the back of the mirror. This being no good, she contented herself with barking sharply. Finally, she gave up but never again did she try to unravel the mysteries of the looking glass. She avoided all reflective surfaces for she knew it to be something beyond her comprehension. If she did, by some misfortune encounter a mirror, she would sit with her back to it, just as she had done now. I wondered what it was she did not understand about Madeleine. For the third time in twenty four hours I decided to put a thought behind me. Like Nell herself, I metaphorically turned my back on it. I led the way up the incline towards the woods.

2

It seemed curious to me, walking up towards the copse without Nell. I couldn't think of a time when she was not with me on a walk before. We stopped here and there as we climbed up the slope to look back and regard the ever-increasing panorama as we went higher up the hill. White clouds billowed up and over the horizon and I knew that the weather was due for a change once more, but not for a few hours yet for the breeze was gentle. We moved out of the sun into the dappled light of the woods.

Madeleine proved to be an expert mushroom hunter. She could spot ones I had never noticed and looked in places where I would never have thought to find any. There were several different kinds and she was quite excited by one or two of the less common ones. She pointed out the differences and described the flavours and what they might be used for in France. There were other kinds, too that she did not know and these we left alone but made a note of their colour and position in order that we might look them up in a reference book when we returned to the house. She was very knowledgeable about fungi and talked about the different poisons that could be obtained from them and their symptoms.

I remarked upon her knowledge. Was it a hobby, perhaps?

She shook her head. "No, although they are fascinating, it is true. No, as we use many natural things in the preparation of our food at the château we have to know what is what. Both of us, that is my brother and I, have to know these things. We cannot have a reputation of sending our guests home with food poisoning. They would never come back. It would not be good for business!"

"No! Particularly if you killed them off in the process. They'd certainly never come back then!"

I showed her the group of Fly Agaric I had noticed a few days before. She squatted down beside them, turning her head this way and that to admire them.

"These are very poisonous, Rober-rt. And... and how it is made the... what do you call it... the Magic mushrooms."

"Yes. Even I know that!"

Her eyes were steady as she looked at me. "Drugs."

"Yes. But I don't partake. I never have. Just legitimate ones - drink, and a bit of tobacco." I smiled reassuringly.

She didn't smile back. Just looked at me, quite expressionless. "They are very beautiful. Only a mouthful would make you terribly ill and a whole dish could possibly kill you."

"It's odd how beautiful the really poisonous ones are. Either beautiful or innocuous. It's small wonder people are taken in by them. They look so innocent." I turned one over with my shoe. They did not snap off easily but half of it remained attached to the stalk. "Such is the stuff that fairy tales are made of - beauty, the perfect cover for wickedness and to commit the prefect crime."

She stood up and wandered off down the pathway, looking here and there as we went. "You have been with too many policemen of late, Rober-rt. Life is not like that. You will see bad in everything, I think."

"On the contrary, life IS like that, I'm afraid." I swung my basket over the top of the stile as we came to it, and I vaulted over it, used to it. "Think how easy it would be to catch bank robbers if they walked about with name tags on saying, "I rob banks". The police would have a much easier task of it, catching my brother's murderer if he went round with a stick of dynamite in one hand and a timing device in the other. But these people look so ordinary. It is the best cover of all, even better than beauty, it occurs to me."

She approached the fence, vaulting it, as I had done, rather than climbing over, and walked beside me down the hillside. It was unusual for a woman and amused me. She was pretty fit, then, I thought. "Are they any closer to finding who it was did this thing?"

The first cloud reached the sun and drew gently across it. With it came a freshening wind and I shivered suddenly. I looked towards Madeleine. "Are you cold?"

She shrugged. "No, not particularly but in France it is still quite warm at this time of year. You should visit again, Rober-rt."

I glanced at her. "Are you inviting me?"

She looked back at me. The green eyes were steady. "If you come to France, of course, we shall be happy to welcome you to the Château Viezy." She spoke like a hotelier welcoming a coach party and I was irritated.

I turned sharply away and quickened my pace a little. It heard her laugh. "Rober-rt! I am only teasing you! You are so serious, always! You know you can come to Viezy whenever you can get away."

This time I stopped and looked at her. She laughed again. "Come on, Rober-rt, be happy. Now, tell me about your wonderful British police. You haven't told me how they are doing."

I walked on again but more slowly now. I did not say anything for the moment. For a brief second, as I met her gaze, there had been something cold and calculating before her usual bland, unreadable expression returned, which disturbed me. As I had shivered when the sun had momentarily been hidden, so I felt a slight chill in the air as I had seen her face, the guard for a moment let down. The reserve she had demonstrated so clearly since she had arrived had, inexplicably, blossomed into animosity. It seemed to me that she did not really want me at the château and I wondered why. Maybe the boyfriend was there, in residence or something but whatever it was, I, too, was suddenly on my guard. I made light of the police enquiry, saying they had no firm leads as yet and changed the subject.

If she didn't want to share important things with me, then I was damned if I would share mine with her.

3

As the day progressed the weather changed and with it my mood saddened and darkened. After a wonderful and protracted lunch, which we all seemed to enjoy (my mother included) Madeleine asked me to show her the whole house. We wandered about all over the place, taking a long time over it and as we did so, the moment for her departure drew nearer and the clouds grew greyer. Tea in the drawing room only served to make me more morose and tense.

By six o'clock it was raining, drops of moisture driven against the windows in furious gusts as the squally wind moaned and twisted its way around the house. It put me in mind of Wuthering Heights, some sad, demented spirit, desperately trying to return to where it had once been happy and seek some sort of solace. But as this analogy only made me think of William, and horrified at the possibility of him trying desperately to get home was so appalling, I became more depressed and increasingly silent.

Finally, we ended up in the drawing room once more, watching the news over a glass of Mother's sherry, which I did not drink, knowing I had to drive Madeleine to the station at some point. Mother herself had disappeared once more, trying to find Helena as was her custom early on a Sunday evening to talk about the coming week and its requirements. Madeleine was staring into the fire which I had lit to distract us from the increasingly miserable weather. Suddenly she looked up.

"Rober-rt?"

"Oui?"

Again, "Rober-rt?"

"Well?"

"I wonder, before I leave, is it possible for me to meet your father? Somehow, I have seen all this house and learned so much of you all, it...it does not seem right not to greet him. It is his house, is it not?"

"It is indeed." I was surprised and pleased she had asked. Immediately my spirits lifted. "I will have to check with the nurse but I see no reason why not. He received some visitors yesterday and that seemed to have had no adverse affect on him." On the contrary, as a matter of fact. After Sam's visit, although tired, he seemed happier and more relaxed. "Shall we see him now?"

She stood up. "Why yes, that would be wonderful for I must leave in a short while for my train, if you will be kind enough to take me to your funny station again." The smile was winning in the flickering firelight and the dimming evening light. I turned sharply on my heel, not wishing to dwell too closely on the vision of her before me.

"Come on, then. We'll see what Nurse has to say."

The nurse on duty for the night had arrived a short time before. She was a woman I had known all my life, related to one of the tenant farmers, an old friend and a wonderfully efficient nurse of whom we were all fond. She bore not the slightest resemblance to the fat-faced, over-sugary creature of the day shift who made me cross just by looking at her. "Hello, Bella."

She beamed at me and the years slipped away. I remembered her smiling at me just that way as I was recovering from chickenpox at the age of seven. She had come over to look after me while everyone went out somewhere, leaving me behind, in quarantine.

"Hello, Robbie, my love." She glanced past me at Madeleine, giving her the once over. "Good evening, madam." (Very formal! I was amused!)

"Bella, can we see my father? Is he up to visitors? I would like to introduce..."
I glanced at Madeleine, whose intense gaze left Bella, rested on me a second, and returned to her once again, "Madeleine, from France."

Bella looked at me, smiling. "Very well, but only a short visit. I want to settle him down in half an hour or so. He's had a reasonable day and I want to keep up the good work with an early night." She tapped on the door, listened, opened it and we followed her in.

The television was on and some hymn or other had just begun after the News was over. Father had the remote control unit in his hand and, seeing it was me, he pressed a button and the television went quiet, the sound off but the picture still there, silent but restless. His eyes were sleepy and his body relaxed. He beamed at me.

"Rob. Dear boy, this is nice. The last thing I wanted was to look at a lot of funny old biddies in their best hats singing hymns for the glorification of the BBC!" He looked at me keenly. "Sam gone?"

"Yes, Dad, Sam went last night. We went to dinner with Inno."

"Ah yes. Now, she's a lovely girl. I often thought..."

"Dad," I interrupted quickly. It was anyone's guess what he might come out with in his present state of mind and that was all I wanted with my relationship with Madeleine so much in the balance. "Dad, I've just come to say good night and to introduce you to a friend of mine, before she returns to London."

Madeleine was standing quietly behind me in the shadows for the room was getting quite dark now, the only light being the glow from the television. I stepped to one side and she moved forwards a little. "Dad, this is Madeleine. Madeleine, my father, Sir William Berkeley."

"Good evening, Sir William," her voice was huskier than ever and I saw him frown as he tried to see her face.

"Let me put on a light." I turned to switch on the beside light but she put her hand on my arm.

"No, leave it, it might be too bright for him." Her voice was very low, close to my ear. "My aunt had this condition last year. The bright lights upset her. Leave him, Rober-rt."

He shifted in his bed. "Madeleine, did you say? I don't think I know a Madeleine." Again he was frowning as he peered up at us.

Madeleine spoke. "No, Sir William, we have not met. I am a comparatively new friend of Robert's. I just came to say good evening. I have been visiting today. Your house is very beautiful. Robert has been a very good guide."

He smiled and relaxed back on his pillows. "Yes. When he has practised a bit more, we shall let him loose on the coach parties!" He chuckled and Madeleine turned a questioning face towards me.

"What does he...?"

"Don't worry. I'll explain later," I said under my breath, "just go along with it. He get's confused."

He looked up again, trying to make out her face. "Come here, a bit closer. Have you been hunting?"

"No, Dad, no. We went to pick mushrooms in the wood."

He continued to study Madeleine. "Catch anything?"

"No, Sir William but we found..."

"You found, did you?" His face lit up, as lively as a two year old. "Get the fellow, did you?"

Madeleine looked mystified, "What...?"

I intervened, "Madeleine doesn't hunt, Father," I turned to her, "'Found' in that sense is a hunting term. It means found a fox. No one is allowed to hunt foxes with dogs in this country any more, though." I turned back to him. "We just found some mushrooms."

Madeleine came closer to him, smiling, leaning over the bed. "They were wonderful mushrooms, Sir William."

He stared at her, looking into her eyes for quite a long moment. Then he put out a thin, frail hand and plucked at my sleeve. "Rob," he whispered.

I leaned closer. "Yes, Father?"

"Don't let your mother know. It isn't right. It is too late now." He looked at Madeleine, sadly with a troubled face. "Why did you come, Dominique? Why now...? William..." He twisted and turned in the bed and I saw, with a growing apprehension, sweat break out on his brow.

I knelt down beside him and tried to soothe him. "It's all right, Father. This is Madeleine, not Dominique." I had to play the game, whatever it was. God knew who Dominique was. He began to look quite wild, suddenly. I shushed him, gently, like talking to a frightened horse. I stood up again. "I'll get Bella, Dad and send Mother to you. Would you like that?" I motioned to Madeleine that we should go. He just looked at me and there was tragedy in his face. I stroked his hand for a moment and we left the room.

I looked up and down the corridor. Bella was nowhere to be seen.

"She must have gone down to the kitchen for something. Can you stay here while I look for her? Just listen out for him, can you? I'm sorry he was so odd." I felt frightened, suddenly. The recollection of his troubled expression and his sudden lack of composure disturbed me greatly. She nodded and pushed at me.

"Go on, Robert, hurry, if you are worried. I will just stay here. Go ON!" Her voice urged me on and I ran down the stairs.

I found Bella alone in the kitchen. She had just made a tray up with something on it. She looked up at me, startled, as I flung open the door.

"Bella, can you go back? I'm bothered about him. He was fine and suddenly he started to ramble on a lot of junk. He seems really distressed and very peculiar all of a sudden."

She smiled. "Don't worry, lovey. That'll be typical, the confusion. By the time I get there, he'll be watching the television again as happy as you please. His mood changes very fast. Did you not notice that yesterday?"

"Yes, but it seemed to change even quicker tonight. Go on, Bella, please go back."

"Come on, then and carry my tray for me. I'll go and look at him straight away."

I felt relief. Dear Bella, straightforward and no fuss, not like that stupid woman yesterday, patronising me. I picked up the tray and walked out of the room with it. We retraced our steps and as we came up the stairs, I saw Madeleine coming out of his room again. She glanced up as we crossed the landing. She was smiling, faintly, I noticed. She put her fingers to her lips.

"I went back to see him. I left my bag behind in the room. He is nearly asleep. He asked for a drink and I gave him one. He is quiet now, Robert. It was the same with my aunt - worried one minute, docile the next. It is the condition, is it not, nurse?"

Bella looked at her with a certain amount of disapproval. "That is so, Madam, but it would have been better if you had waited for me before you retrieved your bag. He is not very keen on strangers on their own with him." She silently peeped round the door. She watched my father for a moment and then softly closed it again. "He's fine. As peaceful as you like, nearly asleep in front of the box."

She took the tray from me and put it on an old Tudor linen chest that stood outside the door. "Don't worry. I'll take good care of him. Off you go and I'll come and find you and report on him in an hour or two." She smiled, patting my arm, "go on. You always did worry about things, even when you were a little boy. Cute, you were... gorgeous..." she gave me a sly smile, "still are, but it wouldn't do to tell you. Give you a swelled head."

"Me, cute? No way! And I don't worry. This is the first worry I've ever had in all my life."

She gave a short laugh and said nothing more. She stood at the top of the stairs, watching us descend to the hall once more. We went back into the drawing room.

I went over to the fireplace. I felt uneasy, something out of sorts and couldn't tell what it was. I put it down to anxiety about my father, although I had been instantly appeased by Bella's pronouncement. "I'm sorry about that. I didn't know he would get so strange so suddenly. I hope it didn't disturb you too much."

Her eyes were very bright and she seemed to be breathing faster, I thought. She walked round the room, looking at things, ignoring my invitation to sit down again. "No, no, it is fine. As I said, I am used to this condition. But I feel it imperative that I leave as soon as possible. You do not want strangers here when your father is so sick. It is not right." She fingered her bag which hung over her shoulder, the catch open, glinting in the firelight. "If we go now, I will catch a train that leaves at 6.45. Then I will get to Heathrow at a reasonable time." I looked at her dubiously. She became impatient. "Come on, Robert. I shall miss it and that will be a nuisance." She stopped and smiled at me suddenly. "Do not forget, I will be back in just over a week. Yes? That is, if you want me to..."

"I want you to, yes." I felt cross but the inevitable was going to happen. I sighed. "All right. Let's go. You're right, if we go now you will just catch the train. Do you have everything?"

"Yes. I only brought my bag with me and here is my jacket." She picked it up from where it was casually lying over the back of a chair near the door. "I fear I cannot wait for your mother to come back. Perhaps you can say goodbye to her for me."

I felt in my pocket for my keys which, surprisingly were there, where they should be for once. I was a notorious key-misplacer. "Yes," I was short. "I'll say goodbye for you. Now then, come on or you'll miss the bloody thing."

Silently, I led the way out of the house and down the steps from the front door. I pressed the button on the key fob which opened the locks. The lights flashed at me and a single rather mournful note escaped from the waiting car. We climbed in and I drove off, fast, down the drive and out into the main road. I continued to drive too fast all the way to the station and we arrived with several minutes to spare. We said nothing as we got out and walked onto the platform.

The rain had stopped but the wind still blew fitfully round our feet as we hopped up and down in the chill air, waiting for the train. Some half a dozen other passengers waited with us, hunched up into jackets to protect them from the sudden drop in temperature. Madeleine looked at me. Her eyes were still bright. "I will not ring you, Robert, but I will see you at your flat next Monday at eight o'clock. Is that all right with you?"

I nodded. "It's all right with me." Suddenly, more than anything, I wanted her to go, although I couldn't say why. "But don't bother if you can't. It's of no consequence." I genuinely suddenly hoped she wouldn't. She shot me a sudden and startled look, surprised, I could see, by my coolness and could see it was genuine. From wanting to be all over her if I had been given the opportunity, she could see that now, that was the last thing I wanted. It pulled her up short. As if in answer to a prayer, the train rounded the corner of the track and slowed as it approached the station, grinding noisily to a gentle halt. Briefly we shared a look and suddenly I knew what was going to happen. As before, she kissed me swiftly on both cheeks and jumped into the open door of the train that someone had opened behind us. I said nothing at all to her cheerful, "au revoir, cheri!" but turned on my heel and left the station before the train did. It pulled off slowly, gathering speed and the tail lights disappeared into the gloom.

I swore obscenely, once, loudly, to the surprise and deep disapproval of a passing elderly lady. "Self-centred... FUCKING twat..." I returned to the waiting car and drove, slowly now, and in a depressed state of mind, back home.

Chapter 14

1

My mother was waiting for me when I returned from putting the car away in the open barn we used as a garage. She held out a drink and I took it, flinging myself down into one of the large club armchairs that dwelt there in the television room. The covers on the top of the arms were worn and faded but I was fond of this room and the old material reminded me of childhood, curled up in a chair, watching TV on a Sunday evening before we were chased upstairs to bed or back to boarding school. Even as I sat there this evening, listening to the rising wind, it was as if I were once again a small boy, half hidden by the hugeness of the furniture, hoping against hope they would forget I was there and leave me for another precious half an hour downstairs. She stood there looking at me, hesitating. I knew she wanted to say something and I knew it was about Madeleine. Obstinately I said nothing, forcing her to speak first.

"Darling...?"

"Yes, Mother?" I stared at the television, flicking the remote through the channels.

"Darling, how long have you known Madeleine?"

"We... met some time ago, but I can't say I've actually known her very long. Why?"

"Oh, nothing, darling, nothing... I... think I must have not been a good hostess today."

I looked at her, surprised. I had never known my mother not be a good hostess. It was second nature to her. "Rubbish! What DO you mean?"

My mother twirled her glass round in her fingers, staring at the fire. "I don't know. She... she seemed so uneasy, somehow, I thought it must be me."

So, she had noticed it, too. "Oh, I think you imagined it," I lied. "She had a wonderful time. She loved the mushrooming and looking at the house." Why was it impossible to get anything past my mother? But was it? I thought of my father. He believed he had, all these years. Suddenly, I wondered. Did she know, after all? I looked at her quickly but she was just staring down into the flames, thinking, I could see. She looked up, smiling brightly - too brightly.

"Silly me! I expect I am over-sensitive at the moment. What a nuisance I am to you, Robert darling."

I leaned forward and grabbed her hand. "You are never a nuisance to anyone, me least of all. You are the king pin in this house. None of us could function without you, you know that, don't you? And if you don't you ought to! Come, Mother, don't be downhearted, it's not like you."

She stood up quickly and came and put her arms round me. "Darling boy." Her voice was very shaky. "Well, as long as there is a use for me, I shall be around. But bless you for saying it, anyway."

I hugged her. "But it's true." I felt her kiss the top of my head.

"I think I'll go up. I get so tired these days and I sleep so badly.

"Do you?"

"Yes... dreams and... restlessness generally and getting up to your father, of course. But I don't mind. As I said, as long as I'm needed."

"We need you, all of... both of us."

She stroked my face and left the room. I sat there staring into the fire as she had done, thinking. Funny. Mother always seemed to like my friends and yet I knew she hadn't liked Madeleine. I knew it as we sat at breakfast and at lunch and I knew it was the reason why she hadn't appeared later in the afternoon, until Madeleine had left, in fact. She had been polite and welcoming and kind as she always was but even before she said she had noticed that Madeleine was uneasy I knew it was no good. The unbelievable had happened. Mother, who had always liked my friends, didn't like Madeleine for some reason and I was more disturbed by this than anything that had happened that strange day, for sitting there in the cosy familiarity of our drawing room, I knew it had been strange, strained and false. I had been aware of it all day long but it was only now that I admitted it to myself.

I looked round. I had heard a noise. I got up and opened the door. From nowhere Nell had appeared. She marched in, tail waving and flopped down on the hearthrug giving out a huge sigh. I sat down again, looking at her. It seemed to me that Mother was not alone in her dislike of Madeleine. She had Nell to back her up. I leant over her, holding her by her long nose. "You dreadful dog! What terrible manners! What do you mean by behaving like that?" She just looked at me, blissfully contented to find me alone. She lay down on her side, her tail thumping on the carpet. I pushed at her ribs with my outstretched foot. "Fat lump. Look at you." She closed her eyes and the tail went on drumming the floor. I continued absent-mindedly to stroke her velvet head as I quietly drank my sherry. Outside, the moan of the wind rose higher and the jasmine bushes that adorned the terrace scratched and tapped at the windows. I kicked at a fallen log and the sparks flew up. I leant over and threw another branch onto the fire. Now I knew it, if I hadn't done before. Autumn was here with a vengeance. How swiftly it had arrived this year.

I watched the flames begin to lick round the new log. It hissed and smoked and then suddenly it caught, leaping into life. And as I sat watching and stroking Nell, I found myself dwelling on something, something that up till that moment I had not felt able to address although it had been in the back of mind all the time.

When I had left Madeleine, that first evening in London, she had disturbed me by knowing something she was not supposed to. I had put the thought aside till then, for, like Nell and her looking glass, I could not, or would not comprehend it. If Madeleine had not known about William's death she could not have known the bomb exploded here, in Hampshire. Why had she pretended she did not know about William? And now, tonight, there was something else. Madeleine had said she had gone back into my father's room to retrieve her bag. As soon as she had said this I knew there was something wrong with this statement although, until now, I did not know what it was. It was a simple enough thing to say but now, I knew.

As I came up the stairs, carrying the tray for Bella already I had begun to look for a place to put it down. My eyes alighted on the Tudor chest and on it, was Madeleine's bag. But at that moment she was coming though the door from the dressing room. Why had she said she had left it behind when it was quite plain that she had not? So now, quite by chance, I had discovered her to have lied to me again.

I sat there, brooding over the fire, wondering about it. I knew now she had not told me the truth. But for the life of me I couldn't tell why.

<h1 style="text-align:center">2</h1>

At about eleven o'clock, I climbed from my reverie amongst the remains of the Sunday papers, empty glasses and a sleepy dog and went upstairs. Bella was sitting watching a dreadful romantic film in the small room we had allotted for her as a sitting room-cum-sleeping quarters. Here she would watch late night television, make some cocoa, doze for a while and every hour or so, or more often if she felt it necessary, visit my father to see if he needed anything or get up to him if he stirred, or called out.

"I looked in on him just five minutes ago. He is fast asleep. Rather on the warm side and very restless tonight, so I shall keep a strict eye on him - 15 minute obs. I shall stay in there with him tonight. The armchair is very comfy and there is that lovely footstool. Luxury! And I'm used to dozing in armchairs!"

"You know my room, Bella. Be sure to let me know if there is a problem. Have you seen my mother this evening?"

"Yes dear, don't fret. She was sad and tired tonight. I have given her a sleeping pill. I think it will do her good." She nodded, looking up at me. "Nothing like a good night's sleep. It seems to me you could do with the same."

"I don't want any pills!" I was appalled.

"No, no, no, not pills, just the sleep. Go on, off you go. It's been a difficult weekend, by all accounts." (How did she know that, I wondered? Somebody must have said something or maybe it was just putting two and two together. Nurses got high marks for observation, I thought). But still I hesitated.

"Do you want to see him yourself?"

"Yes. I think perhaps I do. Is that all right?"

"Of course it's all right. Come on, lovey." It was like being ten again, I thought, smiling to myself and followed her out of the room. I was surprised she didn't take me by the hand and lead me in there.

The bedside light was on now, a dark burgundy shade sending out subdued light. It was peaceful and still in the room - a sharp contrast to the increasingly wild night outside. My father was propped up on his pillows, breathing rather fast. He was hot and I looked at Bella anxiously. Her hand was on his wrist taking his pulse, her eyes on the watch on the top corner of her apron. She nodded, but regarded him solemnly for a while, frowning slightly. We silently left the room, pulling the door to but not closing it.

"He's not too bad, but his breathing is a bit on the erratic side. Now, don't worry, go to bed and go to sleep. I'll call you if I think it is necessary." I still stood there, hesitating. "Go on, shoo!"

I laughed. "I'm on my way. But you will...?"

"Don't be daft. You know I will. Go on."

I felt the responsibility leave me and settle on her ample shoulders. Just for a few hours, I thought, with relief. The bed was wonderful, even though I was alone in it, and found myself thinking of Inno, not Madeleine. Ah well, not to be... and I must have been asleep in seconds...

3

"...Robert, Robbie, love...! Wake up...!"

I struggled back into the world again and forced myself into a sitting position. Sleep filled my mind but words came to me from somewhere far away. "Rob, listen to me! Robbie..." It was Bella.

As soon as I realised it was her, I was instantly fully awake. It was still dark and in that second between sleep and consciousness, everything came flooding back. I grabbed her.

"Bella. What is it?"

"Get up, Rob and come with me. I have sent for Eddy Farley. I haven't yet woken your mother. He is worse, very much worse. I fear he has had another stroke."

"Oh, shit!"

I was out of bed as she was speaking. I was shivering and my teeth started to chatter. My heart was thumping and I felt a mixture of awful dread and a curious, terrified excitement. I rummaged around, searching for clothes I could fling on but I was unco-ordinated and dropped things, lurching against the furniture.

I managed to scramble into jeans and a sweatshirt, my mind racing, trying to cope with waking out of such a deep sleep and the horrors of reality as opposed to nightmare. I ran, barefoot, down the corridor and into my father's room.

I leaned over the bed. He was barely breathing and looked dreadful. "Father? Dad?" I whispered. His eyes moved but did not quite open. He took another deep breath and seemed to make an enormous effort. He opened his eyes. His voice was gone, not even a whisper. He recognised me, I could see and his mouth silently formed the word. "Rob..."

"I'm here, Dad. Is there anything you want?"

I took his hand. It was as hot as a furnace and I could feel the bones sticking through the paper-like skin. His face seemed to be crumpling up, his mouth working, trying to say something but I could hear no sound.

Bella's hand was on my arm. "I'm going to get your mother. Stay here."

I didn't take my eyes off him and merely nodded as she swiftly left the room.

Seemingly, with a huge effort, he tried again and this time the words came. "The girl with green eyes, Rob... Be careful... William..."

I spoke, close to his ear. "I promise, Dad, I'll be careful."

"Look after your... mother..."

"Of course. You know I will. But you'll be fine..."

His eyes were closed again and he sank back into his pillows but only for a moment for almost instantly he started to turn and twist and his chest heaved with the effort. I tried to soothe him, stroking his hand and he became a little quieter. It seemed to me that he was listening, listening for someone or something - waiting for something, that was it. I knew, suddenly who it was he was waiting for. I felt a panic starting to rise. My emotions turned a dozen knives in my stomach but still I stayed there, talking quietly and gently, holding his hand.

His erratic and laboured breathing went on but he said no more as I waited there. I was desperate to be with him and yet almost had to forcibly hang on to the side of the bed to stop myself from rushing from the room. The pain of seeing him like that was nearly unbearable. I needed to be there and yet could hardly stand the strain. Those minutes were like days as I waited there, frightened, helpless beside this man who had given me life and whose own life I knew was now slipping away from him.

The door opened again and my mother was there, kneeling beside him and taking his hand from me in hers.

"William. Darling William. It's me. I'm here."

I turned away from the bed to the window. The curtains were still partly opened. I could see the headlights of a car turn into the drive from the road and drive fast up towards the house. Eddy, if I knew anything, I thought.

"Phyllis, forgive me. I love you." I heard the whispered words and her gentle response, loving and gentle, hasty. I swiftly walked from the room. This was no place for me. This was their private moment.

Bella was on the landing. On the chest outside the room was her nurse's bag, open and she was pulling the wrapping off something she had taken from it. She filled the syringe, watching the liquid climb up it.

"Eddy's here, Bella, I think."

"Good. I'm just going to give your father this."

"I'll just nip down and let him in."

"There's a good boy, now. Thank you, dearie."

I ran down the stairs as Bella walked into the room behind her. I ran across the hall and opened the door as Eddy was climbing the steps, two at a time. He passed me and I shut the door, following him back up the stairs again.

"Bella rang me. I know all about it. She says he's had another stroke."

"She's giving him an injection of something."

"Yes, I told her to." He pushed open the door and went in.

I heard my mother greet him. I turned away outside the door and sat on the window ledge on the landing, staring out at the rain-lashed night. Water droplets coursed down the pane.

Then I heard it - that primitive, Godforsaken sound from below. It was Nell and my father's dog, Jess, both their voices raised together in a long, mournful eerie howl, in unison, inexplicably crying suddenly from another part of the house.

As I listened to it, with my flesh beginning to creep, I knew. I stood there, rigid, waiting for I knew not what, fixed to the spot, rendered immobile by the extraordinary sound made by the dogs.

"He's gone, Rob." Eddy stood there quietly in the doorway.

I nodded. Staring in front of me down the dimly lit staircase. "I know. Listen."

He stood, watching me. "Yes, I've heard it before. I've never understood how they know."

As he spoke, the howling stopped as suddenly as it had begun and taking a deep breath I went back into my father's room where my mother still knelt on the floor, her head bowed. Together we stayed beside him, so peaceful now and ageless, suddenly. Then her tears began to flow down her face and fell onto his hand and we knew enough was enough for the moment. Between us, Eddy, Bella and I raised her up and guided her back along the corridor to her own room. Bella motioned to me that they would see to her and I turned and went downstairs, to seek the inadequate comfort of a glass of brandy. As I sat there, waiting for the dawn to break, trying to feel something through the numbness that had settled on me, a wet nose pushed its way into my hand. Both animals stood there, looking at me and I stroked their gentle velvet heads and gazed in a sort of wonderment into the sad brown eyes of those two remarkable harbingers of Death.

Chapter 15

1

The day, when it came, was bleak and the sky streaked in differing shades of charcoal. Eddy had gone, to return later but Bella remained. She would stay all day, she said, as there was much she could do, final attentions for my father before the undertaker took him away and also to care for my mother, sedated now and resting fitfully in her room.

The great grey gloom that I had got to know so well over these past days, rested ever greyer and heavier on me today. My thoughts were a mixture of nothing at all, or fragmented reminiscences of childhood and more recent memories all jumbled up together. I bit my lip in worry about my mother, so shocked and small and struck down that it made her unrecognisable. What hell was she going through now? I was glad that Eddy had promised to knock her out for a few hours. It would give her some time to gather a little physical strength before consciousness and all the horror that came with it, returned. I sat waiting till the clock struck seven and then I picked up the phone.

"Sam, it's me."

"What's wrong, Rob?" No preamble or explanations, Sam knew instantly that something was amiss. I knew it would be like that. I think that was why it was Sam I rang first, I needed to ease myself into the dreadful day with someone I could trust implicitly and whose reaction I could predict accurately. I needed that security to make this first telephone call.

"My father died in the night, Sam. He had another stroke."

"Oh, Rob... what a tragedy... How sorry I am, how very, very sad I am for you. What a thoroughly delightful man he was. How is your mother?"

"Shocked, appalled, disbelieving. She is under sedation. Eddy says he will gradually let up on that but not just at the moment."

"Is he very worried about her?"

"No, not really, just concerned she should not overtax herself at this present time. A second shock so soon after William, it is a situation he needs to watch. But she is very healthy, you know and has a constitution similar to an ox."

"And you, Rob? How about you?"

"I'm all right."

"No, you're not... Robbie, let me do whatever I can. Don't shut me out." I could hear an appeal in Sam's voice.

I closed my eyes as I held the receiver to my ear. Hot tears pricked my eyelids. I brushed them sharply away. "I won't... I'm not... You are helping. It is you I rang before anyone. I've spoken to no one else yet."

"Well, thank you for that. I'll ring you later and I'll be down if you need me."

"Thanks, but I think we need you up there. You have a murderer to catch. I suppose you might say he has just claimed another victim. My father would not be dead if it weren't for that fucking bastard killing William." My voice was flat. I spoke the words but felt nothing as I said them. I dare not feel - not yet - it was too soon for mortal man to bear.

Sam's voice was quiet and soothing but even in my shell-shocked state I could hear the steel thread contained within that gentleness. "Do not fear on that score, Rob. We will catch him and make no mistake, he will account for this too, in conscience at any rate. Is there anyone I can speak to for you?"

"No, I don't think so at present, but I will let you know if there is anything you can help me with."

"Promise?"

"I promise. Goodbye for now, Sam."

I put down the receiver. The ice had been broken but I waited a full half hour before I summoned up enough strength to ring Martin and Jane.

I decided that was enough for the moment, I would make some more calls in about an hour. There were relatives, friends, business associates, dozens of people. I'd done it before. I would do it again. Then, suddenly, I thought of Madeleine. She was going back to France first thing. I had better call her now. I called directory Enquiries and for the number of the Heathrow Hilton.

"Miss de la Flèche, please."

"Is she a guest, sir?"

"Yes."

"I cannot see that name on our list, sir. I will put you through to Reservations."

A click or two, then, "Miss de la Flèche, did you say, sir?"

"Yes. She was to arrive last night, or so I understood."

"Yes, sir but she cancelled the reservation. She called yesterday evening and said she would not need the room."

"Did she say why?"

"I spoke to her, as a matter of fact. She said her business was finished earlier than she expected. She caught the last flight to Paris last night instead."

"I see..." but I did not. I didn't see at all. Still... "Thanks for the information."

I put down the phone. And suddenly, I found I was angry, very angry although I couldn't say why. What the bloody hell was this woman playing at, I wondered and although I was curious as to the reason, as far as I was concerned, at that moment, Madeleine could rot in hell. I stood up and walked down the corridor to the kitchen. I would think about Madeleine some other time. Maybe. Or maybe not bother to give her another thought. I had considerably more important people to care for today.

2

Through the haze that enveloped my mind I did everything that day as if I were a sleepwalker. I made telephone calls - to the undertaker, the solicitor, various relatives. I held the sobbing Helena and received a stunned and shocked Inno. Charles was with her, solemn and kind. He was a great help - getting things like cups of tea and fiddling about in the freezer for meals. Eddy came in again to visit Mother and gave me the death certificate. I stared at it, the second in a matter of days to bear the name of William Berkeley. I placed it on the desk in the library with a sort of wary reverence to give to the undertaker. I knew the order of play now, I thought grimly to myself.

And then the phone began to ring - friends, acquaintances and the press. Reporters seemed to descend on us from everywhere, just as we seemed to have got rid of then. Did I mind if they print this, that or the other? How seriously ill was Lady Berkeley? Could they come and take pictures? Exclusive this and special feature that. In the end I referred them to the family solicitor but not before the television cameras had once again taken possession of the front lawns. The police presence increased all of a sudden and all this when all I wanted was to be quiet and alone with my thoughts.

Eventually I escaped for an hour and, as was my wont, I set off up to the copse with Nell and Jess. They were subdued and trotted close beside me, not even an errant rabbit could entice Jess away from me although Nell made a half-hearted stab at running it to ground. I stopped by the stile, leaning over and watching the activity below me. Jess stood beside me, her ears drooping, her tail hanging straight down behind her, the picture of dejection.

"Poor Jess. You loved him, didn't you?" She just looked at me, her eyes dull and sad. Dogs knew, all right, I thought. I climbed over the gate and turning up my collar at the wind and the rain set off back down the hill with a heavy heart.

I walked up the front step. There was a policeman on the doorstep, arguing with someone who had 'press' written all over him. He dodged the policeman and oiled his way over to me.

"Julian Sparrow, sir, freelance journalist. I wondered if you might give me a few words on your feelings at this tragic time so soon after the murder of your brother."

I stared at his shorthand notebook and the stubby bit of pencil in his hand. I gave him a few words but they are not printable in any British newspaper unless punctuated liberally with asterisks. Furthermore, they related to him and his intrusion rather than any feelings I might have cared to share with him over this recent tragedy. He disappeared down the steps rather rapidly, assisted by the hand at the end of the long arm of the law on his collar.

"I'm sorry, sir, I was just about to get rid of him when you turned up." He looked woeful indeed and I couldn't help but smile.

"It's all right, officer. I'm sorry about the few words, though. I simply couldn't resist it. Stupid bugger! What did he expect me to say?"

The policeman gave me a sympathetic nod. "No more than he deserved, sir. He's the last one to get through here today, though, that I promise."

"Thanks. I'll send you out a cup of tea."

"Thank you, sir, that'd be just the thing. Your doorstep is getting rather chilly."

I nodded. "I'm afraid summer is over, well and truly, now." I turned to go inside.

"Just let me know if there is anything you need and we're only too happy to oblige, sir. Everyone here on the local force has been very upset by the events of the last weeks. Both your brother and your father was very much cared for by us, all your family is, if you know what I mean, sir."

I nodded again. "Thanks. Thanks a lot. That's kind of you to say so and means a great deal to me and I know my mother will feel the same when I tell her. Good evening, officer."

"Good evening, Sir Robert."

It wasn't until I had gone inside and shut the door that I realised what he had said, what he had called me. Slowly, I made my way into the drawing room and closed the door. I leaned on the mantlepiece, staring down into the fire that had been lit there, one foot up on the fender. It was still smoking, the match not long having been applied to it. My father's title! And William's too, or should have been. All I could think of was how uncomfortable it made me feel and how curious it was that after all the death and destruction some little glimmer of life remained - something no one could murder, something no one could remove. I was humbled and proud and angry, all in a strange jumble of feelings. This thing I had never expected to be mine, much less ever wanted, now was mine, mine to hold till in turn I handed it on to my son, if I should ever have one. Responsibility! Well, I should just try my best to be worthy of it, that was all. My father, the mildest of men and as unambitious as they came had wanted that more than anything, I think, for why else had he groomed William so meticulously for the task. It was a curious moment for me, that sudden need for self-examination and I was glad I was alone for it was an aspect of this business that had not, strange as it may seem, until that moment, occurred to me.

Above the mantelpiece was a mirror. I straightened up and looked at my reflection in it and regarded it critically. My hair, as ever, fell into my eyes. They were dark with suffering. I badly needed a shave and I suddenly felt grubby and unwashed, which was not surprising, that being the first I'd thought about it for heaven knew how many hours. The door behind me opened and I turned.

"I had to come, Rob. Selfish of me, I guess, but...well..."

"Don't be daft." I smiled an exhausted smile. "It's good to have you here."

It was Sam.

3

Sam answered the phones, chased away strangers, organised the household. Bella came back for another night on duty and I found them whispering together outside my mother's door, laying plans for her welfare for the coming hours, which would be difficult. I had sat beside her for part of the early evening, holding her hand while she slept fitfully, tossing and turning. But she did not wake fully and I just kissed her gently on her forehead and quietly crept downstairs again.

We raided the larder, having sent poor Helena to bed early, too and sat in the kitchen, eating a strange collection of bits from the fridge, the remains of a pie, some cold pasta and a small helping of what we thought was probably destined to become part of a risotto or something. Throughout the evening the phone rang and Sam answered every call. Some were for me and some were not, Sam having moved temporarily to Hampshire, the headquarters of the police operation moved to us, too, for the moment. It was over coffee that Sam brought up the subject of the enquiry again.

"I've looked at the videos, Rob."

"Oh, yes?" I looked up. "Anything?"

"Yes. I rather think there might be. Jane can help with the security firm's tape. There's something funny about that and the other one is a film of William's. Will you feel up to looking at them tomorrow?"

"I expect so. It's got to be done, so there it is. But wouldn't you rather I had a look tonight?"

Sam looked concerned. "Rob, I don't think that would be wise. I think you need to get some sleep."

"I had some sleep last night, before Bella came to get me." I wondered how many years had passed since that moment. How curious to think that in fact it wasn't even twenty four hours ago. I needed sleep but I didn't want it. The brief moment of forgetfulness wasn't worth the agony of the first recollection when one next woke. I shuddered inwardly, made fearful by the memory of waking the day after William's death. I was brisk. "Come on, Sam. You don't have to spare my feelings. Let's get on with it. I don't suppose I can feel any worse than I do already. Besides, what else can I go through that I haven't endured these last few days. I think I can cope with some bits of old film."

Sam looked very dubious. "I don't know. I don't know what Eddy Farley would say."

"Well, don't tell him, then." I drained my glass of wine and poured myself another one. I stood up, heading for the television room. "Come on, let's watch your films." And I led the way out of the kitchen.

Sam sat on the floor and fiddled with the recordings. "Let me show you the security disc. There's someone who appears on it who isn't a member of the helicopter engineering team. They have seen it and don't know who it is. I wonder if you know. And I shall want to ask Jane if she has seen him before." It spun and whirred and clicked as it coursed its way through the disc player. It jerked to a stop. Sam peered at it. "This is the spot. Now, watch."

The camera was set up in such a way as to watch the helicopter and an area all the way round it. The date appeared in the bottom left hand corner. Two days before the fête. People came and went. Figures in white overalls were hanging about, one was in the cockpit and they were discussing the blades, shading their eyes against the sun as they peered up. Sam pointed. "This fellow. Look. He comes in from the left, here, from the direction of the house."

He was tall, thin and the overall made him anonymous, or, at least I imagined it was supposed to. To anyone who didn't know he was just a helicopter engineer. "Why don't the others say anything? If he was a stranger, why didn't they ask him what the hell he was up to there?" I watched them greet the new arrival. They were nodding and indicating the helicopter.

"I spoke to the technical director of the helicopter engineering firm. He said the men had said he had turned up and said he was the expert on this type of machine who had been taken on to help for the duration of the fête. This is quite normal, apparently. They are often very busy in the summer months with displays and whatnot and engaged extra staff. The only trouble was no one was taken on for your event."

"And they've only just discovered it now? That's extraordinarily efficient!" I sneered with sarcasm. I frowned at the screen watching the thin figure walk under the body of the helicopter, only the legs visible as he examined the engine. The difficult thing with the film was that the camera moved slowly over everything all the time, there were no helpful close ups or even a constant still picture. Maddeningly, he went out of shot as the camera sent back its harmless record of hills and fields, a few worthy locals scurrying here and there before it slowly panned back to the helicopter again. The legs were still there. The film continued in the same vein for some time and the man moved about here and there working on this bit and that bit, most of the time with his head just out of view of the camera. He had a box of equipment and tools and he took things out and applied them to the helicopter in the normal way. I couldn't see anything that looked like a bomb and said so.

"It was very small and highly sophisticated. Bombs don't all look like Scud missiles, you see." Sam ran the recording forwards a short way, the figures rushing and jerking this way and that as the film galloped on at an unnatural speed.

"Here he is again." He came out from under it, wiping his hands on a rag. As he ducked beneath the tail, he caught his head on the underbelly of the helicopter and it dislodged his cap, pushing it forward and flicking it onto the ground. He picked it up off the grass and put it swiftly back in its proper place, low over his eyes. Surprised, I noticed he was bald.

"Oh!" I looked at Sam.

Sam nodded at me and put the film on hold. "Odd, isn't it? He's obviously young, so it's quite a shock to see someone so completely devoid of hair like that. Now, do you recognise him?" Sam fished in a large brown envelope and handed me a photograph. "This has been printed from the film so we can see more easily. Have a good long look for that's the only picture we have."

I stared down at the photo but I was thinking about what Sam said, more than looking at that precise moment. I looked up and saw those grey eyes regarding me with a curious intensity. "Sam, are you saying that this is... this is William's murderer?"

"Don't know, Rob, but he is there, on film, doing something to the helicopter. He is unknown to the engineers. He does not appear again and no one else has such intimate dealings with it, if I can put it that way. These films go on for hours and all night with infra red. No one approaches the helicopter after this crew have done their preparations here. I have sat through hours of tape as have the security firm and the helicopter team and they have all been rigorously interviewed. This is the only section which is in any way dubious. Personally I feel that is a little more than circumstantial evidence but I can only say at this moment, this man must be found and questioned as a matter of extreme urgency."

Sam stopped speaking and I was aware of the silence in the room. The DVD was silent, still on "pause", the wind had dropped for a while, even the ticking of the clock seemed to have been dulled by that moment as I stood staring at the screen trying to assess my thoughts. I felt odd, jumpy, my stomach churning and I could feel my hands were shaking slightly.

I pulled myself together. I frowned. "Run it again."

Sam obliged.

"And again."

I shook my head. "I thought, just for a moment that I did know who it might be, but now I think I do not. It was something... something about the walk, I think, somewhere I've seen someone walk like that but... I don't know anyone as young as that who is bald as he is. It's pretty unusual, isn't it? And to shave your hair off is not the best form of disguise, is it, if it was done on purpose."

"I agree, so I think he must really be bald and that is why I have very high hopes about tracking this person down, Rob. But whoever he is, he's been appallingly daring. Clever, seemingly lucky and with one hell of a lot of nerve. But it can't just be luck, you know. He must have had some kind of inside information. This was two days before the fête. Two days, Rob! For two days that bomb was sitting there, counting itself down to the moment William climbed in it. Now this... this..." Sam waved a hand at the screen, "this creature must have known all about the timings and everything."

I nodded. Who was it this person reminded me of, I wondered? I was surprised, too, at my own dispassionate observance. I was capable of tearing the screen to pieces in a frustrated attempt to rip apart the calculating bastard who stood there on the film, silently picking up his baseball cap to cover his smooth, bland head. I found my hand was wet and my arm ached from the tenseness of the muscles and I drank my wine down with a sort of violence. Again, I poured another glass.

"Two days, Sam. Two days before that fucking thing blew up."

The date was clear on the screen and the time. It was 4.45 in the afternoon. It was a normal, sunny, late August afternoon in the middle of preparations for a little bit of modern English pageantry. It was so casual and friendly and the people round about were relaxed and laughing and there in the middle of it was this monster, this calculating, evil... I felt sick, really terribly sick and in that second I knew I was going to be. I dived for the French windows that opened out onto the terrace.

The cold of the night hit me like a shaft of ice and slowly I recovered myself, taking in great gasps of air. I leaned against the doorpost and shut my eyes. Slowly the spasm subsided and I closed the doors, quietly and once again sat down beside Sam on the floor.

The screen was blank again. Sam had removed the disc.

"Better?"

"Yes." I blew my nose. "Sorry. I just felt, well... terrible all of a sudden."

Sam got up. "Poor Rob. I'll get you a special drink - port and brandy. It calms the nerves and stomach like nothing else. My mother used to drink it before a first night performance."

I smiled faintly. Sam's mother had been an actress, a very famous one. It had rocked the aristocracy to the core to think the Earl should actually marry his mistress. Unheard of! Sam's family had not been afraid of controversy, it seemed, at any time in its history, and here was Sam, carrying on the tradition, jolting them out of their complacency and joining the police.

Sam handed me the drink and I sipped at it. It didn't taste as bad as it sounded and it was remarkable how well the medicine worked. I said so.

"My mother knew what she was talking about." Sam nodded gravely.

I glanced at Sam, whose mother had died when we were at school, I recalled. The newspapers had been full of it, tribute programmes on television, interviews of her laughing over absurdities in her professional life or seriously talking about plays and playwrights and how much it had meant to her, what roles had been her favourites, her family, her son and her daughter... All this I remembered in that tiny moment. "Do you still miss her?"

Sam stared ahead. "Yes, of course. I shall always miss her. Most of us get over people dying, Rob, death is a natural part of life, after all, even though the method of bringing it about may be unnatural or premature as it was with William but it changes you. You are never the same person again, you know. There's a loneliness there that will never be filled again, wherever you go or whoever you meet or..." And here Sam hesitated, "... or find to... love." Sam drained the drink in the glass which I realised was a port and brandy as well. "Now, this is the other film I need you to look at. And this was the film I suggested you might find a bit tricky to watch."

I nodded. That conversation we had had seemed about half a century ago as well, I thought grimly to myself. I felt I was being scrutinised carefully again.

"Are you all right, do you think?"

I sighed. "Come on, Sam. I'm OK. I said I was. This is a film that William took. You have seen it. Tell me about it and what it is I can help you with?"

"I want you to look at the film and tell me if you recognise any of the people there or, indeed, tell me anything about it you can. All right? There is one sequence that has William himself in it. I think you ought to know that."

"Oh." I turned off the emotion, ready for the onslaught. I was quite calm.

Sam gave me one more quick look and pressed the play button.

I watched the film. As it rolled on, I recognised things. I began to speak. "This is Paris. It is Montmartre."

"Hmm. Yes. I recognised it, too."

I paused and watched some more. The date was on the corner of the film again. I noticed it was earlier in the year, in February. A girl came into the shot. She was tall and very slim and had long, blonde hair, straight, hanging down her back. I could not see her face because she was walking away from the camera, slowly, in the middle distance, looking down over Montmartre. It was obviously cold because she was wearing a long winter coat and had boots on. Her face was hidden by a sort of sombrero and the whole effect was very striking. She looked an expensive sort of girl, I thought. It would be difficult to recognise anyone from such a shot unless you knew who they were, or were supposed to be and could make an educated guess. The camera followed her obviously deliberately. She was the subject of the film as much as the setting, more so, in fact.

"Who is that, Rob, do you know?"

"No," but I frowned, there was something about her...

The picture changed and so did the date. It was now May. This time the scene was in London, on the Embankment. In the background was the familiar shape of the Savoy. The plane trees were out and there was the same girl, leaning over the parapet. She had on dark glasses and a floppy hat, obscuring her face as she fed the pigeons. She walked away from the camera and her feet twisted, swivelling her hips and spine, as if she were on a catwalk.

"She walks like a model," I said.

"Yes, I thought that. You don't know her?"

I shook my head. "No. I don't know her..." I hesitated. As in the last film of the man with the helicopter, there was something familiar about this girl. She reminded me of someone. I said so.

The film went on, a different location now. And here at last, was William, his head thrown back, laughing at the camera. The date was July and the location was...

"Christ, Sam, that's the Château Viezy!" I was stunned.

Sam paused the recording. "Are you sure?"

"Yes. But why did he... Why did he go back there and not tell me he was going?" I couldn't believe it. It was so... so, what was the word? Underhand. That was it. And William had never been underhand. WHY? "And who is filming it?" A peculiar sensation crept over me, it was like my flesh creeping in a sort of thrilled horror. Maybe even Madeleine had filmed this. But never, never would William have gone there, not told me and met Madeleine, surely. Surely? My head reeled and I put it in my hands. I looked up again at the film. It was on "play" again, for Sam had rewound it to the Savoy clip. This girl. Now I came to look at her again, I was not wrong, was I? Didn't she remind me of Madeleine herself?

As before, I asked Sam to play it again. I was uneasy, the more I looked at her, the more she reminded me of Madeleine but was it merely some kind of auto-suggestion?

William at Viezy when he hadn't said he'd been there, one strange thing after another, the previous clip with a tall, slim girl with long blonde hair - I didn't know but I felt deeply uncomfortable about it.

Sam put the film on pause and ran it back again, let it play a few minutes and then pressed "pause" once more, leaning forward to observe the screen more closely. "Rob, look, there in the background, just going out of shot up the steps towards the Savoy."

I looked where Sam indicated. "Sam... no. It isn't, is it?"

I stared hard at the picture. Slowly, the realisation came to the surface and formed words. Surely I was not mistaken. I felt a thrill of excitement and dread and fear. "Sam," my voice was very quiet, "that fellow. That's the one you mean, isn't it?"

"Yes, him. Tell me what you think, Rob."

"Surely I'm not wrong. Isn't it...? I think it's the helicopter engineer."

Chapter 16

1

Sam and I stared at the flickering film. We played it back about a hundred times, it felt like and compared it with the still photograph we already had. I was positive and Sam was cautiously optimistic. Sam picked up the phone and rang someone.

"George? Yes, it's me... No, I'm in Hampshire still, yes... at Forbridge. Now listen, this is urgent. We've looked at the DVDs again... yes... that's right... Now, it's the one I've showed you... yes, the most recent film William made. I'm sending the disc back to you now on a bike. I want you to make stills. I've stopped the film where I need it done... yes, that's right. There's a fellow going up the steps in the distance. I want them enlarged. OK?... A dozen... Sorry, yes, tonight and send them to me at once... Email first then the hard copies, yup... No, London, I'm coming back. Got that?... Yes... I think it's the same bloke and Robert thinks so, too. I'm pretty sure... I don't know about coincidence, George. There ain't no such thing in my book with something like this. Yes, at once... good man, George and I love you, too..." A grin, "Piss off!" another grin as the receiver went down. "He's a terrific chap. I'm extraordinarily fortunate to have such a team working for me."

I watched Sam's animated face. "I don't imagine it's coincidence and I don't believe in them in a case like this, either."

Sam looked confused. "Bollocks, Rob."

I smiled to myself. So Sam still couldn't take a compliment, even when it was nothing more or less than the bleedin' obvious!

"Rob?"

"Yes?"

"Listen, I've discovered a bit more today. How are you going on the strength stakes? Can you take a bit more questioning?" The grey eyes were full of anxious enquiry, earnest and concerned but a steely determination there underneath, I perceived.

I was beginning to flag in a serious way. Exhaustion, both mental and physical, not to mention a mixture of various alcohols, were beginning to make their mark but I hadn't the heart to deny Sam this moment. I summoned up as much energy as I could muster. "I'm OK, Sam. One more bash and then I'm going to leave you for tonight. I am totally exhausted."

"Of course you are. It's been hell. Now are you sure?"

"Positive."

"OK. Just a sec, then." Sam went outside and I heard the handover of the disc and some instructions. The front door opened and closed. I heard the police motorbike start up and shoot off down the drive into the distance. The recording was on its way. Sam came back and sat down again, this time in the armchair, hunched up before the fire. The flames were dying now, the heat still fierce and the embers glowing red and yellow. I watched a log fall and the sparks fly up. Outside the charmed circle of intense heat, the logs had turned to grey ash. Sam looked up at me as I sat, hunched on the sofa, my feet on the fender, wondering what was coming now.

"I have been to what was once the old War Office. I know what your father did in the war."

I was struck immediately by the strange irony that his secret war record should be revealed on the very day he died. Genuine coincidences were often stranger than engineered ones, it seemed to me and my thoughts strayed briefly to Sam's earlier conversation with the unseen George.

"Go on. Tell me."

Sam said nothing for a moment and then began to speak, rather as if telling a story to a child. It could easily have started, 'Once upon a time, in a land far away...'

"Your father was given a commission not long after the war started, in spite of being very young. It was discovered he could speak fluent French and they transferred him to the division that dealt with underground activities. To put it simply, they trained him to be a spy." Sam glanced at me to see how I was taking it.

"Bloody hell!" I nodded sharply. "Go on."

"He was sent on several missions. He spent, in total, close on four years in Occupied France but not all at one fell swoop. He had about six or seven separate sorties of varying lengths. To mention the main ones, he was responsible for conducting a party of Dutch scientists through enemy lines under the noses of the Nazis. He flew planes out to equip and renew supplies to the Underground Movement, hopping from airfield to airfield right the way down to the Riviera and then back. They nearly got him then, several times. He blew up an enemy destroyer whilst in the harbour in Honfleur, taking with it one of Hitler's major naval men and..." Sam hesitated briefly, "...and he was involved in the attempted sabotage of the German war machine's weapons' depot at the Château Viezy."

I sat up, the tiredness abandoning me in an instant.

"Christ," I said.

Sam held out an empty glass. I filled it from whatever bottle I had beside me. It might have been meths for all I knew at that moment but Sam drank it, staring at the fire.

"He was in the little village of Viezy-sur-L'eau for seven months. He was disguised as the cousin of one of the local farmers. His story was that he had been rendered homeless in another part of France and given a home and work by this supposed cousin. He worked on the fields all the Summer but in fact he was the leader of a group of men who planned, organised and carried out the blowing up of the Château. At least, that was what was to have happened, but in fact it did not."

"I know. I've read the brochure about it." I was staggered, thinking. So clearly it came back to me, Madeleine walking back from the Reception area and handing us the little leaflet about the history of her home. I could almost hear her voice, and William's, discussing the story. And yet we, that is William and I, had not known how close was our involvement in this tragedy.

But what of Madeleine, I asked myself. Did she know? I recalled the look on her face, her horrified expression when she read our names. Was that the reason? I told Sam this now who sat listening attentively opposite me.

"But why should she be horrified to think the two sons of a friend of the Resistance should be staying in the hotel? I should have thought they would have welcomed you with open arms, wouldn't they?"

I frowned. "Maybe... But, Sam, the mission was a failure. The château stayed standing and the village was blown up. It was a disaster. It said in the leaflet that they believed the fuses were rerouted by a saboteur who was never found. Perhaps, there, where it all happened, the last thing they wanted was to be reminded of one of the people who carried out the attempt. After all, if the attempt had never been made the village and all its inhabitants would have survived." I shook my head. It was a mess and the sadness reached me, down the years, even as it had touched William and I when we first heard the story, eighteen months ago. And to think our own gentle, loving father had been part of that horror... It was impossible to believe.

All I could think of was his hands, showing me how to quieten a frightened horse, or prepare a rod to catch an elusive trout, to mend my teddy bear when his arm had fallen off, touching the head of the rocking horse to make it rock. To think those gentle hands had twisted fuses and laid dynamite. They had planted mines and bombs - maybe they had even killed people, creeping up in the silence of the night to garrotte a sentry, off-guard for a moment. One swift movement and then dead... nothing... This quiet, loving man had been all these things and now he, too, lay upstairs, still and silent and as he did so, his past was rising before he was in his grave. I buried my head in a cushion and put my hands over my ears. I wanted no more. I shut Sam out.

I don't know how long I sat there but when I raised my head, Sam was still sitting, staring into the fire. I had recovered. I knew there was more and I must know it all. "Sorry, Sam. You can go on now."

Sam looked at me with concern but a certain amount of determination. "Are you all right, Rob? We can wait till tomorrow if you would rather."

"No. I wouldn't rather. I would rather now."

"Very well... As you say, this last mission was a failure and they have never discovered who it was who was the saboteur. It has to be said, they felt at the ministry of Defence that it simply had to be one of the four people involved for it was those four and only those four, who knew where the fuses were laid. Now these men were all tried and trusted and proven in their idealism. They had run, or were running terrible risks to help the Resistance and yet one of them must have been a traitor."

I slid onto the floor, leaning back against the sofa. I stretched my legs out and ran my hands through my hair. I felt some sort of change was needed to help clear my brain and focus on things. This conversation was vitally important. Nearly on the point of physical collapse after all I had suffered that day, on top of all that had gone before and with barely any sleep, something was driving me on, not merely Sam, but something within myself.

"Do they have any theories or evidence, for that matter, who it was?

Sam leaned over and threw another log on the embers. The fire was in need of revival as well as myself. "There was much discourse on the subject but there is something else..."

"What?"

"The names of your father's team. They say a lot in themselves, Rob and say a lot to me."

The room was quiet, all of a sudden. I had been staring up at the ceiling but now I shut my eyes. "Who were they?"

"The first was a Belgian. He had carried out many raids with your father and some on his own as well. He had escaped from Brussels early in the war and got himself to England. He was a radio operator and his name was Pierre DuPont."

I could feel Sam's eyes on me. "Pierre DuPont, " I repeated. "And the next?"

"The next was a Dutchman. He was a double agent. Taken into the German army but working for the Resistance. His name was Hans van Cleef."

My eyes flew open wide. "Van Cleef? My God!" I sat up.

Sam nodded. "Yes, Rob," but pressed on, "and the last was a Frenchman, a very famous Frenchman and his name was..."

But I knew it. Of course I knew it. I said it myself. In fact Sam and I said the name in unison.

"Jean-Yves de la Flèche."

Silence. Then, slowly,

"Oh... fuck," I said.

I woke next morning on the sofa in the drawing room. The fire was merely a heap of ash now. I was stiff and uncomfortable but I found Sam had covered me up with a blanket. I struggled into a sitting position. There was a note lying on the coffee table beside me and I picked it up.

"Rob,

I have left you, tucked up and sleeping like a baby and have gone back to London. As you will gather from our conversation last night the pace seems to be hotting up and I must get back to town and organise the interviews that are going to have to be conducted. Now we start the foot-slogging and mind-blowing paperwork in earnest! I will, of course, keep you informed and I will see you soon.

My best love to your mother.

Sam"

I looked at my watch. It was only 6.30 and I heaved myself upwards and out to the kitchen. Nell and Jess greeted me sleepily from their baskets and I pottered about making a hash of brewing coffee and toast as I dropped first the coffee jar on the floor and then the butter dish.

Helena came in. "Oh, Robbie, it's you making a din. I thought we had burglars."

"Funny sort of burglars, Helena, who go about making breakfast."

She took the dustpan and brush from me and pushed me gently to one side. "I'll do this. Really, dear, I know you meant well but you stick to your job and let me do mine. We'll have no china left at this rate!"

I grinned at her and sat at the table watching her as she put things to rights. Out came frying pans and eggs and bacon. "Do you want some?"

I eagerly agreed and she laughed. I hadn't eaten much the day before and brought back up most of that which I had eaten. She put things on plates and fished out table napkins and within a minute my mother's breakfast tray was ready, as if by magic and no fuss at all. I was impressed.

"I'll take it up."

She looked at me dubiously. "All right, but don't drop it."

I gave her a look. " Really, Helena, as if I would..."

She held the door open for me and as I passed she put her hand on my arm, "Darling,

Rob. I don't know whatever any of us would have done without you, really I don't."

She stretched up and kissed me on the cheek and I had to bend over sideways to let her. "Helena, you'll be the one to make me drop this stuff! Well, as my mother would say, as long as I'm needed..." I winked at her and went out leaving her rather damp round the eyes.

Bella was there, faithful as ever and took the tray from me at the top of the stairs. "My, you're up early, lovey."

"Is she awake?"

"Yes, dear and quite perky. She has absolutely refused any more medication but has promised to stay in bed this morning. I'll see if she wants to see you."

She disappeared down the corridor and opened the door. After a moment she opened it again and beckoned to me. "She's sitting up in her second best bed jacket. Come on, lovey boy."

I smiled. Bella would always make me feel about eight years old.

My mother was sitting there, propped up with the tray on her lap. She was pale but her eyes were bright and she greeted me as she always did, cheerily and as if I were the only person in the world she wanted to see. She always made everyone feel like that. She patted the edge of the bed and I sat there, holding her hand a minute while she regarded me.

"Darling! Now did you sleep well? I have to confess I did. Eddy and Bella's potions did me the world of good but this can go on no longer. The world still spins, dearest and I'm still spinning with it, so there will be no more sedatives and whatnot, although I don't doubt they have been very valuable."

I saw her chin set in a determined way and I knew that no power on earth could dissuade her from her decision. It would take a lot more than Eddy and Bella, that much I knew and not myself, either, if I were any judge. I smiled. "All right, Mother, if you say so."

She gave a quick, sharp nod and a bright smile.

"Now, I've been thinking. After the funeral, which will be dreadful, but there it is, these things have to be gone through, I have decided that I will go away and take our dear Helena with me for a couple of weeks. I hope you don't feel I'm deserting you, darling, but I must get out of this house for a bit. Do you think you understand?" She looked at me anxiously.

"Of course I understand and I think that is a wonderful idea. But where do you want to go? I can get Jane to make all the arrangements."

"No." She poured out a cup of tea and put in the milk. She took a sip. "Ah, that's good!"

"You don't want Jane to help? She's very good at it, Mother."

"Oh, of course she is, darling. Jane is wonderful. No, I don't mean that, I mean I have planned it already and it only needs a phone call. I have decided we will go and stay with Grace Thornbury, down in North Cornwall. It seems right, somehow. Her husband died last year and so Helena and Grace and I will be together as we used to be, back at school before we were married! We shall be girls again together, Robert darling, and it is just what I need. I will sort this out," (here she tapped her head) "and then we shall come back and get on with the rest of our lives."

I leaned over and kissed her, endangering the safety of yet another piece of china. When I looked at her again there were tears in her eyes but she was still smiling.

"You see, darling, you can get on and organise everything much better if I am not here and you and Martin can do all sorts of things I wouldn't want to do, like..." and here she spoke in a big rush, "like... getting rid of Father's things, which should be done soon. There... I hope that is all right and you don't think I'm being domineering or whatever but I've thought about it and I believe it will the best for all of us."

I stroked her hand. "It's fine. If it's good for you, then it's good for everyone. I don't know what Helena will think of me being left to make a mess in her kitchen! I've already broken two things this morning and I was only I there on my own for five minutes!"

"Idiot boy!' She smiled at me, smoothing my cheek with her forefinger, "but no, darling, I've thought of that, too."

I groaned, "Oh no, what now? Don't tell me your going to get in some awful harridan from the village to "do" for me while you're away. I'd rather replace all the china in the kitchen, Mother, really, I would!"

"Just wait and you'll hear! I'm going to ask Jane and Martin to come and move in for while I'm away. They are a delightful couple and will be company for you. And besides, if you want to pop off up to London and buy a couple of pictures, they'll be here as caretakers. What do you think?"

"Well, yes, it sounds fine... I think it's a marvellous plan. But will they agree?"

To this my mother only laughed and sipped her tea and, of course, I knew. She might not have asked any of these people yet but it would all happen because she was like that, and had always been so. It was part of her charm and it was from her that William had inherited it. It bore the same hallmark.

I kissed her again and went downstairs feeling much happier and strengthened, too. I glanced in the mirror and was appalled to see the stubble on my chin and lank, unwashed hair. I headed for the shower and 15 minutes later sat down to do justice to Helena's eggs and bacon in a presentable state.

3

The phone began to ring at about 9 o'clock and didn't stop ringing till the evening. We organised everything, Jane and Martin and I. Father's obituary would appear in the following day's Times and Telegraph. It would mention his distinguished war record without going into any real details. The Commander of his old regiment rang and said they would be at the funeral and provide a guard of honour. Also, if I wished, they would help to organise a memorial service for him in London in six to eight weeks' time. I was touched and said so. I pointed him in the direction of the undertaker to arrange the pall bearers and guardsmen.

At five o'clock I had a very unexpected call.

"Rober-rt?"

"Madeleine?" Her voice was light and clear again, the remains of her cold had left her.

"Rober-rt, I have just heard the news. I understand your father died. It is all over the French papers. I had to say how sorry I was."

I was staggered. "Thank you."

"How is your mother? She must be so broken up and sad."

"Er... yes. Well... she's managing all right. She's very strong."

"There was a lot in the paper about the work your father did in the war. Did he tell you much about it?"

What a curious question. "I know a bit about it, yes. Why?"

"Oh, no reason. The papers print so many awful lies these days it is hard to know the truth from the stories." She changed the subject. "I shall be over then, next week. Will I still see you?"

I thought hard for a minute. "Yes, yes, I'll be back in London then, probably Sunday evening, in fact. But in case something crops up, I'll ring you. What is the number?"

"Leave a message for me at the Grosvenor House on Monday and I will pick it up whenever I arrive. Then I will come over. I have the key, remember? À bientôt Rober-rt!"

The phone went dead and I felt foolish, sitting there with the receiver in my hand, the dialling tone ringing out for nothing. Why was she always doing this? Blowing hot and cold. She was the oddest girl I had ever met.

I think that was the moment I suddenly realised I didn't want to go on with this charade any more. She was using me like a cat with a mouse and I wasn't going to have it any longer. But I would meet her next Monday. I would try and find out some of the answers to my questions and then I would let her go. My mother's words came back to me, "I must sort this out and then we can get on with the rest of our lives." I summed it up. A brief encounter such as that must not dominate me any more. It happened. A thrilling, untypical physical experience and that was all. It was over. I must move on and I knew where to, as well, if she would have me... If I was honest with myself I had known it from the moment she had walked back into my life after so many months out of it but how serious was the seeming rival for my affections?

Whistling for Nell and Jess, I braved what was left of the day and climbed the hill to the copse. I sat on the stile for a moment or two looking down at this land that was now mine with sorrow and pride in equal measures and came down the slope and went indoors.

4

The second funeral in such a short time after the first was always bound to have been an ordeal. My father's regiment made the whole thing very different from William's and this somehow made it easier to bear. There were police all over the place. I was almost getting used to them, I found myself thinking, rather grimly. Adrian Merchant had organised it all but to Sam's demands, for this was his beat. He'd done it before and he'd do it again. I stared at one of the stained glass windows, my favourite ever since I was small. Acorns and squirrels, primroses and robins adorned it, creeping round a picture of St Francis of Assisi. It brought back memories from my childhood, standing there, making patterns in my mind while the sermon droned on. I'd imagine the names of the animals, what they said to one another and why they had come to be immortalised in glass in a tiny church in England, far away from Italy and Assisi. We sang a hymn, 'I Vow to Thee My Country', one of my father's favourites and I tried to think of something else. I didn't look at the coffin. Outside, with "Dust to dust, ashes to ashes," I stood holding my mother's black-gloved hand and a chill wind blew round our feet. The plot next to where we stood was still without its headstone. Now there would be two for the stonemason to finish, two for people to read in years to come and father and son dead within less than a month of each other, and wonder at the story.

We were accompanied back to the house by I don't know how many people but I had refused to get caterers in.

"This is not a fucking wedding, for Christ's sake!" I had shouted at poor Jane and had been instantly sorry but would not back down. In the end, how she did it I don't know, she organised people from the village to make vol au vents and sandwiches and things on sticks and I just gave them all glasses of wine or cups of tea or coffee. I received condolences and listened to stories about my father that people found it necessary to repeat. Some were even quite funny but all were caring and well-meant. I recognised this and felt guilty about resenting them all. After having made peace with myself, so to speak, I began to feel a bit better about it.

At last they all went away leaving us alone with our policemen. It had been a milestone. We had passed it successfully and although I felt drained and exhausted I knew it had been a turning point, the way now must only be forward.

The next morning, Mother set off, with Helena driving, for Cornwall. I waved till they were out of sight and turned and went up the steps. How small she had looked and in spite of Helena, so alone. They had so rarely been parted, my parents, hardly more than the odd day or two in all their married lives. I was glad she had gone away for a while, though. I hoped, fervently, that it would do her good and I could get on with the unpleasantness of disposing of his personal belongings without her distressed countenance watching me as she regarded first one suit and then another - all with their own special memories for her, I had no doubt.

Martin helped me, in his usual quiet way. We parcelled up shoes and boots and riding things, military uniforms and dress suits. I kept a couple of the military uniforms and all the trimmings that went with them. We could have a memorial to my father on display for the coach parties. I was learning this new job pretty swiftly, I thought and caught Martin's impressed expression as I put the things to one side. I went carefully through everything, looking for the letters but I found nothing of importance or relevance. Finally, someone came with a van and took it all away. Jane organised it and afterwards Martin and I had large whiskies and I wondered if I was as pale as I felt. I missed Inno, I was forced to admit to myself, but wondered if it was her sweet, generous nature that I missed or her soft, round little body stretched under or curled next to mine and put the thought away. Now was not the time to think of this.

The next day, Sam turned up. I was eating breakfast that Jane had cooked. I was glad of their company and they knew, too when to make themselves scarce, I realised, a great quality in friends. Sam sat next to me and put a file on the table top.

"What's all this lot, Sam?"

Sam's voice was quiet. "Rob, I think I might be getting somewhere." The voice was very serious.

I looked up sharply. "God! Really? Sam, that's marvellous..."

"Here, hang on a minute, don't get too excited. It's just that I have a feeling that... oh, I don't know, you get feelings in this job, but I feel I have got a lot of pieces of this jigsaw on the table in front of me. Not all, I know, but like everything else with these cases, I don't have the picture in front of me to copy to work out where the pieces go, if you follow."

I followed.

"Now, let me tell you what I tracked down."

I poured coffee for us both and sat back and waited.

"First of all, Mr Hans van Cleef. Now, he's a nasty piece of work, and not just recently, either, I can tell you. Basically, he was a double agent in the forties and after this failed mission at Viezy (it was his only one, although he got out plenty of information somehow that was pretty vital and all proved to be completely valid) he came back to England for the rest of the war. As soon as it was over, he went abroad again. These agents were paid, incidentally, in rather a curious way. They were given confiscated works of art, sculptures, paintings, antiques, etc. They couldn't appear on the payroll. Your father, although a regular soldier was also presented with one or two paintings for his work behind the enemy lines. He must have appreciated that. One of the paintings given to van Cleef was the Stubbs." Sam glanced up at it, hanging at the end of the dining room. "It is odd that it should end up here in this house, when all is said and done. But I don't know, quite, what you'll feel about it after..." Sam hesitated, looking at me gravely for a moment.

"After what?"

"Yes... Right. Now then, after the war the trail on van Cleef went cold but in the late sixties we began to hear his name mentioned again here and there. He was beginning to be very wealthy - yachts, girls, fast cars, several homes, you know the sort of thing. He was supposed to be a diamond merchant but the police had other ideas about him. He was suspected of smuggling, amongst other things but no one could prove it. Anyway, as the years have gone on his list of associates has become ever more dubious. Quite simply, he seems to have had a finger in all sorts of pies, drugs, robberies, prostitution, arms dealing and..." again Sam hesitated, "...bomb making."

"Bomb making?"

"Yes. And the man who made the bomb that killed William, we are absolutely certain was a known associate of van Cleef."

I was quiet, trying to assimilate my thoughts and, at the same time, not explode with rage. This man was supposed to have been on the same side as my father, they had risked their lives together, and now it looked as if he, for some inexplicable reason had tried to kill his son. "Is this the man then, Sam? Have you found him?" But then a thought struck me. "But he's dead, isn't he? When did he die?"

"We know it wasn't he, himself. Don't forget the helicopter engineer is a young man. Van Cleef died the day after William. He was found on his yacht in the Dutch West Indies and he had been shot through the head, as had his wife. He had been out there a couple of weeks."

"Right, so, he didn't actually have his finger on the trigger, so to speak. But, well, that still makes him a murderer, doesn't it?"

"If he is the man we're after, yes. But don't forget, Rob, there is something missing from all this. Motive. What possible motive could he have had for killing William? Not because he had a row with him over the price of sandwiches for a clay pigeon shoot, surely, or that he had sold his Stubbs to the Berkeleys, I think."

I got up and started to walk about the room. "No, not that, of course, but, well, you said once, in fact Mother agreed with you, someone might have killed William to get back at my father, mightn't he?"

"Yes, that's perfectly true. But what motive would he have for that?"

"Well, if he's the sort of man you say he is, it is pretty likely he was the man who sabotaged the mission in Viezy in the war. Perhaps my father knew that and he wanted to make him keep quiet or something."

Sam continued to look dubious. "After all these years, Rob? I think not. If that had been the case then surely your father, if he had known it, would have spilled the beans years ago. He wouldn't have waited all this time, would he? Now think back to what he said about his letters. He didn't say Hans was the saboteur. All he said was, "he sold out to him." Now we know his finances were in a parlous state. He was a gambler and a lot of his deals had come to nothing. However, I don't like the sound of all this. It is all too close for comfort and there are too many of these bloody coincidences.

I nodded. "All right. What now, then?"

"Oh, that's fairly easy." Sam's grey eyes regarded me levelly. "I have to go and interview someone, the only surviving member of this little gang - Monsieur Jean-Yves de la Flèche."

Chapter 17

1

On Sunday afternoon I returned to the flat in London. My postponed meeting with the Chinese jade man would take place the following morning, early. It was easier to go up on the Sunday night and besides, with Jane and Martin in charge in Hampshire I felt it was almost like giving myself a treat. Also, there was Madeleine on Monday and I wondered what precisely I was going to say to her and what exactly it was I felt. One night of electrifying sex wasn't enough as a basis for a meaningful relationship. All I was after, really, was another but that was all. It was difficult to admit that to myself as I wasn't really a casual person, neither was I as selfish as that scenario suggested but most particularly I had discovered that what I was beginning to know of her now, I simply didn't like. I was to snap out of it and get on with a proper life. How I put it, though, and what questions I needed answers to I had not yet worked out. I would wait and see.

I spent the evening alone, working a bit and in front of the television. Jess still seemed so low-spirited that I left Nell to keep her company. Sam had gone to France, the police presence was not so much in evidence but I had informed Sam's right hand man, one Sergeant Evans, that I was back in London for two or three days. I was getting well trained now.

I woke suddenly, at about three in the morning and lay there, in the dark wondering what it was that had wakened me. I was aware that my senses were sharpened and I was tense, instantly straining my ears to hear something. And then, from the pale light of the street lights outside, falling onto my bed, I saw someone, standing at the foot, looking at me.

I didn't move but I spoke. "Who the hell are you?"

A soft laugh came across the darkness. "'Ello, Rober-rt. I 'ave come to give you a surprise!"

"Madeleine!" The tenseness left me, I lay there, bathed in sweat, my heart hammering in my chest. "Dear Christ alive, what a fright you gave me!"

She laughed again and I put out my hand to turn on the light. She took a step forward and put her hand on my wrist. She knelt beside the bed. "No! Leave the light. It is fun in this half-light. Ver-ry romantic, I think. Just like last time, in Viezy."

Slowly, as my nerves returned to normal levels, I began to realise what she was talking about. "Madeleine...?" I put out my hand again and slid it round behind her. I realised she was naked. "What...? Why the change of heart?"

She stoked my chest with her hand, pushing the duvet down to my waist and beyond, looking down at me, smiling. Her voice was low, seductive. "I thought you needed a little fun, that is all..."

In the dim glow from the street lights outside I could see her fair hair hanging away from her face and her wonderful green eyes, flirting with me, narrowing sexily as she looked at me, reminding me of last time. I thought maybe I was still asleep - this was a dream and said so. All she did was reply with a low, sensual laugh and she began to kiss me, all over my face and down my chest.

And beyond...

Lower...

Where she stayed...

I pushed my fingers into her hair, holding her head. Oh my God, but she was... so... bloody... good at this...

2

I woke about 7.30 to the sound of the alarm and stretched and rolled over. She was not there. I lay still a moment, thinking about the night, a grin on my face. More extraordinary sex. Then I got up and pulling on my dressing gown, went out into the sitting room. "Madeleine?"

There was no answer and the flat was quiet, just the sound of the distant early morning traffic beginning. In the middle of the coffee table was a note.

"Thank you for last night, Robert. It was all very sexy. I hope you liked your treat. I have to go back to France this morning but I will be over again soon. I will be in touch. Love, M."

I frowned as I read it again and shook my head. She was a curious girl and no mistake. If she used mystery as an enticement, it certainly worked. I showered slowly and got myself ready for the day. I made my severely tumbled bed, pulling the duvet cover over. It wouldn't do to shock my redoubtable cleaning lady. There were several long blond hairs on the pillow as I plumped them up and I smiled to myself once more as I thought about her.

The morning was successful, the jade was wonderful and I bought some. I had a call from Inno to see if I could go over for supper that evening with her and Charles and, as Madeleine had been to see me the night before I was now free and went over to her flat about eight.

It was a small party, some ten or twelve guests. I was seized and kissed and hugged, which was all very pleasant. I was given a glass of champagne and on the hand that held it out to me sparkled a rather large diamond. Suddenly I twigged. "Hey! You're engaged!"

Inno nodded, her eyes sparkling to match her ring and I kissed her again. "Well, he's a lucky man. I'm so pleased for you. Have you told the aged ones?"

"Yes, we radioed the cruise ship which was very exciting. We thought it was more momentous than texting or simply a big standard call on a mobile! They were thrilled to bits."

"So, we are to expect a great big do in the village church then, are we?" I grinned at Charles who was watching me fairly closely, I thought, but smiled his quiet, shy smile.

"Well, not too huge, if I can hold Mummy back from the brink which will be hard, being the only daughter!"

It was a happy occasion and I was glad I had left my car at the flat and got a taxi as it would have been a shame to let the champagne stay in the bottle. My cab dropped me at the end of Putney Bridge at my request and I walked the rest of the way. The wind was chill but there were a million stars shining down. I looked up at them and thought about recent events. So, Inno engaged. Well... did I mind? Maybe not so much as I thought I was going to, after last night. It seems she really was off the list now. Life goes on, I mused and in the midst of sadness, happy things happen, too, to stop us going quite mad and once again I thought of Madeleine and her green eyes, full of passion, looking up at me from the pillow and her moans of pleasure as we had sex. And now what, I wondered, as I put my key in the lock? I was back at square one for it didn't seem to me that I was about to tell her that I couldn't see any point in continuing our relationship. After last night, I could see the point very clearly indeed, as a matter of fact. Her timing was pretty good, though. It was almost as if she had guessed I'd had enough messing around and was about to call it a day. Maybe she had, as I had been pretty cool and disinterested last time we spoke. I got into bed and slept soundly till morning for I was tired, unsurprisingly.

3

I was just about to set off for the gallery in the morning when there was a ring on the bell. It was Sam back from France. I held the door open and we stood, in the hallway looking at each other for a moment. Sam spoke.

"So, you had a visitor in the small hours of Monday morning. You didn't tell my sergeant."

I might have known! Where were they all, these coppers? Did they disguise themselves as potted palms? I gave a half-grin. Sam's grey eyes were their usual enigmatic selves but, oddly, I found I couldn't look into them for long. "Yes. I... er...well, I didn't know I was going to get a visitor that evening, so..." I shrugged.

"I see. Did she say anything interesting?"

I turned away towards the window. I could have made several answers of the flippant or suggestive kind, if I had so chosen but decided against it. "What sort of interesting?"

"Did she mention I had visited her grandfather, at all?"

"No. Did she know?"

"I don't know, that's why I asked really. Anyway, I came to report back to you, keep you in the picture."

"Thanks." I indicated the sofa and Sam sat down, crossing the designer-trousered legs. "Well?"

"Well... He's charismatic, all right, you can say that for him. He was shocked to hear his old friend had died, he said and he had written to you. He listened to what I had to say about Hans van Cleef and he got very agitated and excited. He said it explained many things and it was ironic to discover who it was who sabotaged the mission after all this time. He seemed to think Hans had always been capable and he, personally, had always suspected him but he had had no proof. He said he had always doubted if he really was a double agent. Once got at by the Nazis, they kept you, he said. In spite of the fact that I said it didn't really prove anything, it was merely circumstantial, he would have none of it. He told me about the raid and your father's part in it. He was the leader, your father, that is, apparently. Jean-Yves also told me about the war from his point of view. His missions for the Underground Movement and how he had been caught by the Nazis and then talked his way out of it." Sam grinned. "I can believe it, too. I should think he could talk his way out of anything. He's a natural politician and about as devious as a..." Sam stopped, suddenly, thinking, I could see. "... as a... weasel. Anyway, I thought I'd tell you."

"Thanks. So what now?"

Sam was sunk in thought again, staring out at the river.

I tried again. "Sam? What happens next?"

"Oh, sorry. Miles away! I was just... mulling over stuff... Anyway, we are trying to find the bomb maker but these people are as elusive as hell. We may not find him for years, they are extraordinarily well protected or he may blow himself up with one of his own devices and we'll never get to talk to him. That happens, too. No, we continue to search for the bald engineer. His face will be all over the papers in a few hours." Sam frowned, staring at the floor.

"What's the matter, Sam? I should have thought you would be pleased to see light at the end of the tunnel."

"If I thought that, then I would be pleased."

"But surely...?" I was surprised. I realised there was a lot more to do but it seemed now only a case of catching this fellow...

"I'm not happy, Rob. There's something too easy about it. It all fits too well. I'm also bothered about motive. However, I shall press on, never fear. I'd dearly love to get hold of the widow of the other man, Pierre DuPont but we've drawn a blank finding her, so far, I have to tell you."

"Oh, you want to see her, too, then?"

"Oh, most certainly, so I want you to go on looking for that letter. Can you do that?"

"Of course."

"Right." Sam stood up. "I'm off, then. You know where I am. When are you returning to Hampshire?"

"This afternoon."

"There's something I need to do first," Sam hesitated, "maybe you would like to come with me."

"What's that?"

"I am going to the Savoy. I have an appointment with the Reservations Manger. I want to find out what I can about who it was William was meeting. Maybe they can give us the name of his companion on those dates. We must follow every lead and this is fairly personal business, I think, as well as helping me with my enquiry."

I was slightly taken aback but, well, yes, I wanted to know what it was William hadn't had time to tell me. I wanted it very much. If we could trace her, whoever she was, then maybe some light might be thrown on grey areas. "Yes, thanks, Sam, I'd like to come."

Sam nodded and stood looking at me for a moment and then turned, sharply and left the room, calling, "See you later then, Rob. Three o'clock in the front Reception of the Savoy, the entrance from the Strand," over the shoulder of the black designer suit. I followed slowly and locked up, going out into the street, thinking. I was wondering why it was that Sam had the effect of making me feel guilty. Perhaps members of Her Majesty's police made everyone feel like that, even if it were only a twinge of conscience about a night of semi-debauchery one was harbouring.

4

I finished my business in London. I found a buyer for the jade and sold it on. I was well satisfied with this deal, gleaning a sort of extra satisfaction that, in spite of all the horrors of the last weeks, I hadn't lost my touch. Jenny looked up at me from her desk, holding her head on one side when I confided this fact to her and gave me a funny smile. "Oh, I can't imagine you ever losing your touch, Rob." I couldn't think what she meant, nor what was amusing about it and set off for the Savoy, oddly refreshed.

By a miracle I found a parking slot just off Covent Garden and made my way through the black revolving doors and into the main foyer of the hotel. Sam was already there, leaning on the counter talking to a formally clad, grey haired man who took us to his office at the back. There were books spread out all over the desk in preparation of our visit. Sam introduced me.

"This is Sir Robert Berkeley. I know you will not mind his being here, Mr. Davies."

"Oh, indeed not, Chief Inspector." He inclined his head with precisely the right amount of deference to my social status. I hid a smile behind my hand as I sat in the chair indicated. I wondered how he struggled with the diverse nature of Sam's.

Sam gave the dates we were interested in and he turned back the leaves of the books. He had the restaurant bookings as well. We quickly found his reservations for the days in his diary, both in the River Room.

"Oh, here we are, Chief Inspector."

He turned the Room Reservations' book round. Sam looked at it for a long moment and gave me a quick glance before pushing in my direction. William's writing was there, signing himself into the hotel and underneath, same date, same room, there it was, M de la Flèche and the address said, c/o Château Viezy, Viezy-sur-L'eau, France. She had signed the register, too, it appeared, just below. The signature was of lovely handwriting, clear and curiously unlike her, I thought. I had not seen Madeleine's handwriting but I would have imagined it to be much more scrawled and flamboyant, somehow, not this beautiful, carefully-formed lettering.

I sat and stared at it. Sam was talking to the fellow, but I just looked at William's handwriting and said not a word. After a little while, Sam got up to leave and I followed, obediently, like a child trailing round the shops with its mother and we went out, this time on the terrace that led to the Embankment, taking our leave of the correct Mr Davies.

We sat on one of the benches and I watched the pigeons strutting about. Sam touched me gently on the arm and I looked into those troubled, grey eyes. "Hmm?"

"Rob - are you all right?"

"Yes." I gave a short laugh. "You've done a lot of asking if I'm all right, lately."

Sam said nothing but just went on looking at me. I sighed and started to speak. "Why, Sam? Why in God's name didn't he tell me. Surely he knew I wouldn't care, not really. I might have been a bit taken aback but, well, if he loved her, then that was great. I cannot bear to think he wouldn't trust me. It is that that makes me sad, not about him taking her away from me." I stood up and walked over to the parapet, looking down into the water and Sam followed, leaning over beside me but watching me, not the Thames. "I never had her, really, anyway, for him to take away. One night stands don't fall into that category. But why didn't she say something? Perhaps it was too hurtful. The whole thing is a worse mystery than before, in a way. I will ask her, though, when she comes over again."

I thought about the other night. Not a word about William and she climbed into my bed and practically seduced me. Well, perhaps that was a bit too strong a word for it but she had taken the initiative even if I did catch up pretty damn quick. I looked at Sam again and found the expression hard to read but it was troubled and pained and anxious. I smiled. "Don't look at me like that, Sam. I'll try and get to the bottom of it."

"Ask her. Ask Madeleine."

"Maybe it wasn't Madeleine. It only says M de la Flèche."

"Oh, Rob! How many M de la Flèches live at the Château Viezy, hmm?"

"I know how it looks but..." I hesitated,"... it's so unlike him I sort of think it couldn't be what it appears..." Sam continued to look bothered. "Come on, Sam, there's nothing for it, is there? We don't know anything about it. It's not as if he had confided in you any more than he had in me. I, at least, saw him most of the time and he didn't tell me. When did you last see William?"

This time Sam turned sharply away from me and started to walk off down the Embankment. I caught up. Sam's profile was set hard and I was surprised at the expression. "Sam?" I could have sworn there were tears in those grey eyes. Surely I must have been mistaken. Sam didn't cry. William and I had done so when needed, still did - well, I still did, but not Sam, not that I had observed, anyway. "Sam, what is it?" I was deeply troubled.

"It's all right, Rob. It's just that once in a while I find it more difficult than I thought I would, delving into the murder of a friend."

We left each other at the foot of the steps that led back up to the Strand. I was still bothered and felt awkward but we parted amicably, Sam would be coming to Hampshire in a day or two, maybe tomorrow if the investigations went the way they were supposed to. I got back into the car and followed the one way system round, past the Aldwych Theatre and Australia House and out and over Waterloo Bridge. I had to find out more about this and Madeleine was the person to ask. I wondered when I might see her again, precisely. She hadn't said.

I drove out of London and onto the A3 and put my foot down flat on the floor. I needed the speed to purge my soul, I felt, and the cold, cleansing air, whistling past me provided just the right effect.

5

Nell was waiting for me on the front steps. As soon as she heard the engine of my car turn into the foot of the drive from the road, if she was outside, she'd come racing round to be there to meet me. If she was indoors, she'd be waiting just inside the house, tail wagging furiously, unashamedly delighted for me to be home. When I changed my car, which I had done a couple of times since I'd had Nell, within a day she'd learned to recognise the new engine note. I had no idea how she knew this or had worked it out. She was a remarkable dog. A policeman was still there, two of them in fact, stamping their feet to keep warm in the chilly autumn air and Nell regarded them solemnly through one of the long windows beside the front door. I pulled up and there she was, jumping round, pleased for me to be back. It was rare for me to leave her behind and she obviously felt she had had enough of playing nursemaid to poor Jess. I picked up my case and glanced round to see if there was anything else I needed to take indoors. Caz, one of our cleaning ladies, had heard the commotion Nell was making and opened the front door for me. She said something briefly to the policemen who nodded, agreeing with whatever it was. One of the wax jackets was on the floor behind the seats. I pulled it out. As I did so I saw, sticking out from one of the pockets, was a piece of paper. It was the poster I had rescued from the board some time ago. It had stayed in the coat pocket and I had forgotten all about it.

Now I opened my briefcase and put it on top of my papers. I would ask Jane later about the printing error. Nell, frantic to get at me, was standing with her feet on the passenger door and I climbed out to greet her, set the alarm and went inside.

I went straight over to the office to find Jane and Martin and dumped my case on William's desk - my desk, now, of course, although it was still too soon to think of it thus. We had some tea as we looked over various bits of mail that needed my attention and then I turned once more to those that were marked, 'personal'.

These were mostly letters of condolence for myself. There were a lot more addressed to Mother and these I left for her. She would be home in a few days. I found the one from Jean-Yves, in French, of course. It was flowery, rather, overly dramatic, typically French, using fifty-six words where five would do. I put it on one side to show Sam who was coming down tomorrow again, Jane told me, having received a message from the ubiquitous Sergeant Evans. Eddy Farley had called in, too, apparently but finding neither Mother nor myself here, he, too would call in tomorrow. I was being looked after, all right, I thought.

Sam arrived early the next day and went straight over to the office. Jane was already there and they were sorting out files as I came in. She left us to answer the phone in the outer office. I remembered my poster now and opened my case and pulled it out.

"Here, Sam, look at this. I took it down from a billboard the other day. I meant to show it to you but I forgot. See?" I pointed out the error. "It says my father is flying the helicopter instead of William." I put the poster on top of the desk and Sam smoothed it out.

"What the...? Sir William?"

"Exactly. Why were they advertising my father flying the helicopter if it was William doing it? I can't understand why William allowed the mistake to go unaltered. It wasn't like him."

"Perhaps Jane will throw some light on that point. But these posters were everywhere, were they?"

"Yes. There was also a programme. A glossy magazine thing. We gave them out at the entrance. It worked like a ticket. If you didn't pay, you didn't get a programme. I expect there is a copy somewhere. We usually keep a few copies of everything like that when we have a special do."

Sam rifled through the appropriate file. "This looks like the thing you mean." Out came the brochure.

It was A4 size and was adorned with a picture of the house, the title

'400 for Forbridge'

and the date. Sam opened it. There were the usual advertisements and photographs, a history of the house and the family. In the centre page was the programme for the Bank Holiday Monday. And there it was again - 'A helicopter rescue performed by Sir William Berkeley and members of the Air/Sea Rescue team...' etc. We looked at each other.

"It's there again! Sam, this is bloody odd!"

Sam stared, grim faced. Then, slowly... "Oh... fuck..."

"What is it? What's the problem?"

"Problem? Yes, well, we'll find out why in a little while. Jane will know. But if these advertisements were everywhere then it will have been believed that Sir William was to be piloting the helicopter. Well, at least we've got one thing straight now, that's for sure." Sam stared into space.

"How can we be positive about anything until we talk to Jane?"

"On this particular point I don't have to in order to form an opinion, Rob. You see, I'm trying to put myself in the position of the murderer. It's the only way you'll catch someone who commits a crime like this."

"What particular point? I don't understand."

"But I do. You see, we've been looking for the killer of William, haven't we?"

I looked blank, nonplussed. "We still are."

"No, Robert, we're not. We're not looking for someone who successfully achieved the murder of your brother. We're looking for the person who tried, but failed to murder your father. And that's a very different thing, believe me."

I stared at Sam, stupefied. Although we had discussed the possibility of someone trying to do damage to my father, I had never, never thought that they had, in fact, killed the wrong man. Mixed emotions and feelings poured in on me and I felt hot and cold by turns. I got up and started to pace about.

"Oh... my... God...!"

Jane came back into the room. "Sorry about that. Somebody on about milk quotas. I referred him to Mark. Coffee won't be long and I spy Martin wandering along the path. He must have smelt the coffee pot!"

Sam held out the poster to her, on top of the brochure, open at the events' page. "Jane, Rob found this poster the other day on a board somewhere. In your absence we've dug out the publicity file. Why does this poster and the programme say the helicopter was to be flown by Sir William? This was not the case, William was the pilot not his father."

Jane shook her head. "Well, Sir William was to have been the pilot, Sam. Didn't you know that? However, he hurt his wrist a few days before the Bank Holiday and William said he'd fly it instead. It was too late to alter any of the publicity so we decided to leave it till the day and make the announcement then. William didn't think anyone would mind, particularly. Besides, there was nothing else we could do about it."

Martin came in and started to distribute the mugs of coffee. He perched on the desk end and listened, picking up the brochure and turning its pages as we talked. Sam walked round the office, pausing to look out of the window, leaning on the sill. "Who else knew of the change of plan, Jane?"

"Well, not many people, I suppose, when you come to think about it. Lady Berkeley, William, of course, Jack Porlock (he's the policeman who was to be rescued - I think we rang him up and told him) and Guy and Solly, the Air/Sea Rescue boys. I assumed William had told you, Rob," she turned her questioning and anxious face towards me.

"No, Jane. No one told me. But then I wasn't even here until the Sunday evening. I had been organising the Antiques Roadshow thing. I had been with the BBC on Saturday and then came down here to help organise bringing the larger items for display for discussion on the programme. I was buzzing about all day with that and it kept me occupied well into the evening. Everyone had their own job connected with the fête and that was mine. If anyone mentioned it to me then it certainly never registered. However, I'm pretty sure no one did mention it."

Sam sat in the chair again, frowning at the desk. "Did you not hear any loud speaker announcements? They were made, I presume?"

Jane nodded but again I shook my head. "No, I didn't hear anything because I wasn't listening. I was only there because I was crossing from one side of the park to the other, talking to the TV producer girl. The quickest way was past the lake. I'd seen this stunt before in the past and the BBC people were ready to begin in about 15 minutes. Will said something about "watching him fly" at breakfast. I said I would if I happened to be around but it would depend on the scheduling of the Roadshow. But he didn't say he was flying instead of my father. I had always thought he was piloting the thing. My father was old, you know, to still have a licence to fly and I knew that would cease before too long now, so if asked, I would assume it was Will flying it. I had no idea this was, in fact, a change from the advertised programme."

Sam got up and started to walk slowly about again, staring at the floor. "So apart from the immediate family (less Robert) and the policeman and crew, you don't think anyone else knew of the change of plan. Is that it? Can you think of anyone else?"

Jane thought, biting the corner of her lip. "I don't know, that's the trouble. Some of the staff in the house, I suppose, maybe the doctor but actually I don't think anyone told the doctor. In fact we didn't think there was anything too much wrong with Sir William's wrist at all. I think he had wanted the glory to be William's and that was his way of engineering it." She smiled fondly but the expression changed as suddenly as switching off a light. "Oh, God, if he hadn't, Sir William would have been killed instead of... Oh, God!" She buried her face in her hands, appalled at the outspoken thoughts, half-casually thrown away, each remark as bad as the other.

Martin's arms were round her. We all made soothing noises, trying to ease her pain. They all looked at me. I raised a hand. "Don't worry, Jane, it's all right," it wasn't but I gave her a half smile, "Sam and I have talked about this. I... it's not such a shock for me at this moment as it is for you. I have had a little while to think about it." It wasn't true, of course. Inside I was both numb and in a turmoil, if it is possible to be both at the same time. I glanced at Sam, uncertain and from the expression rested upon me it seemed I had done all right and Martin's hand on my shoulder and his quiet, "Poor old Rob," seemed to be proof that it had been. I swallowed hard and fished for the now inevitable cigarette.

I smiled at them with difficulty but managed it, as I lit it. "By the time this business is over, I'll be kicking myself I didn't buy shares in the tobacco company, I reckon. I'd practically given up, would you believe." They smiled faintly back and I was conscious of their collective careful and anxious scrutiny and Jane's attempt at trying not to cry in any way other than silently. "I'll make some more coffee."

I went out to the little kitchen. I could hear the faint murmur of voices in the office behind me. I deliberately didn't listen. I leant on my elbows, staring out through the small round window that had once been a source of light to a tack room. The rain that had begun in the night, was slackening off at last and even as I watched, a damp and bedraggled piece of blue sky appeared briefly before it was hastily covered up again by a stray rain cloud. But the blue was winning. Here was another patch, and another just visible over the trees of the copse where I had wandered earlier. A childhood rhyme came into my head and I glanced at my watch. Two minutes to eleven. "Rain before seven, shine before eleven." Still true, apparently. I unplugged the percolator which had stopped making its plopping noises and carried it into the other room.

"Here we are? See how domesticated I am!"

Jane came over and took the pot from me. "Dear Rob," and she hugged me, nearly upsetting the scalding coffee all over both of us.

"Idiot!" and we smiled at each other. A tear still lingered on her cheek and I wiped it off for her with my finger. I poured the refills with a steady hand. I was amazed at myself.

Sam was back on the train again. "So, to all intents and purposes, practically everyone believed it was Sir William who was going to fly the helicopter. The only people who knew were close friends or family and precious few of them, too it seems. Right?" We nodded. "So..." Sam looked at me, "I come back to what I said to you earlier, Rob. We are looking for someone who wanted not to just harm your father but actually kill him. And since he led such a quiet, gentle existence it has to go back to his days in the war. Surely it must. Besides, all those old wartime associates rearing their heads - letters, phone calls, etc. I know he's a minor public figure but only connected with family entertainment. He doesn't make outspoken statements about religion or the Middle East or any other controversial topics. And besides, Lady Berkeley suggested something of the kind." Sam banged the coffee cup down on the desk. "So, we come back to Mr van Cleef."

I was thinking. "So, when I said he might have done it because of getting my father to keep his mouth shut, I might very well have been right."

Sam stared at me, but I felt the eyes were looking straight through me, not at me, at all.

"Sam? Is that right?"

Sam got up and walked to the window. "Maybe..." It was a very doubtful 'maybe' and sounded much more like 'no'.

I pressed on, almost desperate. "Sam, really, it must be. You said he was, well, if not a terrorist, then a man who walked with terrorists. Jean-Yves himself told you he had been got at by the Nazis."

Sam turned round and this time I found the grey eyes were looking right into mine. "Yes, he did, didn't he, and he also said once you were got at, they kept you..."

Sam appeared to make some sort of decision. "Jane, can I borrow your office and use your computer and stuff, please?" She nodded and they went out together, leaving Martin looking at me with troubled gaze.

I sat in the chair again and started opening one or two letters that had arrived that morning. "It's all right, Martin. Don't look at me like that. I can handle it."

He nodded but said nothing and after another furtive glance my way, which I affected not to notice, he went off to his own office, leaving me to light up yet another cigarette to assuage my raw and battered nerves.

Chapter 18

1

Sam stayed over at the office. Jane made sandwiches for lunch and we ate them in various locations around the house, Sam on the phone most of the time, receiving and sending messages and emails and printing things off the computer. Jane and Martin just got on with the usual running of things and I wrote letters.

Early in the afternoon I went back up to the house. The leaves were beginning to fall quickly this year, I thought, as I rustled my way along past a row of horse chestnuts. I stared at the ground as I walked, hands in pockets, kicking at the yellow and brown skeletons of leaves, trying to piece all the bits together and realising it was hopeless. As soon as I thought I might be able to understand it, something else cropped up to make my vision cloud over once more. And William? I tried to imagine why it was he thought he couldn't tell me about Madeleine, let alone she, herself. It was all so pointless and unlike him or unlike the man I thought I knew, at any rate. I still couldn't believe it. And now, our attention was turned to my father, the man they had really wanted to kill. They had made a mistake and I tried to examine my feelings here. But it was too hard to think about, the choice too terrible and besides, what did it matter now, with them both dead. We cannot dwell too long on what might have been, or that could drive us mad. I had to go on living and do my best to help Sam avenge them both.

As I walked up the steps, I saw Eddy Farley's car turn into the drive from the road below me and I waited for him. He parked and climbed from the car.

"Hello, Rob. I just thought I'd pop by and see how you are and how things are going."

He was a good friend and I was touched. I ushered him into the hall. "Thank you, Eddy, that was very kind. I'm fine."

"And your mother? Have you heard from her?"

"Oh yes. She seems to be coping all right, as far as I can tell, but you know what she's like. It's difficult enough to break through the veneer when she's here but over the phone..." I shook my head, "but she'll always be like that, so there we are."

"Yes, yes, indeed. I know."

"Coffee? Tea?"

"Just a quick cup now I'm here. Coffee, thanks."

I led the way towards the kitchens. We continued talking as he followed behind me. "I think I will turn into some sort of caffeine addict sooner rather than later. Along with nicotine. I was saying earlier this morning I should have bought shares in the cigarette companies. I must add coffee growers to my list of wise investments."

He smiled. "Don't worry about all that at present. Things will simmer down in a little while and then you can give up smoking."

"That's what I figured."

Eddy sat in one of the wooden kitchen carvers that had stood at the kitchen table for as long as I could remember. I used to play trapping pirates in them, I recalled, as a small boy, turning two of the chairs to face each other, creating a small round prison. Sometimes I was the pirate and sometimes William. If we were very lucky we might catch unsuspecting visitors in them, too and then we could be on the same side, which we preferred.

I filled the jug, covering the grounds with boiling water and we sat, looking at it, waiting for it to brew. He looked up at me carefully, observing me critically. I knew some sort of medical-type question was on its way.

"Have you a girlfriend at the moment, Rob?"

"Not a regular one, no. Not at present."

"Hmm. Nothing still going on with little Inno Harcourt?"

It was interesting how people who knew adults as children still thought of them as 'little', I mused. Inno was at least five foot seven. I liked tall girls. "No, no. That's run its course. But we're still very good friends and hopefully will always be. She's engaged to be married now, to a very nice guy - a fellow member of her chambers, actually."

"Hmm," he said again, still looking at me closely. "And how do you feel about that?"

I was casual. "Fine... fine. He's just right for her." I wanted to say nothing more on this subject. You never knew how much you could find yourself giving away to questioning from an expert like Eddy. He was as good as getting information out of you as Sam was, I thought.

"You parted on good terms?"

"Yes, very. I went to the engagement party. I have no doubt I'll go to the wedding, too. As I said we're very good mates."

"Or were - mates, I mean...?" There was innuendo in his expression now and I grinned.

"Yes... were." I was light in my reply, carefully presenting how casual and laid back about it all I was. "Plenty more fish and all that."

He changed the subject. "Your father's funeral - that was a most dignified and touching service, Robert. I think you must have been pleased with the way it went."

"Yes, I was, thank you, Eddy."

"Quite tricky, making it different from William's, something special for each of them."

"Yes. I don't know if I tried to do that consciously, I have to say but it worked out in the end. Mother did all right, too, bless her, getting slightly tipsy. Did her good. Helena will keep an eye on her and so will I, of course, when she returns. She's not an easy patient, as you must well know!"

He smiled, "I do, to my cost."

I pushed the plunger down onto the grounds and poured out the coffee, handing first milk and offering sugar. I was amused to see him put in two spoons whereas I took none. Balanced the cigarettes a little, I thought. "I'll tell you one thing, Eddy. I'm so glad he was able to have just one word with her before he died. And me. It would have been awful if that had been denied to us. It means a lot to humans to say goodbye. I think that was one of the most awful things about William being killed. No time to..." I stopped. He was staring at me. "Whatever's the matter?"

"You say your father spoke to you before he died? When do you mean, exactly? That afternoon or just before you went to bed?"

I was disturbed by his expression. "Well, neither. I mean just before he died - literally. Bella came and got me and..." I stopped again. He looked increasingly dreadful. "Eddy? Whatever is it? You look..."

He got up and walked across the room, shakily, holding on to things to help him keep his balance, it seemed. He looked grey and old suddenly. "Now listen carefully, Robert, I want you to tell me exactly when your father spoke to you and also to your mother."

I felt I was beginning to lose my grip on reality. I took a deep breath. "I told you. Bella came down the corridor to my room. To wake me up. I went to my father's dressing room with her and then she went to fetch my mother. Dad spoke to me while we were waiting for my mother. Then she came in and he spoke to her."

"Did Bella hear him?"

"I don't know, you'll have to ask her. She wasn't in the room, I think. If I remember," I screwed up my face in an effort to recall it all and any trivial details from such an important moment to me, "she left me alone with him as she got my mother out of bed and then went next door to get something. I heard my father say something personal to my mother and I thought they should be alone and left the room. Bella was on the landing, fiddling about squirting liquid through a needle. Then I heard you arrive and went down to let you in. Eddy, what is all this?"

He had gone quite white and was staring at me. "Oh Jesus Christ! Rob..." He was transfixed and I shook him.

"Eddy! Tell me!"

He straightened himself up from where he had slumped over the front of the Aga, hanging on to the rail. "Rob, I don't know how to say this to you. I think it is quite one of the most awful things I have ever said to anyone." He took a deep breath and I thought I was going to smack him. "I am deeply afraid that I have made a mistake in the cause of your father's death. I am therefore going to have to go to the police and tell them. That means, I believe, that if there is no death certificate, your father's body will have to be exhumed and a postmortem carried out."

I felt myself go white. I hardly had a voice and it came out in a whisper. "Oh... Jesus Christ, no... But why? What has changed your mind, now, after the funeral and everything?"

He looked at me. "You have. By what you have just said. I believed your father died of a massive stroke, a second one. I believed all the symptoms were there, particularly coming on top of the other one, paralysis, loss of control of bodily functions, apparent loss of hearing and," he paused and swallowed, "loss of speech, Rob."

I looked sharply at him. "But he...?"

"Exactly. If you hadn't told me he had spoken to you and to your mother, I wouldn't have known this. If he had died of a stroke as big as the one I believed he had had, he could not possibly have been able to speak."

I turned from him and sat staring out in the direction of the stable yard. There were several horses' heads nodding over the doors - William's horse, my father's, mine - mildly regarding their familiar world. They looked so commonplace and normal. How were we going to stand this new horror, I asked myself. I turned back. He was staring miserably at me.

"Are you going to get your mother back from Cornwall?"

"I don't know. I shall take the advice of the police. I want to spare her this as long as possible. I shall probably ring Helena." Dear, faithful Helena. He still stood there. "Go on, Eddy. You'd better hurry up. You don't have to go far, it's knee deep in police out there still. Take your pick. One of the senior representatives of the Anti-Terrorist Squad is in my father's office or use the phone and call the Chief Constable of Hampshire, whose personal number is permanently on the pad beside it these days."

He turned and left, half stumbling down the hall and out towards the of stable block where Sam would be, chewing a pencil and quietly giving instructions down the phone.

I sat in a chair again, or rather on the edge of it for what seemed like an eternity. Then the door opened again.

Sam's face was very grave. "Rob, this is very serious. Eddy Farley cannot stand by the death certificate. Therefore..."

"It's all right, Sam," I interrupted, "he has explained it to me. Basically, I was just sitting here till you came so that I can make plans about telling my mother."

Sam nodded. There was a long pause. "I don't know what we shall find, Rob."

I nodded. "No. I realise that. What I can't understand is, if he thought it was a heart attack or something why he can't just change the certificate. Surely it had to be something like that, doesn't it, if he died so quickly?"

Sam stood looking at me with a deeply concerned expression. "I don't think it could be a heart attack but I don't know, Rob. I don't know. I am not a doctor but I do know they cannot just change a death certificate without further examination."

I stood up. "I had better put a brave face on it and call Helena. Will you wait here for me, Sam?"

Sam nodded and the ghost of a fleeting smile hovered there briefly. "Yes, Rob. Of course I'll wait for you."

I turned and went out to phone from the library, the quiet tranquility of the room soothing my fraying nerves as I dialled the number in Cornwall.

2

There was more than a small element of black comedy about it all, I thought. No sooner had my father's coffin been reverently placed in the grave than the police came along and dragged it out again. The only trouble about it was, I wasn't laughing. They took the body away to Winchester to the mortuary and we had to wait. After some discussion my mother decided to stay in Cornwall for the immediate present. There was nothing she could do and I wanted her out of the way while this new horror sorted itself out. I wasn't sure if this was for her sake or mine but finally decided it was probably for both of us, at least, I talked myself into thinking that way.

The house seemed like a morgue itself, those two days, while we waited for them to make their pronouncements. On the afternoon of the second day after the exhumation, Jane called me to the phone. "Robbie, it's Sam."

"Hello."

"Rob, I'm coming right over and I'll be with you in less than an hour. I'm only in Winchester. I was checking to see you would be in."

"I'll expect you shortly, then. I'll be here."

"Yes. You will." The phone went dead immediately. I stared at the receiver briefly before I put it back on the rest. Sam never ever signed off like that, no word of goodbye, abruptly. And the 'Yes. You will,' was actually an order, I suddenly realised. I frowned, puzzled and disturbed.

The weather was damp and unpleasant, reflecting the mood of myself and the whole atmosphere of the house. While waiting for Sam I wandered up to the old nursery. Once again, I perched on the window seat, looking out over the rain-sodden countryside, no break in the clouds today, greyness from horizon to horizon. I smoked and watched the grey smoke mingle with the blue as it wound its way upwards. I glanced round the room, its familiar look, comforting and safe. The rocking horse stood between the two long windows, its back towards me. The ever-faithful Nell came pushing in and brushed past it as she came and sat next to me, poking her black nose into my hand.

She turned suddenly and started to bite violently at her back, a busy flea having distracted her momentarily. She sat on the end of one of the curved rockers and as she moved her position again, she set the horse in motion, gently tipping back and forth. I watched it.

Something caught my eye and I sat up. As the horse rocked away from me, I could see under its back hooves. This was impossible while the horse was standing still. A small piece of paper seemed to be there, protruding from under the wooden hoof. As I bent towards it to see what it was, something came back to me over the years.

It had been somebody's birthday, Mother's perhaps, maybe even William's. I had something to hide, a secret and I asked my father a good hiding place. I could see him, in my mind's eye, as clearly as it had been then. He had taken me by the hand and brought me here, to the nursery and we had stood together, excited by the conspiracy.

"Look, old chap, see here, under the hoof at the back. If you slide this little plate away, there is a gap underneath - a secret hiding place." He stood up, looking at me solemnly. "Now this is a great secret. I found this when I was a boy, not much older than you are now and I would hide special things in there. No one knows about it but me and now you, Robbie, now you. Even little chaps like you need to hide things sometimes, even from William. So there you are. That's my secret and now it's yours. You won't tell, will you?"

I put my finger into the little gap. It went up inside the horse's foot. I was very thrilled. "No, Daddy, I'll never tell. It's our special place, just yours and mine."

"Just yours and mine, Robbie. Don't forget."

I had used it as a child but then I had forgotten. I had forgotten until now. I had hidden all sorts of things in there over the years but I had never told, not even William, as I had promised and now I bent down and pulled out of the hiding place a wad of paper. It was wedged in tight and had been rolled up to go up inside the hollow leg of the horse. I sat back on the window seat and unfolded them. My father had said I would know where to look and he had been right. It was I who had been slow-witted. They were the missing letters.

The first one was from Pierre's widow and was written in French, the handwriting clear on the crumpled paper.

"21 Rue de Saint Cyr

Limoges

Dear William

I am writing to tell you that Pierre is dead.

I know you have not corresponded since the end of the war and I know you were supposed not to contact one another again but I wanted to tell you. It does not seem to matter now. It was all so long ago.

We have run a mission in French West Africa for years, since the war ended, in fact. Last month, we came home to our little house in Limoges that was left to me by my mother.

Jean-Yves is running for President. When Pierre found out he went to see him at the Château. Hans was there and he was very surprised. Jean-Yves said it was an extraordinary day for he had not seen Hans for years, either. Pierre stayed at the little auberge that used to be just outside the village and in the night he was taken ill. The doctor was called but he was dead. They said he had had a stroke.

I can't believe it, William. Pierre had had a medical only a few weeks before. He was fit and healthy, his heart was strong and the cholesterol levels were low. It is hard to think of him having a stroke but it was true. I am so lonely. And sad. I loved him so much, he was everything for me, as we had no children. Now I have brought his body back to Limoges for burial.

Take care of yourself, dear friend. I know we have never met but I seem to know so much about you, Pierre so often spoke of you to me. I have written to Hans as well. I felt I owed him that much.

Pierre admired you so much always. And he loved you, William.

Goodbye,

Agnes DuPont."

I stared at this letter. Yes, no wonder he was sad, hearing his old friend and comrade in arms had died. And no wonder he couldn't show it to us. They were not ever supposed to contact one another, it appeared. How strange, this world of espionage, right here amongst the ordinary people like myself whose brush with spies was in the cinema or John le Carré books - fiction, every last word. And yet...? Perhaps that is always what is needed, the perfect cover being the most ordinary, why, I had even said as much to someone recently.

I read the other. This one was in English.

"Amsterdam

Dear William

I have had a letter from Pierre's widow. She says she has written to you. It is sad to think of him gone. He was a wonderful man and a superb radio operator.

I am soon to leave for the West Indies, sailing my yacht. I have had terrible times and I have been a fool.

I am desperately short of money. I have an extravagant lifestyle and it costs a fortune. My art dealer told me he had sold my Stubbs to a young man called Robert Berkeley from London but it was to be sent to Hampshire. Could it be possible that this is your son? I hope so. I would love for you to have the Stubbs after all we went through together.

I am on the run though, William, from the law, from so-called business friends but mostly from myself. I was stupid to get involved with all this but it is too late now but it was only ambition, nothing more. I saw Jean-Yves when Pierre was there. He is a hero, you know, and will be the next President of France. It is so strange to think of that, when I can still see him in my mind, pedalling along on his old bicycle, friendly with everyone, even a cheery greeting with the Nazis to put them off the scent. Will we ever know who sabotaged our mission? Certainly not Pierre, unless he took the secret with him. It must have been an outside job, not one of us was capable of betrayal.

I had to tell you I am leaving Europe, never to return. They may catch me, I don't know. You cannot help me, but you must know.

Take care. Look after Elsa if you can, when I die.

You were always the best of men.

Hans"

I stared at this letter and I read them both all over again. This van Cleef was a cool customer, I thought, writing letters, claiming he didn't know who was the saboteur and all the while arranging for a bomb to be made to kill my father, that "best of men" and getting William instead. My hand shook as I read it. Sam would be pleased, I knew. There was even an address to interview Pierre's widow, Agnes, now. I put them in my pocket and went downstairs. I could see from the nursery Sam's car turn into the drive and wend its way swiftly up the hill towards me. Well, we would both have news for each other, I thought but I would have Sam's first, I decided. The letters could wait.

Chapter 19

1

And so I sat in the library and waited. I heard Sam walk up the steps and ring the bell. Someone answered it and I heard footsteps in the hall. The door opened and I stood up.

Sam walked in quickly and stood by the fire, looking at me. It was the impersonal, blank police-image, give-away-nothing face that regarded me and my heart sank.

Sam came straight to the point as I would have expected. "Robert, the examination is complete. The pathologist is in no doubt what killed your father. He was poisoned."

I stared at Sam, disbelieving. I had thought he must have had a heart attack but what was all this? Perhaps I had misunderstood. "Poisoned? What, food poisoning, do you mean?" I thought of the invalid slops he'd been eating prior to his death. They were all so harmless...

"No, not food poisoning. It was a rare poison and that is why they have taken some time to track it down but they know its name and where it comes from. It will be up to me, however, to find out how it was administered... and by whom."

I didn't move. No, this wasn't true. "Sam, what are you saying to me?"

"I am saying that your father died of a rare poison that must have been given to him. I do not believe it possible, considering his frail state, that he could have given it to himself deliberately. It wasn't suicide. Therefore, we have to assume that it was murder."

I sat down. "Holy Mother of God." I said it without expression and I think I actually meant it. There didn't seem to be anyone more suitable to address at that moment.

Sam moved opposite me. "Right then, you understand I am now having to open a second murder file on this family, Robert. I must take statements from everyone who was in the house leading up to before he died."

I stared, light slowly dawning. "Are you actually saying to me that everyone in this house is under suspicion of murder? Do you really believe any one of us here is capable of killing a man who we all loved as much as he was loved?"

"I don't personally believe you killed him or your mother killed him, even though there are motives..."

"What?" I shouted, outraged. "Motives? What... fucking... motives?"

Sam snapped back at me. There was nothing calm, kind or measured now. "Of course there are motives. Listen, who benefits from the death of both your brother and your father? You do, don't you? You inherit a title, a 7,000-plus acre estate that's worth a fortune from your father as well as a very tidy sum from William." I started to swear violently but Sam shouted me down. "Shut up and let me finish. That has been true from the outset. A lot of people have been under suspicion but there are some theories that simply don't hold water."

"What do you mean? You're talking like a maniac as far as I can see!"

"No, I'm not, I'm talking cold logic. Take your mother, for instance. Many a man has been murdered by his wife because she thought he was too ill to live any more. See what I mean? It doesn't mean I think she did it any more I think you did it but I have to eliminate you both or the whole thing would be a complete farce. I have to protect myself too from any form of suspicion or favouritism, not just for myself, but for the enquiry. I have to think of the defence lawyers who would pick up immediately on any area that was glossed over or a personal vendetta against someone else or trying to save you... or, or, a... family from prosecution for any personal motives of my own." I still glared, furious and disbelieving. Sam thumped the chair in fury, to get through to me. "Let me spell it out for you, if you fucking killed your brother and your father you'll go to prison and I will put you there. Willingly. I don't believe you did, but by Christ you'll have to clear yourself far and away beyond all reasonable doubt, not just for me personally, or for yourself, but for the courts and to help me track down the bastards who did do it, right?"

"Are you telling me I, myself, have actually been under suspicion? How could you... how could you... ever... fucking think..?"

"Quite easily, all things considered. In fact, for a long time you were the prime suspect."

"What?! How could you... how could anyone..?" I wasn't sure if I was angry or horrified or terrified. I sank onto the sofa, staring at Sam in a black haze of disbelief. Something of my actual physical pain at this must have registered.

Quieter now, Sam let up on me slightly. "In any murder case, do you not know, Robert, that the first people under suspicion are always the family? The vast majority of murders are committed by members of the victim's immediate relatives. Or close friends. Think of Martin. One can make out a case against him, if one tried, and without trying too hard, either."

"Martin?"

"Yes, of course. He has married one of William's ex-girlfriends, a man she still worked for. Suppose he was jealous? Maybe she compared him unfavourable with William, anything. Hurt pride is a very powerful emotion, particularly where love is concerned. And even more especially, sex. Was William better in the sack than Martin and she made it clear he was or even implied it? Many men have killed for less. And now, also, as a result of William's death, Martin has a damn good job and just when he needed one, too."

I was speechless by this outburst, enraged and shocked. But yet Sam was right. Of course these things were, in a crazy way, plausible and had to be investigated, simply because of their plausibility. Not for the first time I thought of Sam, elegant, cool, refined, dealing with the dregs of humanity and I was amazed by it. Even in the midst of personal hell I was aware of it but Sam went on talking and I listened, calmer now, to the rest of it.

"Now here, in this case, none of these possibilities seemed really likely. Not because I know you, you understand but because after the initial investigations were made by the Hampshire police and it was discovered very quickly it was not an accident but caused by a highly sophisticated designer bomb, it was felt it had to be some kind of terrorist attack and we were called in to take over. After some initial investigations I didn't believe it to be a terrorist motivated murder and I told my superiors so. I thought it was something more personal. They didn't believe me but I kept on with it. Now we know the bomb was meant for your father and not William and we have had to build up a profile of his past and present, rather than William's. With the discovery that your father was advertised as the pilot and he was poisoned, I think this proves it. They really killed the wrong man when they murdered William. Seemingly, now, after this forensic report, they have the right one."

I was chastened by these last remarks but my feathers were severely ruffled as well as the shock of the whole dreadful business. I was gruff, as I spoke, grudgingly, I could hear it in my voice.

"All right. So, as I understand it, we'd all been under suspicion of murder to a greater or lesser extent until you discovered it was something basically beyond the scope of a normal law-abiding English family."

Sam nodded. "More or less."

"So, have things changed by this... this new monstrosity?"

"Probably not in fact, but here we have a curious conflict. Bombs are not every day methods of destruction for ordinary people to use but poison is not generally a terrorist weapon. It is a domestic one. However, be that as it may for the moment. I have to make enquiries in order to eliminate people, as I said. There is one thing, though. Whoever it was who blew up the helicopter wasn't going to leave it to chance that your father might die of shock or a stroke. It seems to me they were determined he should die, so they killed him. Maybe it was even more important when it was known they killed the wrong person, the son of the wrong person, what was more. Maybe the past would not have been enough to keep him silent now. It sounds simple enough but I have now got to prove how it was done. I have the method but not the opportunity or, God damn it, the reason, although maybe I think I am beginning..."

"Sam, can I ask you something?"

"Of course. I may not be able to answer it though, even if I know the answer."

I took in the implications behind that short remark and was chastened by it in a way that nothing in our previous conversation had managed to achieve. The status quo between us had altered suddenly. I knew it and knew why. The chasm was huge. "Wha-what sort of poison is it?"

"As I said, it is very rare. It produces symptoms very similar to those of a stroke with, of course, the exception of loss of speech. It is a natural poison, that is, one that occurs in vegetable matter and is not manufactured by man. It would poison you if you ate the plant or if you dried the plant and administered it as a powder. It is the latter method that was used as your father had only liquids in his stomach. It kills in about 6 to 12 hours after being consumed.

"Which plant? Something like laburnum seeds or yew berries, do you mean?"

"Well, in a way but laburnum seeds and yew berries don't produce symptoms like that. No, this particular poison has only one source. It comes from a rare and deadly form of mushroom."

2

This terrible thought and its implications filled my mind and I swallowed hard. I needed time to think about this. I pushed my hands in my pockets and felt the papers. I had forgotten about them in my misery. I pulled out the letters and handed them over silently.

The grey eyes registered what was there and looked up at me sharply. "Where? When?"

"Just now, while I was waiting for you." I explained about the secret nature of the rocking horse. "He said I would know and he was right, or rather I should have known. It's been a long time since I hid something there, though."

Sam was reading them and there was silence. I could hear the clock in the hall ticking quietly to itself and then the whirring started as it gathered itself into some sort of order in which to release its striking mechanism. Sam looked up at me but still said nothing.

"Well? What do they tell you, if anything? I think van Cleef was a bloody cool customer."

"Very." Sam's voice and gaze were far away. "I must get on, Rob. I'll be back to talk to you later. There are things for me arrange and what not. Don't leave the estate at all, please and the house only with permission."

"What?" I was outraged again.

"Of course. Think about it." Sam snapped back. "For my purposes you need to be under observation, to make sure you cannot skip off or hide anything or bribe anyone or administer to yourself some kind of suicide pill. Then..."

"Christ!"

"Think about it some more. This protects you as well as myself and also the validity of the enquiry. If the bastards who did it can find a loophole they'll use it. They would get off scot free, I'd be out of a job or worse and you'd be under suspicion for the rest of your life." The grey eyes were like steel. I nodded, meekly. I saw, all right. Sam went on, "I need to take a statement from you and I'll take a look at the rocking horse myself, if I may."

I nodded again - Sam knew the way to the nursery - and left me staring at the empty grate. Quietly, a policeman slipped into the room and stood impersonal beside the door. He was like one of the guards on duty outside Whitehall or Buckingham Palace, almost unreal, but if challenged, I knew would be a determined and formidable foe. I shivered and found matches and lit the newspaper, watching it catch the kindling, the clouds of smoke pouring up the chimney. The flames caught and the scent of log fire was soon pervading the room and I stared, mesmerised, into its depths as I thought of Sam and the postmortem. There was nothing else for it. When Sam came back I was going to have to speak my mind, purge myself of my suspicions and I didn't know if I was glad or sorry.

Sam was with us for the rest of the day, taking statements from everyone. The police presence was everywhere, less discreetly now, though, aware that once again turmoil had come to rest in peaceful, rural Hampshire. One thing they had done was keep the news about the exhumation out of the papers. I was grateful for this and said so. Sam said that they weren't going to tell them anyway which surprised me a little and I asked why.

Sam regarded me coolly. "It would warn the murderer that we suspected him, of course. So far he'll think he's got away with it. Complacency is dangerous for those who break the law."

I nodded, grimly, impressed in spite of myself. And now my mother was on her way home, her little break to adjust to a new world was at an end. There were to be more statements now from her and from Helena.

Sam went round the household one at a time eventually coming to me last of all. We sat there, once again in the library. The silent watching spectre had been relieved of his duty. Sam smiled a weary smile.

"Jesus, what a day! But you're the last, thank God!" A young policeman had come in at the same time and sat a small distance away from us in order to piece together in a suitable fashion for the courts to read what I had to say.

I had been up in the woods, accompanied, at a short distance, by a policeman. I had thought about it all very carefully and I knew what I must do. Perhaps I realised I should always have been more open about Madeleine with Sam but something held me back. While walking with the dogs, I tried to address the whole thing as dispassionately as possible. I knew now I must tell Sam everything about our relationship since she had come into my life again and also some thoughts I had had that might be useful.

So, I started to speak. I told Sam everything about that Sunday, my father's last day on this earth. It took a long time for the policeman had to write it all down and I had to initial pages and sign things. I told Sam about my disquiet over Madeleine knowing about the bomb exploding in Hampshire when she was supposed to know nothing about it and about how she lied about leaving her handbag in the room.

Sam made little comment as I talked but stopped me here and there to clarify a point or two. Eventually it was all done and we sat there, staring at each other. I felt drained and purged as if I had been to a lengthy confessional.

Sam leaned back in the sofa, hands behind head and looked up at the ceiling.

"So, Rob, now we come down to it. Madeleine was here and she was on her own with your father. She told you she had knowledge of poisons from fungi and you actually went mushroom picking that day, right?"

I was grim. "Yes. If it is proved she killed him I shall never forgive myself, bringing her here like that. Why, I suppose she even killed him with one of his own mushrooms."

Sam looked at me sharply. "No, that's impossible. I told you, they were dried and powdered. She couldn't have done all that in the time. If Madeleine gave him the poison, she must have brought it with her and her intention was to get at him somehow or other or she would not have come prepared. You say she accepted your invitation with alacrity. She intended to get an invitation here and would have engineered it eventually. Furthermore, if she is that determined and that ruthless then she would have made the attempt without you inviting her here, in any case. You must not feel guilty, Rob."

But I would have none of it. "I suppose you must be right about the mushrooms not being ours but I shan't ever think I could have prevented it if she had never been invited. But listen, Sam, are we any nearer as to the reason why she wanted to kill my father?"

Sam stared out of the window at the autumnal world for a moment. Soon the clocks would go back, I thought and then it would be crumpets for tea and going home to the Putney flat in the dark and then next it would be Christmas. And how we had always looked forward to Christmas, William and I! It was always the highlight of the year at Forbridge. The enormous tree in the hallway that rose up through the stairwell, the house full of visitors, carol singers and laughter everywhere. Even when we grew up we kept on with the traditions. But what this year? The future was only grey and bleak, like living in a swirling, freezing fog. No light penetrated that fog, not even Christmas tree lights, I thought morosely.

Sam stirred and looked at me. "Well, yes, I think I know it all now. I have to prove it though, of course, and that is going to be very difficult but we shall see what we shall see but before you say any more," for I had leapt to my feet, "I don't think I am in a position to talk about that just for the moment. There are lots of things to prove. There are your letters, too and well, let's say tomorrow, after I've spoken to your mother, I shall be leaving for France again. I shall have to speak to Madeleine. It is always difficult dealing with foreign police forces, even helpful ones. And the French police! You should have heard them rant and rave last week when I said I wanted to rake up the past of their beloved Jean-Yves! However, now, as then, they have little choice."

Sam leaned over and threw another log on the fire. The young policeman had left, melting into the shadows and out into the hallway and we stared in silence for a while at the cruel but cleansing flames, each of us with our own thoughts.

Chapter 20

1

My mother, shocked and quiet, had returned and made her statement, alone with Sam. I didn't know what they said to one another but she was sad and drawn afterwards and I did not question her. Sam left, flying for Orly as soon as was possible. We agreed to meet back in London.

Some three or four days later I had a phone call. The police team would be back that afternoon. Sam would seek me out later in the evening at the flat. I gleaned nothing from the quiet voice, all the way from over the Channel. I would have to wait.

Nell and I speeded up the A3 and arrived at lunchtime. I went to the pub and had a passable steak and kidney pie. She sat beside me, thrilled to be up in London with me again. She revelled in the country life, of course, but it was in London that she had me most often to myself and she loved that. I went up to the flat and dumped some things into the kitchen - the ingredients for the suppers I was to prepare tonight and tomorrow evenings. I unpacked the bags and put things away in the fridge and I opened the balcony windows and the bedroom windows and let the wind blow through as it had been shut up for several days.

I was restless and decided a brisk walk along the river would do us both good. I closed the flat once more leaving the bedroom windows open at the top and ran down the stairs and out into the fitful autumn sun. The hall was deserted, no policeman was on duty now. The victim had been eliminated finally, I thought darkly and I was in no further need of serious protection. They left the bug on the phone, though, they said, just for the moment. I felt suddenly uneasy, rather in the way one does when one has a plaster cast taken off after weeks of a bone mending. The joy of freedom and then the fear of vulnerability - the lack of protective covering, somehow.

It was good to be back in anonymous, grubby London. The Thames was as grey as ever. I watched it, throwing an old tennis ball I found in my pocket for Nell. This was supposed to be the cleanest it had been for many years, was it? Salmon came up it now and otters lived on its banks, supposedly. There were the boats, most of them on the water this afternoon, a mini regatta in progress, and I watched them for some time with some amusement, idly throwing the ball for Nell at regular intervals, as one crew shipped in water by the gallon and attempted to bail it out using a pair of leaky old trainers. The water fell out of the holes in the bottom of the shoes but it fell down inside the fellow's shirtsleeves and hence back into the boat. It was like slapstick in a pantomime.

We walked a long way, Nell and I, and eventually turned for home. By the time I reached the flat, it was dusk. We climbed up the stairs and I put the key in the lock. The door stuck a little for some reason and I shoved at it.

It was then Nell growled, deep in her throat.

She pushed open the door in front of me, determined, her hackles were up and she scraped at the door of the lounge which was closed. I hadn't remembered shutting it. Maybe the wind had done it. "What's the matter, Nell? It's all right."

But it wasn't.

Madeleine was standing by the fireplace. The room was dim, lit only by the street lamps that shone in from outside the windows but I knew it was her, even though I couldn't see her face.

"Madeleine? Is that you?" I walked to the corner of the room opposite the door and turned on the standard lamp that stood there. It gave out a gentle, apricot glow. She was standing with one hand on the mantelpiece and the other was in the pocket of her loose jacket.

"Hello, Rober-rt. I was hoping to surprise you." Her cold had come back, her voice was husky as before.

"Well, you did." I looked at her with a large degree of unease but she appeared quite relaxed. "How did you get in?"

"The key you gave me." (God, what an idiot I was, I thought. Why had I not got that back from her or changed the lock?) "I was going to make you a great big beautiful meal and serve it to you. But now you have discovered me. I have only just got here. That is why I had not even put on the lights. I was looking for the light switch."

How easily she lied, I thought. She made it sound very plausible. But I knew she was for I had not said I would be in London. I wondered what she had really come for. Perhaps if I strung her along for a while I might find out. I decided I'd better play it her way for the moment and made a mental note to eat nothing.

Nell was making a fearful racket, grumbling and snarling.

"Shut up, Nell. She is a funny dog, isn't she? Be quiet, Nell!" But still she rumbled on. I took her by the collar and pushed her out into the kitchen and closed the door. I turned to the sideboard.

"Now you're here, would you like a drink, Madeleine?"

The green eyes regarded me placidly. She smiled. "That would be love-lee."

"Gin and tonic?"

"Yes, thank you, Rober-rt."

I selected a glass and filled it for her. I chose a bottle of beer and pulled off the serrated top with an opener. I didn't bother with a glass but drank it from the bottle.

She sat down and I sat opposite her. I felt curiously calm and began to talk easily of this and that. All the time I watched her and I could see underneath the casual exterior was supreme tension. I had caught her out in the process of about to do something. I knew I must not let her know I knew. I had to persuade her her story about surprise meals had convinced me, too. It suddenly occurred to me that this was a really dangerous situation. But I was taller than she and stronger and also I had the advantage of a certain wariness.

I leaned back in the chair, simulating relaxation. "So, what is all this about a beautiful meal? It sounds too good to be true."

She smiled. "Yes, everything is in the kitchen. I went in there first." That was true at any rate. When I had pushed Nell in through the door I had seen carrier bags and whatnot all over the work surface.

"Well, shall we go and have a look at everything? Perhaps I can help." I got up and walked to the door of the kitchen. She followed me. Nell flew out like a bullet, cannoning violently into Madeleine, knocking her off her feet.

I shouted at Nell but stopped, frozen into silence. I couldn't believe the hell of what was happening in front of me.

It seemed to me that Madeleine began to fall apart. The essence of the person is often encapsulated in the outward appearance and though that may change as years go by, you cope with it easily as the change is so gradual. But this was different. This was like the unmasking of the Phantom of the Opera or Dorian Grey or some such character for she stopped being Madeleine and became someone quite different. But not, as I stood there in ever-increasing horror, watching, God help me, someone I did not know.

It was simple, really, an illusion, all of it from start to finish. As Nell flew at her, she fell. Nell snapped at Madeleine as she started to get up and the part she got hold of was her hair. And her hair came off. Just like that. In one piece. It was left hanging from Nell's jaws. It wasn't real. It was a wig. And as I looked at Madeleine I knew she wasn't real, either. She wasn't Madeleine at all. She wasn't even a woman.

She was a young man, with false eyelashes and woman's make-up and eyebrows painted on and no hair. She was as bald as a coot.

Madeleine was the helicopter engineer.

2

"So..." The voice was the same, I thought, staring at this monstrous thing in front of me. "So, your horrible dog has uncovered my disguise. No matter. I am going to kill you anyway and it doesn't matter if you still believe me to be Madeleine or not."

I could barely take it in, but my mind was beginning to move pretty fast through these new facts that presented themselves. "Who are you?"

"Well now, Rober-rt, I will tell you. But give me another drink for this repulsive animal of yours has spilled mine and just in case you think of doing something you might regret, perhaps this will persuade you."

I couldn't believe all this rubbish. It was like something out of a poor quality gangster film. I stifled the desire to laugh but found suddenly that was not too difficult. I found myself looking down the barrel of a hand gun.

My mouth couldn't form any words for a moment. I opened it to say something and nothing came out.

"And put that creature in the kitchen again."

I bent down and slowly put Nell in the kitchen and shut the door. She looked at me, her tail drooping, she sensed something had happened and it was her fault. I stroked her ears. "It's all right. Good girl. Stay." I shut the door and felt as if my last friend had deserted me.

I walked over to the sideboard again and poured out another drink and handed it over. My brain stopped being a numb and useless thing and I started to think fast. I had to find out who this monster was and I wanted to stay alive. And I had to get hold of Sam.

I smote my hand to my brow. "God, I've got a friend coming round in half an hour. I've only just remembered. That is why I came back to London tonight, so we could meet."

"Madeleine" or whoever it was, stared at me. "You had better ring and tell them not to come. What is your friend's name?"

"Sam. Sam Stewart."

"How chummy! Is that the word? Makes a change for a womaniser such as you to spend an evening with the boys!"

Evenings with on-duty senior police officers weren't chummy at all and I was angered to be called a womaniser when I wasn't. I opened my mouth to say something but changed my mind. The helicopter engineer was speaking again. "You know the number?" I nodded. "Then call. I will stand next to you so I can hear the conversation the other end and if there is a problem I shall shoot you. Is that clear?"

"Very."

"Get on with it, then."

I pressed the buttons and held the receiver to my ear. Sam answered. I spoke before Sam had a chance to say something else.

"Hi... This is Robert Berkeley speaking. I wonder if you would be good enough to give Sam a message for me?"

I heard Sam's voice, instantly on guard. There was only the briefest of hesitations. "Yes, of course. What is the message?"

I glanced sideways at the grey metal, like a child's toy, resting on the engineer's arm. "Can you tell... him... um, tell... him..."

Sam's voice was sharper now. "What? Can I tell him what?"

"Can you tell him I cannot meet him at the flat tonight after all. An old friend has dropped by - from France, so..."

"Right. A friend from France. I have got the message. I can assure you that he'll get it. Goodbye."

I put the receiver gently down...

... Just...

He waved the gun at me and I went back to the sofa and sat down again. "Good. Now that is all right. But I hope for your sake he gets the message."

I prayed, so did I, but said nothing. The phone was just off the hook and I sent up another prayer to the Almighty that he wouldn't notice. I had done all I could for the moment for outside help. I now had to keep him talking and see what else came out of it. If I could get him to give me some sort of confession, even if he killed me, it would be something. But I wasn't going to give up yet...

Chapter 21

1

Extracted from Police records (7)

Sam stared at the phone, frowning hard and began to listen to the recording going on a few miles away but not for long. "Oh... shit..."

"Boss?" Sergeant Evans looked up across the desk.

"Robert Berkeley. He's in serious trouble!"

"Christ!"

Sam leapt across the room, heading for the door, screaming orders into a radio phone. "Cordon off Putney High Street, Putney Bridge, Lower Richmond Road and Waterman Street. Armed response unit to Robert's flat. No sirens in the immediate area. Emergency support vehicles. Go, go, go! Now!"

2

I cleared my throat. "So, who are you?"

He drank a little more and smiled, swilling the contents round and round. "Ah yes, well I don't see why you shouldn't know. I am Madeleine's brother, Jean-Marc. Jean-Marc de la Flèche." He spoke the name with obvious pride.

I stared at him, taking it in. He put down the drink and pulled off his false eyelashes one after the other. I watched him. His arms were brown and hairless. I glanced down at his legs below the calf-length jeans he wore. They were smooth and hairless, too. I wondered why he shaved his hair off. It can't have been a disguise. Women didn't shave their arms, as far as I was aware. And as I thought it a picture came into my mind, a picture of Madeleine as I lit her cigarette on that first evening, the little pale gold hairs shining on the back of her brown skin.

He was watching me. My train of thought appeared to manifest itself to him. "I was born with no hair and I never grew any. It is a medical condition. I have no hair anywhere. Naturally, it does not bother me but since I had to pretend to be Madeleine, I had to wear a wig."

"Why did you pretend to be Madeleine?"

He have a short laugh. "I hardly imagine you would make such efforts to keep the friendship of a man and a stranger, at that. I do not doubt Madeleine would have succumbed to your attempts at seduction without delay. Even if you had been interested in a man sexually, which I presume you would not be, I would not be the one. I am a virgin. Sex is a repulsive, disgusting activity no matter which sex is one's preference. That is not what I am here for. I am here for revenge."

"Revenge?"

"Yes. To us, the family de la Flèche, the family is everything. Someone hurts one of us and we never forgive and we hunt them down and make them pay. Your family has done terrible hurt to mine. I would not let it rest."

"Hurt? What hurt? What are you talking about? My father is dead. You killed him and my brother. It is you who have hurt my family not the other way around. Why, my father hasn't even spoken to your grandfather in fifty something years! I have never heard such a load of balls about revenge. What have we, the Berkeleys, ever done to you?" In spite of my fear, I was shaking with rage.

His voice was like a quiet snake. His green eyes, those eyes I had thought unique, glittered in the darkened room. "So, you believe that is the truth, do you? You should have talked to your father, mon ami, when you had the chance. He could have told you a story or two about that. My grandfather cares about only two things, the honour of France and the honour of his family. It is the code by which we all live. I have accomplished two thirds of my mission. When I have killed you I shall have succeeded in avenging it."

I sat there, curiously detached. I found myself thinking how he must have rehearsed this nonsense. It was over-dramatic and ludicrous. But I realised he was in real and deadly earnest and by saying what I had, I had touched a nerve and now this dangerous man was bitterly and terribly angry. I had to calm him, somehow, or it would be too late for Sam.

"Please tell me what it is we have done, then, that you hate us so. Maybe I can make amends... do something... I don't know, but I can't do anything until I know."

He stared at me. He smiled. "It was so easy, killing William. The helicopter engineers were so easy to dupe. Your security firms are a joke in England."

"You meant to kill William?" I couldn't believe what I was hearing.

He stared at me coldly. "Of course I meant to kill him. What ever did you think? I don't make mistakes."

Was this bravado or did he really get the right man? "But why did you want to kill William?"

His eyes registered cold and bitter fury. "Because of the damage he has done. She was as dear to me as any sister could be. He took up with her, seduced her, made love to her, the disgusting, immoral bastard, sex, always sex, and then threw her away as soon as she fell in love with him. And without a true word of explanation. I don't believe she

220

will ever get over it. He took everything from her and cast her aside. If he had thoughts of her at all he must have known what he was doing. Such behaviour, it is worthy of death and so I killed him."

His sister! Madeleine was his sister. I felt a shock of real, physical pain. I had tried hard not to believe William had been in love with Madeleine in spite of the evidence to the contrary but he hadn't had the courage to tell me. That's why it had been a secret. Oh, God, William, as if it had mattered... I struggled to get back to some sort of reasoned questioning. "But how did you know he was flying the helicopter?"

"He told her, like a fool. She was coming down to see him fly it. Then a little while after he told her to get out of his life for ever and never see him again. He broke her heart. The fact he cried as he told her meant nothing. They were false tears. I told her so. She was staying in London ready to go down to Hampshire to meet you and the rest of his family. I was in England, too and I met her and she told me. I was coming anyway to kill your father and so I planted the bomb so it would kill William. I succeeded. I killed him first, that was all. It did not matter but I certainly meant your brother to die that day."

"Why then," I struggled to get out the words, "why then did you wish to kill my father?"

"Your father?" He spat on the floor. I wanted to hit him but dared not move. "I do not believe you do not know. He sabotaged the mission at Viezy. It was he who killed our villagers and wrecked the plan of the Resistance. He was a mass murderer of the most vile sort. He had to die. Jean-Yves said so."

"My father...? You lying bastard! My father wouldn't have hurt a fly! He was an honourable man, you..."

He leaned forward, the gun pressed against me. "He was a traitor. Jean-Yves told me." His eyes glinted madly again. Oh God, I must be more careful! I swallowed. I just had to keep him talking.

"So, now you want to kill me..."

"Yes, of course." He sneered at me. "You and your brother are just the same. You take advantage of Madeleine. You turn her into a prostitute. She was pure and sweet, untouched by men and their disgusting lust." Not the girl I slept with, I thought. She was the most experienced female I'd ever encountered, without a doubt. "She is nothing now. Yet she had to come back and see you that one night. I asked her not to come, begged her, but she got away from me. She said it would keep you interested so I had continued access to your family. I knew you had decided you didn't really want to see me again. I tried to keep her from you but, no, your body, your bed, the vileness of the sexual practices you encouraged her to perform on you and with you..." Jesus, I thought, he's completely crazy. Madeleine might have been experienced but she performed a quite normal range of variations on the theme of sex. She simply had been very good at them. "I made her tell me all about it, what she did to you, what you did to her..." His eyes were wild and his breath came shorter. Oh, he was that sort of nutcase, was he? Condemning sex one second but actually getting off on it vicariously. This got worse, I thought. "Poor Madeleine, she is not to blame. You seduced her, turned her from the path of righteousness and made her a whore..."

I stared at him. It explained that which I had not yet dared to contemplate, for I knew with an absolute assurance that it was a woman in my dimly lit room and in my bed the other evening and everything about her had been supremely feminine, curvaceous and soft. Her hair, too was very real - all of it - everywhere... I remembered running my hands through it, holding her head to me and it was certainly no wig, as well as all the rest of the hair on her body. So that night the real Madeleine had returned and yet she had said nothing of William, it had all been about what had been in our past, hers and mine... it was all pretence. In spite of what Will had thought, I doubt if she had loved him at all. She probably set him up for Jean-Marc to kill him. She had laughed with me and thoroughly enjoyed herself. Experienced Madeleine might have been but I know enough about it all to know when a woman is enjoying herself in bed and I knew she had.

He went on. "The men of the Berkeley family have ruined our women, murdered our villagers and betrayed France. You deserve to die. My grandfather agreed with me and applauded the plan."

"Your grandfather?"

"Oh, yes. When I told him what you and William had done, he said I was to seek you out and kill you. Hans got us the bomb." He gave a terrible laugh, high-pitched and wild. He was getting more worked up, I could see. "He did not know who it was for, though. He even talked to my grandfather about him when he saw him. He said he had always loved William Berkeley!" He laughed again.

I was puzzled. "I thought it was Hans who sabotaged the mission in France."

He looked at me and smiled, slowly. "So, you did not know. Well, well, that is strange, then. But it does not matter. No, Hans was a fool, dangerous to some and useful to us but it was not he who was the saboteur."

I was trying to piece things together. I wondered if Sam had met this lunatic or only the real Madeleine. "Where is Madeleine, Jean-Marc?"

"At the Château." He leaned towards me. I could see a pulse beating in his head. His eyes were wild and I suddenly knew, he was mad, completely insane. His reply seemed to confirm it, oddly for he said, "she is unwell sometimes. She is a, a... I don't know the word. She thinks she is two people. She says I am but she's wrong. Very wrong."

"Schizophrenic," I muttered. I thought there are probably two of them in the family.

"Yes, that is it. I am pure. She is defiled for always now. It is you who have driven her into this state, you and your disgusting, immoral, depraved behaviour. I am thankful you will rot in hell, away from her for ever."

He's a religious nutcase, I thought, as well as all the other sorts of craziness he displayed. He thinks he's some sort of avenging angel. What in God's name am I going to do now? You can't argue rationally with lunatics.

I don't know if I heard the noise first or he did but it was a tiny one and I knew it to be the door to the hall opening outside. He knew it, too and was on me like a limpet, arm round my neck and the gun at my head. And that was how Sam saw me as they pushed the door aside and stood, three of them armed, Sam seemingly not one of them, guns pointing.

One of them shouted. "This is the police! We are armed! Drop your weapon!"

3

The arm round my neck was tight and I could hardly breathe.

"I do not think so. When there is shooting, I will do it."

In a sort of despair I saw them carefully, slowly, put down their guns and I saw them swiftly take in the scene. Sam started to speak. "Jean-Marc..."

"You know who I am, then?" There was pride in his voice.

"Yes, of course. I have just returned from France. I have talked to Madeleine and she told me all about you."

The gun dug further into my neck. "She is mad. Unbalanced. You cannot believe her."

"Must I not? Listen Jean-Marc, your grandfather has given up his bid to be President. Madeleine has told me everything. You just stop this now, before you hurt someone, or you get hurt yourself." Sam's voice was like silk.

I felt Jean-Marc start to tremble. When he was in charge and the plan going well he was relaxed and sure of himself. If it started to unravel he did, too. Now he was being forced to listen to another viewpoint, one he was not prepared for, or contemplated as a possibility. He was always right. He was being made to listen to the beginnings of relentless persuasion and he was not capable of holding his ground and he knew it. He was now at his most dangerous and I could hear it.

"Let Robert go, Jean-Marc. It can only make things worse for you now and the British courts will understand, believe me."

He screamed at Sam. "He would never give up! He has always wanted to be President. I do not believe you! Get down, you!" He forced me to the floor and put his foot on my neck. I could feel the cold of the metal on the back of my head.

Sam went on, there was hardly a tremor there, almost like a hypnotist, quiet and coaxing. "But it is true, Jean-Marc. He is getting old now, he said. He wants the quiet life so he can live with you and Madeleine at the Château. He looked very tired and I think he has made a wise choice. He thinks the past should lie down. There has been enough killing. Give me your gun and then we can take you home to see him and you will see that I am telling the truth."

Suddenly he removed his foot from my back and stood up. I didn't know where the gun was pointing but I didn't dare move. Blood was hammering through my head and I thought my heart would burst through my ribs, but I tried to breathe as quietly as possible. The room was still and quiet with tense expectancy, no sound from the river, no rumble of the traffic in the distance. God, this was... hell...

"I will telephone him. Get me the number."

"That's a good idea, Jean-Marc. A very good idea... Now..."

He dug me in the back, "Get up. You can get the number for me. I shall not let go the gun."

I got up slowly. Sam was standing in front of me, slightly to the left, outwardly relaxed and smiling at Jean-Marc. "Fine, that's fine..."

I picked up the handset and put my finger on the little glowing red light to disconnect the previous call and get the dialling tone. I started to dial the international code for France. He gave me the number and I repeated it, slowly, after him, one number at a time.

Sam sprang like a cat, knocking his arm upwards and away from me as, off guard momentarily, he watched me pressing the buttons. The gun went off and the bullet hit the window to disappear outside towards the swirling black waters of the Thames. The policeman nearest to me shouted and pulled me downwards and away and suddenly there was mayhem, a chaotic, seething mass of people and in the middle was Sam, on the floor now with Jean-Marc screaming with rage and madness, the gun still in his hand, but now held above his head as Sam forced him onto the floor on his back.

I couldn't see anything, only hear the terrifying sounds of bitter physical combat. I tried to get away from the policeman but he held me tightly and I couldn't move. He told me to stay still. I felt desperate. I was afraid, terribly afraid but more than anything I wanted to help Sam. Then deafeningly loud and close there was a second shot and immediately a third and then a silence, broken only by firstly a male scream that immediately lapsed into agonised groaning, that lasted half an eternity.

"Sam! Sam!" I was frantic and scrabbled at the policeman who was holding me. He let me go and I stood up.

Sam was standing now looking down at Jean-Marc. His head was torn open by the bullet and blood flowed out over the carpet in a violent red stream. It was a sick-making sight. One of the policemen was on the floor, blood pouring from his thigh and it was he who was in agony. Sam was breathing hard, dishevelled, jacket torn, gun holster exposed now from under it, hand bleeding, the gun in it, just standing there, almost reverently, it seemed and glanced at the sergeant who was staring down at what remained of Jean-Marc, his gun still trained at the shattered head. He lowered it slowly.

"I hate killing people, Jock, even... fucking madmen like this one," and the huge policeman who towered over everyone there leaned over and rumpled Sam's hair as one might a child who had said something rather touching. It was an extraordinary moment to witness but the mood did not last for more than a split second.

"Don't think like that. You done well, Chief. Couldn't let this one get away with it." He turned immediately and fell on the floor beside his colleague and started to help with the attempt to stem the bleeding. Someone was talking into a radio demanding an ambulance.

Sam snapped out orders. Police radios sprang into use, photographers appeared from nowhere and it swarmed with police and white-overalled forensic teams. I sank onto the sofa but they moved me off to the bedroom and people looked after me. Sam, swiftly and confidently in charge, gave me a quick smile. "OK, Rob? You did brilliantly, keeping him talking. You'll get a medal, I shouldn't wonder!"

"Bollocks."

And to my dismay, I leaned back on the heaped up pillows, relief rushing through me and tears began to roll down my face and I did nothing to stop them.

4

The mess was indescribable but they assured me someone would eventually clear it all up. The flat swarmed with all sorts of official people, uniformed and otherwise. Eventually, they took away Jean-Marc's body and in a slight lull in the proceedings I managed to have a brief conversation with Sam, now with a hastily bandaged hand, the second bullet of Jean-Marc's actually grazing it.

"Is that true then, all you told him? Has Jean-Yves given up his attempt to be President?"

Sam looked at me. "Oh, yes, well, forced to, to be absolutely accurate. I'll tell you all the actual details later. Now, can you come over to my office, Rob? We must take your statement and it's going to be ages here, so we need to get you out of it. These guys are going to be around for hours."

"Sure. I'll get my jacket and bring Nell, if I may."

"Bring Nell, yes, of course. Don't drive, though. We'll take you in one of the cars."

"I'd rather be independent. I might actually go back to Hampshire after you've finished with me, if that's all right. Just for tonight, anyway. Then I'll come back."

"All right. Yes, of course that's fine."

I found a jacket and my keys and Nell, who was quite unfazed by everything. She was used to guns, of course. Some dogs would be shaking like jellies for days but not a Labrador and together we left the flat. Outside the road was closed off and there were determined, neck-craning spectators here and there that the police held back and TV cameras arriving and all sorts of activity. I slipped off behind the building and into the car park, away from them all.

"My car, Nell. Find my car!" Nell ran in front of me, excitedly looking about her, delighting in the game we had. I could see her ahead of me, tail wagging beside it in the gloomy lights that lit the area. I called across the space to her, fishing in my pocket for the electronic key which slipped from my hand onto the ground. "OK, Nell! Well done! Clever girl!" Her tail wagged faster. I bent down behind a car that was between us, masking me from her momentarily. I picked up my escaped keys. I pressed the remote control and the world exploded into pain and blackness punctuated by brilliant lights and deafening noise. And then, mercifully for me, it went black again.

.

Chapter 22

1

The world was pale now as I opened my eyes and there were funny little squeaking blips going on around me. I wondered if it might be the dawn chorus as I was obviously in bed but they didn't sound like any birds that I knew. I was quite relaxed and drowsy but gradually became less so, coming back to reality. I turned my head sideways and found myself looking straight into some bright brown female eyes. This was rather pleasant. I wondered why Inno was in my bedroom. Maybe she'd had a change of heart. I hadn't expected that. Oh well, why not? I reached out to her.

"Hello, Inno. Come here, beautiful..."

"Rob! Darling Rob...!"

This was decidedly encouraging but when I looked at her again, I found she was crying. Not so good.

"Don't cry, sweet. There's nothing to cry for, silly old you."

"Oh, Rob!"

Someone else came and stood beside Inno. Another girl, pretty, but I didn't know her. "How do you do? Are you a friend of Inno's?"

She laughed and took my hand which was unexpected but rather nice. "I'm a friend of yours, Robert, actually," and I heard Inno laugh as well, through her tears, rather a watery sort of laugh.

I looked round me. I was nowhere I knew. I glanced back at them. "Where the hell am I?"

The girl I didn't know but who seemed to know me sat on the edge of my bed. "Can't you remember anything?"

I stared at her. Something was there and I struggled to recall it. I moved and found my hand was wired up to something. I looked at it. It was an intravenous drip. I became aware there were wires and tubes all over me and then took in the fact my right arm was in plaster. I looked back at her, anxiously now. She was a nurse, I suddenly realised.

"Here, who are you? I seem to be in hospital for some reason..." I stopped. And then I remembered. It came back to me in a rush, Jean-Marc and his bloody gun, all the death and blood and carnage and Sam standing over him with a revolver and then... nothing... Nothing at all... and now I was here.

I took in a sharp breath, the horror of it all hitting me sharply like diving into icy water. "Oh Christ! Sam killed him! He tried to... he... oh, my God!"

I began to shake all over and the blip things I could hear started to go faster. The girl soothed me and stuck something into the drip above me and I became drowsy once more. Inno disappeared for a while and then I woke up again. I remembered everything that I remembered before but I was calm about it. I saw more people I didn't know, doctors, surgeons, more nurses and they talked to me about myself for ages, it seemed and I listened but said little. I shifted uncomfortably in the bed and looked about me.

"Hello, Rob."

It was Sam.

We looked at each other for a moment. "Hello, Sam. You got him, then, that lunatic bastard."

"Yes. We got him. You helped. Helped enormously. Do you remember?"

"Yes, I think so. But why am I here? I didn't think he shot me, did he?" I was puzzled.

Sam's face was tragic. "No, Rob. It was a bomb. In your car. Don't you remember?"

"No."

Sam tried again and I could see it was an effort. "It was my fault. I should not have removed the watch so soon. I thought you were safe. I thought they were after your father and killed Will instead but after murdering your father that was it. I didn't know they were after all of you, you see. Jean-Marc planted a bomb in your car. I don't know if he knew you were on to him or not, he probably did but he was going to make sure of you if he could. He wired it to the door lock. Your remote control triggered it instead of a physical key. He chose the wrong mechanism to set it off. If he had been better schooled at his task you would be... d-dead, Rob." Sam's voice shook. "I'm so sorry you've been hurt. It was my fault."

I denied this forcefully. "No, no, Sam. You've been wonderful. You caught him. That's all that matters. They tell me I shall be able to leave intensive care later today and then go into a room of my own on an ordinary ward. I'm getting better, see? They told me all that and I can remember it all." I was restless, though, trying to recall something that was there in my mind somewhere but I couldn't find the trigger to release it. "I can't remember the explosion." But I felt instantly desperately tired and I went to sleep again.

In a few days I was sufficiently well enough to walk about and sit up and read the papers, turning the pages with my left hand, my broken upper right arm in plaster beneath a bandaged broken collar bone. Visitors began to pour in and I had had a look at my cheekbone which had been sliced in one place with broken glass but would mend well with virtually no scarring, if any, the surgeon told me. I grinned, for I had a bit of a reputation in the family for being on the vain side. Served me right, probably.

Flowers filled the room and it smelled like a florist's shop and one day Sam came back and we continued our conversation. This time I was properly awake and could take things in better. Sam sat in the high-backed chair next to my bed and I listened.

"Jean-Yves is in prison, awaiting trial. Madeleine...", Sam sighed. "Madeleine was arrested but what we didn't know was she managed to take some of her own poison. She killed herself in her cell. The French police are very fed up with themselves but I can't blame them. It was hidden in her earrings, of all things. It doesn't take much of it to kill someone. Jean-Marc had some in his signet ring. It was probably where he kept the dose he gave your father."

I nodded. I knew it hadn't been in the handbag. I had seen it outside his room on the chest. I watched Sam as I listened. It seemed unreal, all of it. I could hardly believe it was all part of me and my life. It seemed like someone recounting the story of a film they had seen recently. "I see. So we'll never know about her and William, will we? If it was true, I mean."

"Not from her, Rob, no, I fear me. However, we'll see if we can't find out something else when you're a bit better."

"Hm. There's something about it I simply don't believe, Sam. I really knew William and I actually don't believe this of him. To begin with I was hurt he hadn't confided in me and I was sad about that. I didn't give a damn about Madeleine."

"Didn't you?"

"No. Not in that way."

"I thought she was special... I mean, you reported much of your meeting with her to Adrian Merchant and..."

"Yes. But he was insistent I recall anything about France, associations, people etc, that's all. That episode was all I could think of - well, all there was. Just one holiday, one... one encounter. That was all. All she'd been was an extremely experienced one night stand."

"And you said nothing after the revelations at the Savoy, when we left, I mean. I was concerned you really loved her..."

"God, no. Really. I was just thinking about Will and not accepting it. I couldn't believe it and I still don't. If Will genuinely cared for her, then that was fine with me. I was simply sad to think he thought he might have caused me pain, and misplaced guilt made him keep it all from me. That was all. But later, lying here thinking, as I have been, with nothing else to do, I think there must be another reason. There must be another explanation that is staring us in the face, somehow. I cannot believe she was the girl who Will would want to spend his life with. Really. We liked the same sort of girls, yes, but she didn't fall into that category. She truly didn't. Not in mine and therefore not in his. He'd have spent the night with her in the way I did, if it had been offered, I'm sure and that, too would have been the end of it."

"I see. Well, we'll see what we can dig up."

"Anyway, go on. Tell me about how you caught Jean-Yves. Did you suspect him at all or did he confess or what?"

Sam watched me. "No, not really, or rather, not at first. But I suspected him, all right. I had done for a while but my difficulty was trying to prove it without leading you into saying things you thought might fit, if you follow me. It was Jean-Yves who gave himself away to me to begin with. He said a very vital thing. It was when I was talking to him about Hans being the saboteur. He said once the Nazis got you, you were theirs for ever. It was true. But it wasn't Hans he was thinking of at that moment, it was himself. Let me go back a bit further."

I lay back on my pillows and went on listening to this extraordinary tale.

"You will recall the letters you found in the horse's leg?"

"Yes, I remember that, all right."

"I went up to the nursery after I had left you and had a look at it myself. I tipped it onto the floor and a bit further up inside the leg was something else. I hooked it out with a wire coat hanger that I took from the wardrobe in the next room. There was another rolled up piece of paper in it, two pieces, in fact. I have photocopies here. Perhaps you would like to read them."

I took them. They were both in French but undated. The hand was unmistakably foreign but they were easy to read. The first one was quite long.

"15d Rue de St Denis

Paris

Dear William

I am writing this now for I am safe. As you see I am in Paris. Even here, I am safer than at the farm but the Nazis are beaten, the British have come and the Americans and all will be well in France again soon. Jean-Yves does not know my address.

You must know this now. It was Jean-Yves who betrayed you. I always suspected him of something underhand. He was always like that, even as a child. I overheard him talking one night when I could not sleep. He was talking to Celestine and he was laughing and he was proud. She was not. He was taunting her with the knowledge. I was horrified and felt sick but then I was afraid, too. He is rich for they paid him a fortune to do it. One day, though, he will be a hero. France will not know the truth, he will see to that.

I don't know if you should tell Pierre or Hans, maybe not, I don't know. I leave that up to you. But you must never return to France, my beloved William, not now. He will kill you, for once he has discovered I have gone he will know why and he will know that I have told you. I had to go. His fervour terrifies me. I suppose, really, he is mad, in a way. This knowledge will put you in danger but you had to know for if you come to France, he would not be sure you knew or not and he would have you killed anyway. To protect you, I am telling you. In the end I expect you would have worked it out, maybe you have already.

They will tell the rest of the family and what neighbours there remain in Viezy that I have left to hide my secret from the world. I have, but it is not the secret he suggests.

I have been so happy with you but there can be no future for us now. I think I have always known that. Now, with Jean-Yves waiting for you, it can never be. I will not leave France to be with you because I know you cannot marry a peasant girl like me. I don't mind. I never did and understand completely. I love you and I will always. I cannot leave France and you cannot come here, but I will never forget you and our child when it comes in a few weeks' time will always, always be something to remind me of you for ever, my beloved.

Adieu, dearest William. I love you so much,

Dominique."

I read it twice and looked up to see Sam watching me. "So, it was him. That was why my father never returned to France."

"Yes. It must have been terrible for him. But I imagine he knew it would be difficult to prove and also, I suppose, he didn't tell Hans and Pierre because they would have been in danger as well as himself. Read the other letter."

This one was very short and this time there was no address, it simply said, "Paris" at the head.

"Dearest William,

Our baby died. He was beautiful but only lived a few hours. I am so very sorry. I will never get over this sorrow, for the baby who did not live and because you and I have nothing any more that binds us together.

My love to you, always,

Dominique."

I was moved by this pathetic little note. "Poor Dominique. First to lose her lover and then her baby. Do we know who she was, Sam?"

"Yes. She was Jean-Yves' cousin. She became your father's mistress during his stay in Viezy."

"Did Jean-Yves tell you that?"

"No, Rob. Your mother did."

I nearly flew out of bed. "My mother?!" Pain shot agonisingly through my collar bone and I sank back onto the pillows, swearing.

"God, are you OK?"

"Yes, yes. Shit, that fucking hurts! Jesus! Sorry... sorry... Oh my God!... Just - Oh Christ! Just... G-go on..."

"Are you sure? Shall I get someone? God, Rob..."

"I'm OK. I just have to remember to be more careful of myself yet awhile. Just... go on."

Watching me anxiously, Sam continued, rather more cautiously. "After I found these letters, I realised there was a lot missing. I had to try and find out as much as I could before I left for France. As you will recall your mother returned from Cornwall with Helena. I interviewed her alone. Amongst other things I asked her if there was anything else she could tell me about his life in the war that she hadn't told already, however unimportant it might seem or... however painful. After a moment she got up and went to her room. She returned bringing with her a very old, crumpled letter. She told me it had been written to her shortly after she married your father and it was from Dominique. It was a sad little letter but full of affection. She introduced herself to her in the letter as the cousin of a colleague and someone who had been very fond of your father during the war. She said she wanted to tell her to be happy and make William happy. Her connections with him finished the moment he left France and the baby they expected had died. She had met someone else and she was expecting another child. Your mother never said anything to your father. She said she could see it had gone deep at the time but it was in the past and she would neither think of it further nor refer to it. She never heard from Dominique again and that was that. So coupled with the other two letters it was easy enough to piece things together."

"Why had she not said anything before?"

"Because she couldn't see any connection. She had no reason to suppose that the person who wrote to her had any tie in with terrorists, either past or present and indeed, the thread was pretty thin in reality let alone in imagination. Why, she might even be dead, your mother thought, as she might, of course. We can't trace Dominique, you see."

I spoke slowly, taking in this new development. "How strange. It is like we were saying some time ago, about our parents not having a life before we appeared on the scene. And Will and I would have had a half-brother somewhere, too, if the child had lived."

"Yes, that's true."

Another thought struck me. "Why did she not say anything to me when I turned up with Madeleine, or Jean-Marc rather, pretending to be Madeleine? She must have seen the connection then."

"No. Why should she? There were no surnames mentioned in the letter and your father had never once referred to Jean-Yves de la Flèche."

I mused for a while, Sam watching me, waiting till I was ready before going on with the tale. "This was what my father meant when he was ill about not telling Mother. He still believed she didn't know. That is remarkable, really, after all those years. I wonder how it was she never said anything." I remembered something else, too. "He thought Madeleine, or Jean-Marc, rather, was Dominique. There must have been a very strong family resemblance between them all. Do they look like Jean-Yves?"

"No, not particularly, something in the walk perhaps, and he is tall, as they are but that was all. He certainly doesn't have green eyes. They were bright blue and very piercing."

"So, what then, you confronted Jean-Yves with the letters?"

"No, not straight away. I went to Limoges first and, after a lot of bother, got them to exhume Pierre's body. I wasn't happy with that letter from his widow's. I met her and talked to her and she was shocked and horrified but keen to have justice done. Pierre didn't have a stroke any more than your father did. He was poisoned by the same poison, administered by the same hand, too."

"How? Surely Jean-Marc didn't sneak into his hotel room and force him to drink it?"

"No. In fact, when I say the same hand, I was forgetting for the moment that it was Jean-Marc who came to Forbridge that day, supplied with poison by Madeleine. It was Madeleine who killed Pierre. She simply put it in his drink while he was at the château with Jean-Yves and Hans. It is possible he implied he knew who was the saboteur and they simply had to eliminate him. Your father certainly never told him, his widow was emphatic about that but he may have worked it out as Dominique said Sir William might. I don't know. But anyway, Madeleine killed him. Madeleine knew the truth about Jean-Yves, she said, she knew he was the saboteur but not Jean-Marc. He believed him to be a hero. Jean-Yves told him it was your father who had done it. He did it on purpose to manipulate Jean-Marc into murdering your father. And it worked because Jean-Marc was seriously unbalanced, you realised, of course."

I thought back again. "That was why she was so appalled when we turned up at the château. Here were the two sons of the man who knew her grandfather was a fraud."

"Yes, indeed. It was a dreadful moment for her but she got round it all right, as you know!" Sam gave me a quizzical look.

"Yes. I can remember that, whatever else I may have forgotten! Though to be honest, I'd prefer not to! And Pierre, he died at the auberge, then?"

"Yes. He was already feeling unwell when he arrived there for the evening. The contents of his stomach were analysed and he had eaten only in the late afternoon - while he was at the château. It is fortunate that the vast majority of Catholics are buried and not cremated. It helped our case a lot, as you can imagine, with two poisonings. The mushrooms grow on the estate. We found them and there were more in Madeleine's room. She was the chemist, it seems."

"My God, what a family."

"Yes, dreadful. Latter-day Borgias, every last one."

"And Hans?"

"Well, his death is not down to the de la Flèche tribe, at any rate. Someone else did that for them. Jean-Yves commissioned the bomb through Jean-Marc who went to Holland to meet him. We got that much out of an informer in Holland but it was going to be difficult to use as there was no way this fellow could come to court. He'd be killed and his whole family, instantly. But we used it to put pressure on Jean-Yves and it worked. You see, once we kept coming back at him with more and more information that we substantiated, he could see he was beaten. It was then he gave in. He wasn't specially clever, I think but he used his power to his advantage all the time, backed up with the heavy stuff, like the Mafia. He didn't tell Hans why the bomb was needed. I don't know if Hans would have supplied the information if he had known, we can only speculate. Probably he would, considering what else we know about him but we can't ever be sure."

I was silent for a while, taking it all in, up-dating my thoughts. "No, we can't be sure. But what then?"

"I now had all sorts of information about them. I called on him and talked. I produced the letter from Dominique and I thought he was going to have a fit. Madeleine tried to run for it but the Gendarmerie caught her in the grounds and they were both arrested. The French papers are outraged. I think they would rather have not found out and made him President, as far as I can make out."

"Why did he try all this now? Why did he not try and kill him before?"

"I think that is not too hard to work out. You see, it is only comparatively recently he has tried to be President. When she told him you two had turned up at the château he wasn't sure if you knew about him or not but he couldn't take the risk. He had to eliminate you all and, fortunately for him, his grandson was a madman and easily suggestible. Madeleine wasn't much better either. He told Jean-Marc about you and William and that you were the sons of the saboteur. The rest Jean-Marc did on his own, with a little help from his friends."

"Oh, God, Sam, if we hadn't stayed at that bloody place, you mean..."

Sam frowned. "No, Rob. Don't think like that. He almost certainly would have had a go at your father, you know. He knew that Sir William knew his good reputation was a false image. Don't dwell on things we can't ever prove. Fate is a curious creature. Jean-Marc, as you know, is dead."

"You knew who he was?"

"Yes, we established that earlier before arriving at the Château. We simply showed the photo of the helicopter engineer to people in the local village, including Gaston, his father. And Gaston has helped us, too. He has a strange story as well."

"Gaston is Jean-Yves' son?"

"That's right. I interviewed him quite without his knowing his father had been arrested and also his children were alive then, too. He is supposed to be divorced, but he is not. His wife lives in an apartment in Dover. She works as a translator for UK Border Control. Every four weeks or so, Gaston comes over to Dover for the weekend which he spends with her and then goes back to the farm. They had to set up this lunatic scheme because they were terrified Jean-Yves would kill her. You see, Gaston's mother, Celestine, knew about Jean-Yves' little wartime games, as we know from Dominique's letter. She couldn't live with this and left him, saying she was going to live with her sister in Toulouse. But she never got there. She arrived by train, and walked to her sister's house in the suburbs but before she arrived, she was mown down by a hit and run driver who was never found. Gaston knew it was his father who had killed her. He wasn't at home that evening, saying he was at a meeting with some business associates in Tours, who corroborated it - they were known criminals - but Gaston knew that to be a lie. He knew his children were totally in his clutches but he could and did protect his wife from him. She is now back with him in Viezy."

"Christ! It gets worse!"

"I know."

"Still, Jean-Yves will stand trial and..."

"Well, he's played the crazy card. He's now been admitted voluntarily to a secure hospital for the criminally insane. He'll never get out for if he tries he'll be arrested and sent to prison. He's chosen a terrible end to his life, really. Those places are hell on earth. Still, he made the choice. All the other people he killed had none. I have absolutely no sympathy."

I sat there, thinking, thinking.

Sam went on, "The villagers recognised Jean-Marc from the photograph of the helicopter engineer, as I said but I hadn't worked out that he was pretending to be Madeleine. He gave us that information on the tape when you left the phone off the hook."

I nodded, recalling things, piecing it together and filling in the gaps. I smiled at Sam. "That was Nell's doing, really. If she hadn't gone for him, unmasking him that way, it might have been a very different story. Disney had better make a film about her - the Dog who Unmasked a Gunman! Clever girl! Where is she, by the way? Has someone taken her back to Hampshire?"

Sam's hand closed over mine as it lay on top of the white sheet. The grey eyes were troubled and sad as they looked at me. "Oh Rob, I'm so sorry. Didn't you know?" I stared and said nothing, just shaking my head, knowing, and yet not wanting to admit that I knew for just a few more seconds. "Nell reached the car before you did. She didn't stand any sort of a chance. She's dead, Rob."

Chapter 23

1

So, he had claimed another of us, finally. I was deeply saddened and angered afresh about my poor dog. Inno came to see me again and we talked about her quietly, Inno holding my hand.

"Poor, sweet Nell. She was a lovely dog, Robbie. You will miss her."

"I will. There'll never be another one like her, I know that," and I lay there, thinking about her, running free in the copse, driving up the A3 happy to be with me on my own, her cold, wet nose pushed into my hand when she thought I needed comfort and in sad and eerie chorus with Jess. But there had been no such song for Nell, who had been responsible for saving my life. If I'd been on my own I wouldn't have pressed the remote so soon. It was her signal that she had found it, my acknowledgment of her cleverness. She was a dog in a million.

The door opened and Sam came in again - a very faithful visitor.

Inno smiled. "Well, well, and who's a famous detective again, all of a sudden?"

Sam looked highly embarrassed, giving me a quick, half-smile before turning away again, leaning on the radiator and looking out of the window. "Oh, I don't know, Inno..."

"What's all this?"

Inno looked at me with mock-severity. "Really, Rob, all the time in the world and you don't read your morning newspapers. Right on the front page, too, of all of them, not just the Daily Mail! All the ones I've seen, anyway."

"What is, for heaven's sake? I've been with the doctors all morning. I can go home this afternoon, by all that's wonderful!"

There were exclamations of joy and delight. Inno nodded, pleased with everything. "Excellent! A double celebration."

"Will one of you tell me what is in the paper, now this minute, or I expect I shall have a relapse."

Inno picked up the unopened Times and pointed. "There! Read it!"

I read.

"Following the successful solving of the murders of Sir William Berkeley
and his son, also William, of Forbridge Park, the Police Appointments Board
have announced the promotion to the rank of Superintendent of the officer in

charge of the case, Sam Stewart, formerly Chief Inspector. This startling and shocking case has brought about the arrest of Jean-Yves de la Flèche, who, as well as being charged as an accessory before and after the crime has also been questioned about his role in various wartime atrocities that the case has brought to light. He is currently detained in a high-security mental institution after claiming diminished responsibility. This well-deserved reward is a remarkable appointment for the police..."

and once more Sam's past and aristocratic private life was all over the papers again, just in case anyone had missed it first time round.

The new Superintendent sighed. "Just as I thought they'd got used to me. I actually thought I was beginning not to be a freak at long last! Ah well. That's what comes of being a pioneer, I suppose."

We smiled indulgently and said all the right congratulatory things that Sam would like to hear, at least, I tried and it seemed to evoke the right response, so that was all right.

Inno slipped away, off to hear Charles in court that afternoon. She was very devoted, I was pleased to see and said as much. Sam grinned.

"Oh, yes, besotted, I'd say. Both of them."

We talked for a while. Suddenly a thought struck me. "Since we're both celebrating, why not have dinner together, Sam - this evening, if you're free. I owe you a meal anyway after that Thai takeaway at the flat all those moons ago," I hesitated, "you might have a date, of course..."

Sam smiled. "All those moons ago... Well, yes, all right, why not? And no, I don't have a date, Rob. But I promised you a meal at my flat, too, once. Let's go there. Better for an invalid just out of hospital than gallivanting about on the town! I have something on this afternoon but I'll send a car to fetch you to the office and then you can come back home with me. I think the lads want to give me a celebratory drink first, or something. You could come to that, too."

I smiled, "Oh, the lads do, do they? And the lasses as well, by any chance? But that sounds marvellous! Perhaps I can stop off for some champagne to swell the feast after the booze-up with the lads, that is, as you call them."

Sam wagged a finger at me. "I think you're certainly recovered if you've got that wicked sense of humour back. Anyway, I must be off. I'll see you about six, then."

I smiled and lay back on my pillows. What an achievement for Sam, I thought. I stared out of the window at my view of London, things moving now, taxis, buses, cars all heaving about on a normal day's work while up above them lives were changing all the time. I picked up the phone beside me and called my mother. I would be back in a day or two, I said and smiled as I heard her excited squeak of delight, like a child who is pleased with its birthday present.

I had one more visitor that afternoon, before I left. Word got round that I was to be discharged and the staff nurse from the intensive care unit who had looked after me to begin with came down to say goodbye.

"I'm glad to see you looking so well. You gave us all a fright when you came in, I can tell you." She had bold eyes and a sexy manner, set off rather well by the starchy uniform.

"Did I? I don't remember that."

"Just as well, I always think. Well, we'll miss having our celebrity around. And all the famous people you've attracted, too - novelists and artists and people from the BBC, not to mention your own newly appointed Superintendent!"

"I know! That was pretty good, wasn't it?"

"Yes. Think of it, all that aristocratic background, probably loads of money, successful career and stunning to look at. Some people have all the luck."

I laughed. "Sam hasn't any money! Aristocrats don't, you know!"

"Oh well, stunning to look at, though, nonetheless. Surely you must agree there?"

I thought. "Well, Sam and I were at school together. I think it's difficult to see people like that when you've fished them out of ponds and rescued them from an irate Matron, or something!"

"Really? Well, you look again. Maybe you'll think differently when..."

The door opened and in came the Sister.

"Angela? What are you doing down here bothering Sir Robert?"

I sprang to her defence as she leapt to her feet. "Oh, she's no bother, Sister, really..."

"I just came to say goodbye, Sister."

I grabbed her by the hand and pulled her over the bed, kissing her. "Bye, Staff Nurse and thanks for... everything." I gave her a wink and she scurried from the room, giggling, under the frosty gaze of her superior.

"Well, really, Sir Robert...!"

But I grinned at her and I was pleased to see she was human at last for I saw a faint smile in return before she left me to make up a prescription of pain killers for me to take home in case of need.

The day progressed and Sam's police driver arrived and thus it was quite an escort that took me down in the lift and to the front steps of the hospital. I was hugged and kissed by various nurses which was all quite delightful and, to my embarrassment, I found myself agreeing to come and open their new accident wing early next year. I had never been a celebrity and suddenly I discovered I was one. I squirmed inwardly and knew how Sam had felt now.

We drove through the darkening London streets. It was a fine, clear cold evening and the shops and theatres were bright with lights and bustle and noise. It was good to be out in the world again. The traffic parted obediently before the police car, even without the siren. I was impressed.

I walked along the corridor to Sam's office, trailing in the wake of the constable. He stopped in front of a door where a fellow was unscrewing the nameplate. There were sounds of revelry inside and we went in, and there was Sam, surrounded by a cheerful, irreverent crowd, cans of beer and glasses of wine for some in their hands. Denied alcohol since my admission to hospital, I gratefully took the offered drink.

I looked about. So this, then, was Sam's working environment - desk littered with papers, posters, mug shots, bog standard computer, printer etc, nothing spectacular and nothing grand. There was still a picture of me pinned up next to Sam's desk, one I had given Adrian at the start of it all. Will had taken it, I recalled. He had just made some kind of irreverent, mildly salacious comment, I recalled and my amused expression reflected it. I imagined eventually I would get it back. I joined in with conversations - most of those there I recognised and they all knew me, even without the photo by now probably, which was not surprising. It was pleasant to see them in a different setting, not grave-faced or tense or apologetic, particularly not alarmingly dead-pan or with guns in their hands, just normal, decent people sharing in the success of a colleague. The door opened again to admit a late-comer and another cheer went up, Sam standing in the middle of them all, looking mildly embarrassed but quietly pleased as they admired and applauded the new nameplate, pointed out loudly to the assembled company by the newcomer.

Sam glanced at me. "What do you think of that, then, Rob?"

I nodded, very impressed, looking at the neat black writing embossed on the white background, plain and simple and dignified. "Very nice. And very alliterative, too."

Sam laughed. "So it is!"

I walked over to Sam and put my drink down on the desk beside me. "I think it's time I said thank you for everything. Not much compared with your promotion but, well, it's the best I can do, really, just at this moment. So... thank you for catching those evil bastards, thank you for avenging Will and my father, thank you for saving my life and being there for my mother and... and for me. You and all your team are... well, amazing... the best... and as long as I live I'll never forget what you've done... so, thank you, Sam and... and..." and I bent and kissed the full, soft, sexy mouth, for rather a long time and increasingly not very chastely, amidst a crescendo of cheers and other rather more basic comments, from the clearly smutty-minded attendant colleagues.

Sam came up for air, with a slightly bemused, disorientated look. "R-rob! Really! What sort of authority am I going to have with this lot now, after that?"

"Plenty," I smiled, my good arm tight round that slim form. "Just remind them of the name on the door. See?" I waved at it, "Superintendent Samantha Stewart."

Chapter 24

Sam's large, quiet flat, overlooking St James's Park was as I expected - lovely soft lights, huge, comfortable squashy sofas and carefully chosen pictures, all of which I liked. I opened the champagne very inexpertly with one hand and the bottle clutched to my chest in the crook of my other arm and she fiddled about in the kitchen while I prowled around and looked at things, relaxed and thankful to be out of hospital, however kind they might have been. I needed to put all the pain and suffering behind me for ever. Sam had changed from her designer suit into something soft and black and, to be honest, distinctly alluring, showing off her perfect figure in a way that made my recently returned to normal pulse shoot up again. She called to me every now and then, I wasn't permitted to help, while she prepared things for our meal as I walked about and admired the decor. The sofas were soft velour in pale grey, the lighting subtle and relaxing, an eclectic mix of artwork on the walls, all restful and tranquil and as different as it was possible to imagine from Sam's working life and environment. If this represented the real her, it made it ever more remarkable she had become so successful in the rough and ready world out there, filled with the low-life, dangerous, obsessed, insane dregs of humanity. In the middle of the mantelpiece was a little snuff box, Louis Quinze, that I recognised. I picked it up and took it into the kitchen.

"Sam?"

"Yes?"

"Where did you get this?"

Sam glanced at me swiftly and then put down the knife she was holding and walked slowly towards me and took it. She turned it over and over in her hands. Her head was bent low over it and her long hair, released now from the clip that held it back behind her head that she wore when she was working, fell forward like a curtain, obscuring her face.

"Sam?"

She lifted her head and looked at me. She was suddenly very tense, I could see and there were tears in her eyes. "William gave it to me, Rob."

I remembered it well. "Yes, he bought it from me when I first opened the shop. He said he was acting as an agent and I teased him about it. He said one day I'd know on whose behalf he'd bought it. It was the first item on the list I showed you relating to my business and its sales and purchases, remember? We mentioned it, briefly."

She nodded.

"You didn't say anything about it when we talked about it."

"No. I... no."

"When did he give it to you?"

Sam continued to turn it over and over. "Just after he bought it."

Suddenly I thought I understood, "Oh, Sam, did you and William...? Oh, God, I'm so sorry, I never knew. He didn't say... Oh, Sam."

She spun round on me, fierce suddenly. "No, Rob, no. You've got hold of the wrong end of the stick. I never had an affair with William. He was my friend, my friend... that was all." She shook me to make the point go home. "That was all..."

"But you wished he had been more, is that it?"

Sam took a long breath, shuddering inwards. "No, Rob, I didn't wish he had been more to me. We kept in touch because... because... Oh God, this is it. This is where it ends, before it had a chance to begin and I so wanted, so desperately wanted it to..." she stopped again, appearing unable to find the right words but something seemingly was torn from her, "oh, Christ, was that it? All of it? One very public, wonderful kiss - to last me... a lifetime...?" I took her hand and led her into the sitting room and sat her on the sofa. She was very tense, her hand rigid in mine. I sat beside her, turned sideways to face her. She was staring fixedly at the snuff box.

"Come now, Sam, tell me. What is it? What ends before it begins? Surely you can tell me anything? Bloody hell, you saved my life! Surely that makes us pretty special to each other, doesn't it?"

"You're special to me, Rob, yes... very special..."

"Well?"

Sam simply gazed at me, wanting to talk but not knowing how to say it, whatever it was, I could see. She was very fearful about something.

"Why don't I start you off? If you weren't in love with William, then what was he? A confidante?"

She took another deep breath. "Yes. He was." She held out her hand with the snuff box in the middle of her palm. "He bought me this when you opened your business. I asked him to buy me something, a little something and I would pay him back and I did. I wanted to be your first customer. And I was, he said. I've had this box ever since. I treasure it."

"Yes, it was the first thing I sold. I've always remembered it and always will. It was special to me for that reason." I stared at her, puzzled. "But why? Why didn't you just come and see me and buy it in the shop yourself?"

Sam wriggled. "Because... because you didn't care about me, Rob and I loved you so much. I'd always loved you, even when we were very small, I think. I think I fell in love with you when your parents came up to stay for a Highland Ball when you and William and I were little. I remember we had a feast in the minstrels' gallery and old Duncan brought us plates of food. I don't suppose you remember that. But I do. I thought you were wonderful."

I stared at her, unable to take in what she said. "Yes, I do remember, actually. I was thinking about that evening only a short while ago. I had such a good time, hiding up there with you and Will, when we shouldn't have been. It was just after he died I recalled that, as a matter of fact."

"Did you? I'm glad you remember. And remember happily. Well, that was it, really. When I was old enough to go to boarding school, I begged my parents to send me to Milldale because you were there. They agreed. They didn't know the real reason but they were happy to go along with it. It might have been a break in our family's traditions but it was a good school and they were happy to indulge me. William always knew what I felt about you and he kept in touch to see how I was. He always said," she hesitated and turned away, "he always said... one day you would come to your senses when you had stopped sowing your wild oats. He kept an eye on me and I... well... I needed to know about you, really. Will told me to go out and sow a few wild oats of my own until... until... So... I had an affair or two with other people but it didn't work, it was you I wanted, Robbie. In fact the last guy I went out with asked me to marry him and I said no, I couldn't, because I was in love with someone else. He called me a whore and said I'd used him and every name under the sun and I felt really guilty. He was right, really, you see."

"No, he wasn't. It's reasonable to try, isn't it? He was wrong. He should never have said that. You're just lovely, Sam and..."

"Anyway, I couldn't risk anything again, it was too awful. That was well over a year ago..."

"Oh, Sam! All that time and... nothing... no one?"

"No. No one... so I flung myself into my job. I had a couple of very high profile cases one on top the other..." I nodded. Everyone had heard of these two and had made Sam a household name, "...which took every minute of my time and exhausted me and I didn't have the time or the inclination to try again so I simply waited and hoped, that was all and just kept in touch with Will when I had a spare moment..." Sam stared at the fire in the grate that we had lit as soon as we had arrived. The flames flickered and danced on the soft, pale peach-coloured walls. "And now... Oh... Christ...!"

"Sam..."

She pressed on, the confession, if that is what it was, seemed unstoppable. "When Will was murdered and we knew it was a bomb, I knew we would be called in to take over the case. I was asked to investigate it. They knew I knew your family but I had to say there was no special attachment to any of you. It was a lie but if I told them I cared they wouldn't have let me be in charge and not only did I want personally to discover who killed William, it gave me a chance to see you, almost every day, and to protect you from the world, the intrusive press and from danger." She looked away. "I made a complete balls-up of that bit, though - that shit and the car bomb..."

"No, you didn't. It wasn't your fault. He was a lunatic, and obsessive..."

She shook her head but continued without a pause, tense, desperate, clutching the snuff box close to her. "And now I've told you and you'll leave. I wasn't going to say... I just... just..."

I watched her. She had always been beautiful but it seemed to me that I hadn't really noticed until recently. As I had said to the nurse earlier, although I didn't think it now, Sam had always been part of the furniture. How could I have been so... stupid... My brother had been right. And now, at last, I had come to my senses. But maybe she didn't still want me. All this conversation was about how she had felt once. Something else struck me.

"Sam?"

"Yes?"

"Is that what my father meant that afternoon? When he said something about loving me? I thought he was talking about my mother but..."

She gave rather a sad little smile. "Yes. William knew, as I said, and had obviously talked to your father about what I felt. It was me he was talking about when he said 'she had always loved you,' not your mother, as you thought." She stood up. "I'm so sorry. I never meant to tell you, but well, I thought, now, with the case over and no more excuses to see you, I would just ask you for dinner, this once before you went out of my life again and maybe this time for ever, with no William to, to... no one to plead my case... No one to..." She turned away from me and I knew she was crying.

I moved closer to her and put my good arm round her. "Sam, Sam, don't cry. Plead your case? You don't need that. I'm not going anywhere, my beautiful Sam. I've had a lot of thinking to do and lying in a hospital bed when you've nearly died is a pretty good time to think, believe me. Come here. If I don't this now, I think I'm going to explode..." I tipped her head back and kissed her again, as I had earlier, but it was nicer without an audience, particularly such a very vocal, smutty-minded one, at that.

She was dazed, "Robbie...?" and I could see she couldn't believe it, so I kissed her again, to prove it and I instantly felt her respond, her arms sliding round behind me, holding me close to her. The kiss ended and she looked at me, in a sort of wonderment. "Do you mean... you actually... like me, a bit... in that way?"

"Like you? A bit? Is that all? Sam, I adore you!"

"Oh, God, do you mean it?"

"Yes, of course I mean it. You asked me here this evening but don't forget it was my idea to eat together tonight. I didn't know how you felt but I had to ask you. You see, I realised a while back that I wanted you, really wanted you but it was impossible to say anything then. You were investigating two murders in my family. I was even the chief suspect, it seems, for a while although I didn't know that till you spelled it out so forcefully. We had a...well, only a professional relationship although there were times when I wanted it to be so much more that I didn't know what to do. I was often short with you, dismissive, let you go from me with barely a word of goodbye or an au revoir. I never dared touch you, not in any way - not even shook your hand. It was how I prevented myself from putting my arms round you, kissing you... I hated myself for it but I was in a real state on every level, to be honest. I genuinely thought you were simply wedded to your job and your career and that was the rival for my affections, if you had any for me at all..."

"Oh, Rob, of course not... never ever... Never has there been a rival of any kind. Let alone my job. I..."

"I remember that first evening, and the take away and at the end of it I just let you leave. I wanted to hold you, keep you, kiss you, ask you to... to stay with me... be with me... all night... always... but-but I was frozen into a kind of stupor. And I let you go, I had to, of course, and I stood behind the door and heard your footsteps going away from me. All I wanted was to pull the door open and call you back, beg you to stay with me... th-that night... for ever... for always..."

"Oh, my God...!"

"I hated having to tell you about Madeleine and going into the minutiae of it, what's more, was hell. I wasn't ashamed of the event, simply not in any way proud of it but I didn't want you... you personally... to have to learn about it in any kind of detail and I was forced to - Adrian made me and you had to clarify stuff. I didn't really like talking to you about Inno, either. I even tried not to but you wouldn't let me stay silent in any area. I understood but it was very difficult and..."

"It was all right. I had to know. It was part of the job. I didn't..."

"Then a couple of days ago I knew I had to ask you out - properly, I mean. I wasn't sure how I was going to get through the rest of my life without seeing you every bloody day so I knew I had to try - try and see if you cared a little, that was all and if you did then, maybe... maybe take it further, if you wanted to."

"Oh... Rob...!"

"I knew I had to ask you. If I've learned anything at all from this fuck-awful business, it's that life's even bloody shorter than is believed already, nothing is guaranteed, and if you wanted something really badly then not to muck about not taking the odd chance every now and then. I didn't know what you felt but I knew I couldn't let you go off into the world without my at least trying. I knew I'd never forgive myself."

"Oh God, what have I ever done to deserve to be this happy!" Tears were still in abundance but her face was radiant.

"No, my darling Sam, that's my line."

Later on, replete with the best Spaghetti Bolognese I had ever had outside Italy and champagne and a sticky chocolate thing she admitted to having bought in Harrods that afternoon, which wasn't bad but not in the same class as the Spag Bol and I said as much, we sat on the sofa in the firelight, curled up together like cats, my good arm round her shoulders. We had to share a glass of whiskey (stunning stuff - made on her father's Scottish estate) as I hadn't got a free hand and she fed it to me sip by sip as I wouldn't let her go and she didn't want me to, either. We talked, made confessions to one another and tried to work out which one of us was the more stupid about not doing anything about this before now. I insisted upon winning that argument and I meant it. Other things occurred to me.

"Sam?"

"Hmm?"

"Did not William confide in you, about Madeleine, I mean?"

"No, he didn't. I've thought a lot about it, as you can imagine. All I knew was he had found someone special. He told me that much. He said he wanted to tell you first, if he could, but that was all. He was in love with her, Rob, I knew that but not her name or address, nothing. I asked him, of course, several times and he teased me. He said, if I wanted to be a great detective then I could find out for myself. It was a joke between us."

I sighed. "I see. Well, I shan't dwell on it or let it mar my memories of him in any way. Besides, if it really was Madeleine, I'm glad he never knew what she was really like. He was spared that," I frowned, "but in spite of the evidence, I don't really think it was. She really wasn't his type at all in any way, she was too bold and obvious. She wasn't mine either, apart from... well, we won't go into that again. I have no idea who it could have been but... there, I don't think we'll ever know so I must let it go and forget about it." I leant back, staring up at the ceiling briefly, thinking some more. "Also, the way Jean-Marc talked about her, thinking back on it, he actually made it sound as if he was talking about two separate people. He said something like, 'She was as dear to me as a sister could be'. He didn't say, 'she was my dear sister'. He blamed me for seducing Madeleine, which was clearly rubbish, but thinking about it, it's almost as if there were two women he was talking about."

Sam inclined her head, but I could see she wasn't totally convinced.

I had to let it go. "We'll maybe never know. So I must just remember him the way I really knew him to be. My lovely, straightforward, very up front big brother who I loved and admired very much."

And Sam simply stroked my face and gazed at me as if she could never stop.

We played favourite music and talked and quite often I kissed her, still utterly disbelieving of my good fortune. I suddenly realised it was late, really late and I had nowhere go. I had made no arrangements, stupidly and the flat no longer had any appeal for me. I was going to sell it, and had already made the necessary approaches for that to happen from my hospital bed - Martin and Inno's cousin was a very smart, slick London estate agent, who'd already found two people to fight over it for an embarrassingly enormous price. I made a move to get up off the sofa. "Sam, sweetheart, I must go. I must find a room somewhere. I'll ring one of the big hotels, I think. They'll have something and are used to people turning up from all over the world in the middle of the night."

Sam's grey eyes were large and dark, looking at me. "You don't have to go, Rob. You can stay here."

"Can I? Are you sure? That'd be wonderful. Have you a spare room? If not, this sofa is extraordinarily comfortable and I..."

"No. I don't mean the spare room or the sofa. I mean with me. Sleep with... me... Be with me... If... if you'd like to, that is..." She was still unsure of me and my feelings but to indicate it further, she slid her hands down my chest, slowly unbuttoning my shirt, making it very clear what precisely she did mean.

I looked at her and smiled, stroking her face, feeling the weight of her hair in my hand. "Darling, of course I'd like to... want to... that would be perfect but, well, I don't want to rush you. This is, in effect our first date. I thought you might think it was assuming a bit much on my part and a bit soon after..."

"Too soon? We've known each other since we were six or something. That's long enough, surely?" She was laughing, happy now, flirting with me. She stretched out along the length of the sofa, sliding down into it, inviting and beautiful. Well, more than beautiful, actually. She looked quite breathtakingly sexy, too.

I knelt down beside the sofa and kissed her again and this time I knew I wasn't going to leave. Certainly not tonight. Actually, not ever...

The kiss and all attendant, pre-sex activity became much more involved. The feel and sight of her body was wonderful, soft in all the right places, inviting me. She stopped the kiss and got up and pulled me gently to my feet. "Come on. You're the one who's been in hospital. I'm trying to look after you! You should have been in bed hours ago!"

"Well, then. Let's obey the doctors' orders which luckily coincide entirely with my own desires, I'll have you know. Let's go to bed, my lovely, darling, Sam." I stopped. "Oh damn and blast it."

"What's the matter?"

I put my arm round her as we walked out of the room together. "It's my arm. You'll have to be indulgent of any failures on my part in this exercise. I can't see how I can make love to you properly with only one arm."

A small giggle escaped from behind the curtain of hair and she pushed it back, her eyes glinting with wicked fun, enticing and to me, increasingly erotic. I took a deep steadying breath. My pulse went up several notches. I was about to have sex with and spend the night with the most beautiful, clever, desirable and adorable girl in the whole world. She walked backwards into her softly lit bedroom, gently pulling me with her. Her laugh was low and thrilling. "Well, then, Sir Robert, darling, you will just have to make love to me IM-properly, won't you?"

Post Script

Six years on...

1

Having taken a remarkably long time to get off the ground (entirely my fault, I insisted still) our courtship was of the whirlwind sort. We had such a lot of lost time to catch up and my God, did we catch up! Having decided I could no longer return to the Putney flat, too much blood and horror and losing my dear Nell there was all too much, Sam suggested, in her shy, tentative way, anxious not to pressurise me, I should move in with her and I needed no second invitation. In fact, I never spent another day in the Putney flat again. We went back once, Sam and I, to collect the few things I wanted - my clothes, a line drawing of a black Labrador, so like Nell she might have sat for that picture, some beautiful wine glasses and a couple of Louis Quinze chairs (moved into Sam's flat, to go with the snuff box) and with the art work all going as stock to the gallery, I sold everything else with the flat. After that first night together, I didn't leave till the following Monday. In fact we didn't get out of bed much at all, to be honest. Well, I had been injured and in hospital - believe that to be the reason and you'll believe anything! Then, with Sam taking a well-earned week off, I took her down to Forbridge with me in a kind of triumph. It amused me to see how restrained my mother was about this, although clearly desperate this new love affair of mine was to be "it". But I didn't disappoint her.

We kept ourselves out of the limelight as much as possible, partly because we'd both had enough inquisitive searching into our private lives but also to ensure there was nothing personal to jeopardise the successful outcome of the various up and coming court cases the murders were going to throw up. We were happy, though, hiding from the world. It gave us the excuse we needed just to be alone together as much as we could.

One afternoon, a couple of weeks after the court hearings were finally over, I took Sam for a walk up to Will's and my special place in the copse one fine, cold winter's day and asked her to marry me. I suppose it could have been more romantic but it was right for us, muffled up in jumpers and scarves, all amongst the fallen leaves and frost-covered branches, looking down over Forbridge.

We were married in June in the tiny church on her father's estate in Scotland and then just came back home to Hampshire and it was all wonderful. But Sam, the darling of the women's libbers, disappointed them all by leaving the force and coming down to be a full time wife and assistant in the Forbridge business. As she had said a long time ago, it wasn't the sort of job you could combine with being a wife, particularly when our daughter Catriona entered the world at not quite a decent interval after the wedding. People generously said she was a slightly premature honeymoon baby but she wasn't! A year later, almost to the day, she presented me with a second lovely daughter, Lexi. Two years later we completed our family with William Charles - we called him Charlie - and from that first electric night together my life turned from darkness into light in a matter of hours.

But we didn't find out anything more about Madeleine and her seemingly strange association with William, though Sam tried hard and got nowhere.

One late March day, Charlie now nearing two, I was in the library, poring over some old prints of Forbridge. We were having an exhibition of Hampshire through the ages and there were pageants to organise and costume displays and all sorts of things of an antiquarian nature, which suited me very well.

A firm rap beat a short tattoo on the door behind me.

"Yes?"

Into the room came the severe and dutifully correct, Mrs Ava Smithers, Jane's temporary replacement while on maternity leave.

"Excuse me, Sir Robert, but Lady Samantha is asking for you. She is in the nursery and wondered if you would kindly go up."

Why the hell she found it necessary to talk to us like that, I couldn't imagine. To everyone else we were just Rob and Sam. Oh well...

"Thanks, Mrs Smithers," (she had us at it, too, in return. I think she would have thought Britain as she knew it would have come to an end if we had ever addressed her as Ava). "I'll go up straight away."

Sam was looking anxious and ruffled, unusual for her.

"Hey, what's all this? You look all in a stew..." I put my arms round her. "Hmm. In spite of that you are looking just gorgeous this afternoon, do you know that?" It was nice, working in the house with her around all day. Occasionally, if all was quiet and the children out or looked after, we would sneak off somewhere to one of the many, many bedrooms and have sex. We planned to do it in every one possible, we promised ourselves when we first married and we were getting there, but this was not one of those occasions as she wriggled free from me.

"No, Rob, darling, really. I'm bothered."

"Yes, I can see that. What's up?"

"It's Charlie. He's disappeared. I can't find him anywhere and I've called and I've looked and Vikki can't find him either." Vikki was the nanny.

He was an imp, if there ever was one, this third child of ours, into mischief such as could not be imagined previously. In comparison, the girls were akin to angels most of the time. My mother maintained he was just like me at that age but I think her memory was failing a little. Sam remarked it hadn't failed in any other area yet. Still... "Where was he when he disappeared?"

"That's the ridiculous thing, in here. He can't have gone far. I was in the other room.

And he was just playing about with the wooden blocks and the train. Then it all went quiet and I came out to look for him and he was gone. I've been looking for about half an hour."

I grinned. "I bet I know where he is, the monkey." I led the way into William's old room. It was still not used by anyone. We didn't keep it as a shrine or anything morbid, it was just not used at present, though Charlie could have it for his own later on, if he liked.

I walked to the old double doors where we had so often hidden as children. I pulled opened the first door, it couldn't be secured in any way, and there he was, curled up like a dormouse and fast asleep, his thumb in his mouth. Sam sank down onto the bed.

"Oh, thank God! I thought something dreadful had happened to him. The wretch! Just wait till he wakes up! I shall leave him for the moment. He seems quite comfy and it is his time for a nap. I'll go and tell Vikki to call off the search. I've got everyone looking for him - Helena, Phyllis, Martin - even Mark. I didn't dare ask the Smithers. She seems far too superior to look for missing toddlers and she'd clearly think I was a terrible mother."

I laughed and Sam went out to call off the search, much relieved, and I sat and watched my son asleep in the corner where William and I had so often hidden. It was dusty and he was grubby, no one having swept in there for years, if ever, maybe. At his feet was a small wooden box, a little carved Indian thing that William used to keep stamps in for swapping when he was about ten. I picked it up. Inside was some loose change, an old Poppy badge left over from some Remembrance Day celebration, a pair of cufflinks of William's and a couple of ten pound notes. Odd bits of this and that. It used to stand on the tallboy in the room once. By the look of it, he would turn out his pockets into it and then sort it out from time to time. I picked up old, unused, now defunct Tube tickets and a receipt from a restaurant and at the bottom I found an unfamiliar computer disk. I turned it over and looked at it. It was labelled "WB Letters". I put it in my pocket to look at later. The money I collected. I would put it in Charlie's money box. He had found it, after all.

He stirred and looked up at me, smiling and relaxed from sleep. I picked him up and carried him into the nursery where we started to play with his wooden blocks again. I helped him pile them up in a high tower. His fat, baby hand whacked at them and he screamed delightedly as bricks flew everywhere.

A little later, before dinner, the girls in bed having been read to by me and Charlie being fed, Sam was still breast feeding him at night before sleep, I took a glass of wine in one hand, the bottle in the other and sat down at the old computer in the library and put the disk into it. I pressed the contents button and stared at the list on the screen in front of me. It was not long, on the contrary, it only had one item and that was entitled, "Rob". I pressed the relevant keys and instantly the letter was displayed on the screen. I read it and then I read it again. I sat in front of the screen and it was here that Sam found me, ready for dinner now and wondering where I had got to.

"Hello. This is where you're hiding. First Charlie today and now you! Vikki is settling him down. I've done my bit. What are you looking at so earnestly?" She poured some more wine into my glass and drank it herself, leaning over my shoulder.

"It's this disk of William's. I wondered what was on it." I got up and wandered away to the window, looking out over the park. "Read it, Sam."

I could feel her glance at me quickly before she looked at the screen.

"Sunday, 29 August

Dear old Rob, (it said)

I can't say exactly why I'm writing all this down. Of course, I intend to tell you tomorrow after this great and glorious bunfight is over. I think perhaps I am just practising what I need to say. Here goes then.

After all these years, I've found myself a girl - the special one. You know, the one to please Mother, the works. She is beautiful and clever and I'm just so glad I saw her first because if I hadn't and you had, then I wouldn't have stood a chance! How do you charm the pants off them, dear boy? Literally, more often than not! And I don't even think you realise it.

I haven't said anything to you - not because I don't want you to know but because I thought it would break the spell. I simply had to keep her a secret. I couldn't believe this lovely girl was mine, really and truly mine. Then I knew this was it. I wanted to marry her and she said yes and I thought I'd tell Father. I invited her down for this weekend. We were going to make the announcement after we'd told you and the parents at the end of the fête. We thought it would be suitable and fun - you understand, I'm sure.

Last week I decided was the moment and I told Father first - I wanted to tell you, but you were in Madrid, buying stuff. Mother was out at the time. I thought he was going to have a heart attack. He said it was impossible because of who she is. Let me explain.

Her name is Marie Fletcher. Well, that is the name she uses for work. She is a famous model. To keep some sort of privacy from the world, when out and about she uses her real name. That name is Marie de la Flèche."

Sam looked up. "Marie?"

"Yes, go on reading."

"Her second cousin is a war hero in France, or supposedly. Our father knows better. This man was the saboteur of the mission we first heard about at the Château Viezy. You will remember that, all right, with Madeleine and your night of unbridled passion etc! Marie is Madeleine's cousin, too, Madeleine

254

being this man's granddaughter. I'm glad that never came to anything, by the way. Marie says Madeleine and her brother are wild and difficult characters, the brother definitely unbalanced and Madeleine herself has the reputation of being a complete tramp - a real bike, it seems and something akin to a nymphomaniac as far as I can gather. Anyway...

Father said he was a murderer and a cheat and it was impossible for me to marry into this man's family. We had the most terrible row, you know the sort of thing, his past nothing to do with us and so on, you can imagine, but God, was it dreadful. I didn't know what to do. But this much I do know, if I had gone ahead it would have destroyed him.

Furthermore, and after the things he told me about this terrible man, and I believe him - he showed me letters from friends and a cousin of his, too - if Marie went back to France and told him who she was intending to marry, he would kill her first. Father cannot return to France because of this monster. The evidence is not enough for a court of law, he felt, but it made sense to him, piecing things together bit by bit. I understand what he is saying and therefore, and this is the hardest part of all, I have to let her go with no real word of explanation. If she knew she would have understood (I hope) but if she knows, he will kill her because she has knowledge she must not have. Dangerous knowledge indeed. This man now is trying to become President of France. He is likely to kill anyone to keep them quiet if they try to stop him. What sort of dilemma is that for me, for God's sake?

When Jean-Yves de la Flèche is dead it will be safe to find her again and tell her what was behind it all. If I cannot do it, for some reason, say, because the years will have rolled by and I am married to someone else (and it would hardly be right to upset my wife with such a thing), seek her out for me, Robbie. Tell her I loved her with all my heart, that I didn't just drop her when I got tired of her, or had had enough sex with her or whatever and tell her the real reason behind my abandoning her. She has a flat in Paris, Apartment b, 16 Petit Rue 24 just off the Rue d'Alma. She hides her identity not just by using her real name but giving the Château as her address, to keep her own life more private, though she very rarely goes there. Show her this letter, maybe, or just use your own words.

You were always good with words, especially with the girls. And talking of which, there's a girl for you out there! I know her, so do you, an old school friend, but she's the one for you, you juggins! You'll kick yourself you haven't done anything about her up till now when I point her out!

Thanks, Brother Rob. This is the most important and the most difficult thing I have ever had to ask you.

Always yours,

Love,

William"

There was silence as Sam stopped reading and stood up, staring at the screen as I did. Then she looked at me.

"You must go and find her, Rob." There were tears in her eyes and on her cheeks.

I nodded. "Yes. I will. I must do it for William and for her, too." I looked down into the glass in my hands and turned it back and forth, watching the light catch in it.

"Darling, are you all right?"

I sighed. "No... yes... Oh shit, sort of. I just feel... oh, dreadful that I doubted him... that I could actually believe he had walked off with an ex-girlfriend of mine and not said anything. I feel... just awful, Sam."

She shook me. She was nearly as tall as I was and I didn't have to look down at her too far. She reached up and held my face between her hands. "No, Rob, you didn't. You know you couldn't believe it, not really. You said so, many times. But look at the evidence. There was the video and the girl on the film looks a lot like Madeleine in many ways and if you were led into believing it was her on the film, the mind makes up the rest. That always happens. We take what we know, or think we do, and add in the missing pieces to fit. He referred to her as 'M' in his diary and you saw her signature in the registry of the Savoy as M de la Flèche of the Château Viezy. You had every right to think it was she. I did. It was only you who had any real doubt, who never quite accepted it. Don't forget that, darling."

I nodded sadly, and kissed her before we walked through into the dining room to start our meal. "I suppose not. But well, now I must make amends to William, mustn't I? I must go and find her, or try to."

"Yes, certainly. When will you go?"

"Tomorrow."

"Fine. After dinner I'll help you pack. I wish I could come with you but I can't leave the baby - all this breast feeding!"

I smiled, looking at her as I picked up my soup spoon. "Mother love suits you."

"I'm glad you think so. Better than killing people, giving them life," and she smiled back at me in the candlelight and I was content.

2

I stood outside the door to the flat in the tiny backstreet just off the Rue d'Alma. I had been there once already but there had been no reply. The concierge said she thought she would be back later, about six thirty. It was now nearly seven and I could hear sounds, a radio on and china and cutlery clattering and a quick, light step coming down the corridor within, in answer to my knock.

"Yes?" She looked at me, brown eyes, not green, I saw with relief. I'd seen enough of green eyes to last me for ever.

"Marie?"

"Yes. Who are you? Press? If you are, you can..."

"No, nothing like that. We haven't met but you probably know who I am, but it may be a shock for you. My name is Robert Berkeley. William was my brother."

She stared at me and went white. "Eh, mon Dieu...!" She swayed slightly and I caught her but she recovered herself reasonably well and I led her into the living room, closing the door behind me. I put her down gently on the sofa and looked round for some brandy.

She grasped what I was looking for. "On the sideboard in the decanter. You have one, too."

I poured two glasses and she drank, thankfully. After a minute colour came back to her face and she composed herself.

"Why have you come here, after all this time?"

"I only found about you yesterday. Or rather, I knew you existed but I didn't know who you really were or how to find you." I told her of the letter and how I had come across it.

"You have the letter?"

"Yes. I printed it out in case you didn't have a computer handy." I handed her both the letter and the disk. She read it, at least twice and I sat there and looked at her and wondered what she was going to say to me.

So this was the girl my brother loved. She was pretty - blonde hair, I knew that already, and tall with a carefully made-up face. She was expensively dressed and her flat was beautiful. A small black cat sat in a chair, its front paws neatly curled beneath it and regarded me solemnly with yellow eyes. Marie looked up at me. Her eyes were bright and hard but she was not crying.

"So... at long last, I know... At last I understand... Oh, God, oh my God!" and then she did break down and I let her cry and cry and as the sobs diminished, I urged her gently to drink a little more which she did, drawing in great hiccuping breaths in an effort to calm herself.

"Thank you, Robert. Thank you for coming as soon as you did. I would not want to think ill of my William for another day longer than I should. And now, I can begin again. You have given me... Oh God, you cannot imagine what you have done for me, coming here."

I watched her, leaning back on the sofa. "I can. I felt dreadful that I had misjudged him myself. It is a great relief to me, so I understand your torment has been much worse than mine. Can you tell me about yourself and how you met William?"

She smiled now, at last, and her face lit up from within and she started to talk and as she spoke of him I knew he had chosen her well. She was lovely and she would have made him very happy. How could the past be so cruel, how could it have been? Old sins cast long shadows, the saying goes. How true that was for us - all of us embroiled in this affair, its roots in the past, its terrible fruition in the present and its legacy in the future. But she was talking and I listened.

"I met William at a promotions thing for the French Tourist Board - a Holidays-in-Europe do. I used to be a model but I gave that up some time ago and run an advertising and promotions firm. We met in England originally and then he came to France and then... well, there we were, in the middle of an affair and head over heels in love. We were very happy together. We went to the Château Viezy once. I was using it as a location for some photos. He only met me there for lunch and we left immediately afterwards. Madeleine wasn't there that day, though Jean-Marc was prowling around. I didn't see him, he was busy doing something else. Besides, I hated my cousins. And now they are dead, but it was deserved, you know."

"Yes, it was."

"Anyway... We were going to be married and everything was wonderful. William came up to London to meet me and, so I thought, bring me down to his home but he told me it was over. Finished. Just like that. He cried and said he adored me and would for ever but he couldn't marry me and I must go away and never come back. It broke my heart and it has not mended yet, Robert." I nodded. Poor bloody girl. "Then I heard he was dead - killed by a bomb. I was horrified and glad all at once but later I was only desperately sad. I couldn't, in the end, hate him. I loved him too much for that. I went abroad shortly afterwards to set up a business in America. I had to get away. I returned to France only last weekend and have just taken possession of this flat again. It is very strange that you should find this letter now for if you had come before you would have found it very difficult to find me, I think, in New York."

She asked me about myself. William had talked much about us all. He had even told her about Sam who he said would make me the perfect wife when I got round to realising how marvellous she was. She laughed when I told her Sam and I were married now. "That would have made William very happy! I hope you are, Robert."

"Just blissful, thanks," and we smiled at each other, happy for William, although he could not be, pleased he had been proved right.

She had heard all about the unmasking of Jean-Yves, dead now, ending his life in the high security psychiatric care unit, after only a couple of months in it, having pleaded guilty on the grounds of diminished responsibility as a result of so-called brainwashing by the Nazis all those years ago. He had had a clever lawyer and supported by psychiatrists they were only too pleased to appear to believe him. It made the authorities who had heaped him with glory look less foolish, it was cynically believed. He had been shut away and that was what mattered to us, my father and brother avenged. And now he, too was dead.

I took her out to a restaurant and we ate a simple but delicious meal and still she talked about William and I let her, she needed to, I could see, after years of silence. She would have been my sister-in-law, I thought idly, watching her intense face in the soft light of the restaurant. I suddenly thought of the letters.

"By the way, Marie, who is Dominique?"

She smiled. "You don't know?"

"No, not really. I know she is Jean-Yves' cousin and she was my father's mistress in the war. That's all, really."

She nodded thoughtfully and lit a Gauloise. I declined, having given up years ago but I liked the smell still, particularly that brand, so French and with so many memories for me. William often smoked them. "Dominique was my grandmother, Robert."

"Your grandmother?"

"Yes. She had an illegitimate child - your father's, it seems - and he died. She then met someone else - he was married but waiting for a divorce. She became pregnant but just before they planned to marry he was killed in a train crash. It was very sad. After that, she just had one or two lovers, I believe and she died when I was about twelve, something like that. Hers was not a happy life but she did not complain and worked very hard to bring up her son, my father, on her own. He married my mother, who is English, and they now live in Cornwall."

"Really?"

"Yes. He is an artist - quite a good one and quite well known, but I returned to Paris when I was 19 and worked for a model agency and made a lot of money. I am very successful, you know."

I was amused by her frankness, it was not boasting, it was a statement of fact. She may have been half English, but it was very French that attribute, I thought.

I walked her home and I could feel her relax at last, her contact with her dead lover's brother brought a nearness to him she had not felt since he left and mine with her seemed to bring William closer to me, as well. She turned on the doorstep and one more question came to me.

"Did William come here?"

"Oh yes. We often were together here, happily away from the world, just the two of us."

It was a good thought. I was happy to imagine them here together. It made this a place where love had blossomed and continued, intimate to me, too. I nodded, pleased and she smiled at me, realising what I was thinking for she said, "We were always happy here, just loving each other."

Now she held out her hand to me and I took it.

"Goodbye, Robert. You have done more for me today than anyone since William fell in love with me. I would like us to keep in touch. I want to meet Sam and your babies. Bring them to France one day."

"I will. You'll come to England?"

"Oh yes. I come to visit my parents sometimes." She hesitated, "but I don't think I am ready yet to come to Forbridge."

It would have been her home, I thought, looking at her. No, it was too soon, yet. Maybe a lifetime would be too soon for that hurdle to be overcome...

I put my arms round her and held her for a long minute. She kissed me on both cheeks. She stepped back over the threshold, smiling, eyes bright and I turned away and left her, watching me. I ran down the stairs and at the foot, looked up, and raised my hand to her once more in farewell. I made my way out to the Metro, the long shadows with their roots so far in the past gone at last, back to my beloved Sam and home.

The End

ABOUT THE AUTHOR

Elizabeth Housden is a professional British actress who started writing first plays for her theatre company and then branching out to write novels for children and later for adults as well. Her writing crosses several genres and this book is her first detective novel.

As well as running her own theatre company she has taught drama at Bedales School and many of her former pupils have gone on to be professional actors. She lives in Hampshire with her husband and between them they have four children and seven grandchildren.

Printed in Poland
by Amazon Fulfillment
Poland Sp. z o.o., Wrocław

67620124R00152